THE HUNT

A Crystal River Pack Novel

BY AMY WORCESTER

TITLE: The Hunt

By: Amy Worcester

Cover Design: Publishing

afworcester@gmail.com

ACKNOWLEDGMENTS

When I was a little girl, I always dreamed of writing stories and becoming an author. But, of course, life and everything else happened, and that dream got put on hold. About a year ago, after our son graduated high school, my husband encouraged me to get out and find my tribe.

The Writer's Club that meets at our local library welcomed and encouraged me through this process. They guided and helped me along the way. Angee Costa has been a wonderful mentor and teacher.

But I also have to give a lot of thanks and love to my husband and son. They encouraged me despite my incessant "tippy tappy" on the keyboard and didn't object to the late nights and early mornings.

This has been an incredible journey and I hope that you enjoy the story as much as I did while bringing Celeste, Wyatt, and the were world to life.

With much love,

Amy

CONTENTS

1 – WYATT'S HUNT

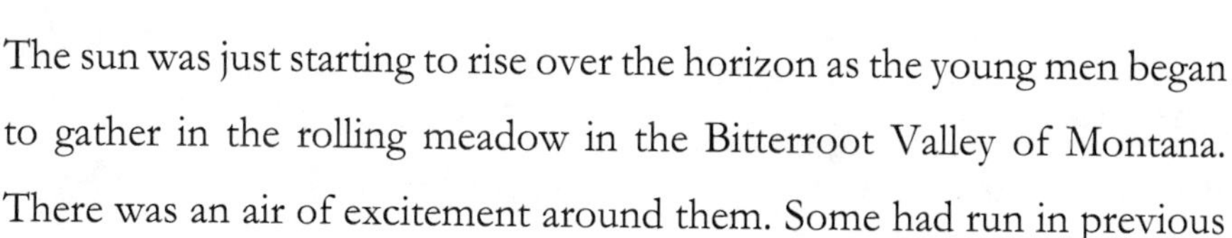

The sun was just starting to rise over the horizon as the young men began to gather in the rolling meadow in the Bitterroot Valley of Montana. There was an air of excitement around them. Some had run in previous Hunts before while others were novices. They were all anticipating finding their mates.

Shadows were still being cast from the jagged mountains and tall trees precariously perched on them. The short grass in the meadow was already trampled by the many feet of both man and wolf. A mix of both meandered around waiting for the opening ceremonies for the Summer Solstice Hunt of the Mates.

Some preferred to hunt in their beast form, while others remained in their human form. Some of the Lycans were in a partial shift making them look like the stereotypical Hollywood werewolf. Several men flocked to one of the Lycans who had made it big in the movies, wanting to get a picture and be able to claim to know him.

Wyatt walked out into the large open meadow with the other Hunters from the Crystal River Pack. He was the youngest of the eleven Hunters that he had traveled with. Being the son of an Alpha, the only son of an Alpha, he was used to a lot of attention from the she-wolves. His height, bright green eyes and short dark mahogany hair were inherited from his mother. The caramel coloring and easy temperament came from his father. At seventeen, he stood just under seven feet and could see over most of the crowd.

Using his height to his advantage, he took in the sights around him, wanting to commit everything to memory. Today could be the day that he met his mate and he wanted to remember all the details. The pine trees growing high on the mountains and the light fog that clung to the grass at the tree line.

Looking towards the West, he noted the stage that was draped with the blues and whites of the West Wind Pack. The large Alpha throne sat in the center with the crest carved into the back. Wyatt remembered it from his childhood, sitting in the huge chair with the blue velvet cushion and ruling over his sisters.

Whitney, as the oldest, always wanted to rule. Wenona was a few years younger himself and preferred to play with their grandmother's jewelry. Wynn, a surprise when Wyatt was eleven, was just happy to be included. With a smile on his face, he caught the eye of another, equally as tall.

Alpha Sampson of the West Winds pack, one of the last Lycan packs, grinned at his nephew who returned his smile. Wyatt and his uncle, his mother's brother, shared a few family traits, including height, broad shoulders and bright green eyes. Sampson's light brown fell loosely around his head just brushing his shoulders before he pulled it back into a low ponytail. The older Alpha had a pale complexion that was lightly sun kissed.

Your mother is telling me that we are dressed as twins. Sampson's voice came through the family link and echoed in Wyatt's head. It was new to hear a different voice along with the others that had become as familiar to him. Now that they were on Sampson's pack lands, the family link had extended to him and his young children.

Wyatt looked down at what he was wearing and chuckled.

Sampson wore khaki slacks, a navy-blue polo shirt and tennis shoes. Wyatt sported khaki cargo shorts and a dark blue, Naval, recruit T-shirt and well-worn, thoroughly abused, gray running shoes.

Wyatt gave a soft laugh causing those around him to look at him. I'm the younger and better-looking twin. Sampson's laughter echoed across the meadow. Seeing the host Alpha caused a ripple of excitement to run through the crowd of Hunters as the breeze carried the scent of the female wolves, called Maidens, from the other side of the orchard.

Yips and howls filled the air as the tall Alpha of the West Winds pack mounted the stage.

Motioning for the crowd of males to settle down, Sampson waited for the area to fall silent. "Thousands of years ago on the Seven Hills of the city that we now call Rome, two brothers were tended by a She-Wolf and suckled from her milk with her own pups. As they grew much slower than their wolf brethren, the she-wolf grew more attached to them. At the end of her life, she howled at the moon, begging the moon goddess, Selene, to watch over her pups."

"Selene blessed the two human brothers with the ability to run and hunt with the wolves that they had grown up with. But they could not keep up, and she then gave them the ability to shift between the two forms. When it was time for them to take their own mates, they chased them down, hunted them. Selene again blessed their mates to be able to shift and run with their mates and the wolves."

"The women of Rome wanted to be chosen as a mate for one of the wolf-men. To find who would best suit the sons of Reemus and Romulus, they hosted the first Hunt on the longest day of the year. As the old world slowly fell away and the new world took over, our ancestors were forced into the shadows."

"Undeterred, we continued to gather on the Summer Solstice and Hunt for our mates." There were more excited howls and yips echoing off the valley walls. Wyatt threw back his head and howled long and loud.

"This is why you are here today! To find your mates!" Sampson pointed to the tree line. "The eligible Maidens have been taken into the trees where they will be running through the woods! At the sound of the horn, you may pursue them."

Wyatt smiled. Somewhere in the woods was his older sister doing her third Hunt. And maybe, if he was lucky, his own fated mate would be in the woods too.

Alpha Sampson stepped aside, and a bugler stepped up. He looked towards the trees as if he was waiting for his cue. Faintly, the sound of Wyatt's mother's voice echoed in his head as she said that they were ready. The musician raised his instrument to his lips and blew a three-note signal. The male werewolves surged forward towards the trees as one, each with a singular goal in mind. Find their mate.

Halfway through the orchard, Wyatt already knew that his mate was not there. There was no scent from her. No pheromones. No tingling sensation. No pull. Even if his mate was not here, there would be plenty of maids that would be willing to be his for the night. It was a long-standing unofficial tradition. Any females who had not found their matches by the end of the Hunt would wait at the far end of the course. Unmated couples could hook up for the night and there would be no harm done when they parted ways the following morning.

Like so many of the other unmated males, Wyatt was lost in the excitement of the hunt. The scent of so many females, excited females, were driving them all harder and faster. In the excitement, some of the other hunters were also letting their wolves lead as they pursued their prey. Giving into the animals that lived inside them, becoming the beasts that the world feared.

Laughter filled the woods that lay on the North side of the meadow. Wyatt entered the woods and his eyes shifted as Demon pushed to the front. With his Lycan wolf now pushing his human form through the woods, he let out a howl of excitement. Loud, excited cries echoed around him as he pushed his body forward. Demon wanted to take control and shift completely into his were form. If Demon had not been so close to the surface of their shared mind, the cry for help probably would not have pushed through the haze.

"NO! HELP! WYATT!"

It was a cry through the mind link shared by the Crystal River Pack members. But it also came through the family link and carried across the air. Whitney was crying out, her voice filled with so much fear that all of Demon's Alpha instincts took over. Being a Lycan-dominant were, he could do a partial shift with his wolf taking control, but he remained mostly in his human form. Continuing to run on two feet, his human body sprouted wolf fur as his claws and fangs extended.

His body stretched to his full Lycan height, standing at just over eight feet tall. Muscles bulged and rippled as he slashed his t-shirt off and his shorts stretched at the seams. The old shoes on his feet flew off in shreds, his ankle socks tearing, leaving patches of cotton caught on his claws and cuffs stretched around his ankles.

Another cry for help came across the links and through the air as he jumped over another hunter, using a large tree trunk to push himself harder and faster towards his sister. Her cries grew louder, more terrified. The tree trunks he bounced off left claw marks in the bark.

As Demon took control of their body, Wyatt felt stronger and faster than he had ever before. Although he had done a partial shift before, Demon had never been in full control. Nor had he ever been reacting to one of his sisters crying out for help.

Whitney came into view and Demon propelled them towards her attacker. Her light green eyes were wide with fear. The crimson red shirt to indicate the pack she belonged to was torn and stained with dirt. just as her dark colored leggings.

Landing on all four paws before standing to his full height and yanking the Beta off her terrified form. The older wolf was a darker skinned man with golden brown eyes and short black hair. He growled angrily and swiped at the intruding male.

Demon roared and forced his Alpha authority out. The Beta recoiled and whimpered in submission as his feet dangled a few inches off the ground, slowly sliding towards the dirt beneath them as the Beta's shirt ripped. The sound of material tearing under the weight of the Beta's body and the sound of the scrape of Demon's sharp claws pulled Whitney out of her shocked stupor.

The drive to protect her mate was suddenly stronger than her fear. "Wyatt!" Whitney screamed as she stood up and forced herself between the two. Placing her hands on her brother's fur covered chest, she hoped that her touch would ground him.

"Demon, please." She pleaded with her brother's wolf. "Please. He is my mate."

Her fingernails dug in slightly as his muscles shifted under her hands. Whitney could feel the battle being waged within her brother as his breath was hard and ragged. The wall of muscles on his chest rippled and then trembled as he took a deep breath.

Looking down at his sister, his face softened, and his snarl faded. Demon tossed the man away from him and pulled Whitney close to him. Slowly, with his arms tightly wrapped around her and inhaling her scent, Demon subsided so Wyatt could return.

"I'm okay, Wyatt." she said softly as a tear trickled out of her eye.

"She is your mate." Wyatt growled at the Beta wolf, resuming his human form. "You should treasure her, not abuse her."

"I'm sorry, Alpha." The man said as he lowered his head in submission. "I was excited from the Hunt and I… I lost control of myself." Shame filled his face with a red blush and a tremor in his voice.

"It happens, Wyatt." Whitney told him. "Mom told me it might. I just panicked."

"He nearly raped you." Wyatt said looking down at his older sister.

"But he didn't." she pointed out. "You came to help me. Others are not as lucky."

As if to emphasize her point, another scream ripped through the forest. Both men turned towards the sound, deep protective growls emanating from their throats.

"You can't protect all the Maidens from their mates." Whitney whispered. "Not even a Lycan like you. Not even a full-blooded Lycan like Uncle Sampson." She glanced at the Beta male that her wolf, Jewel, recognized as their mate. Once again, Jewel was panting and yipping in excitement inside Whitney's mind. "If I had known him, I probably would not have been as scared."

This was not her first Hunt. She had been sent to them ever since she turned seventeen, whether she wanted to or not. Like all other females, she had no say in the choice of her mate. It was determined by the moon goddess and whether the male accepted or rejected her. As the daughter of an Alpha, she attended as many council events as possible and still had not met her mate.

Once again, she had been told that she must participate in the annual Hunt. This time, when she sensed him, both the woman and wolf had been excited… until they weren't. The beta had approached, growling possessively as he stalked her, intent on claiming what he believed was his. Fear washed over her and not even Jewel could make contact with his inner wolf to calm him as she had seen her mother do with her own mate. Whitney had pleaded with the male; his eyes were glazed as his wolf had the lead. Fearing that she had no other choice, she had called out for her younger brother with every option that she had.

"I'm sorry, mate," the man said as he stood up and offered her a hand. "I'm Nathaniel Taylor, High Plains Pack."

"Whitney O'Donnell, Crystal River." She took his hand and a small step away from her brother but kept a light protective hand on her shoulder. "And my brother, the next Alpha, Wyatt."

They were surrounded by howls and screams as the three of them made their way to the end of the course. The following day, when the newly mated couples presented themselves before the Elder Alpha's and the council, Wyatt noticed how many of the females looked terrified — how many of them cowered from their mates.

More importantly, he saw how many of the Alphas and parents approved of the matches and forced their daughters and female pack members to leave the pack that they had known their entire lives and start over with their mate in a new and unknown pack. There was even one, the daughter of the Silver Lake Alpha, who was sent to live in Mexico. She did not speak Spanish; he did not speak English. It was deemed a good match, and a terrified girl was sent live with a man at least ten years her senior.

Wyatt swore then and there that he would never participate in another Hunt. And that when he became Alpha, he would work hard to change how the annual Summer Solstice Hunt for Mates was done. Whitney had said that he could not save them all. But he sure as hell would try.

.

2 - SUNRISE

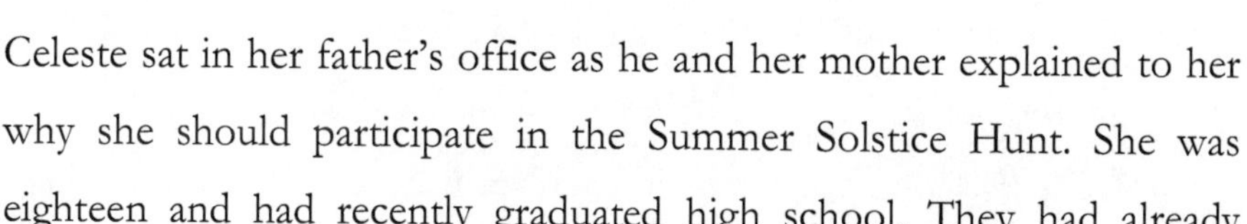

Celeste sat in her father's office as he and her mother explained to her why she should participate in the Summer Solstice Hunt. She was eighteen and had recently graduated high school. They had already allowed her an extra year. Now, they felt it was time for her to find a mate.

Nope. It is not going to happen. There was a little bit of guilt at her deception. But they were refusing to listen. Tradition dictated her life. And tradition could kiss her ass.

It was nearly midnight when her parents decided that they had lectured long enough. Finally. She went to bed and slept for a few hours. She was up before the sun, anxious to run, needing to burn off some of her Alpha energy. Starting her running playlist and putting in her earbuds, she stepped out of the house and stretched. Her black leggings hugged her legs below her baggy t-shirt, which was required by her father to protect her modesty.

She couldn't help but smirk when she thought about how the only wolves that would take her on as a sparring partner were now her brothers. The rest of the warriors in the pack had already learned that she would take them down. Like her oldest brother, she too was Lycan dominant. Her height, strength and power only grew as she matured.

Her modesty could be damned. As she ran and got hotter, she would strip off the T-shirt and tie it around her waist. When she was warmed up, Celeste stepped off the second-story deck and started her run. Malachi, her father, and the pack Alpha allowed her to run, for now. He allowed a lot of extra activities. And he liked to remind her how generous he was. She had participated in sports at the local human high school. Reluctantly, he had even allowed gymnastics and tumbling, later cheer squad, and then competitive cheer.

Her freshman year, he had declared no more. Trapped inside the house, with no way to expel her energy, she was driving everyone crazy. Then, within a week, he let her go back to all her activities. Even now, with no sports to play, she was getting restless. Her runs were getting longer. Following the pack law of having a male family member with her, she would keep one of her brothers at the gym more than he wanted.

None of the warriors of the pack had any interest in her. She knew it wasn't because of her looks. She stood just under six and a half feet, with an athletic body and a full chest. Her pitch-black hair hung past her shoulders and topped her tanned body. She had a slight sprinkling of freckles across her face and full lips that the human boys said were kissable. High cheek bones and a pert nose gave her a striking profile. But her eyes were what everyone always commented on. They were silver. Most assumed they were pale blue until they got closer.

The pack members gave no opinion. Even the men in the pack that didn't pursue her, always watched for her at the picnics and pool parties.

Celeste reached the overlook at the lake just in time to watch the sunrise. With the warmth of the sun on her upturned face, she felt her senses heighten. Closing her eyes, she focused on everything around her. The wind picked up across Silver Lake and kissed her skin. Taking a deep breath, she could smell the morning dew on the green grass. Her senses heightened and she could smell the fresh dew on the grass as it blew over the lake and onto her skin. Even her hearing was enhanced as she perceived the tiny sounds of all the little critters starting their day. A rooster crowed to greet the morning and birds chirped in the distance. As a shifter, she stood between their world and the human one, much like where she stood in the well-kept grass. There was a running path that went from the town to the overlook and then back around to the training grounds. It completely encircled the town and was usually used by the warriors during patrol.

The sound of footsteps approaching caused her body to tense up. But then a familiar scent filled her nose and she smiled. Her eldest brother wrapped his arms around her shoulders and rested his chin on her head. This was their ritual. It was their time. And it was here that she had confessed her plan last fall.

Like Celeste's other siblings, Sirius had reddish brown hair and green eyes. He stood a little over six and a half feet with about four inches between them. They both had athletic builds and tanned skin. Sirius wore running shoes, black basketball shorts and a gray tank top. His neck had his mate's mark, and the Silver Lake Pack Crest was tattooed on his left upper arm.

The rising silver moon reflected on the water of the lake flanked by ancient oak trees with the limbs creating an arch with the pack motto emblazoned on them. Argentum Lupus, Custos Nocits – Silver Wolf, Guardian of the Night. Celtic knots encircled the crest entwined with the lunar phases across the top and a single paw print at the base.

"When do you leave?" Sirius asked, breaking the silence.

"Two more days," she replied. "I'm going to miss this."

"Me too. Just promise that you'll come back whenever you can." He squeezed her tight and kissed the top of her head.

"I will. As long as dad will let me," she said with a catch in her throat.

"He will. It may take a little while."

"Did I do the right thing?"

"I can't tell you that. But I completely support you. I didn't meet Laura at the hunt. To be honest, I agree with you. I'm glad I met Laura before she was part of the hunt. I'm dreading the thought of having to host it now that I'm Alpha."

"I don't envy you," she whispered and they fell back into silence.

"Can I take you?" he whispered, fighting back the tears.

"I would love that."

"I'll tell dad you're staying over at our house. What time do you have to be there?"

"I meet the recruiter at one at the office."

"Tomorrow?"

"Yeah. I'm getting nervous."

"Too late for that, the Marines aren't going to let you go so easily. Come on," he said, leading her back to the trail that went to the training ground. "You only have two more chances to kick my ass."

"And I plan to. Race your sorry ass!" she laughed as she took off running.

"My ass is not sorry!" he retorted as he took off after her.

It was close, but Sirius beat her. She made up for it by beating him several times while sparring. Their brothers, Aries, Phoenix, and Caelum joined them. Just before eight, Sirius kissed his sister's cheek and told her to stay strong. He offered a salute to his brothers and then headed home for a shower before work.

3 - HAIR DO AND DON'T

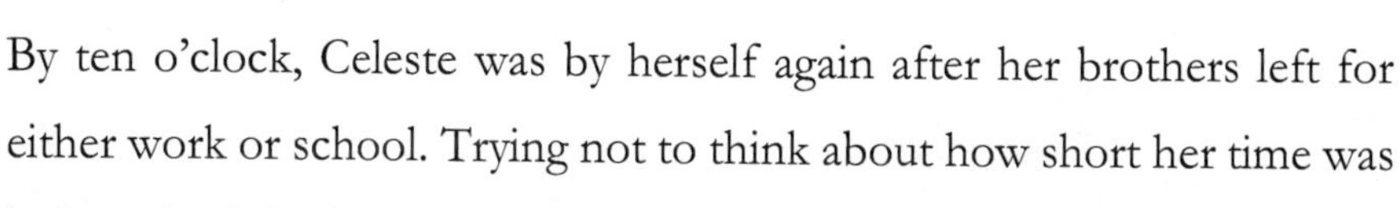

By ten o'clock, Celeste was by herself again after her brothers left for either work or school. Trying not to think about how short her time was before she left, she ran the five miles to the 24-hour gym in the human town.

She spent two hours on weights then took a shower and emptied her locker. Her parents didn't like her using the pila or human gym. Pilas, a crude name for humans taken from a breed of hairless dogs, were unaware that the nearby city was inhabited by werewolves. Celeste remembered the rumors from high school that it was a cult of some sort. Frequently she would assure her friends and teammates that it was not a cult or strange religious sect.

However, there were times that she thought that it was exactly that.

Females had few rights that were not guaranteed by the federal government of the Werewolf Council. Most families, including her own, opted to send their daughters to the public school in the pila town, Peony Village. This was done for their protection because as a male came into his prime, he could sometimes be unpredictable and in a moment of lust and desire, attack an unmated female.

For the same reason the pack had laws that her father refused to change. One of which was that females could not use the pack gym by themselves. And she, even as the daughter of the Alpha, was forbidden from the gym and training grounds unless one of her brothers was with her.

As was her regular routine, she went to the little café next door and had a quick lunch. Before heading back home, she went to the beauty shop and had her hair cut into a pixie style and donated the long black tresses before running back home for another shower to get the remaining traces of hair off her newly sweaty skin. She was walking out of her bathroom as her mom walked into her room.

Aislinn was quite beautiful and did not look as if she had borne thirteen pups and was approaching her fifth decade. Her brassy auburn hair fell in tight curls down to the middle of her back. Her golden tanned skin was flawless after a lifelong strict skin care routine that she passed on to her daughters. She stood five feet four and had a slender build, with soft brown eyes that were currently focused on her daughter.

"What did you do to your hair?" Aislinn screamed, the deep Irish lilt from her childhood slightly tinging her words.

"I got it cut. I wanted something different," Celeste said, going into her closet to get dressed.

"But why now?" her mother squealed. "Do you really think that cutting your hair will change the way your mate feels about you?"

Walking back out in yoga pants and an oversized t-shirt, Celeste glared at her mother. "Did you ever consider that I did it because I wanted a haircut? That I wanted something different? That it has nothing to do with my mate? Or that horrible hunt?"

"But your hair. Why? Your mate -"

"Are you not listening?" Celeste yelled. "It has nothing to do with that fucking hunt! I wanted something different! If it won't affect my mate finding me, why the hell do you care? My looks shouldn't be why they want to be with me! With me! Not my damned hair!"

Celeste grabbed her gym bag and walked back into her closet to put her dirty clothes in the basket.

"Don't yeh walk away from me, girl!" Aislinn yelled back, her Irish accent a little thicker.

"Why the fuck not? You're planning on sending me away with a fucking stranger in just a few days!"

"He's your mate!"

"Well, who the hell is he?"

"Your mate!"

"A fucking stranger!"

"Celeste Starr Moore!" her father said, walking into her room. "You do not talk to your mother like that!"

"Then you tell me who you're going to sell me to!"

"We are not selling you," Malachi said, trying to calm his daughter. He didn't like her yelling or cursing at her mother. But she was his strong daughter, just as strong as her brothers. Perhaps even stronger. Celeste was the one who could take on the world. And win. The tears that she refused to shed would be his undoing.

"Am I not good enough for two cows and a goat?" she demanded angrily.

"I would never sell any of my daughters." Malachi walked towards her.

"But you have no problems with them being raped."

The instant his hand hit her cheek, Malachi regretted it. There was no shock in her face. Her eyes radiated with anger and rage.

"Celeste," Sirius said walking into the room after clearly overhearing the heated discussion. "Why don't you pack a bag and come stay with me for a few days. Let everyone cool off. We'll talk about all of this in a few days."

Celeste stepped back into her closet and grabbed a change of clothes and the old running shoes, shoving them into the newly emptied gym bag. Then she walked out of her room, down the stairs, and out of her parents' house for the final time.

"I… I…" Malachi tried to apologize as his shoulder slumped, and then locked eyes with his son , "tell her I'm sorry."

"I will. But she's not wrong." Sirius glared at their father. "Two of my sisters have been raped at the Hunt. And your response both times was to get their bags and make them go with their rapist. Aria is dead. And Sky fears her husband. Still, you wonder why Celeste doesn't want anything to do with the hunt?"

He turned on his heel and followed his sister's path. When he got to the circular drive, she was nowhere to be seen. Her scent told him that she went in the direction of his house and hoped that was where she went. As he was getting into his car, his wife's voice came through the mate link saying Celeste was at their house, crying. His sister was hurt badly. Celeste never cried.

4 - FAMILY MEETING

The following morning Celeste refused to go for a run or even to the training ground to beat up her brothers, even after Sirius pointed out that it would be her last chance for a long time. Instead, her oldest brother crawled into the twin bed beside her and held her close as she waged her internal battle. She knew that she would be breaking her family's hearts, and that was not what she wanted.

Always the protector, he had said that she would be staying at his house for a few days knowing that she would be leaving before that time frame was up. But with their parents believing that she was there, they would not question her sudden disappearance from the family quarters of the pack house.

However, they may notice her silence from the family and pack links. Now with the fight between her and her parents yesterday, it would simply be chalked up to anger.

"I feel guilty," he whispered to her brother, pushing long black strands away her eyes and wiping her tears.

"You shouldn't," her brother assured her.

"Not enough to stay," came the soft admission. "But maybe enough for some cookie dough ice cream."

"Laura is making cookies. Does that count?"

"Only if she saves me some cookie dough."

Chuckling, Sirius reached his wife through the mate link and then kissed his sister's hair. "She has some set aside for you."

When she had decided that the pity party was over, Celeste took a shower and ate the lunch Laura had made, along with a few cookies and a spoonful of cookie dough.

Sitting at her brother's home office desk, she tried to write a goodbye letter but couldn't. Nothing came. How could she explain that the death of her oldest sister at the hands of her fated mate terrified her of what her own might do. Only weeks after they buried Aria, Sky had been attacked at the Hunt in the West Winds pack and was now afraid of her own mate.

Celeste finally wrote two simple sentences in bold block letters on the elegant paper with the pack crest embossed at the top.

"TELL THEM THE TRUTH. I LOVE YOU ALL."

She sealed it in an envelope just before Sirius took her to the recruiting station in the human town. He hugged his sister and kissed her forehead, bestowing the blessing of the Alpha on her.

"I love you. This is the bravest thing I've ever seen you do. And I've seen you do some brave things. Some pretty damned dumb things, too." Laughing, they hugged each other even tighter. "Now go find the biggest, baddest motherfucker and go kick his ass."

Chuckling, she agreed to do just that. A few minutes later, she was in the car with her recruiter. And then… she was gone.

Sirius waited until the day before the other packs would begin arriving for the Hunt, coolly refusing to answer his father's demands to tell him where Celeste was. He might not live in the pack house, but since he had turned twenty-five last year, he was the Alpha. No matter how much Malachi demanded, ordered or threatened, his son would no longer bend to his will.

Celeste had been gone for nearly a week, would already be on Parris Island. She was on her way to becoming a Marine. Not even their father had enough power to stop that now. It was all up to her.

Laura had gotten a babysitter for their pups, insisting on being there to support her Alpha as any Luna would do. She would support her husband and his sister. Goddess knew they both needed it.

"Where is she?" Malachi asked when he did not see Celeste with the couple as they entered the family quarters of the pack house.

"Is the rest of the family here?" Sirius asked, going to the living room.

Looking around, Sirius saw his divorced grandmother, mother and all but two of his siblings as they sat in confusion. He had called them all. One after another. They needed to have a family meeting without the youngest generation. It was important.

Now they all sat there, from nine-year-old Portia, all the way to twenty-five-year-old Phoenix. The only ones missing were Celeste and Aria. One was at Marine boot camp and the other had died after being sent back to her mate in Mexico. Sirius noted that each of his mated brothers held their mates in a loving embrace. Sky flinched every time her mate barely touched her. Andromeda, or Andi to family and close friends, sat alone.

All eleven of these siblings were a perfect blend of their parents. Bright with amber-colored eyes from their dad and pale skin with a dusting of freckles from their Irish mom. Their hair ranged from mahogany to dark honey, all with red undertones. The brothers were all around or above six feet, even twelve-year-old Leo already stood at six feet even.

They all looked like their parents. Like each other. But the sibling who was missing looked nothing like them. She had been marked by the Moon Goddess to stand out from the others in her family.

"Andi, where's Drew?" Sirius asked. He could have reached out through the pack link but preferred to grant his siblings and their spouses privacy in their relationships.

Her eyes glazed over for just a moment before saying he was nearly there. A few silent and tense minutes later, Drew entered the house and came to find his mate. He kissed her gently before picking her up and putting her on his lap as he sat down.

"Everyone is here." Malachi snarled. "Where is Celeste? The ceremonies for the Hunt start tomorrow. We have packs arriving at sunrise."

"That's your concern? The damn Hunt?" Sirius asked.

"Our pack was chosen to host. I do not intend to look like a fool," their father snarled.

"For the past two years, your daughter has been telling you that she's scared of the Hunt. And what have you done?"

"We gave her an extra year. Told everyone that she wanted to do the Hunt when we host. Now for the last time, where is she?" Malachi snarled, and Sirius' wolf, Ranger, offered a low growl in their chest as a warning. The older wolf and former Alpha of the pack, Brutus, whined in submission even as the man refused to back down.

"That was so kind of you to give her a year to get used to the idea that she might be raped. So noble." Sirius sneered at his father, standing tall and fighting to keep his composure. Since Sirius had ascended to the position of Alpha, he was the only one who would dare to speak to Malachi so directly. He dared a lot lately.

"Sometimes the males get so excited that they can't control themselves." Aislinn said trying to soothe the situation. "I've tried to prepare all the girls for this."

As it clicked with his brothers and the other males what she was saying, there were low protective growls filling the room. Sirius could only hope they remembered this anger when it was time for their own daughters to go to the Hunt. Generations ago, when the Hunt started in Rome, all the unmated females were forced to attend. Now they were sent out of tradition and honor, often against their wishes to prevent their family and, by extension, their pack from looking weak and breaking tradition. It was the one thing that he had no control over as an Alpha. If the father decided that his daughter was doing the Hunt, the Alpha could not interfere.

Shaking his head, he walked over to where Sky sat. He knelt in front of her and gently took her hands in his. "Sky, my beautiful brave sister. Will you tell me what happened at your hunt?"

She looked at her mate warily.

"He won't hurt you. And if you don't want to go back home with him, you can come and stay with us. But he needs to know what he did to you. He doesn't know how he hurt you. And he needs to understand."

She sighed and then spoke so softly that they could barely hear her, even with super sensitive hearing. "I was excited at first. Mom always said that I'd meet my mate at the hunt. And I was excited about it but afraid if I didn't find my mate, I would be one of those wolves that goes crazy. We were running through the woods when I felt the first tingle, and I knew my mate was there."

Nodding, Sirius encouraged her to continue. He too had heard the stories all of his life. If you did not find your mate, your inner wolf would become more and more beastlike. Unable to control. For the lack of a better description, they would become feral.

Sky let out a shaky breath. "Then, suddenly, I was face down in the dirt. One hand was holding my head down to the ground. It was hard for me to breathe. With his other he ripped my pants off. Then my leg was twisted and pulled out of socket."

Joseph sat stunned. He remembered catching her scent. And then the next thing he remembered was the howl that he made just before he went to claim her, but she was unconscious. When she came to, her parents had given her a change of clothes and her suitcases. Three years later and he had yet to claim her because any time that he got near her, she would have a panic attack. Now, he knew why. She saw him as a monster and not a mate.

"Aminah told me that he was our mate, so she wouldn't fight back. She was too weak to fight back, even if she wanted to." Sky said softly of her wolf with a tremor in her voice and body. "Before … before the Hunt, we were, we were given a drink laced with," she closed her eyes and swallowed hard, "with wolf's bane. She was scared." Her voice became even softer. "We're still scared."

Sirius brushed some tears off her cheeks. "Tell me the rest." He knew that some packs still subdued the she-wolves before the Hunt with wolf's bane that weakened the inner beast.

Nodding, Sky told the worst part of her story keeping her eyes closed, unable to meet anyone's eyes. "Th-th-here… there was a tearing pain, down…" she shook her head and Sirius squeezed her hand to remind that she was safe, "there. And again, I…I…I tried to call out, but there was dirt in, in my mouth. S-s-some st-started going up my nose. The pain was unbearable."

Tears began to fall heavily from her closed eyes as her head hung in shame. "Now, not only was I being…I was ripped, but I was being hit too. Over and over and over." Her voice rose as panic set in along with the shame. A sob racked her trembling body and she lifted her fist to bite her knuckles before returning to a softer voice. "The pain… it hurt so, so bad. It all became too much to bear. I couldn't breathe. It all went black."

When I woke up," her voice was accusing now, and she looked at her parents with hatred and anger. "When I woke up, mom gave me a set of clean clothes. She told me that she was so happy that I had found my mate." She spit venom with her words and Sirius saw their mother flinch.

"I tried to tell her what happened. How much it hurt." She sneered at her mother. " She didn't care. And she just told me that sometimes the first-time hurts." Sky's anger was now directed at their father. "Neither did dad. He was only concerned with what other packs would think of us. And how we upheld the damned tradition."

Guilt filled Aislinn's face and she could no longer look at any of her daughters. Malachi seemed unmoved. But Sirius saw the slight tick in his father's clenched jaw that appeared when he was angry. Or when he was uncertain of his decision.

"Then dad said that my suitcases were in his cabin, and I needed to go to him. I tried to tell dad about it, and he just told me it was a good match… And then, then…" her voice softened and her head dropped again as her shame returned, "I was sent away. A painful sob was ripped from her chest. "Nobody loved me enough to listen."

Sirius gathered her into his arms and sat on the floor rocking her in his lap. "I love you, Sky. I will always love you. I'm listening. We're all listening now. Go ahead and cry. You cry as much as you want."

"I am the monster of her dreams," Joseph said quietly. He got down on the floor and looked at his beautiful mate. "I never wanted to hurt you. I don't even remember anything. I remember catching your scent and then finding you. The next thing that I remember is howling, and I was going to mark you. But you had passed out. So, I took you to the first aid tent." He was the one crying now. "They said that your hip was out of socket. That you may have fallen and that the fall probably did it. I am so sorry. I've never wanted to hurt you. I just want to treasure you. You are my mate, my soul. You are the best part of me. I love you so much. And now that I know that I caused this… this pain for you... Oh, goddess. I would completely understand if you wanted to reject me."

"How about if she comes and stays with us for a while," Laura suggested. " You can come see her and maybe you two can start over. When Sirius and I first met, he always brought me coffee in the morning. I fell in love with my mate over really bad coffee."

Sirius gave a little laugh remembering all the coffee he had bought and made. He did not drink it himself and did not know that there was more to it than ground coffee beans and water. His wife, a self-proclaimed coffee snob, drank the coffee because of the man who brought it.

"Does that sound good to you?" he asked his sister, and she nodded and sniffled.

Joseph started to reach out to touch her cheek but he stopped with his hand raised only a few inches away from his wife and unmarked mate. Sky reached out and touched her fingertips to his and gave a small smile.

Hope overtook him.

The rest of the room remained silent for several more minutes.

"I was afraid that it would happen to me." Elisabeth, Phoenix's mate said. The other women in the room agreed.

"It's not like a female can reject a mate as easily as a male can." Laura said and, when her father-in-law questioned this, she gave a small smile. "If a male rejects a female, everyone points out all her flaws, justifying why he rejected her. If a female rejects, they still point out all of her flaws and his attributes, telling her that she just screwed up her life and will never get a better mate."

"Even if he's a monster that beats her," Malachi's mother, Bridget, admitted.

"This is why Celeste didn't want to do the Hunt. She was terrified of what would happen to her. She tried talking to you over and over and over again. But you two never listened." Sirius told his parents.

"Where is she, Sirius?" his grandmother asked quietly.

"She's gone." He turned to look at her. "There's nothing that can be done about it."

"Is she safe?" his mother asked.

"I'll check on her," he answered. Although Celeste had blocked the pack and the family, she left her connection to her eldest brother.

Sirius reached out through the mind link before answering, "She's fine. She said so far, she's liking boot camp." He smirked, "The humidity sucks."

"Where is she?" Malachi demanded. "And why can I not reach her?"

"She's at Marine Corps boot camp and she blocked the pack."

"Boot camp?" Aislinn asked. "When did this happen?"

"She signed up in November, after her birthday. She left for boot camp two days after you slapped her."

"Did you know?" Malachi asked.

"She went with my blessing."

5 - PACKHOUSE MEETING

"Are you really going to let this happen to me?"

The simple question from seventeen-year-old Wenona cut Wyatt to the core. She had demanded an answer from him the day before the Crystal River Pack was leaving for the Hunt in the nearby Silver Lake pack. He had agreed to go, but refused to participate, stating that he had business with the other Alpha. Quite simply, he wanted nothing to do with the Hunt. Because of this, Wenona knew that Wyatt would understand her fears.

He did understand her fears. He clearly remembered the terror in his older sister's eyes causing the deep need to protect his sister. The hunt sparked her need to protect her mate and the Beta's need to mark his. The only thing they could hope for was that once their youngest sister was old enough for the Hunt, it had changed. In the meantime, he made a concoction and told her to drink it with a simple warning.

"This will make you sicker than a dog. Pun intended."

She downed the drink and regretted it almost immediately. By morning, Wenona was too sick to go with the rest of the delegation. Luna Elizabeth stated that she would stay with their daughter, and Alpha Jonathan declared that his son could handle the Alpha responsibilities by himself.

At twenty years old, Wyatt knew that he had five more years until he could assume the position of Alpha according to the laws implemented by the Council. There would also be a few more years before he would be released from the Navy. But he had been training for this position his entire life. As the only son of Alpha Jonathon and Luna Elizabeth, he knew his responsibilities.

The dreams that he had of becoming a Navy SEAL would never come to fruition. But as a medic embedded with the Marines, he still felt useful and had the opportunity to train with them. He took advantage of this every chance that he got.

Wyatt found himself approaching the Silver Lake packhouse for the meeting that he had with Sirius during the Hunt. The opening ceremonies for the Hunt had already taken place and it was approaching midmorning. The sky was slightly overcast with the first thin bands of the hurricane coming up the eastern seaboard. It was expected to turn out towards sea and be clear by early to mid-afternoon.

The buildings were all traditional colonial style, as were so many in New England. The light rolling hills made the whole area picture perfect. His own pack was west of Philadelphia and had plenty of their own colonial buildings. But here, it appeared that the pack held tightly to tradition and barely grasped for the future.

Wyatt was stopped by the sentry at the door who insisted on checking his ID and a list of appointments. He appreciated the thoroughness and the relaxed uniform of the polo and utility pants over the formal livery that he saw in other parts of the pack. Perhaps the new Alpha was looking towards the future.

Once he was inside the packhouse, the subtle scent that had Demon perking up in the back of his mind surrounded him. Intoxicating. Sweet and spicy with just a little hint of tanginess. It was everywhere. He had to find who it belonged to.

"Mate." Demon practically pranced in the back of Wyatt's mind with his nose tipped up in the air inhaling the intoxicating flavors.

Ignoring the office to his right, he followed the scent up the stairs in search of his mate. On the third floor, it grew stronger. He started down the wing to his left but quickly turned around as it got weaker. Halfway down the other wing, he found a door that was closed. Opening the door, the scent overpowered him. Demon rolled around and howled in Wyatt's mind.

"That's our mate" Demon declared. "Find her!"

"Patience," Wyatt told his wolf.

Stepping inside, he was enveloped in the best scent he had ever smelled. Along with the typically feminine and submissive scents was also a very strong dominant scent of strong, tangy spice. Sugar sweet like cookies mixed with strong aromas of cinnamon, cloves, and a touch of ginger.

Walking through the room, man and beast continued to argue. Demon wanted to go find their mate immediately. Wyatt agreed but kept thinking of how Wenona had begged him to make her sick so she could avoid the hunt. He thought of Whitney screaming for help. He could not be the reason that any woman had that look of fear on her face.

Certainly not the face of his mate.

Wyatt walked around looking at his mate's stuff. Trophies from cheer and tumbling competitions. Medals for track and field and a few for marathons. Championship trophies for soccer, fast pitch softball and basketball. There were even a few championship rings.

Pictures of teams, friends, and special events covered a poster size corkboard. He scanned the images, wondering which one she was. He stepped into the bathroom and opened the three small drawers. Mascara, lip gloss and lotion were the only pieces of makeup he found.

There was a drawer full of hair ties and barrettes. The third drawer was empty.

On the back of the door, he found a pair of pajama pants with Cookie Monster and a matching tank top. Wyatt stepped out of the bathroom and did not see the man standing in the doorway to the hall, watching him. Wyatt continued around the room and came across certificates and martial arts belts. There were two belt holders; both had all slots filled all the way to from beginner to black. There was a certificate showing that Celeste — now he knew her name — had earned the rank of third-degree black belt in Tai Kwon Do. Next to it was the same rank for Brazilian Ju Jitsu.

A bench sat in front of her window with a bottle of bright purple nail polish and sparkly blue toe separators on the windowsill. On the other side of the window were kickboxing and boxing gloves. He was having a hard time connecting the feminine nail polish, cheer pictures and jewelry with the violent activities associated with the boxing gloves, medals and belts. The twin bed sat in the middle and was tightly made with a bright blue comforter. When he peeked at the pillowcase underneath, he again found Cookie Monster grinning back at him.

"She loves Cookie Monster. Always has, " Sirius said from the door. "I would ask what you're doing, but the lovesick look in your eyes tells me."

"Is she in the Hunt?" Wyatt hoped that the other man would say no. The beast inside him growled at the other man. The older wolf huffed at Demon before offering a low warning growl himself.

"If you're hoping to meet her, I'm afraid you're out of luck." Sirius leaned up against the doorframe, studying the man only a few years younger than himself. "Before I tell you anything else about my sister, tell me what you think about the Hunt."

With Wyatt stating that the woman was a relative of his, Demon backed down. But he still wanted to go find her, claim her, and mate with her. The moon goddess made mates perfect for each other, therefore, the wolf decided she should submit to them without question.

The moon goddess has made her perfect for us. Wyatt thought to himself. She will challenge us and keep us on our toes.

Demon chuckled in the back of Wyatt's mind. A completely submissive female would bore us both within a short period of time.

Sirius smirked at the other man standing in his sister's room and knew that he was talking with the beast within him.

"Do you want the 'its tradition' bullshit answer?" Wyatt finally asked. "Or do you want my honest opinion?"

"Honest."

"It's archaic, sexist, sadistic, and downright cruel. I think it needs to be eliminated."

Sirius smiled and glanced at the crest on the other man's polo. "Crystal River. Your pack encourages military service, right?"

"Yes, sir. I am in the Navy as a medic." he extended a hand. "Wyatt O'Donnell."

"My ten-thirty." Sirius chuckled as he accepted the other man's hand. "Sirius Moore, not more serious. You like Marines?"

Wyatt laughed. "I better. Not only is my best friend, and future Beta, one, but I am embedded with a platoon."

"Really?" Sirius asked and the other man nodded. "Why?"

"Every Marine is a rifleman." Wyatt quoted with a small chuckle.

"Every Marine?" Sirius clarified.

With a nod, the younger man expanded his answer. "Yes, every Marine has to qualify on the rifle range, noncombatants do not. Therefore, they don't have medical personnel because Devil Docs, such as myself, are traditionally considered noncombatants."

"Great. She can already kick my ass. Now she's going to be able to shoot it also, " Sirius mused with a grin.

"She's very active, " Wyatt observed, motioning towards the belts and awards.

'Let's get her active under us.' Demon suggested and Wyatt warned him to calm down. 'Or what?'

'Wolf's bane.' Wyatt warned and Demon retreated to the back of their mind. A shot made from the extract of the Wolf's bane plant would subdue the beast inside him, knocking it unconscious.

The flower was typically used to make the suppressants that many in the were community used to control their inner beasts. Witches and alchemists made the suppressants for most packs. The Crystal River pack had a healer that custom made Wyatt's specifically for Demon. After all, no one wanted him to get a bad suppressant and the future Alpha of the Crystal River pack be killed or seriously maimed.

Sirius smirked as the other man's eyes cleared indicating that the inner conversation in his link was done. "Extremely active. The longest she would ever willingly sit still was when she would paint her toenails. And that was a struggle."

"When did she go in?"

"I dropped her off last week."

"She's at Parris?"

"Yeah. Don't think that you can just go there and get her; the more you try to force her, the more she will fight. Our dad was forcing her to do the Hunt but was kind enough to allow her an extra year to get used to the idea." The venom dripping from that statement was almost palpable. "She had just graduated and since we were hosting this year, he thought it would be okay. But she described it as an extra year to prepare to be raped."

"That's one of the reasons I don't like it. Seems like there are more and more every year."

"Two of my sisters." Sirius shook his head sadly. "And they are the daughters of an Alpha. With my older sister, Aria, her husband liked it so much that he continued to rape her, right up until she died."

"And because it was her mate, no one did anything, " Wyatt stated.

Sirius nodded in agreement. "She found out that she was pregnant, refused to have a child like him, took a large dose of wolf's bane and silver. She was…" Sirius sighed. "Let's just say it was horrible. Aria died only a few weeks before Sky did her hunt. She was also attacked and now lives with us while her mate courts her."

"I'm so sorry, " Wyatt said, swallowing his emotions as he thought about his sister calling out for him. "My sister, Wenona, was supposed to be here for her hunt, but she told me that she was scared of being raped. I made up a concoction that made her sick like crazy. My parents stayed with her, and I came with our delegation. I have two females hiding in the cabin being guarded by some of my most trusted warriors."

"They didn't want to be in the hunt?"

"No. I told them that they could do the events after. If they met their mate then, what would it matter?"

"I think Celeste will like you, " Sirius said straightening up and walking around the bed and past Wyatt into her closet. "Because of that, I'm going to do something that she may not like. At least not right now."

Wyatt watched as the other man opened a drawer and pulled out a large, plastic, sealable bag. Arching an eyebrow in a silent question, Sirius just grinned and shrugged.

"My mom has a thing about sweaty clothes and makes us carry bags for after workouts. I thought it was a mom thing, I didn't know it was a 'my mom' thing."

Sirius dug through his sister's dirty clothes basket. The majority of what he pulled out were exercise clothes which caused him to make a face after giving the cloth a good sniff. Then he picked up a blue shirt that he approved of. Touching it as little as possible, it was folded up and placed inside the bag before he sealed it. "It's not as good as having her," Sirius admitted, "but at least you can have her scent. Just don't let my parents know. In fact, don't let them know that she's your mate. Dad is pissed at her. Mom now understands, I think. Pretty sure all of us kids support her."

"Do you support her?"

"I gave her the blessing of an Alpha, helped her block the pack and family so she couldn't be tracked, and dropped her off." He cocked his head, listening to the faint footsteps down the hall. "My dad is coming. P lay along." He mouthed.

Wyatt nodded and then accepted the t-shirt and yoga pants that he was handed.

"That should fit her." Sirius was saying as his father walked into the room. "If not, let me know and we'll see if we can find something else."

"What are you doing in here?" Malachi demanded, anger rolling off him.

"Alpha O'Donnell has a girl with them that didn't pack anything in case her hunt outfit got messed up."

"She tripped against a tree and both her shirt and pants were ripped. You don't think that your daughter will mind, do you?" Wyatt asked politely.

"She left it here. Take what you want." With that, Malachi turned and left. Even after he was gone, his anger could still be felt. Along with shame and an undercurrent of hurt.

Once he was far enough away from the door, Sirius whispered, "Let me have your phone number and I'll keep you updated on her."

Wyatt nodded, took Sirius's phone, and put his number in it. Since they were from different packs and had no familial connection, they would have to rely on technology and not the mind links to keep in touch.

He then took the extra clothes he was given to Devlin, one of the girls hiding in the cabin. Devlin would appreciate the fact that the other woman's scent would help mask her own as she also planned on going into the military when she turned eighteen.

If Devlin found her mate today, he may not allow her to live her dream.

The shirt in the sealed bag remained a secret between the two men. From then on, even after it lost the scent of his mate, it went everywhere with Wyatt. Keeping him grounded and staving off the bloodlust that lesser wolves would succumb to without their mates.

6 - COUNCIL CHAMBERS

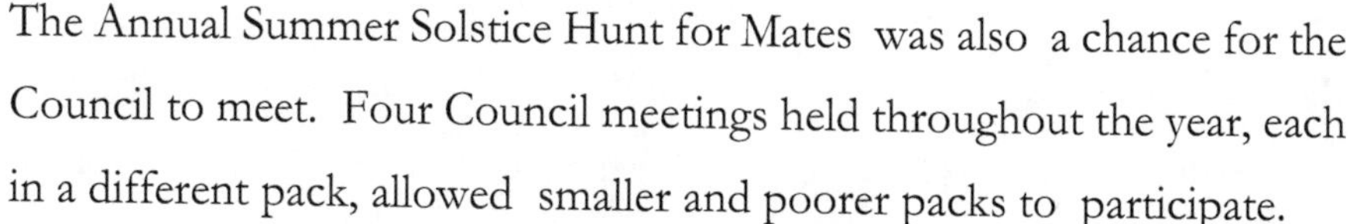

The Annual Summer Solstice Hunt for Mates was also a chance for the Council to meet. Four Council meetings held throughout the year, each in a different pack, allowed smaller and poorer packs to participate.

It was just over an hour after Sirius found Wyatt in his sister's bedroom that the council chambers began to fill with the Alphas and Betas. The chambers for the Silver Lake pack were in a building adjacent to the pack house.

Old colonial style buildings complimented others with their red brick and dark shutters. The former Alpha and his family still lived in the current pack house while Sirius and his family lived in the older and smaller previous pack house. Just like the other official pack buildings for Silver Lake, they were all red brick colonial style. At least from the front.

The new packhouse was nearly three times the size of the old one with pack offices on the first floor, the top two floors were for the Alpha family and their guests. The previous packhouses did not need to house so many offices. Now with the family and offices being kept in one building, it simplified everything.

But as with so many things with the Silver Lake Pack, everything was rooted in tradition. The plumbing improved. The buildings went from whale oil to gas and then electricity for lights and heat. Wi-Fi and internet could be used throughout the buildings.

Every single official pack building was made from the same basic design. Chuckling, Sirius thought about how his mother had described them to her family in Ireland. 'Basic American colonial, standard American colonial and deluxe American colonial. Red brick, trim in cream or black.'

After Sirius ascended to the position of Alpha, he could have kicked his parents and siblings out, or at least taken over the master suites. However, he had no desire to do so. With no offices being housed in the old pack house, they did not have to worry about random pack members walking into their house.

Sirius and his wife took the smaller and older house for more privacy to start their lives and family together. Plus, there was not another house big enough to house all his siblings when he ascended to the position. Malachi had insisted that Sirius and Laura take the bigger house – it was tradition.

It was also tradition that currently had him walking across the small field between the two buildings to attend the Council meeting. He was tired of some of these traditions and had no issues with refusing to kick his family out of their house just for tradition.

"Tradition. Smedition. Fo-fana-fedition, " Sirius muttered just before opening the large wood and glass door and entering the lobby. Taking a deep breath, he steeled himself and plastered a smile on his face.

So many Alphas in one space who were each trying to show that they were more powerful than the others was something that he could live without. This was the hierarchy of werewolf society.

The Omegas as servants and manual laborers were at the bottom of the food chain and were forced to submit to everyone. He had seen the way they were treated — almost like second class citizens. His own wife, Laura, had been Omega- born and living as a Luna of the pack was a drastic change.

Her parents had worked the greenhouses, a necessity for New England winters that can see more than a hundred inches of snow. Because of this, they had been lucky and had always had food, even in the depths of frozen hell. Other Omega families were not as lucky. While he courted his wife, he had seen it all.

Multiple families lived together to take care of children and older generations. Parents went without meals, sometimes days at a time, to ensure their pups could eat. Children were not allowed to play in the snow because they only had school clothes to wear. Houses without heat had only a single fireplace that everyone slept around.

The Omegas were in the twenty-first century and yet the lowest level of their pack lived like they were still in the sixteenth century. And his predecessors had allowed it. Because, once again, tradition.

The Gammas were, according to Malachi, nothing more than glorified Omegas. Their station in life was a little better, but not by much. There were several Gammas who worked in the trades and for the city. Many lived in the pack city, Silver Lake, but went to the neighboring city, Silver Lake Township, to work.

The Betas were all upper middle class by pila standards. But they insisted on separating themselves out into different sects and cliques. Not that the Alphas were any better. The bigger and richer the pack, the higher in rank they believed themselves to be.

How often had Sirius heard his father bragging about their lineage going back to Romulus himself. And his mother's Lycan heritage … Sure, he enjoyed the height and strength that came from being of Lycan blood. But there were so many issues that came with it.

Entering the foyer of the building, Sirius was assaulted by hundreds of scents from all the Alphas and their staff members. Ranger gave a warning growl at the back of Sirius' mind. All of these males. powerful and authoritative Alphas, were on his lands, his territory. Even if they were invited, the beast still saw them as a threat to his position. His title. Possibly even his young pups.

With the internal struggle in his head, he was having a hard time paying attention to what was being said. Or even who was saying what. Realizing that he needed to respond, and not just smile and shake hands, Sirius nodded at something that Alpha Sampson of the West Winds pack said. He continued to remind himself and Ranger to keep control of their thoughts and emotions. He was still new to his position and did not need to have the Elder Alphas question his ability to control himself and his wolf.

Shaking the older Alpha's hand, he continued to circle the room. The older Alphas and their Betas were regaling the younger ones with tales of their Hunts. Looking over at the tall man that he now knew to be his sister's mate, he could feel the anger building.

The conversation around him not only angered him. but it made him sick. These were the men that were raising the boys who would take his younger sisters, and possibly his daughters as their mates. He refused to look at the crests on the shirts, afraid that the knowledge would make the upcoming meetings even more unbearable.

"She couldn't get enough of me, " one Alpha said and another laughed.

"My mate put up a fight, actually for quite a while, " a third grinned. "Now that I've put a few pups in her, she's the perfect docile Luna."

His Beta laughed. "Was it the pups or you correcting her behavior?"

Several of the men laughed.

"That's something that these younger generations need to learn again. Bitches need to be put in their place, " the Alpha of the Dark Sky pack declared.

His pack lands were in northern Maine and the pack was known for being hard. They clung to old traditions and consequences be damned. While the Omegas and Gammas were treated barely above slaves, it was rumored that the Dark Sky pack still practiced slavery. It had been outlawed by the Elder Alphas of the council long before any of the pila governments had done so.

But once again, tradition.

"Maybe we need to learn a new place for ourselves, " Sirius interrupted to a round of laughter.

"Boy, I've seen that wife of yours, " one of the older Alphas said lewdly. "There's some places that I'd like to put her."

There was another round of raucous laughter. Before Sirius could do something stupid, Wyatt crossed the room and grabbed his new friend.

"They're not going to touch her, " Wyatt reminded him softly. Ranger was still growling in Sirius' chest and Demon echoed the sentiment. "This is not the time or the place." He nodded towards the chambers where business would be handled. "In there. That's where we can make changes."

"Not with these Alphas, " Sirius pointed out and Wyatt nodded.

"But they won't be in charge for much longer. It's our generation that will make the changes that are needed." Wyatt tilted his head and the other man followed where he indicated.

Standing only a few dozen feet away was Alpha Henry of the Harbor Moon pack in North Carolina. The man had no sons to take the position of Alpha. His oldest daughter was now the Luna of the Autumn Hills Pack in New Hampshire. But his second daughter, twenty-one-year-old Amber, stood in the place of the next Alpha. Whether it was to learn the duties of the Alpha, or to find a mate, neither man was not certain. But the fact that she was here at the meeting, and not at the Hunt spoke volumes.

Sirius nodded and Wyatt stepped back to let his hands fall away, clasping them behind his back in what the Navy had told him was a normal stance.

After a three-hour session, the Elder Alphas called a recess until the following morning. The Hunt was over, and couples were getting ready for the feast later that night. The new mates would present themselves to their new pack Alphas and the Elder Alphas. Very rarely were the matches denied; if they were, it was typically ignored.

Wyatt's closest friend and future Beta and second in command, knocked on the door to the master chamber in their pack cabin before entering the room without waiting for an order to enter. Rolling his eyes at his friend, Wyatt finished tying his tie as Stephen held his own out to his friend.

"Seriously?"

Stephen shrugged. "Marine dress blues don't have these stupid fuckers."

Finishing his own tie, he took the other one and tied it quickly. "I know you didn't agree with my decision to leave Devlin and Charissa here."

"I just don't think it's that big of a deal."

"Maybe because you've known your mate since she was born."

"Some of us are lucky." Stephen grinned as Wyatt slid the tie over his head and passed it to his friend. "Thank you."

"Yeah." He grinned and his friend closed the door and activated the white noise machine.

"You found your mate. See? Some traditions are worth keeping." Both men looked in the mirror to tighten their ties before reaching for the suit jackets with the Crystal River crest on the breast pocket.

"Where is she?" Stephen asked.

Wyatt's eyes landed on the crest that he had seen all his life. An elongated shield with a crescent moon hanging with golden constellations of the night sky. In the center stood a majestic werewolf, his golden fur lit with hints of deep red and light blue. Willow trees that were adorned with golden threads in their branches and leaves with a pale blue-ribbon banner ran along the bottom with the motto emblazoned in scarlet red. Flumen Crystallinum, Custodientes Noctis – Crystal River, Guardians of the Night.

"She's on Parris Island."

Stephen adjusted his shirt collar before buttoning his jacket and fixing his cuffs. Laughing, Wyatt realized that he and his Beta were doing the same process.

"I'm not sure if I should cheer a fellow Marine or ask what the hell." Stephen told his friend as they both finished the adjustments on their suits.

"Don't say anything about it. It's complicated, but I promise that I'll explain later." Wyatt paused and his friend nodded in understanding. While they were discussing the Hunt, the other elephant in the room should also be addressed. "Stephen, I know you don't agree with my opinions and actions, but thank you for not openly arguing with me."

"I might not agree, and I don't think there's a reason to end this tradition, but you are still my Alpha." Stephen admitted. " More importantly, you're my friend. We haven't always agreed, but we've always had each other's backs."

Wyatt smiled at his oldest and closest friend. His support meant more to him than any blind agreement ever could. Stephen would always tell his friend what his honest opinion was, even if it was not what Wyat wanted to hear. And the Beta might not agree with all the Alpha's decisions, but he would support him and defer to his decisions in public.

"Come on," Stephen slapped his friend on the back. "Let's go eat some good food with some mediocre company."

.

7 - MAIL CALL

True to his word, Sirius kept Wyatt updated on Celeste. When she graduated boot camp, he went and watched but stayed away. He fought against every instinct that told him to go to her. But he smiled when the wind shifted, and she caught his scent. Laura was telling her something and then her head popped up and she looked in his direction. He moved further into the shadows to stay out of sight but was glad that she'd had that reaction.

A few days later, a package arrived in the mail. Inside the box, along with pictures and a letter, was a PT shirt in a Ziploc bag. He moved quickly and closed the door to his room in the apartment he shared with two other shipmates. Then he opened it and inhaled that wonderful scent.

Neither of his pila roommates would understand him sniffing a T-shirt in a Ziploc bag to stave off bloodlust and insanity. He often wondered how his pila would react if they found out that werewolves and shifters were real. And that, unlike what Hollywood says, they could shift at any time.

But just as Hollywood portrayed, they mated for life. And the beasts that they shared their body with, mind and soul, needed their mate. Without it, the animal would take over, and they would become feral.

A mate was found through the scent that each wolf carried. All people carried a scent, but most pila were unaware of the individual scents. The human side of the werewolf would also feel the pull - a tingling sensation felt at a touch, the urge and unexplainable need to go towards something. Some called it a premonition or a sense of deja vu. A base instinct that predated man having a beast, maybe when he himself was more beast than man.

Without their mate, a wolf would give into the bloodlust. They could lose touch with reality and kill indiscriminately. Sirius had seen wolves and cats that were away from their mates for too long and gave into the bloodlust. So many times, it was passed off as a wild animal attack or a mental break.

As with anything else in this world, there were ways around it. Close contact with the mate or family. Keeping their scent close by.

Having pups to care for. Something to keep them grounded and anchored in reality.

The she-wolf across the hall completely understood what Wyatt was experiencing. Her own mate was currently on a float on the submarine USS Texas – not to be confused with the dreadnaught battleship USS Texas.

Both she and her husband were from the Buffalo Bayou pack in Houston, Texas. Thanks to them, Wyatt now knew more about the USS Texas than he ever thought possible. Texans may be friendly and humble about themselves, but when it came to their state, they were anything but.

A few months later, he received another package. The she-wolf from across the hall met him in the hallway with the package that was delivered to their apartment in error. This was a unit shirt. Celeste was an M.P. for the Marines.

This is how it went for the next several years. Anytime Sirius or one of his siblings went to see Celeste, they stole a shirt. And then he would get a new package in the mail with her shirt, a letter and if he was really lucky, sweets. He in turn would send her one of his own shirts and a letter and, sometimes, a care package. If she was going to be close by, he would go and watch from a distance. Every time that she caught his scent and looked for him, he and Demon got excited.

Occasionally, he felt like a stalker. Sometimes he even felt guilty.

But then, he'd catch her scent, and the world would spin upside down.

And when she caught his scent, her head would pop up and those silver eyes would seek him.

Once, he was certain that she had seen him. A few other times, he thought that she might have but wasn't certain. Not like that one time at the bar when their eyes had met. She stared at him with desire in her eyes and started to move towards him. Then her friends got her attention and the desire quickly turned to hate.

Sirius' words from the Hunt that the Silver Lake pack hosted echoed through his mind. Don't think that you can just go there and get her; the more you try to force her, the more she will fight. He did not want her to fight him. He wanted her to come to him, willingly and wanting to build a life together.

Wyatt smiled at her and then left. It took everything in him to walk away. But he did.

He knew that if she had come to him, it would have been under the influence of alcohol. She would probably regret it in the morning. As Demon screamed at him to go back to her, he left.

Being much more careful after that, Wyatt never followed her to a bar again. And since she was a Marine, there were lots of bars. Lots of nights that she could have her pick of men to spend the night with. And he had to let her.

From then on , it was strictly letters and packages. And those made the deployments more bearable. Such as the night, not quite two years since the Silver Lake Hunt, he was sitting in the middle of bombed out building with the Marines that he was embedded with, he pulled out the letter from Laura and reread it yet again in the low light of the moon.

Tucking the latest letter back into his pocket he pulled out his notebook and pencil. With the rest of the men asleep, except for the one walking patrol, a new letter was penned.

My dearest Mate,

I'm sitting here in the glow of a half-moon; the Hunt is only a few weeks away. If we had met at the last one, this would be our second anniversary. There are times when I wonder what it would be like if we had met then.

I remember what your brother has told me about you, and I know that this is better for both of us. You would be miserable having been forced into a marriage you did not want... were not ready for. I would be miserable knowing that you were at home, and I was not.

I understand your need to serve and travel and to find yourself. I have done the same. I have enjoyed seeing the world. I can only hope that you have also enjoyed your time.

As it is nearly two here, I must get some sleep. But not before I ask you the question that has been bouncing around in my head for the last few days...

Neither rain, or sleet nor snow.... But what about mortar fire? Does that keep the mail from being delivered?

As always, I will wait until the moon goddess brings you to me.

AW

Closing the notepad, he tucked it back into its spot and settled in for a few hours of sleep. Thankfully, the battlefield remained quiet, and he did not have to wonder if the mail still ran under the rain of bullets. Folding up a shirt and placing it in a Ziploc bag, he headed for the exchange.

"You got toys for the K9s?" Wyatt asked the man working the small post exchange.

Chuckling the man shook his head. "In the past seven months, the answer has never changed. Until today." A small box of dog toys was placed on the plywood counter. "Had my wife send some just for you."

"How much do I owe you?" Wyatt asked, taking the whole box.

"Don't worry about it, Doc." He smiled, waving the money away before it could appear. "Just…" his eyes cut one way and then the other and his voice dropped to a whisper, "get your luna."

Wyatt stepped back and was surprised to see the man's pupils shift to those of a cat. Taking a deep breath, he wondered why he could not detect the presence of a werecat.

"It's a blocker and shampoo, " the postal worker admitted, seeing Wyatt's confusion. "I'm mated to a Donskoi; I think you call them pila."

"It's a breed of hairless dog…" Wyatt explained.

"Same with Donskoi, but a cat."

.

8 - TRADITION

In less than a week, it would be two years since Sirius took Celeste to the recruiting station before she went off to bootcamp. Now, he was making plans to go to the Nohoch Mul Pack in the Yucatan peninsula of Mexico. The last time he had been in Mexico, it had been to retrieve his sister's body.

Aria was three and a half years younger than him, and seven minutes older than her twin, Aries. Around the same time that Aria died, Aries found his mate. Had he not found Kaliegh when he did, Sirius doubted that his brother would have survived the death of his twin.

Shaking his head to dispel the memories , Sirius once again looked at the list of those who were going. Halfway down the first page were the two names he did not want to see, Aurora Moore and Danika

Moore, his identical twin sisters — both named for the times they were born: Dawn and the morning star.

Smiling, he thought of the two starring in the community play last night. The dig at their father nearly went straight over his head. He thought of Hodel and Chava in Fiddler on the Roof when the two defiant daughters of Tevye and Golde chose their own husbands. He knew his sisters wanted to pick their own husbands themselves; his sisters wanted a chance to make their own choices.

Suddenly, the tunes from the night before were playing in his mind. Whistling, he checked the list again and prepared to send the final count to Alpha Miguel. The Hunt had a different feel for Sirius now. Although it had made him uncomfortable before, he never realized how bad it was for the " Maidens" in the Hunt.

His Omega, Charles, sent a quick warning through the mind link that Malachi was headed into the office just before the door burst open. Hiding behind his papers and computer screen, he rolled his eyes at the impending drama.

"I came to help you coordinate the travel plans for the Hunt."

"It's under control."

"Is it? You told me that you had everything under control once before. And do you know who was not at the Hunt? The one that we hosted. I'm surprised we're not still the laughingstock of the world."

The meme that had circulated around the were-community social media popped into Sirius' mind. A picture of the Maidens walking through the woods with the caption Camouflage so good the Alpha's daughter cannot be found. It and several others ran the typical course of any scandal and then died off with the next one. They had popped up a few more times over the past year and each time Malachi burst into his office threatening to take his position back.

The council and Elders would not even tolerate a discussion like that — Partially because Sirius had not done anything to warrant them stepping in. Although the parents had the ultimate say in whether their daughter participated in the Hunt, Celeste could petition for sanctuary. It was not something that many knew, and there was a process to it.

Celeste's alpha and the host alpha had to agree to offer the protection of sanctuary. Since he was both, it was an easy decision. It would not be as easy with Alpha Miguel. Although he was only a year older than Sirius, he was an extreme conservative and adhered to traditions more than Malachi did.

"I told you, Celeste left with my blessing." It was an old argument, one that they had had many times. Sirius was certain that they would have it many more times.

"Do not say her name!" Malachi bellowed.

"It's my office, I'll say or do whatever I want, " Sirius replied calmly as he made a sweeping motion with his hand encompassing the office and indicating the changes made since Sirius ascended to the position.

The black walls were now a light gray, and the dark built-ins and shelves were now a cornflower blue. Navy geometric patterns were on the wallpaper in the back of the shelves offered a contrast to the lighter colors. He did keep the giant crest behind the desk. Mainly because the large plaster medallion was part of the wall.

Even the imposing dark wood desk was replaced with a sleek glass and metal one. Most everything was on the computer and his papers were filed away in the drawers in the cabinets behind him. All the papers were scanned into the computer system. Malachi refused to use anything on the computer and his new, and much smaller, office was crowded with filing cabinets.

The black leather couch from his father's time as Alpha was the only thing removable that remained. His wife, Laura, had added gray and light blue throw pillows and a matching striped blanket to soften the harsh lines.

The long conference table where Malachi had lorded over the officers of the pack had been replaced with a casual seating area. Four wing-back chairs sat at the corners of a square coffee table in front of the fireplace. A small bar sat at the other end of the room and Sirius wondered if there was a beer in the small refrigerator.

"Are you even listening to me?" Malachi demanded.

His son debated on his answer. Deciding that honesty was not the best policy in this case, Sirius nodded and motioned for his father to continue. This time he actually paid attention to the rant of his father.

"Do you know how long we have been having the Hunt? It goes back generations. This is our tradition!"

Rolling his lips between his teeth, Sirius fought hard not to laugh. He could just see his dad throwing up his hands and doing the choreographed dance as he declared, "Tradition!" just as Tevye did in the play last night.

"Ya ha deedle deedle, bubba bubba deedle deedle dum." Sirius sang under his breath.

"What was that?"

"I said that I needed to get these numbers done." He shifted the papers on the glass top next to the computer.

"You have plenty of time to get that turned in. Do you want to be the one that destroys our oldest tradition?"

Coughing to cover the laugh that almost escaped, Sirius covered his mouth with his fist as he stood up to go to the bar. Grabbing two bottles of water from the minifridge, he offered one to his father on his way back to his desk. As he passed off the bottle, he saw the disapproving look from Malachi as his father scanned at the outfit Sirius wore.

Malachi still wore his dark suits, even though he was no longer the Alpha. The tie he wore today was a bright blue with silver-look thread creating a herringbone pattern. It was one that his youngest daughter, Portia, had given him at the last Yule celebration.

Meanwhile, Sirius wore relaxed faded jeans and a dark burgundy oxford shirt with his collar open and sleeves rolled up to his elbows. After a quick shower following a sparring match with his brothers, he had gone to his office for paperwork and two phone meetings in his flip flops.

He was not like his father; he understood that the world was changing. Traditions needed to be left by the wayside and new ones made. One of which was the damned Hunt.

The cell phone on the glass top rang and both men looked when the screen showed that it was the council offices in Philadelphia. Sirius was waiting on a call from Elder Alpha Marcus letting him know if the Council was going to be opening an investigation into Aria's death. Grabbing the phone, he dismissed his father. The former Alpha needed to accept that his era had ended.

"You can let Charles know that I'm on the phone." Pressing the button, he held the phone to his ear. "One moment, Elder."

Yes, he could just as easily let his Omega know that the expected call had come through. But Sirius took the opportunity to remind his father that he no longer held a position of power. His child did.

With an angry growl, Malachi reminded his insolent son of his rank. "I am-"

"The former Alpha. You have no authority and even less right to be privy to this conversation."

Looking into the face of the man who used to terrify him as a small boy, Sirius saw an old, defeated man. He was no longer fearsome and intimidating. Hanging his head in defeat, Malachi turned and walked out of the office that was once his.

At the door he paused and looked at his oldest son. "As Abraham said, I am a stranger in a strange land."

Sirius smiled. His father may not have understood why his daughters had pushed for that play, but he had at least paid attention. "Moses said that."

9 - BE MY VALENTINE

It was Saturday and Valentine's Day. Celeste lay on the couch in her friends' living room. The rising sun shone through the sliding glass door leading out to the patio. Listening to the bed of the happily married couple creaking upstairs, she considered going out for coffee.

Did she stay and listen to Gunny and Sammy going at it upstairs? Or did she go home and listen to her roommates, Jack and Jill, go at it down the hall? She was certain that there would be no coffee here. But it could be picked up on the way home.

Just as she decided coffee was needed, her phone chirped. Picking it up off the floor, there was a vague memory of tossing it towards the coffee table, obviously she missed. She grinned at the HEY GIRLFRIEND! that appeared on the screen. It immediately chirped again and her best friend and roommate, Jill, asked her to guess what came in the mail.

They had called the large black werecat Jill for so long, Celeste often forgot that he actually had a male name. Even Gunnery Sergeant Williams upstairs had a first name. But just as he and his wife were simply Gunny and Sammy, also an acquired nickname, Jackson and Matthew were Jack and Jill. And somewhere, probably a drunken night when Celeste was too hard to say, she herself became Sles.

Replying, she told her best friend that she was on her way home. Rolling her eyes at the loud moan that came from the bedroom above her head, Celeste grabbed her wallet and keys from the coffee table. The next text was the coffee order for himself and Jack. Celeste considered saying that she wasn't going to stop for coffee. No one would believe that. Sending off a quick text to the couple upstairs that she was leaving, she used the downstairs powder room, she then left the duplex and headed out towards her pickup, followed by her K9 partner, Rory.

Looking at the phone as it chirped, she smirked as she walked out the door. A single word from Jack in the Roommates group text. " HYDRATE!" Locking the door, she gave Rory time to do her business.

The military K9s were usually kept at the base kennel. But the base commander was a were himself and agreed that they needed to spend as much time with their handlers as possible. The time together helped them build a bond that needed to be nurtured and tended if the team was to work seamlessly. Especially the teams that deployed frequently.

Just shy of an hour later, Celeste pulled into her parking spot at the apartment complex near the base. She grabbed the tray of coffee, bag of breakfast food, and her keys. She and Rory were not even halfway up the stairs when Jill flung open the door to their shared apartment.

"Hurry up, girlfriend! I want to see what we got!"

Jill's family could never accept the fact that he was gay. They would rather that he be with a she-wolf than another man. Because of this, they encouraged him to pursue Celeste and for years referred to her as his girlfriend. Eventually, it stuck and became a joke between the two of them.

"We?" Celeste teased walking through the door.

"You know that I'm getting something from in there." He replied, snagging a disposable cup from the cardboard tray. "I hope there's some of those German chocolate things I like."

"There are two certainties about Valentine's Day. Sles always gets something from her Wonder Pup. And chocolate is half price tomorrow." the redheaded Jack laughed from his spot on the couch.

"I like chocolate." The tall, muscular, black man declared as he followed Celeste towards the dining room table.

Celeste shook her head as she slid her knife through the tape along the sides of the top. The return address was Sirius and Laura's house, as always. But the post mark was from the Philippines. The other reason that she knew it was not from her family was that she could not smell them. The overwhelming smell was of him.

Mate! Angel yipped in her mind. Is that not the best smell EVER!?!

Was that a question or a statement? Celeste asked her wolf. There would be no response because Angel was too busy getting lost in the scent.

Inside the box was a small Styrofoam cooler that she handed over to Jill. If there was any chocolate, it would be in there. Jill took the cooler, his coffee, and a breakfast burrito to the couch. Soon there was a squeal as he found the chocolate.

Rolling her eyes, Celeste went back to the box. There were a few plain white t-shirts, some tennis balls, a chew toy and a stuffed wolf. There was also a card, but as always, she ignored it. She threw two of the tennis balls and Rory and Liberty, Jill's K-9, both took off down the hall after them. Making sure that her roommates weren't looking, Celeste buried her face in one of the t-shirts and breathed deeply.

Angel was right. It was the best scent ever.

"When you're done acting like you're not inhaling that shirt, come look at what Wonder Pup sent my cat." Jack called from the couch.

"Bite me." Celeste teased as she went to her chair with her coffee and breakfast sandwich.

The well trained Malinois dogs dropped the balls into Jack's lap. "Yeah, yeah." He replied, throwing the balls back down the hall.

"Here." Jill handed her a piece of plain white paper with writing on it. "Makes you think of the constitution and shit, don't it?"

Looking back at the masculine yet old-fashioned cursive writing, she realized that it did indeed look like the writing on the constitution.

Jill, I have been told that you get almost all the chocolate that I send to my mate. This time, I'm sending you some of your own. In return, I only ask that you keep my mate safe. It is nearly time for me to go home and take over the family business. You are always welcome in my home. Sincerely, AW

"I say we keep him." Jill said, popping a piece of chocolate in his mouth.

"You only want to keep getting chocolate." Jack teased as he tried to get a piece and had his hand slapped. "Ouch."

"Wonder Pup sent the candy to me. Tell Sles to get another man to send you candy." Jill hugged the candy to his chest protectively.

"I don't want another one." Celeste argued. "Hell, I don't even want this asshole."

"So that wasn't you that had her face buried in a t-shirt for five minutes?" Jill asked as Jack grabbed a piece of candy then focused his attention at their friend. Jill gave him a side eye glance before rolling his eyes and shaking his head.

"Angel wants him, " she answered and ignored the beast inside telling her she was a horrible liar.

"Uh-huh." Jill grinned.

"Shut up, you damn cat. Don't make me get the laser pointer, " she taunted.

"Okay, you two." Jack warned as the two dogs fought over a toy.

" You talking to us or the dogs?" Celeste joked as she went for her second coffee.

"Both." Jack replied. "Are you excited to go see your sister?"

"Nice change of subject." Jill grinned over at his mate.

Jack gave him a quick kiss and snagged another piece of candy. "Thanks. I try."

Celeste made a fake gagging sound while grinning at her friends. "Yes, I am. The last time I saw Sky, she was terrified of her mate. And now they have pups."

10 - MIDNIGHT RUN

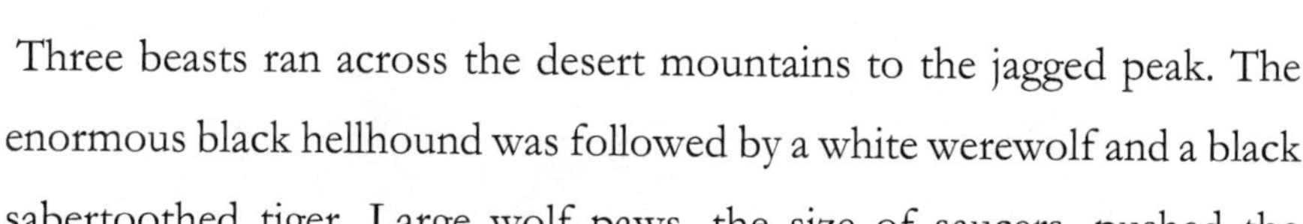

Three beasts ran across the desert mountains to the jagged peak. The enormous black hellhound was followed by a white werewolf and a black sabertoothed tiger. Large wolf paws, the size of saucers, pushed the hound higher and higher with his companions hot on his heels.

Reaching the top of the mountain, the larger wolf skidded to a stop, his tongue lolling out of his mouth. Happily, he howled at the moon as the two other beasts joined him. The white wolf joined him in baying at the moon as the tiger chuffed.

The large black canine head lowered, its eyes glowing red and smoke billowing from his nostrils. Steam rose off his body as he rolled to his back, squirming as he happily scratched .

Feminine laughter filled the air as the large white wolf shifted into the form of a woman. The white fur with black tips on her ears, paws and tail gave way to tanned and tattooed skin and black hair. The eyes of both the woman and the wolf were eerily silver.

"You are a fucking idiot, " the naked woman said as she reached over and rubbed the massive dog's belly.

"Only you could get away with calling him an idiot." The large black man said as he shifted from the saber-toothed tiger.

Celeste looked at her closest friend and grinned. "I'm just lucky like that."

"Yeah, yeah." Jill said as he sat on the other side of the large black wolf.

They sat in silence, enjoying the night blessed by the moon goddess. Light from the full moon shimmered on the clouds above the desert mountains around them. The heat radiating from the hound between them kept the two naked friends warm in the cold night air. The lights of Twentynine Palms blinked on and off to the north. They were in the middle of the Joshua Tree National Park and their favorite place to run free.

Celeste's eyes wandered over to the man with traditional black ink tattoos covering his body. When he came into his prime, the marks were placed around both biceps. By the time he was cast out of the pride, his arms and torso were completely covered.

Slowly, he was covering the traditional marks of his Pride with tattoos that he chose. The marks that had traced his lineage back to the original pride of saber werecats, were now under roses and paw prints. Even the Marine Corps werewolf pack crest graced his upper left bicep.

"Don't." Jill said softly, as he felt her eyes on him.

Her initial response was to look away, guilty that she was caught staring at his markings. She kept her head turned towards her friend and did not avert her gaze. There were times that he would open up and explain what the different marks meant. Tonight would not be one of those times.

The hound between them rolled to his belly and laid his head between his paws, closing his eyes. He looked as if he were drifting off to sleep, but the two friends knew that the hound's senses would remain on high alert allowing the two friends to relax and enjoy the night air.

There was nothing out there that was stronger or scarier than a hell hound. He was what the things that went bump in the night feared.

"I'm just deciding what the next ones that we should get together should be." Celeste motioned to the empty space on her arm between the other tattoos.

"Bullshit." He smiled at her, his teeth shining in the moonlight, almost as bright as his green eyes that easily saw her amid the darkness.

She grinned back, not even bothering to deny the lie. Instead, she gave him a small shrug. "Maybe I am now."

"Now," he agreed.

"You ever thought about doing color?" Her eyes were looking at her own colored tattoos. Instinctively, she touched the full color memorial tattoo of her first K-9, Duke, on her side.

"It won't stay." He said as he turned back to the view ahead of them. It was a conversation that they had skirted around several times. Tonight, it looked like they were actually going to have it.

"Our bodies won't accept color. Whatever your pride, their color is the only color that our skin will accept. Our beasts are temperamental."

"Heavy on the mental." She teased her friend.

"Could say the same about you, girlfriend."

Laughing, she leaned back and rested her hands behind her. "Never denied that."

"You ever figure out who he is?"

There was no doubt about who he was referring to. Wonder pup. She shook her head and they fell back into silence.

"What's it like?" she finally asked. "Being mated?"

He chuckled. "You realize that I'm mated to a man?"

"Well … so am I."

His chuckle turned into a full-blown laugh, and he chuffed a little as his feline eyes turned towards his friend. "Touche, girlfriend. You ever feel that pull and think you'll give in?"

"Sometimes." she admitted. "It's strange. I know when he's close. Angel can sense them; she tries to go to his wolf. Hell, sometimes, I think they talk."

"But…?"

"He doesn't force me. Doesn't pull on that invisible bond that would make me come to him."

"Does send you some great gifts, though."

"You want me to mate with him just so you can get more chocolate."

"And?"

She had no answer, instead she asked another question that they had only ever danced around. "Do you ever regret leaving your pride?"

"We should head back." Jill said as he stood up, pretending not to hear her.

"Matthew." She said using his real name.

He sighed. "Sometimes." He sat back down, knowing they would not be leaving just yet. "We're not as bound as you and your packs are. Shortly after reaching his prime, a male is supposed to find a mate and start producing offspring. Doesn't matter what lovers you have on the side, as long as you mate."

"Do you ever get the urge?"

"To mate? Sure. The beast sees it as his responsibility. The problem is, we mate in beast form. I may have fathered some on the few times that I've given in to the urge. But in the morning, when we're not in beast form, there's no desire… no attraction."

"Kind of hard to have a mate when half of you doesn't want one."

"You know all about that, girlfriend." Jill grinned into the night. "How do the hellhounds work?"

"What do you mean?"

"Well, Teuf is a hell hound, but his littermate, Marley, is not."

"They're chosen. Just like we are. I know the cats don't have the strict structure that we have, but you still have your Alpha born, " Celeste said and Jill nodded. "It's the same. The stronger cats become Alphas and the stronger dogs become hounds."

"Lineage?"

"If a hound mates with a hound, they will produce hounds. They bond to their wolf for life, serve the Moon Goddess whenever she bids them, and have only one mate. Ever."

Jill nodded as he reached over and scratched the hound behind his oversized ear.

"What happens if you do get colored ink?"

"It either rejects or changes."

She couldn't help the laughter that erupted and at his look, it only grew. Finally, she curled in on herself and leaned against the hot body of the oversized hound next to her. Gasping, she wiped tears off her cheeks with the back of her hands.

"Okay, hear me out. I shift into my beast and I'm her color." She said in reference to the white wolf that she shared a body and mind with. "You shift and your tattoos still show."

"Yeah, my fur darkens where the marks and tattoos are." He nodded, wondering where this was going.

"Could you imagine what Angel would look like if my tattoos showed up in her fur?"

Jill roared with laughter while Angel sulked. With the picture fully in her head, Celeste began laughing again. Eventually, even her beast saw the humor in it.

Even the large hound between them began to shake and his laughter filled her mind.

"You'd look like you got dipped in a clown wig." Jill laughed.

The hound was so amused that even Jill heard his laughter. Celeste laughed even harder as Angel growled and snarled.

"Careful, girlfriend." Jill warned as Celeste took control of her own beast. "If you're not careful, she's going to give in to that bloodlust and your beast will be no better than mine."

11 - GRUMPY

Wyatt laid on the deck of the USS Iwo Jima in the middle of the Atlantic Ocean with other members of the Navy Pack. They had done a midnight run around the deck under the full moon. The captain, although not were, understood that they needed this every so often. The ship was performing a drill keeping the rest of the crew and Marines below deck.

This was what Wyatt needed. It had been over a year since he had been around his mate or received anything with her scent. Demon had been restless and irritable. When the beast was irritable, the man was also.

Sirius had let Wyatt know that Celeste was deployed and that it would be a while before they could send another shirt. Or anything with her scent. The shirt that he had brought with him on this deployment had lost all but the barest trace of her scent. With nothing to ground man and beast to their mate, he was becoming more and more irritable.

Grumpy as his bunkmates called him.

But the camaraderie with the other shifters calmed his soul.

The whistle from the far end of the deck signaled that their time was almost up. The few who had not shifted back, returned to their human forms and they all redressed. Within a few minutes they stood as sailors and Marines again in uniform.

Wyatt went below deck and headed to his rack. His day had started long before sunrise with an emergency. One of the sailors walking patrol had leaned over too far to speak with someone on a lower level. As it usually happened after being at sea for long periods, the sailor forgot the laws of physics, including gravity, and the ever-present dizziness that strikes when you're in the middle of the ocean, and he fell over the railing. A medivac flight took him off ship; he would have arrived at Walter Reed by now.

After breakfast, they had a safety briefing before his unit ran through fire drills before lunch. Then the colonel sent the Marines to the gym. Since Wyatt was embedded with them, he was expected to join, after which, he had his daily duties in sick bay. After dinner, all he wanted was to crawl back into his rack and sleep.

But the other corpsman had gotten ill, and Wyatt went back to sick bay for a short shift. At eleven the captain called a midnight drill.

Demon pranced with excitement and even the man was looking forward to the run. It ended up being just what man and beast needed.

He stopped beside his rack and saw the box. Mail call had happened while he was tending to his duties, or during the run. At some point while he was gone, his mail was placed on the rack assigned to him. A large box and thin envelope sat on the tightly made mattress.

Wyatt looked around and noticed that his bunkmates were impatiently waiting for him. One deep breath and he knew why. Quickly, he opened the box and started handing over cookies, brownies, and blondies. The packages with Sirius' handwriting were typically ignored. But the ones from his mother and sisters were watched like a hawk.

And the ones from Laura were practically drooled over.

His family sent a dozen cookies. Laura sent dozens of multiple types of cookies and sweets. At the bottom of the box was a shirt in a Ziploc bag and a letter. Opening the bag, he inhaled his mate's scent. She had been in heat when they took this garment.

Several males close to him perked up and tried to get a better sniff. Wyatt gave a low, deep, and protective growl in warning, and they backed off. The NCO in their area gave a cautioning glare and they settled down for the night. The last thing that they needed was for the humans to see werewolves fighting over the scent of a she-wolf in heat that wasn't even on ship.

Laying down in his rack, he pulled out the letter from Laura.

Wyatt,

I know it has been a while, and we're sorry about that. Celeste just got back to the states a few weeks ago and went to see Sky and Joseph. Their pup has just started to walk and is keeping them on their toes.

Celeste has a new dog. Sirius did tell you that the last one was killed, didn't he? Celeste was quite upset, and the Blue-Sky Alpha didn't seem to care until the Navy and Marine Alphas and Elder Alpha Marcus showed up. Elder Alpha Marcus was not happy that the council had to get involved.

Anyway, she has a new dog and Sky said that he has an interesting personality. Said that he got in the bath with the pup and then would not get out. When they asked Celeste how to get him out, she said to drain the water. He seems to love water, especially showers.

The Corps is keeping her unit together. Not sure if the Alphas had anything to do with that or not.

Her father, Malachi, still won't have anything to do with Celeste, but her mother, Aislinn, went out to see her. Sky sent the shirt home with her. She brought it over to Sirius and handed him a shoe box with at least three layers of tape around it. Aislinn was so confused, but I wasn't going to give her any information.

I have to go get our own pups from school and get this in the mail. Sirius did ask me to tell you that he'll be at Crystal River in a few months. If you're going to be around let us know. Stay safe.

Laura

P.S. I didn't make it to the post office in time, so the kids helped me make a few more sweets for you. Yes, there is a reason I'm telling you this. If you find eggshells in the brownies, it's not my fault. Blame it on the three-year-old.

Wyatt chuckled at the thought of the little pup trying so hard to help. As his sister described her own pups, they were helpful hindrances when trying to do something. He considered warning the guys about the eggshells but decided against it. He would only mention it if it was brought up.

With that decision made, he grabbed the envelope with his sister's writing on the outside. Wynne wrote in meticulous block lettering on the envelope and that told him that she was not happy with him.

To the great and powerful future Alpha of the Crystal River pack,

He caught himself just before he busted out laughing at her sarcastic salutation. If it was starting off with sarcasm, Wyatt needed to brace himself for the ass chewing that was coming. Demon was happily rolling on his back in their mind. The run in the moonlight had caused him to relax and the scent of their mate put him into a state of bliss.

Which was good. The Lycan dominant beast was slowly becoming calmer as they aged, something that did not typically happen if their mate was not around them. But during his time in the Navy, he had learned a lot about himself and the world.

Knowing that his mate was safe and being taken care of helped him. Receiving the shirts with her scent kept the beast controlled. Their experiences forced them to grow up and work together. Wyatt knew that he and his wolf were considered an anomaly. Most wolves at his age without a mate were on the verge of going crazy. Somehow, the goddess had blessed them to retain their sanity and only grow in strength with their bond.

To the great and powerful future Alpha of the Crystal River pack,

How are you doing? Saved many lives lately?

This was not going to be good. He could already tell.

Dad said that I should not push this, that you know what you're doing. But I just want to point out that you are putting more than just yourself in danger by not coming home and finding your mate! What is going to happen to the pack if your wolf goes crazy and bloodlust takes hold???

Folding the paper, he placed it back into the envelope without finishing the letter. His sister had every right to worry about him and the pack. But he did not want to listen to – or even read – another lecture.

In six weeks, they would dock in Pensacola and a few days later, he would be headed home to assume his duties and responsibilities. Closing his eyes, he knew that he would have to tell his sister about his mate… and why he refused to force Celeste to marry him and thrusting her into the position of the Luna and mother of his pack.

12 - WOLF'S BANE

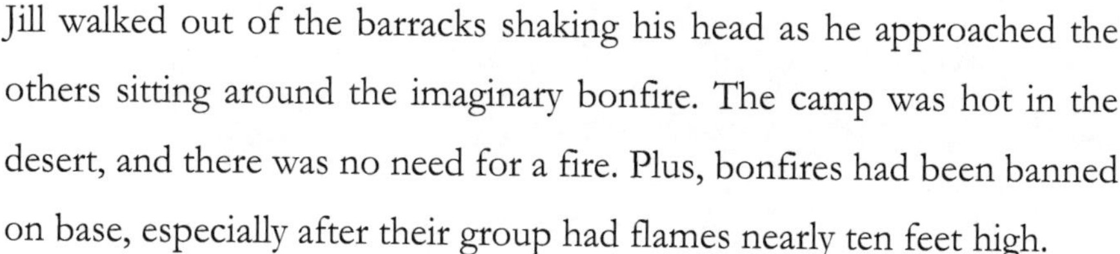

Jill walked out of the barracks shaking his head as he approached the others sitting around the imaginary bonfire. The camp was hot in the desert, and there was no need for a fire. Plus, bonfires had been banned on base, especially after their group had flames nearly ten feet high.

He sat down on the camp chair and accepted the water bottle from Gunny. The bottle had a piece of silver tape on it with BEER written across it. He took a deep drink and then leaned his head back to look up at the clouds. Jill was six feet eight with a linebacker build, his dark skin covered with black ink tattoos. His face and head were clean shaven, and his dark brown eyes glistened with tears.

"Is she okay?" Doc asked.

Jill lifted his head and looked at the newest member of their group. Doc had been an Army medic who wanted a change. He found it with the Marines as a K9 handler. He stood right at six,feet and had traditional middle eastern features. His hair was a little longer than usual and he had a few weeks of growth on his beard. He was muscular and fit, their routine made sure of that.

"Yeah, just have to up her medicine a little bit," Jill said vaguely.

"What is she taking?" Doc asked and the other two men looked at each other. "I was a medic. I know the signs of a were going into heat."

The two men looked at him in surprise. "It's more than just that," Gunny said.

"Wolves mate for life," Jill explained. "If they are separated for long periods of time, they can go crazy."

"She needs to go spend some time with her mate," Doc said.

"She doesn't have a mate," Gunny and Jill said simultaneously.

"Yes, she does," Doc countered. "She caught his scent when we were in Germany."

"Never said anything," Jill grumbled. "Sles usually tells me when he's around."

"You know about him?" Doc asked.

Both men nodded and told him about the many times that they were close to each other. She refused to go to him. He never forced himself on her. One of their favorite stories was Mardi Gras when she nearly did go to him.

"She won't tell us what he smells like, and yes, everyone has a distinct scent. Even you." Jill explained.

Without thinking about it, Doc automatically lifted his arm and sniffed his armpit. With the dessert heat, deodorant did not last long. Making a face of disgust, he put his arm down. "Should not have done that."

The other men laughed at him.

"Your scent can change if you're sick or even your emotions can change it." Gunny grinned and Jill rolled his eyes. "It also changes when a she-wolf is in heat."

"Can you smell the difference?" Doc asked the other human.

"No." Gunny shook his head. "But my wife, my mate, has tells. Mainly popcorn drizzled with chocolate."

"Anyway…" Jill said, redirecting the conversation. "She was at a bar in New Orleans and Wonderpup was there too."

"Wonderpup?" Doc cocked an eyebrow.

Jill shrugged as Gunny pointed at him. "He chose the name."

"We needed to call him something." Jill pointed out. "Wonderpup shows up and she started to go to him. One of the girls that was with her distracted her and he left."

"Now ask why that is Jill's favorite story." Gunny grinned as he took a drink of water from the bottle with silver tape and BEER written on it.

Giving a confused look from one man to the other, Doc turned his attention back to Jill. "Okay, why is it your favorite?"

"Because after that, there was no way that she could deny that she does want a mate. and she wants Wonderpup as her mate." The large man said with what could only be described as an 'I told you so' look.

"What about you?" Doc asked Jill. "Are werecats the same way?"

Gunny laughed and Jill shook his head. "No. We do have mates, but we are not tied to them like wolves are. And my breed is very…"

"He's a damned tomcat," Gunny supplied. "Given half the chance, he'll fuck you and Jack at the same time. And then prowl afterwards."

"I would not," Jill objected. "I would have a snack and then go prowl."

"You must have the correct order," Doc agreed. "Does Celeste need a higher dose of suppressant?"

"No, but she does need more wolf's bane. Angel is getting more aggressive," Jill admitted. "Sles is going to lose control of her someday and Angel is going to kill someone. Just hope it's not one of us."

"You really think it really could get that bad?" Gunny asked.

Jill looked over at his old friend and nodded. "Yeah. Yeah, I do."

"I'll order more," Doc told them and then grinned. "Better topic. Or at least more fun. Why does the rest of camp call you guys the Pervs?"

"What all have you heard?" Gunny asked with a grin.

"Lots of warnings. And I got a lot of side eye looks when I was asking about where to go. And why is our barracks referred to as the Suck and Fuck?"

"Yeah, Jill, why?" Jack asked, walking up to them. He leaned over the chair from behind and kissed his partner.

Watching Jack sit down, Jill replied, "Because Jackin' Shack was already taken."

Gunny handed the large Scotsman a water bottle, with a gray tape with BEER written on it in permanent marker.

"Hydrate!" the three men called out as a toast. Doc decided that he needed to learn about this HYDRATE command that they were always shouting to each other.

But for now, he was going to focus on the newest member of the group around the fake campfire. Jack was larger than Doc, but not as big as Jill. His red hair was in a regulation flat top and face was clean shaven. His issued BDUs hugged his five feet eleven frame. Jack had only been in the country for a week, whereas Jill, Gunny, and Celeste had been in for six. Doc had joined their merry band earlier that day.

"I always knew that Sles was a bit off, but I never saw her as being a perv," Doc observed.

"Stick around; she's the biggest perv of us all." Gunny laughed.

"How do you know my girlfriend?" Jill demanded.

"How do you think I know what she takes?" he queried. "I treated her heats last time we were stationed here together. It was actually at Leatherneck," He said referring to Forward Operating Base they were typically stationed at. It was located in the Helmand Province of Afghanistan while the one they were currently stationed at, Lonestar, was in the Nangarhar Province.

"That was before my time," Gunny admitted.

"Did you know her when Duke…." Jill couldn't bring himself to finish the sentence.

"Yeah. She's the first were that I ever met. Or at least the first that I knew was a were."

"There's more of us cats and dogs than people suspect," Jill admitted.

They all turned as the door to the barracks opened and Teuf walked out followed by Celeste.

"You good, girlfriend?"

"Yeah. Solstice is hard. Plus, I swear I smelled him earlier." She sat on the cooler after getting her own water bottle. "Hydrate."

She tapped her bottle to the four men's bottles before sitting down, they each responded with "Hydrate."

"Think he's here?" Gunny asked offering beef sticks that his wife had recently sent.

"No. I don't feel him anymore." She tossed a meat stick to Jill. "You want to go for a run later?"

"Oh yeah! I need to let the beast out for a bit."

Celeste looked down at Teuf who was looking up at her and watching the meat stick. "Well, of course, you can go too." She handed him an unwrapped stick that he quickly devoured. "Do you even know what the concept of chewing is?"

"Did you not see him with the goat he caught the other day?" Jack asked, absently scratching Marley behind her ear.

"That was more tearing than chewing," Jill objected.

Teuf bared his sharp teeth at the werecat who did the same in turn. The dog growled and the cat roared.

"Enough," Celeste bellowed with her Alpha voice. "I don't need some idiot pila walking by and seeing you two comparing dicks."

"It's all good fun. Teuf knows that I love him." Jill grinned at the Alpha and her companion. "I'm too scared not to love him."

13 - CHANGE OF HEART

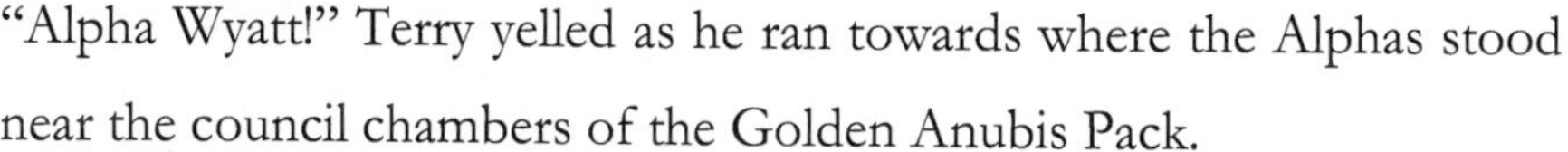

"Alpha Wyatt!" Terry yelled as he ran towards where the Alphas stood near the council chambers of the Golden Anubis Pack.

The new chambers were only recently built when they created the Al-Azhar Park in the center of Cairo. As it was with many other packs that were located inside major cities, the chambers were also used by the pila community. There was a wedding a few nights earlier. A music festival would be held a day after the Hunt was completed and the werewolves were gone.

Typically, Terry did not act like this. He was normally a well put together man who was prepared for anything that Wyatt might need. If he was yelling, and running, then Wyatt could only assume that it was important. If he was using the title in front of pilas, then that important something was bad.

"Terry?" Wyatt asked with a cocked eyebrow as he glanced around to remind the Omega of where they were and that the people surrounding them may or may not be were.

"Forgive me, sir," Terry said, ignoring the other Alphas and Betas. "One of our…" he paused as a group of students walked past. "I need to take you to the medical center."

Wyatt nodded and made quick apologies to the others standing around him before following his aide to the waiting car.

"I tried to reach out to Beta Stephen," Terry said once they were in the car and the door closed behind them. "The medical center," he barked at the driver.

"The one for the Hunt?" the driver confirmed before pulling out into the traffic.

"Yes, and quickly," Terry confirmed.

"Terry, what's going on?"

"I've tried to reach Beta Stephen."

"His mate is in heat," Wyatt explained, hoping that his Omega would get to the point. With a nod, the other man explained that Stephen's sister had been attacked by her mate in the Hunt. After he explained that the healers were not certain she would survive, Wyatt forced his way into Stephen's mind through the link.

'Stephen, I'm sending a car for you. When it arrives, get in the fucking car and don't ask any questions.'

'You said that I could have the day-'

'Any other time, I would not cut into your private time.' Wyatt cut his friend off as the car pulled up to a small house that was being used as a medical center. 'This is an emergency. Damnit, just do as you're told for once. Get in the fucking car.'

Ignoring the grumbles of his Beta he leaned forward and gave the driver instructions to go pick up the Beta from the hotel where they were staying. The dark-skinned Egyptian assured the Alpha that it would be taken care of.

Terry led the way out of the car and into the house. "Adeline and Elder Alpha Samuel are tending to her."

"Alpha!" Roderick, one of his most trusted warriors, called from the hallway behind them.

Wyatt turned and looked at the large blonde man who was currently shirtless with his Viking rune tattoos on full display. "My brothers are holding him at the security station next door."

Nodding, Wyatt turned to continue down the hall. "Thank you, Roderick. Let me know when the Beta arrives."

"Yes, Alpha." Roderick's deep voice echoed in the hall as Wyatt and Terry entered a side room.

Seventeen-year-old Vanessa lay on the hospital bed with the Crystal River healer, the Golden Anubis healer, and all three of the Elder Alphas surrounding her. The formerly white sheets were stained bright red with a puddle of blood growing on the floor.

"What do you need of me?" Wyatt asked of Adeline, the Crystal River healer.

"She's lost a lot of blood," Adeline told him. "There's only so much that we can give her. She has relatives here?"

"Her brother, my Beta. He's on his way.," Wyatt said, feeling his anger and hatred of the Hunt growing.

The five of them continued to work to save the girl's life. Wyatt had known Adeline and her sisters for practically his whole life. They were born when he was not quite a year old, not that he remembered either birth. Imogen, the Oracle of the triplets, insisted that she did remember it.

Frustration built in Adeline, and she closed her eyes and whispered. "Sisters, I need you."

A moment later the door opened, and Wyatt turned, expecting to see his Beta. Instead, the other two triplets entered the room. They were the Blessed Three – the healer, oracle, and priestess. They all had platinum blonde hair, light blue eyes, and pale white skin.

"Her brother is on his way," Adeline said as her sisters gently pushed the Elder Alphas out of the way. The shift allowed Wyatt to see the large gaping hole in the young woman's neck. The skin was torn away exposing the muscles and tendons beneath.

As a Navy corpsman, Wyatt had seen a lot of injuries to soldiers and civilians alike. War did not discriminate on who it hurt, who it killed, who it maimed. The young, old, rich, poor, male, female. But the Hunt? The Hunt targeted young women. And only young women.

The door opened and Roderick stuck his head inside. "Alpha, he's here."

Wyatt moved towards the door and saw that the large wound was now only about half the size that it had been. Stepping outside he closed the door behind him, Stephen needed to be prepared and his sister deserved the decency and respect that small act gave her.

"A Maiden from our pack was attacked by her mate."

"Wyatt, we've been through this, sometimes males get overly excited. She'll recover and be fine with it once the mate bond sets in."

"He ripped half her neck off. The Blessed Three and Elder Alphas are tending to her. But even they may not be able to save her."

Stephen drew a deep breath to calm himself. "No offense, Wyatt, but you should handle this, not me. You're the Alpha now."

"It's Vanessa."

Stephen stopped in the middle of his rant. His face lost all color and his knees buckled. Roderick grabbed one arm and Wyatt grabbed the other.

"My sister?" Stephen asked quietly and Wyatt nodded.

"There's a lot of blood in there. They've given her a lot of blood. The Blessed Three are trying to heal her. But she's going to need a transfusion."

"Okay, take my blood. Take all that you need. Hell, take it all."

"We don't need it all." Adeline said from the now open door. "But we do need some and we need it now."

14 - HYDRATE

Hydrate.

It had started on their first deployment to Iraq in the heat of summer. They had a sergeant that you could set a watch by. Every thirty minutes he would give the reminder – Hydrate.

By the end of the deployment, it had become a running joke. No matter what the question was, the answer was hydrate.

What time is it?

Hydrate.

What's for dinner?

Hydrate.

Why did the chicken cross the road?

To hydrate.

At some point in time the word became a mantra for them. And then slowly, it meant so much more than just hydrate. It was the one word that they all said the most. Over the years, it had taken on a different meaning.

It was the way that they told each other that they were safe. That they needed a break or needed help. A way of telling each other that they loved one another. It became their safe word. Their celebratory word. A curse word when they could not use one.

Somewhere along the line, it became them.

Today, they were packed into the heavily armored troop transport, headed back along the rough dirt road going to Camp Leatherneck. They had been on patrol of a village for a little over a week. The school for the girls had been threatened… again. Though the Taliban did not want the girls attending school, the women wanted more for their children. The unit had been sent because of their ability to persuade the locals to leave the school alone.

The large werecat and Lycan dominant werewolf could be very persuasive. Even in their human forms, they were both imposing figures. Celeste stood just shy of six and a half feet and although her body was feminine, the tattoos and uniform gave her an air of authority.

The local Alpha of the small pack had cowered before the Lycan and Saber.

Jill was one of the few full-blooded Sabers still in existence. In his cat form, he resembled the ancient feline. However, unlike what most archaeologists and artists portrayed them as, they had been dark in their skin and fur. Their northern brethren of the artic sabers had been golden brown, but the southern packs were dark brown and black.

Unlike the wolves, the feline beast did not have a name or separate personality. He had a drive to hunt, kill, and mate. Jill rarely let his beast have full reign when they were in the beast form. When he did, he ended up in situations like he was in now.

His head pounded and his stomach rolled. If he were a mere mortal, he would say that he had a bad hangover. But that's not what he had. He was suffering from the aftereffects of giving into the bloodlust.

Celeste shoved a canteen at him. "Hydrate."

Carefully, he took the canteen and sipped. She had mixed some electrolyte fruit punch flavored powder into the water. He took a slightly larger swig before smiling his thanks to his closest friend and newly commissioned officer.

"Hydrate," Jill replied weakly.

He struggled to drink the concoction since it tasted like someone had used salt instead of sugar in the fruit punch mix. After the disgusting drink was gone, he leaned against Celeste's shoulder and closed his eyes.

Opening them again as the transport vehicle rolled through the gates of the camp, he sat up and stretched. The bulky machine grumbled to a stop and the four Marines and their K-9's piled out of the doors.

"Lieutenant," a Marine called, "General wants to see you and your crew."

Celeste nodded and they all headed towards the tent that served as the camp headquarters for their unit. Just outside the tent, Jill knew that what he had eaten last night in his beast form was about to come up. Grabbing Celeste's arm, he tried to tell her.

"Holy fuck, you do change colors." Celeste's eyes went wide as she turned her friend away from her. "Aim away from me!"

His dark skin had taken on a green hue, and he tried to swallow the rising bile. Failing to stop what was going to happen, he emptied his stomach of its contents, including the red liquid. Doc grabbed one arm while Gunny grabbed the other and helped support the larger man as they tried to guide him to a trash barrel.

"What the hell is going on here?" General Thomas demanded.

"He ate something yesterday at the village that made him sick." Celeste explained. "I gave him some of the fruit punch crap, but it's not…"

"Working?" the general offered.

"Yeah."

"You have a medic?"

"Me," Doc replied to the general's inquiry.

"He going to be okay?"

"We need to get some fluids in him, sir. But yes, he'll be fine."

"Get him tended to," the general ordered and then motioned for Celeste to join him.

She followed him into the makeshift office with plywood walls. He pointed at the folding chair, and she sat in it.

"Do you know Admiral Ian Kingston?" the general asked as he sat behind the desk.

He was the Alpha of the Navy pack, and she knew him. Before he had taken his position, he had been the commander of the Pacific Fleet and she had even served on the USS Peleliu that he had once commanded.

"Yes, sir. I've served under him."

"He's ordered you home. Your whole unit is headed back to Cali. You fly out in two days. Will your man be good?"

"Yes, sir. Some fluids, sleep, and decent food and he'll be good," she said and the older man nodded. "Sir, why am I— are we being sent home?"

"I don't know. That's above my paygrade." He grabbed some papers and waved her away.

On her way back to their tent, she was caught by a Marine delivering mail. "LT. I was told to deliver this to you personally, to place it in your hand."

She accepted the thin legal sized envelope with no return address and only her name. Nodding her thanks, she continued her way to the tent. Inside, he found Jill asleep on his bunk with two IV's hooked up to him. Doc looked up from the camp chair he was in as Gunny remained stretched out in his own bunk.

"How is he?"

"About what you expect." came the reply as he checked the IV closest to him. "That was smart. Giving him red fluids to throw up."

Shrugging, she sat down on her bunk and tore open the envelope, pulling out another smaller envelope. "He always throws up after he gives in to the beast."

Tearing open the second envelope and found yet another. This one was made of thick paper with the wax seal of the Naval pack. It was a simplified version of the Naval crest – a ship's wheel with a wolf head in the center and the pack motto encircling the wheel. Navigator noctis, Custos Maris. Translated from Latin it meant "Navigator of the Night, Guardian of the Sea."

Breaking the seal, Celeste opened the gold foil lined envelope and removed the single piece of paper. The full crest was at the center of the bottom of the page in full color and as a watermark on the full page.

A ship's wheel on a background of deep blue waves darkening to a night sky with a silver crescent moon placed in the stars in the sky. In the center stood a blue and silver werewolf with his golden glowing eyes, vigilantly watching as his left hand rested on an anchor and his right held a trident. Beneath the werewolf, on a flowing banner of red, was the pack motto. The entire crest was bordered by nautical rope.

The few sentences that were written in bold script told her everything that she needed to know.

Alpha Celeste,

I have arranged for you to be released from your service contract early as was requested. The High Priestess suggested that you seek the guidance of the Pendleton Oracle as to where you should go. Your separation from the Marines and the Marine Corps Pack will occur shortly after your return.

Alpha Ian

The last time the High Priestess and Divine Oracle had called her home, it had been to lead the investigation against the Mesa Verde pack. She could only imagine what they wanted her for this time. And why they were making her leave her beloved Corps?

As a Marine, she followed the orders of higher-ranking officers. As an Alpha, she followed the guidance of the Divine Three – the High Priestess, Divine Oracle, and Divine Healer as well as the Elder Alphas of the council. Shortly before this deployment, she had received a visit from the Senior Elder Alpha who told her it was time for her to end her service.

The request had been sent to the Alphas of the Marine and Navy packs. Just before they left the following day, she received a similar letter from the Alpha of the Marine pack. And that was that. Her service with the Corps was coming to an end. It was time to go home.

15 - LOOKING FOR A NEW HOME

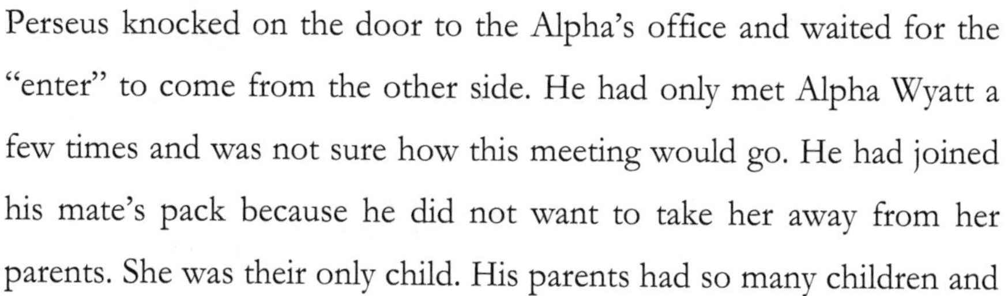

Perseus knocked on the door to the Alpha's office and waited for the "enter" to come from the other side. He had only met Alpha Wyatt a few times and was not sure how this meeting would go. He had joined his mate's pack because he did not want to take her away from her parents. She was their only child. His parents had so many children and grandchildren that their home was never empty.

"Alpha Wyatt," Perseus said, approaching the large desk.

"Perseus," Wyatt replied. He knew who Perseus was. When he had asked to join Wyatt's pack two years ago, he almost hugged the man. That would have been weird, and there would have been some questions that he was not prepared to answer. "How can I help you?"

"Well, sir, several years ago, my sister ran away and joined the Marines," Perseus explained. "My father is still quite upset over it. She has decided not to reenlist and needs a pack. I don't know how long it will be for."

"Our pack has always encouraged service. Military or otherwise. I would be honored if another Marine joined our pack."

"I don't know if she will actually join."

"Why do you say that?"

"My oldest brother knows who her mate is and has been in contact with him for quite a while. I am certain that he will try to get them to meet."

"I understand," Wyatt replied with a grin. Sirius had promised to keep his identity to himself. "She is welcome here for as long as she wants or needs."

"Thank you, Alpha."

"Perseus, why did she run away?"

He contemplated what to say and finally decided on the truth. "Two of our sisters were raped during the Hunt. She feared her own. Our father forced her into it. To avoid it, she ran away and joined the Marines. And to be honest, Alpha, I fear my youngest sister is thinking about the same."

"Why is that?"

"She missed last year's Hunt due to illness. Our father is insisting that she do it. Our mother does not want her to."

"I understand. Tell your sister she has nothing to fear. Our pack is hosting this year. I plan to make many changes to ensure the safety of the Maidens."

"Are you certain, Alpha?"

"Very much so. All Maidens will receive a mated guard," Wyatt said, keeping his voice even. Every time he thought about the fear in his Whitney's eyes, or Wenona begging him to save her, his anger and hatred of the Hunt rose to the surface. Smiling, he reigned in his anger as Demon snarled in the back of his mind. "There were nine maidens raped at last year's Hunt. And about twice as many marked against their will. Personally, I see that as rape also."

"Alpha, how are you picking the guards?"

"Volunteers, with consent of their mates. But I will not let you be the guard for your sister. I know how protective I am over my sisters; I assume you would be the same. The guards are there to step in if needed. Not to stop them from being together."

"I understand. I would still like to volunteer."

"I'll put you on my list. But I still need to speak with Viviane. Although, knowing how much she did not want to do the Hunt, I doubt that she will mind."

"She looked like a scared rabbit when I caught up with her," Perseus said, remembering his mate's terrified expression. "She was really confused when I asked her if I could hold her hand."

"She brags about you all the time. She's my sister's best friend. I hear way more than I want to." Wyatt said with a laugh. "Wynne can't wait to meet her mate. And since I told her that I was changing things, she's really excited for the Solstice."

"I think it gets worse every year."

"Unfortunately, I think that you are right," Wyatt wrote on his notepad. "Do you know when we should expect your sister? I need to let the patrols know to expect her."

"She said sometime before Saturday."

"Okay. And is she staying with you? Or does she need an apartment?"

"I told her she could stay with us. As long as you-"

"She's your family. You never have to ask permission for your family to visit. I just ask that you notify the patrols," Wyatt said, raising his hand.

"Thank you, Alpha."

"You're welcome." He glanced at his watch. "I apologize, but I need to make a call."

"I understand. Thank you for your time," Perseus said before he left the office.

Wyatt was well aware of how sensitive werewolf hearing was and that precautions would need to be taken to prevent his next conversation from being heard. Switching on the white noise machine he grabbed up his smartphone and clicked on Alpha Sirius, SLP, on his contacts. After the second ring he heard "Sirius."

"This is very serious. Perseus was just in my office," he said into the receiver.

"Hang on." It sounded like he sat the phone down and then he heard, "Baby, go close the door." He heard Laura say something and then Sirius replied sounding like he was further away. Then he was back, "Okay. What did he tell you?"

"Celeste is getting out, but she's still not welcome with your dad."

"That is a huge understatement. She told me yesterday that she was getting out. Nothing like waiting until the last minute."

"I was wondering about that."

"She swears that she told me several months ago. If she did, it would have been around the time that the baby was born. I'm pretty sure that the sun and moon continued to rise, and the world kept spinning. Past that, if it wasn't there in the neo unit, I have no idea."

"How is that little fighter doing?"

"Currently, sleeping like an angel. But at any moment, she can start screaming like a demon. We have three white noise machines in here and we blame it on her."

"But it's got more to do with Celeste."

"I always knew that you were smart," Sirius said with a chuckle.

"Not sure about that." Wyatt leaned back in his chair. "I swear I can damn near feel Demon dancing in my head."

Sirius laughed. "Just wait until she's close to you."

Wyatt groaned. Sirius laughed even harder. Laura said something in the background, and he settled back down.

"Sirius, if you don't like me, just say so. You don't have to try to kill me."

"But I do like you. Maybe even enough for you to mate my sister. Maybe."

Wyatt rolled his eyes and chuckled. "I think we passed that point when you gave me her first shirt."

"You're probably right. When does my sister get there?"

"Sometime before Saturday."

"Expect her Thursday night. And I quote, if you're late, you're disrespectful; if you're on time, you're late; and if you're early, you're on time."

"I'll tell the patrol to expect her at any time." Wyatt adjusted the note before leaning back in his chair again. "Perseus also told me about your youngest sister."

"Portia. Yeah, she's not looking forward to it. I would have thought that dad would change his opinion. But no… He's determined that his youngest daughter will do the Hunt." Sirius sighed and Wyatt pictured him rubbing his temples. "She's forbidden to go to the human town because dad is certain she'll run away too. I don't see her going to the Marines, but I can certainly see her running."

"I told Perseus to tell her this, and I'll go ahead and tell you. All the Maidens are getting guards this year. I refuse to have any rapes on my pack lands." Now it was Wyatt's turn to sigh. "That brings us to the second reason for my call. And I'm only telling a few other Alphas about this. So…"

"Silence is golden."

"I'm not having a Hunt."

"How are you going to do that?"

"The morning of the Hunt, they'll go get the hunters and all the escorts like always. And once they are on the training grounds, the guards will go get the maidens."

"Sounds like every other Hunt."

"And bring them to the grounds."

"Not to the woods?"

"Nope. Once everyone is there. I'll make a speech and then let nature take its course. Without rapes."

"Your dad agreed to this?"

"My dad would agree anything to guarantee that no Maidens were raped while under his protection."

There was a pregnant pause. "I started talking about these changes; he didn't like them at first. Then my aunt, his favorite sister, told him that she was raped. And my sister, Wenona, told him that she had nearly been raped. Had I not been in that Hunt, and close enough to smell her fear, she probably would have been."

"I didn't know that you ever did a Hunt."

"One. When I was seventeen. It was her third. After that, I refused to participate," Wyatt explained. "Recently, my dad started talking to the other women here. He completely supports me now."

"I wish more people would."

"You'd be surprised how many of our generation think the same. Have you heard who the new Alpha is for the Harbor Moon Pack?"

"No. Didn't Alpha Henry only have daughters?"

"Yes. His oldest is Luna at the Autumn Hills Pack. His second daughter is now the Alpha. She called me last week to tell me that her pack would not be participating this year."

"What did she say when you told her about your plans."

"Told me to let her know how many guards she needs to bring."

"How many should we bring?" Sirius asked.

"Right now, I'm saying one for each of your maidens and twenty more."

"Got it. Thirty."

Wyatt smiled. "But be warned, your guards will not be with your maidens."

"I get that. A little too protective."

"Exactly."

There was a knock at Wyatt's door. "Sounds like my next appointment is here. I've got to go see the orphanage. Hate this part of the job."

"Agreed."

After they disconnected the call and both returned to their duties, Wyatt found himself waiting to hear from the guards that Perseus' sister had arrived. When the message finally came, he had been having an early dinner with his sister at her favorite restaurant.

The little smirk that she gave him told him more than any words she could have said. He knew that she noticed a change in him, and he was grateful that she did not press him. Much.

"I'm guessing that it's not alpha duties that put that sappy look on your face?" Wynne asked as the waitress placed her raspberry and lemon cake on the table.

"No." Wyatt agreed with the sappy grin she accused him of having.

16 - EXTRA GUEST

Celeste pulled up to the cute little cream-colored house. It was just as Perseus had described. 1940s style craftsman with lots of green and blue accents. She got out of the pickup just as Teuf lifted his big German shepherd head, and then curled back up in the passenger seat. She walked up the cobblestone walk to the wrap around porch. Seeing the rocking chairs on one side and porch swing on the other, she shook her head. Though he was four years younger than her, his soul was old.

She knocked on the wood and glass door. Viviane quickly appeared at the door wearing jeans, a Grateful Dead T-shirt, and no shoes. Her blonde hair had a pink peekaboo that showed clearly through her messy bun. Bright blue eyes held the same smile as her pink lips.

"Celeste?" she said with a sweet voice as the door opened.

"Viviane?" Celeste replied.

“If not, I’m in the wrong house,” she said with a little laugh. “Come on in.”

“Before I do, I have a question,” Celeste said with a nervous little huff. “I didn’t say anything before, because it was just recently that I got the final answer.”

“I'm sure it will be fine. What’s the question?”

“How do you feel about dogs?”

“I’m a wolf.”

“Exactly. Full blooded dogs.”

“Well, I like looking at them on Facebook. But I’ve never really been around any.”

“I have a dog.”

“In that?” Viviane pointed to the pickup with the windows rolled up.

“Yeah.”

“Well, I know you’re not supposed to leave them in the car.”

Celeste smiled broadly and followed her to the pickup. “He’s a trained K9. You better let me open the door,” she said, stopping her sister-in-law from letting Teuf out.

“Oh. He’s not aggressive, is he?”

"Only if he needs to be." Celeste opened the door and Teuf jumped out and stretched before sitting down facing Viviane and holding up a paw. "Viviane, please meet Teufelhunden. Or Teuf for short. He'd like to shake your hand."

"He's beautiful." Viviane said, bending down and taking his paw in her hand.

"And he knows it. He's housebroken but not neutered. Typically, he's a perfect gentleman. Unless he needs to be something else, and then, he truly is Teufelhunden."

"What does that mean?"

"Devil Dog. Well, I think it translates to Devil Hound. The Germans gave the Marines that name during WWI. But you probably don't want a history lesson."

"My dad was in the Army. I've learned a lot about military history."

"Well, I promise not to argue with him too much over which is better."

"Probably a good idea. Let's get your stuff inside, and I'll make dinner."

Celeste opened the back seat and pulled out her rucksack and dog bed. "Where is my idiot brother?"

"He's on his way home. He had patrol today."

"How about I take you guys out for letting me crash here."

A black SUV pulled into the long drive next to the house. Perseus stepped out and quickly walked to his sister embracing her in a bear hug. She returned the hug; she had missed him. She had missed all her family.

"You look good, Sis."

"So do you, Idiot," she said as he stepped away and looked down at the dog at her feet.

"And who is this?"

"This is Teuf. I just got approved to keep him yesterday," she said as Teuf held out his paw.

"At least he's polite." He shook the dog's paw.

"He is. Is there a place he can go? He's been in there for about an hour." She opened the door and grabbed the dog bed and bowl out of the floorboard.

"Treeline, I guess." He took the dog bed from his sister.

"Teuf," Celeste said and he looked up at her. She made a subtle movement with her head, and he took off to the trees.

"He won't run off?" Viviane asked as they made their way back up to the house.

"He said he wouldn't. He'll go take care of business and come back."

"How freaked out were your bosses when you told them that you could talk to dogs?" he asked.

She laughed, following the couple up the stairs and to the guest room. "I went with a K9 officer, he was an Omega, and he said that there was a dog that was about to be put down. He was way too aggressive after losing his handler. I went in and he started going crazy and trying to get to me. I commanded him to sit down and calm down. He did."

"You are of Alpha blood," Perseus reminded her as he set the dog bed on the floor.

"That's what Simmons said. Must be able to tell you're Alpha. Two days later, I found myself in training to be a handler."

"Was that Teuf?" Viviane asked.

"No, that was Duke. He died in Afghanistan. IED. He went with another handler that day. At least it was an LOD," she said with a little smile. "Sorry, line of duty death. After Duke was Rory and then Teuf. And at first, they were not going to let me have him."

"What changed?" Perseus asked.

"He is now my PTSD dog. And as a warning, I have nightmares. Teuf will get on the bed with me when I have them. Awake, I don't typically have any issues. But asleep... That's when my demons come out." She pulled his veteran assistant harness out. "Now, where are we going for dinner?"

"Are you taking him with us?" Viviane asked.

"Unless you want me to leave him in your house alone. I don't advise that. He becomes very destructive if he gets bored. If he has his harness, he can go anywhere I go."

She thought about one of the most common sentences that she would say to her dog while they were deployed. "Quit eating the dozer tires. And tank treads. And the damn tank."

"We're taking your truck," Perseus said. "No dog hair in my SUV."

"Okay."

They headed back downstairs and out the door.

"So, what are we eating? I haven't eaten since breakfast."

"How are you still standing?" he teased his sister.

"Discipline," she said stepping out onto the porch. Teuf curled up to the left of the door. "Teuf," she said, and when the dog saw his harness, he stretched to stand and then shook his whole body before waiting for the harness to be put on.

"He's very well trained," Viviane observed.

"He is. The harness is a lot lighter than the Kevlar. He likes it better. But he's also a diva. He insists on riding shotgun."

17 - EARLY MORNING COFFEE

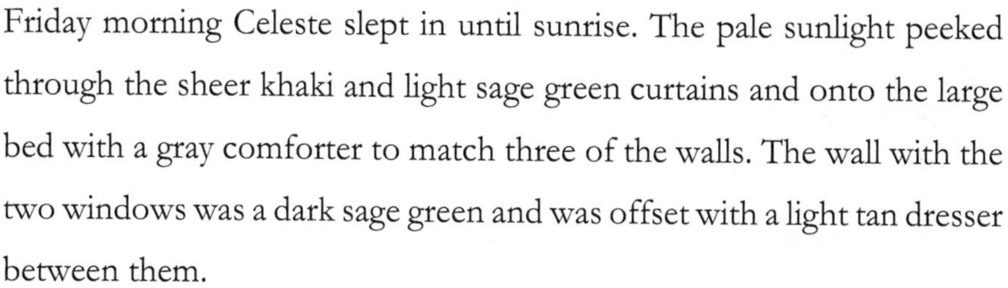

Friday morning Celeste slept in until sunrise. The pale sunlight peeked through the sheer khaki and light sage green curtains and onto the large bed with a gray comforter to match three of the walls. The wall with the two windows was a dark sage green and was offset with a light tan dresser between them.

Teuf's bed sat under the far window, but the dog himself lay on the bed like the diva he was. Absently her hand moved over his head, and he stretched a little closer. Looking through her lashes, she glanced at the overnight bag on her borrowed dresser. Celeste did not bring much with her, but the few other bags and boxes would need to be brought in.

But not yet.

She considered going for a run but wasn't sure what the rules were for this pack. At her father's pack, she could go just about anywhere, as long as one of her brothers was with her. Out of all the Moore kids, her wolf was the biggest. Usually, the first-born son was. She was the fourth daughter, number six of thirteen.

Being that Angel was the biggest, and strongest, Celeste went wherever she wanted, with or without a brother. When she had her first shift, way earlier than she should have, she started getting stronger. And then her need to be busy got even worse. So kickboxing and regular boxing were added to her schedule.

By the time she was in high school, she could lay out just about all her brothers. She could lay them all out by the time she was driving. And by the time she was supposed to do the Hunt, she had perfected the skills to protect herself. But the mate bond could render her stupid. And she feared that she'd end up like her sisters. She was determined that was not going to happen.

Celeste knew that her mate had been close to her before. She could smell that cedar and spice and knew it was him. That one time at the bar in New Orleans during Mardi Gras, she was certain that she saw him. She was drunk. And horny. And that scent drove her crazy. She started to go to him. But then Tameka said something, and she looked away.

When she looked back, she was angry, and she hated herself. She had nearly given into the mate bond. Just given away her life. But when her eyes found him again, he just smiled and left. Isn't that what she wanted? For him to go away and leave her alone? But why did he walk away?

That question bothered her every time she thought about it. Just as she was thinking of it now. Last night at the restaurant, she caught his scent. Not strong enough for him to be there. He had been recently.

She loved that scent.

It was intoxicating. Maddening. Sweet. Spicy. Woodsy. And someday, it would belong to her.

She hated that scent.

It was intoxicating. Maddening. Sweet. Spicy. Woodsy. And someday, she would belong to it.

With a groan, she rolled out of bed. Teuf stretched as he stood and followed her to the hall bathroom where he sat just outside the door. After a few minutes, he heard the shower turn on and he whimpered.

"You're pathetic." Celeste told her dog as she opened the door. He happily trotted over and entered the walk-in shower. She rolled her eyes as Teuf rolled around under the warm spray. She finished stripping before stepping into the shower also.

"Move, ya big lug." She said nudging his side with her foot. Reluctantly, he rolled over and sat up. She lathered up and again he whimpered. "I need to get you some soap. We'll do that today."

His now soaking wet tail thumped on the tile floor. She made a small motion with her head, and he jumped up onto the built-in bench. Now that she had room to easily move, she washed and conditioned her hair and shaved. Once she felt thoroughly clean, she stepped out, leaving the shower running for Teuf. He got back under the spray and enjoyed himself.

Once she was dry, she put lotion on, using a kind that would not cause her tattoos to fade. She paid a lot for them, and she planned on keeping them for a while.

"You know that you might not get daily showers now." He stopped squirming on his back and looked at her. "Sorry, Teuf. Got to pay a water bill now."

She got dressed, pulling on jeans and a long-sleeved t-shirt. When he saw that she was dressed, he got up and waited for her to turn off the water. He gave a good shake of his body and then stood patiently while she ran a towel over his fur. Like always, he had waited until she was behind the glass before he shook, she closed the door a second time when she was through drying him and he gave himself another good shake.

"Shampoo, and a brush. You look like a giant poof ball!" Teuf simply sat down and looked up at her. "You're the one that shook. Poofy. Come on, let's go outside."

Celeste opened the door, and they raced down the stairs to the back door. She opened the door, and he took off for the tree line. Turning around she found three men staring at her.

"Hi there." She said, looking at them. They were all tall and blond and very Nordic looking. They were nice to look at, but the machine behind them was even better. "Oh goddess, you sexy beast." She approached the coffee maker. Pushing one of them out of the way, she hugged the machine. "Talk dirty to me and tell me lies about all the things we're probably not going to get done today."

"Seriously?" Perseus said as he came down the stairs.

"Shhhhh…." She replied with her cheek lying on top of the machine. "We're having a moment."

"Issues. You have freaking issues." He told his sister with a laugh.

"You think I have freaking issues?" she asked as she moved away from the coffee maker and looked to where he was getting coffee cups out of the cabinet. "That is so cute. Are you this adorable on patrol?" she then turned to the other men in the kitchen. "Really, is he this adorable on patrol? Because, Sunshine, I passed freaking issues many years ago. Now I have fucking subscriptions."

"If mom could hear you now." Perseus said with a laugh and then his eyes went as big as saucers. "I'm sorry, Celeste. I didn't-"

"Stop. I knew what the consequences were when I left." She said taking the mug from him and making a cup of coffee. "The way I saw it, I had two choices. Get kicked off pack lands or possibly get raped. I can move. I can't get unraped. Let Teuf in please."

The man that she had pushed out of her way to get coffee opened the back door and Teuf came trotting in.

"Rabbit got away, didn't he?" she asked, and the dog sat down and hung his head. "We'll go to the store today and get you shampoo and a brush and tomorrow you won't smell like a sweet pea poof ball." Teuf laid down and put his head between his paws. "Quit pouting. Hey, idiot."

"I thought I was adorable." Her brother countered.

"Hey, adorable idiot. Is there a Starbucks around here?" As soon as she said the magic word, Teuf sat up and looked excited.

"Someone likes Starbucks?" the man closest to her asked. "There's one in the human town."

"Someone loves Starbucks." She took a deep drink of the still hot coffee. "Sweet goddess. I knew I loved you."

"Who you talking to?" Viviane asked, joining them in the kitchen. "I thought you might sleep in today."

"Coffee. And I did sleep in." Celeste said sipping her coffee. "The sun was rising when I got up."

Perseus started laughing. "What is not the right thing to say first morning of boot camp?"

"It's about time you got here." She said with a grin and the men started laughing.

"Please, tell me that you did not say that!" one of men said.

"I woke up around three. Got a shower. Was dressed. Had my rack made and sitting on my footlocker. DIs come in carrying trash cans flipped the lights on. They saw me and just stood there. I opened my mouth and what came out was 'It's about time you got here.' You ever seen a pissed off Marine DI up close? I have."

One of the men doubled over with laughter. "Damn girl, you got balls!"

"Yeah. It didn't get any better."

"We're all going to run until she gets tired." Perseus quoted with a grin.

"30 miles later and DI Sampson is the only one still with me and he's on the side of the road puking. Speaking of running, any rules I should know for around here?"

"No. And you can go to the gym by yourself." He told his sister in reference to their father's rules. "That was the stupidest rule ever. You could lay Sirius on his ass. I don't think any of the warriors would spar with you. Weren't you a black belt by then?"

"Black in Ju Jitsu and brown in Tae Kwon Do. And junior golden gloves for the state."

"And you couldn't run or go to the gym by yourself." Perseus shook his head.

"Yeah. I wasn't supposed to spar either. It was all to make me a better Luna and baby making machine." She batted her eyes dramatically at the triplets before looking back at her brother. "Aren't you supposed to go on patrol or something?"

"We probably should." The men agreed.

"Well, Larry, Curly and Moe, I'm Celeste. That idiot's older sister. Nice to meet you."

"Oh, shit!" Perseus said and then pointed to each of them in turn. "Robert, Ronald and Roderick. Triplets. Sorry, you were whispering sweet nothings, thought that you had met."

"Yeah. Me and coffee have a very special relationship. I drink it and it keeps me from killing idiots."

"I know that." He kissed his sister's forehead. "I asked if you could train. Commander wants to see what you can do. Hope you don't have plans for tomorrow."

"I do now." She said hugging him. "Kicking your ass. And then the biggest baddest mother fucker I can find is going to get laid out on his ass. Thank you, Pers."

"And you probably will." He let her go and then moved to kiss his mate. "If she starts giving you problems, make her do girl things."

"Viviane, I like you. Don't make me do girl things."

"How about just furniture shopping?"

"Will there be any coffee?"

Viviane laughed. "And food."

"Teuf." Celeste and the dog looked at each other and then he rose, stretched and went upstairs.

"Weirdo." Perseus called to his sister as the four men headed for the door.

"Idiot." She called back as Teuf came back with his vest.

Hours later, as they returned to the little craftsman's house, after yet another stop for coffee, Viviane sent a message to her husband through the mate link. If coffee is the life blood of the gods, your sister must be a god.

You have no idea. Came the quick reply. Ask her what her blood type is.

"Ummm… your brother says that I should ask you a question." Viviane said with a smile.

"What does the idiot want to know?"

"You blood type."

Celeste laughed as she pulled into the driveway. "Dark roast. It's always important to hydrate."

18 - THE ALL-KNOWING BETA

Wyatt walked into his office and found his Beta sitting in front of his desk reading through some papers. He walked over to the coffee bar and made himself a cup before sitting behind the large desk. He studied his Beta for a moment taking in the relaxed look of the gray polo and jeans. His hair was disheveled from running his hand through it, which he did again absently.

Before it had been Wyatt's office, it had been his father's and his father's before him. Their family had ruled over this pack since before the revolutionary war. The original pack house had been a major meeting house for the revolutionaries. It had been an ale house for the community, just far enough outside Philadelphia not to draw attention but close enough to reach on horseback in just a few hours.

Three other buildings had served as the Crystal River pack house since that very first one. The original one was destroyed in the Revolutionary War. The second during the War of 1812. The third burned just before the Civil War and the fourth lasted until the 1940s.

That building still stood, but it now housed the city offices. This building had started as a simple two-story building to hold pack offices. Multiple additions have occurred over the years. The biggest was in the 70's when the round central hub and the second wing was added. Wyatt's dad, Jonathon, remodeled the office during his reign.

Wyatt had stripped the wood paneling and about half of the built-ins. Smooth khaki-colored walls now held pictures of pack events and his time in the Navy. The pale carpet had been replaced with dark hardwood that matched the trim and crown molding. The one remaining built-in at the back of the office held a coffee bar, small refrigerator and, because he was bad about working through lunches, snack foods and take out plasticware that got dropped into a drawer .

The only things in the office that never changed were the portrait of the first Alpha and the ornate mahogany desk. The chair, however, was ergonomic, plush, heated, and very well molded to his body. Settling into his chair he looked at his Beta and lifelong friend. They had never been able to keep secrets from each other. He knew that today would be no different.

"Something on your mind?" Wyatt asked as he gathered up the messages that Terry left on his desk.

"Are you going to tell me about the sister staying with Perseus?" Stephen asked, not looking up from the report in his hand.

"Seems like you know." He called for Terry through the mind link and the Omega quickly entered the room.

"Of course, I do. It's my job to know everything." Stephen replied as he handed a small stack of papers to the Omega as he passed. "I know everything, and you look good."

Wyatt smirked as he also handed a stack of papers to Terry. "Put these on the calendar for next week, get me some research on those two and you have dinner reservations at Miguel's for your wife's birthday." Wyatt handed over the messages. "Oh, at seven. Did I tell you that? And Wynne will be there at six to watch the pups."

"I'll get right on those. And thank you, Alpha." Terry headed back out to his desk.

"That was nice of you." Stephen handed over the report he had been looking at. "Estimates for upgrades to the hospital and bids."

"Preferred bid on top?"

"Always." Stephen wrote a note on his calendar before looking up at the Alpha for the first time. "It's her, isn't it?"

"Yes, " he admitted to his oldest friend.

Stephen nodded and then went on with the morning business. He acted as if his friend had not just admitted that the woman he had been following for ten years was suddenly nearby.

Three hours, and probably way too much coffee, later they had finished up with their work. Stephen closed out the program on his tablet as Wyatt pulled up his email on the laptop.

"What are your plans?" he asked his Alpha.

"I don't know," he admitted, leaning back in his chair. "Nothing about our relationship has been…"

"Normal?" Stephen suggested.

"I was going to say typical, but normal also works." Wyatt chuckled. "Any suggestions?"

"Jewelry? Chocolate? Clothes? Promises that you don't intend to keep." Stephen suggested with a grin.

"Sasha is back on the Clock Man movie," he said, referring to the four-year-old who ruled Stephen's house with an iron fist and adorable smile.

"Do you know how many children's movies have clocks in them?"

"How many did you watch before you figured out that she was talking about Beauty and the Beast?" Wyatt couldn't help but laugh at the fact that his friend's little girl loved the grouchy Clock Man more than the princess.

"Way more than I wanted to." He shook his head slightly. "But you knew exactly who she was talking about."

"Dad always said that Cogsworth was the most realistic Disney character. Ever. Maybe I should reach out to him."

"Mr. Knew My Mate from Birth?" Stephen asked with a cocked eyebrow. "You might as well ask Betty Crocker how to do an oil change."

"Okay, so who do you suggest I ask about courting a woman who ran away from her Hunt to avoid her mate?"

"I'm pretty sure that you're in uncharted waters. I just suggest a life jacket. And in the event of an emergency-"

"Seat cushions may be used as a flotation device."

They both finished it together with a laugh. When they laughed at it as children, Alpha Jonathan had said that it was always good to have a Plan B.

"It's better if it's not useless and bat shit crazy. But never fault someone for having a backup plan." Wyatt quoted his father. "I'm flying blind with no plan, much less a backup plan."

"Then at least have a goal."

"I do have that." Wyatt grinned as he thought of the woman with silver eyes who had haunted him for a decade.

19 - TEN YEARS OF LETTERS

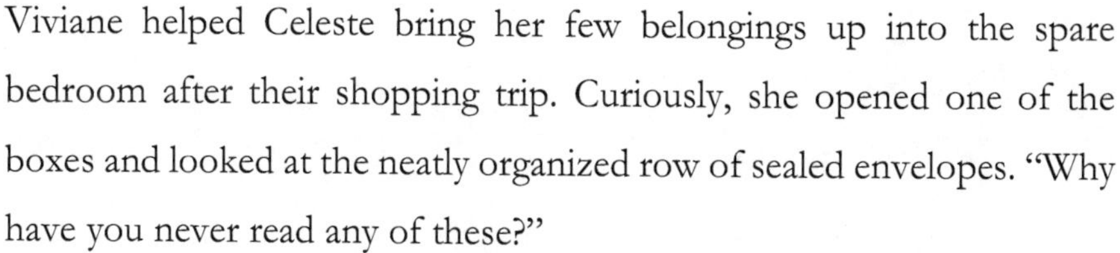

Viviane helped Celeste bring her few belongings up into the spare bedroom after their shopping trip. Curiously, she opened one of the boxes and looked at the neatly organized row of sealed envelopes. "Why have you never read any of these?"

Guilt washed over Celeste as she looked at the box. "I guess I just wasn't ready."

Although she wasn't sure she was ready to read them now or not, Celeste found herself sitting on the meticulously made bed with too many decorative throw pillows in khaki, sage, and gray, looking at a box where Jill had kept all the letters and cards that had been received from Wonder Pup, as her unknown mate had been dubbed. It should not have surprised her; that damned werecat was the ultimate romantic. Now she stared at the box full of one-sided correspondence.

Reaching in, she grabbed a random envelope. In Jill's bold sprawling handwriting she saw that he had marked the day it was received and where she had been. There was a small note underneath declaring that she had groaned at receiving it and then smelled it "like your life depended on it" before throwing it away unopened.

She had done that to most letters and cards. The less she knew about him, the easier it was to ignore the pull. But since she had been here, it was stronger than ever. Granted, it had not even been a full twenty-four hours, but the urge to go find him was growing.

Ignoring Angel as she whined at the pain of the wolf's bane, she tossed the envelope aside and grabbed another. After a few more, she found the one that she wanted. It was the only one that she had ever opened and read. The only one that she had kept.

Opening the envelope, she removed the letter that she had received a few days after she graduated from boot camp. She hated this letter because it reminded her that no matter what she did, she was bound to this man. Yet, she loved it because she felt treasured and cared for.

Her eyes skimmed over the words that her heart and mind already knew.

My dearest mate,

I know that you sensed me earlier. Your gaze found me, even if you did not see me. I have an advantage because I know who you are.

And I know some about you. You should have the same chance to get to know me.

I currently serve in the Navy as a medic, and I'm embedded with the Big Red One out of Pendleton. If our paths ever cross during our service, I promise to do my best to give you the space and time that you want and need. I will wait for you. When you are ready, the moon goddess will bring you to me.

AW

Carefully, she placed the letter back in the envelope and set it off to the side. Grabbing another envelope, she read the note from Jill. Received it on her birthday while they were in California. She had tried to get her dog, Duke, to eat it.

Smiling, Celeste remembered that day. It was her second year in the Corps, and she had called Sirius at the office, having been disowned by her father, she no longer had access to the pack or family links. But her father had answered and once again told her that she was a disappointment to him and the pack. After listening to his lecture longer than she should have, she simply hung up the phone and called Jill. At the time, he was still using his given name, Matthew. It would be a little over a year before he met Jack and another two before he became Jill.

Opening an envelope at random she read the short note.

My dearest mate,

I saw you last night. You were outside the barracks at Leatherneck with your fellow K9 handlers. I think that the dogs sensed me as they all looked in my direction. I had hoped that you would also. But you did not.

The wind carried your scent to me. As always, it is the most beautiful thing I have ever smelled. I am only here for a few days, and they say that you are going out tomorrow. By the time you get this, I will be back in my FOB.

I only have a few more years before I must go home. My duties wait for me, and my father wishes to spend more time with his mate. I understand this desire. But I also understand that you need time.

As always, I will wait for you until the moon goddess brings me to you.

AW

Celeste replaced the letter, set it aside and picked up another envelope. She continued this until she had read them all. They all started with "My dearest mate" and ended with him saying that he would wait for her. None were more than a page long and most were barely half a page.

In those short notes, she learned so much. Unlike her pack, his pack encouraged service. Like her pack, they participated in the solstice Hunt. Just like her, he did not like it.

In his letters she had discovered that he had three sisters and now all but the youngest were mated. He had no brothers, so all the family responsibilities fell to him. His parents were ready for him to find a mate. His mother did not know about her. Only his father, one sister, and a few close friends did. He enjoyed having her all to himself.

She had laughed when she read about his sisters attacking him with silly string the first morning that he was home. Tears filled her eyes when he wrote about losing a patient. There were little stories about his shipmates and the Marines he was embedded with. Anecdotes about his sisters and their kids. He spoke of his fears that he would disappoint his family. Or his pack. But most of all, he feared that she would be disappointed in him.

Once they had all been read, Celeste placed them all back in the box. Teuf moved up and let her hug him as she cried. Not for the first time, she wondered if she had done the right thing.

Angel spoke to her for the first time all day. Only the moon goddess knows.

20 - BREAKFAST

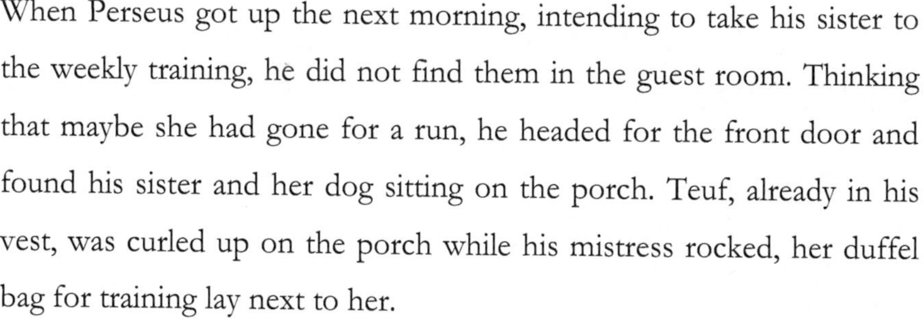

When Perseus got up the next morning, intending to take his sister to the weekly training, he did not find them in the guest room. Thinking that maybe she had gone for a run, he headed for the front door and found his sister and her dog sitting on the porch. Teuf, already in his vest, was curled up on the porch while his mistress rocked, her duffel bag for training lay next to her.

"It's about time."

With a little laugh, he kissed the top of her head. "Come on. We got to go find you a big, bad mother fucker to beat up."

"Finally." She stood and grabbed her bag and Teuf followed them. She opened the passenger door, and the dog effortlessly jumped into his spot. "I told you, that's where the diva rides," she told her crestfallen brother. "I can follow you."

"There's no point in taking two vehicles to the same place,." he said, opening the door to get into the back seat. "I'll give way to the beast."

"You can either give directions, or you can drive," Celeste conceded, offering him the keys.

"I want to drive," Perseus said, snatching the keys and rushing around to the driver's side. "Breakfast."

"What happened to big bad mother fuckers?" she pouted playfully.

"Gives you a chance to size up your competition." The engine roared to life, and he gave a soft sound of appreciation. "Some of us go every week. Think of it as team building."

"If your team is all like you, I won't even break a sweat." They bantered back and forth until they reached the red brick café. "They're busy."

"You okay with crowds?" he asked quietly.

"What?" she gave a little laugh. "I guess I wasn't expecting so many when you said a few of you all go before training."

"Few. Few dozen. Meh,." he said, opening the green wood and glass door. She rolled her eyes at him. "Over there." He pointed out where the triplets from yesterday sat.

Smirking, she followed her brother and sent him a message through the family link. Testosterone…, it's what's for breakfast.

As they approached, the table was much bigger than she had thought, Perseus couldn't help but laugh and shake his head at her. "We'll see about that."

There had to be at least a dozen men already at the multiple tables pulled together. And there were still a few black metal chairs open at the red checked tables. As When the pack members saw Teuf, they got quiet and watched the dog and woman walk past. Most wolves did not have dogs. And they certainly didn't take them with them to breakfast. She sat in an open empty chair and Teuf lay down under her chair with his front pads and face between her feet. He curled his tail around himself and practically disappeared.

"I'm sorry, Miss,." a manager said, approaching the table. "We can't allow dogs in here."

"State and federal laws say otherwise." She started looking at the menu.

"As you know," the Omega said, "on pack lands-"

"Jerry," Perseus interrupted. "The dog stays." Though he was not the Alpha of this pack, he still had Alpha blood. His power rippled through the air as he spoke.

Jerry lowered his head in submission. As he did so, another ripple of Alpha authority rose from another table in the room, obviously telling

Jerry to get rid of the dog. Perseus upped the authority he was pushing out, the air in the room changed, becoming thick and charged. As one, the Betas and Gammas in the room lowered their heads, baring their necks in submission.

Not to be out done, the other Alpha did the same. Neither willing to back down, they kept one upping each other. The few Omegas in the restaurant began trembling in fear.

Sighing, Celeste set her menu down and pushed her chair back. As soon as she did, Perseus quit and put his head down in submission. Several of the other men at the table looked at him in surprise. The other Alpha felt victorious.

But then, Celeste stood silently up. She didn't say anything. Simply, looking looked at the manager and exuding her own Alpha presence. It was stronger than the tooth men. Jerry lowered his head in submission and bared his neck.

Satisfied, she then turned her attention to the other Alpha. In an act of defiance, she met his eyes straight on. This could very easily be seen as a challenge. And it was. He pushed out more of his authority, his fangs extending and eyes shifting to the golden green eyes of his wolf. Celeste pushed hers until it seemed to be oozing out of every pore she had. The man lowered his eyes. And then his head. Then bared his neck.

Celeste sat down and just as quickly as it all came out, she pulled it back in. As if nothing happened, she picked up her menu again. "Jerry, I'd like some coffee, please."

"Yes, ma'am," Jerry said, his. His voice was a little shaky. "Cream or sugar?"

"Black," came the terse answer. Jerry hurried away to get her coffee. She smirked before muttering to herself, "Hydrate."

Perseus waited until she had her coffee and had sipped some of it. Gingerly, the conversations around the café started up again. "You okay, Alpha weirdo?"

"Definitely going to need several big bad mother fuckers," she told him and gave a laugh when several unmated males held up their hands to volunteer.

"You boys don't know what you're in for," Perseus warned. "Here it was, I was worried about the stories I've heard about women Marines, and I should have worried about your vagina turning into a penis."

They shared a laugh with everyone at the table that who heard. Something finally clicked with Perseus. His eyes widened with the realization.

"That's why Dad-"

"Stop. Don't finish that sentence. If you truly love me, you'll forget what you just figured out." Her eyes begged him to ignore the realization that she had the markings of the next Alpha of the Silver Lake Pack.

"Can I ask one question?"

"One."

"Is that why Dad wanted to get you mated as quickly as possible."

"Yes."

He was quiet for a moment and then decided to push for one more question. "When did-"

"Only one." She quietly reminded him.

Perseus nodded at the true Alpha of the Silver Lake Pack.

21 - TRAINING

The rest of breakfast was uneventful. Then they all headed to the training field. The sun was warm in the early spring morning. The snow had already melted, and the training grounds were dry from the spring sun. The wind, still cool and harsh, a reminder that winter was not that far behind them.

After the commander walked out to the center of the fields, he went over the rules of sparring before making a few announcements.

Someone got a promotion.

Someone else had a baby.

The police and fire departments will be holding physical exams in three weeks. The civil service test was on Thursday.

"And finally, Perseus has one of his sisters staying with him. She asked if she could spar. Seeing that she has been in the Marines," there were some ooh-rahs from around the crowd, "for ten years, she can probably hold her own. Can I get some volunteers?"

"What kind of sparring partner does she want?" someone in the crowd called out and the commander looked to Celeste for an answer.

"Oh, you know, the usual," Celeste smirked. "Tall, dark, handsome, well endowed." There were some laughs and a few offers. "But for this, big bad mother fuckers. The bigger, the badder, the betterer." There were a few more laughs and then a man around six feet and nothing but muscle stepped out into the field.

In a show of intimidation, he removed his t-shirt to show off his muscles and tattoos. He flexed and the crowd expected her to decline. Instead, she toed off her shoes. Celeste walked out and looked at the tattoo on his shoulder. She admired the line work and how it seamlessly transitioned from chest to back and then down the arm.

"Takes a real man to get a tattoo this big," he told her with a wink.

"Pers!" Celeste smiled as her brother doubled over in laughter.

"Sorry!" Perseus called out from the side. "Just trying to figure out what that makes you."

She grinned up at her competitor. "I guess that makes women tougher than a real man."

Walking back towards her brother, she removed her own shirt revealing two full sleeves, a nearly completed back piece that spilled around her sides and partially onto her abdomen. She then dropped her jeans revealing exercise shorts that stopped mid-thigh and matched her black racerback sports bra. A half sleeve was on her right leg stopping just above her knee. The left had designs peeking out in a few places.

"I think that we play different games in the tattoo world."

Celeste then walked back out and made a complete circle around him. "You should make a good warm- up."

"Time?" Perseus yelled at her.

"It's first fight., not really warmed up..., he's pretty good size., fits both description-"

"Shut up, weirdo."

"Whatever, idiot." She continued her assessment. She sniffed the air, and then winked, "We'll say fifteen. Tops. First contact?"

"Yups."

Celeste nodded as they. They then started to circle each other. The man reached out to swing at her arm. She caught his arm with hers and used his momentum to throw him over her back while. While she yelled "Time."

On the sidelines, Perseus started his stopwatch app on his phone.

Her challenger was surprised at how easily she tossed him. He looked at her in confusion as someone in the crowd loudly asked if it was sheer luck or if she truly was a good fighter. She smiled at him seeing that he too seemed to be questioning her skills. This irritated him and he charged at her. Right before he reached her, she crouched down and again tossed him onto his back.

Celeste stepped to him and expected her to pin him. Instead, she offered him a hand up. He accepted it and she pulled him to his feet. She started to step away, but he used the close proximity to twist her around, pinning her arm across her chest with her back to his chest. She folded herself in half and wrapped her legs around his neck.

As he started to see black, he let go of her chest and arm. She loosened the grip of her legs. Bending her knees, she unfolded herself and used her hands to gently force his knees to give. As he started to go down, she bent over backwards, landing on her feet. Quickly, she turned and gave him a swift kick in the chest. The air got knocked out of his chest and he fell back. Celeste straddled his waist and pinned his wrists above his head. They had a stare off before. He tried to push his power out at her.

Beta.

She grinned at him and countered with her Alpha power. His eyes widened before he turned his head exposing his neck in defeat.

"Time." Celeste called her brother.

"Thirteen forty-two,." he called back as she stood up and offered him a hand up. "You could have had him a lot sooner."

"Yes. But that would just be rude." She smiled at her challenger. "You're a bit too predictable and you telegraph your moves."

"You don't,." he said grinning at her. "Did not expect any of your moves. I'm Kenneth."

"Celeste," she replied, accepting his hand.

Something in the wind caught her attention and she turned her face towards it and sniffed. It was the wonderful scent that she had grown to love. And hate. Her eyes glazed over before she closed them. She was having an internal struggle.

"You should go," Kenneth advised.

"No," she said between gritted teeth. "I don't want that shit." She took a calming breath. "I'll teach you how to hide your intentions."

"I appreciate that."

Celeste nodded, and turned around and walked over to where her bag was. Teuf sat up as she bent down. He gave a few licks to her face. Smiling, she ruffled his fur, shaking his ears from side to side.

"You thirsty? Hydrate, you asshole." she pulled out a small bowl and a bottle of water. She poured some in the bowl before taking a drink herself. Before she stood up, she grabbed a rope out of her bag. Teuf perked up and reached for it. "You be my good boy."

"Weirdo." Perseus laughed.

"Idiot," his sister replied.

Celeste stood and turned around to find another man standing in the field. She eyed him up and down. Just before she walked out, she commented, "Tasty. Ten."

Perseus rolled his eyes. "Are you giving me a score? Or your time?"

"Time." she replied with a small lopsided smile.

"So, you can flip people around, but can you take a hit?" he taunted as she walked out.

"Can you?" she replied.

"I'll be gentle, I would hate for you to break a nail."

"Oh, feisty." She had an evil grin. "Change that ten to twenty-five."

"Think I'm more than you can handle," he countered, and she caught the innuendo.

"No, baby. I like foreplay." She purred.

Her comment got the reaction she wanted as his eyes glazed over with desire.

"My poor ears!" Perseus teased from the side.

"Guess you don't want to hear about cheer camp then."

"No, I'm pretty sure that's where you learned the banana trick."

"No, learned it from Jill."

"Are we going to fight or are we going down memory lane?" the new challenger demanded.

"Waiting on you, sweetheart."

He charged at her, and she stepped out of the way at the last moment. He turned and looked at her.

"Thought you wanted to see if I could take a hit."

He angrily walked up to her and punched at her, but she avoided his fists. She shook her head and stepped back from him. Celeste held up her hands forming a T, indicating a time out.

He looked at her confused.

"You're emotionally involved. You've decided that I must submit to you. You're not thinking about your moves. Only about taking me down. You're sloppy and predictable. Calm down. Forget the tits. I'm your competitor, and nothing else. You're not going to fuck me, and I'm not sucking your dick."

He took a deep breath and quietly admitted that she was right. Calming down he nodded to her.

"You sure?" she asked. "I'm hoping to be back next week. Don't forget to tip your waitresses."

Chuckling, he asked, "Are you going to take this seriously?"

"Are you going to try to kill me?" she asked, and he said no. "Mate me in front everyone, including my idiot brother over there." Again, he said no but from the crack in his voice, she was certain that an image of just that exact event ran through his mind. "I've been surrounded by perverted men for the past ten years. I know exactly what you just thought."

He blushed, giving away the thought that he just had. "Sorry, I'm a guy."

"Meh." She shrugged her shoulders. "Who doesn't like a good porn from time to time." At his look of surprise, she rolled her eyes. "Please, I have a heartbeat."

"Just not used to a girl talking like that," he admitted.

"She's not a girl,." someone called out behind her. "She's a Marine!"

This time she joined in with the chorus of ""OOH-RAH!"" with the Marines in the crowd.

"Calm down, baby brother. I'm still a virgin."

"Thanks for announcing it to whole pack," Perseus complained.

"You're not the only one who was wondering."

The scent wasn't as strong as it had been before. But it lingered in the air. And she felt the eyes belonging to it boring down into her. She turned her attention back to her opponent. "Since you've already mind fucked me, you should probably tell me your name. That way I know what to scream in your fantasies later.

The fact that he could not meet her eyes as he smirked proved that she was right. He gave a small laugh as she grinned at him. "Will."

"Nice to meet you, Will. I'll be your fantasy later tonight. But for now, I'm here to kick your ass. You ready?"

"Yeah. You're not going to make this easy, are you?"

"Nope." She emphasized the pop of the p.

Will stepped towards her and raised his fists. He gave a nod letting her know that he was ready. She returned the nod. He swung a left hook, and she blocked it.

"Time," Celeste called, and Perseus started the timer. She blocked a few more and then missed one that hit her shoulder.

"Harder,." she told him and hit back with enough force to make him take a step back.

He hit her a little harder with the next few punches. But she knew that he was still holding back.

"I'm hoping that you fuck harder than you hit,." she taunted, and a few men snickered. "Don't make me have to scream "harder" in your fantasies too!"

That got him. He swung hard with a left uppercut hitting her on the chin. Her head was knocked back, and she grinned at him before rolling her neck. He had a horrible look of regret on his face. Celeste spit spat out a little bit of blood and grinned at him.

"There you are. Keep going."

"I don't want to hurt you," Will admitted.

"Bitch, please, I'll heal."

This time he came at her with everything he had. She took a few hard blows and relished the pain. The pain made it easier to ignore the scent which had become stronger and steadier now. She refused to look in the direction that it came from.

Celeste found an opening and the next time it came, she palm-punched on his chest. The air rushed out of him as he fell backwards. Once he hit the ground, she nodded to him, and he agreed. Holding out a hand, she called "time." to her brother.

Will stood up with her help and she bent him to a 90-degree angle. She began to rub circles on his back.

"Little breaths. That's it. Calm down, you're not going to pass out on me, are you? We have a date in your fantasy later."

Will gave a little laugh and slowly calmed down.

22 - WONDER PUP

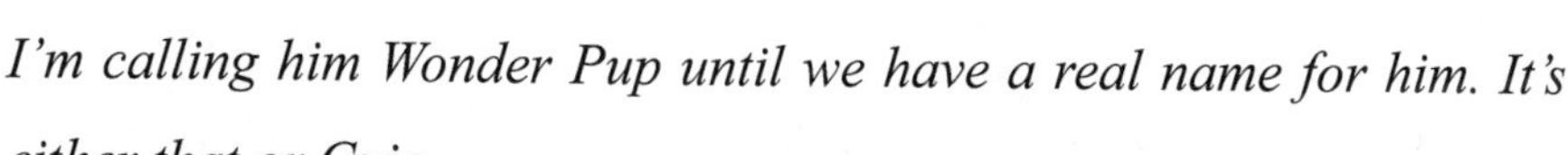

I'm calling him Wonder Pup until we have a real name for him. It's either that or Cujo.

Jill's words from years ago bounced around in Celeste's mind as the scent that would always be associated with Wonder Pup enveloped her.

He was next to her. She took a deep breath to calm herself. All that did was to fill her senses with him. She focused on Will. But he noticed that her hand paused for a moment. And the next breath after her deep breath was shaky.

Will stood up and looked at her. For the first time he saw her not looking confident. Her eyes were closed, and her face looked calm and serene. But her shaky breath and unsteady circles on his back gave her away.

"Better?" he asked, concern was laced in his voice. And what a voice. A rumbling base that wrapped itself around her.

"Yes, Alpha."

Of course. He had to be an Alpha. But would she settle for anything else? Probably not. No guarantee that she would settle for him either.

"Good. Why don't you go sit down, and we'll see if I can't salvage some pride for our pack."

Will nodded and walked off, taking away the only barrier between him and her.

"You're going to have to look at me. Unless you prefer to do this blindfolded," he teased.

"Weighing the pros and cons of that idea."

He gave a light laugh. "You want to give your brother a time for me?"

"No."

"Still calculating?"

"Still debating."

"And what are you debating?"

"Do I fight you, kill you, or run as far away as I can from you."

"I have another option." He offered. "But since you're considering bodily harm, my murder, and you leaving, I don't think you would like that option."

"No. Not really."

"Then let's go with your first option."

"Bodily harm?"

"That's the one."

She finally looked up and was almost undone. Fighting the urge to touch the wall of muscles in front of her, she snapped twice at her dog. Teuf grabbed the blue water bottle and ran to her. Celeste held her hand out, and Teuf put the bottle in her hand palm before sitting beside her.

"I've been hearing about you," Wyatt said looking at the dog.

The dog looked up at him, cocked his head to one side and then rolled over on his back exposing his belly.

She Celeste finished her drink and then looked down at the Alpha rubbing the dog's belly. "Traitor."

"Make a decision yet?" Wyatt asked, looking up at her.

"Bodily harm." She told him and was rewarded with a gorgeous smile. Her stomach and heart were doing weird things inside her. "Teuf."

The dog rolled back to his feet and took the bottle from her before trotting back to the same spot and laid down.

"He's very well trained," Wyatt observed as they walked to the center.

"We've been through some shit together," Celeste acknowledged as she took her place. "Don't go easy just because I got tits."

"Don't go easy on me because I'm only using half a brain."

"Time?" Perseus called.

"No. I can't get a good read on him," she admitted.

"That really never happens." her brother said to no one in particular.

"A read on me for here? Or in general?" Wyatt asked softly.

"Both," she whispered honestly.

He nodded at her. He knew that he had an advantage in having seen her fight. Plus, he knew more about her than she did of him. He knew that she did was skilled in boxing, kick boxing and martial arts. Whereas she knew nothing of him. He knew that her favorite color was blue. Had a fascination with Cookie Monster. Had a stubborn streak that he loved. And strength that he admired.

The problem he was having was finally being so close to her, and still not being able to touch her. The beast inside him wanted to do nothing more than sink his teeth into the soft flesh of her neck. Claim her as his in every way possible.

Celeste made a few quick punches that Wyatt easily avoided. Just as she threw another punch, he moved to the side and grabbed her wrist. Pulling her to him, he turned her around. A quick tug and her back was to his chest.

Striking out behind her with her free hand, she missed as he shifted behind her. Using his longer arms to his advantage, he grabbed her free hand and crossed her arms across her chest. A growl of frustration escaped her, and he couldn't help the grin on his face.

With her now wrapped in his arms, the temptation to mark her was even harder.

Wyatt knew that since he had her arms pinned with her back to her chest, she would aim for the knees. To prevent that, he leaned back causing her kick to miss.

"You smell wonderful," he murmured against the back of her head.

He was too engrossed with her smell and did not notice that she had moved her head forward. The mistake became very clear when her head connected with his nose. The force and his odd position caused him to go backwards. Landing on his back with her on his chest, the blow knocked the air out of him.

As soon as they landed, his grip on her loosened enough for her to roll away from him. Before she could get too far, he captured her legs with his own. He twisted, getting into a better position and improving his hold on her. They were now on their backs facing away from each other. He lifted his hips to put pressure on her legs.

Grinning, she began to move into a better position and then began to walk up on her hands. Quickly, his position was used against him. He released her legs, and scrambled to grab her before she could get away. She was on her back, and he rolled over to trap her.

Celeste slid her leg out from under him and wrapped it around his leg. She picked the place carefully before raising her foot and driving her heel into his inside thigh muscle. He didn't roll off her, but she was able to roll out from under him. She started to straddle his back, pulling his arm with her.

Wyatt caught her off guard and swept her back under him. He pinned her legs with his knees on the outside and his feet on the inside. He then caught her wrists trapping them on either side of her head. Knowing that she had finally been bested, she started to show her neck. She had lost and he was her mate. He had the right to mark her.

"Don't," he said barely above a whisper. "I will never ask you to submit to me. You should be my partner. Not my property."

With that, he stood up and offered her a hand. She rolled over and accepted it.

"You are good. Wasn't sure I was going to get you."

She looked up at him and he watched her and her wolf fight for control. Her eyes never changed colors, they remained silver, but the wolf eyes were more hardened, sharper and clearer. The wolf knew what she wanted and had accepted her fated mate. The woman was still conflicted, wanted to make her own choices and refused to accept what was in front of her.

"I was distracted," she admitted. Just as she said that she heard a familiar low growl of warning. "Teuf." The growl lessened but did not stop. She looked over and saw the Alpha from breakfast. "Teuf,." she said again, but he continued to growl at the man's still approaching him. "Teufel!" His ears twitched but nothing else. "Teufelhunden!"

He still did not respond to her and this time she knew why. There was something shiny against the man's arm. From the way that he held his hand, she could only assume that it was a knife. Fear ran through her, and she did the only thing that she could think of.

"SIT!" Celeste commanded in her Alpha voice, and everyone there sat where they were. Wyatt even started to sit as the power of an Alpha radiated off her. She walked towards the man with the knife and everyone between them quickly moved out of her way. The man started bolted to get up to run. "DO NOT MOVE!!!"

"If you have a problem with my dog, say something to me. Don't attack my dog. I've already lost one dog like that."

She turned to look at Wyatt. "I'm sorry, Alpha. I didn't mean to bring division to your pack. I'll leave."

"No," Wyatt said. "John was out of line. You are my … guest." He caught himself right before he said mate. "You, and your dog, are both welcome here. And no harm will come to either of you." His eyes swept around the crowd as he made sure that everyone there understood what he was saying.

"Thank you," she said sincerely.

"Have dinner with me?" he asked, softly, quietly enough for only her to hear.

Not trusting her voice, she simply nodded.

He nodded at her. "I'll pick you up around seven."

She nodded again and retrieved her clothes. She was excited to spend time alone with him. Even if it was just a car ride. And she was terrified to spend any time with him. Alone.

"Hey," Perseus said catching up to her. "Where are you going?"

"I just need some space." She said looking down at Teuf, and then they were both running for the tree line.

"I know you, Sles. What's going on?" Perseus asked, catching up to her.

"You've got the keys. Take the pickup. I'll find my way back to your house." She started to walk away.

Perseus grabbed her arm and she finally looked at him. Wyatt knew what her brother was seeing. The shifting of the eyes between that of her wolf and then her own again. He would know his sister better than Wyatt did and would be able to easily tell what was going on.

"Oh." He let go of her arm and she and Teuf quickly walked away. Then he walked back to where the Alpha stood. "I do not envy you. She'll fight you the whole way. But she'll be worth it."

"I know. She's definitely worth it."

23 - MOMMA

"She's going to think you're desperate," Demon told Wyatt. "You should never show up right on time."

"You're just as desperate to see her as I am," Wyatt pointed out, stopping his pickup behind hers with California license plates.

"She felt so good under us." Demon practically purred at the memory.

"Keep that to yourself or you may never get to experience it again," Wyatt said, walking up to the front door.

"She likes you," Demon said as the front door opened. Wyatt smiled at the vision in front of him.

She was dressed casually in a black T-shirt declaring Drinks Well with other Marines in bold white script. Faded skinny jeans hugged her long legs and ended in gray and blue running shoes.

"Sorry, I heard the door," Celeste said, grabbing her key. Teuf sat at Wyatt's feet and looked up at her. "Traitor."

Wyatt reached down and scratched him behind the ear. "Do you like Greek food?"

"I've never had it," she admitted as they walked down the walkway.

"It's some of my favorite." He opened the passenger door and Teuf jumped up into his spot. Celeste laughed at the look on Wyatt's face.

"Not who I was hoping to be riding shotgun with me."

"He's a diva," Celeste chuckled.

"I see that. Do you mind riding in back?"

"No," she replied acutely aware of his hand on her arm.

He reached over and opened the back door. Just as she started to get in, he spoke very softly. "Celeste. Please, don't run away from me."

She hesitated slightly as she slid into the truck. It smelled of him, he saw her reaction and knew that she was considering running away.

Once the door shut, she was completely engulfed in it. This was not a good idea.

She was reaching for the door handle to get out when Wyatt got into the driver's seat and started the engine.

"Do you mind going to the pila town to eat?" he asked as they pulled away from the curb.

"No."

The drive into the neighboring town did not take long. And they went to a part of town that she had not yet been to. It was pretty, almost quaint. He pulled up to a small little café. It was so small that if you didn't know it was there, you would miss it completely.

"They're not going to have a problem with Teuf are they?"

"No. Pretty sure Momma is going to love both of you."

"Momma?"

"It's what I've called her since I was a pup." He opened the door. She was assaulted with exotic smells of sunny beaches.

"Wyatt!" a woman called out. "I'll go tell momma that you're here."

"Come here a lot?" Celeste asked as they sat at a table.

"I got lost once. I was about five or six, and I ended up here. Momma fed me, made me feel at home and then called my dad. It became our Saturday place." His face lit up as an older lady approached the table. "Hey, momma."

"There's my big boy!" she said sitting in the chair next to him. "And I see you've brought a friend."

"Friends, actually." He pointed under the table. "This is Celeste, and her helper dog Teuf."

"Teff?" Momma said.

"Teuf." Celeste grinned. "Kind of like tooth but with an F. It's short for Teufelhunden."

"Ohh…" Momma looked under the table and saw Teuf laying by their feet. "Aren't you adorable?" She looked at Celeste. "Does he like lamb?"

"If it's meat, he likes it. If it's rope and will end with strings hanging out of his butt, he really likes it. And if it smells like last week's catch and should have been thrown out two days ago, he adores it. And if it's something that should not be eaten at all, he loves it." Teuf whined. "Yes, sir, I'm talking about you and the tire."

"He ate a tire?" Momma asked.

"Unfortunately, more than one."

"But he's so well behaved now." Wyatt said and Celeste just smiled. "Oh. Go ahead and say it… Duh, Wyatt, she has Alpha blood."

Celeste looked at him in surprise. He smiled back at her knowing that Momma was well aware of the pack.

"Are you an Alpha also?" Momma asked as the girl from earlier started setting food on the table.

"Females can't be Alpha," Celeste shook her head, quoting her father.

"I wouldn't be so sure about that," Wyatt said.

"Well, I let you eat. Celeste, what would you like to drink?"

"Water is fine, thank you." She smiled at the friendly older woman.

"I'm the only one from the pack who comes here," Wyatt said quietly. "I thought that you might like to go someplace where everyone is not going to be staring at you. Or me. The pack keeps waiting for me to take a mate."

"Thank you."

They ate in near silence, with only a few comments here and there. Mainly about how good the food was. He kept asking her if everything was okay. Even in high school, he did not feel this nervous.

"Can I ask a question?"

"You're the Alpha. I'm just a guest."

"Do you have Alpha blood? Or are you the Alpha of the Silver Lake Pack?"

"The Silver Lake Pack is named after the silver eyes of the first Alpha. It typically passes to the oldest son. Up until three generations ago, all first born sons had silver eyes. My great grandfather cheated on his wife and lost favor with the moon goddess. The next two generations did not have silver eyes."

"And then there was you."

"And then there was me. Fourth daughter. Sixth child. And suddenly, there's a chosen Alpha with the traditional markings." She sighed and looked down at her plate. " I've always been active. Always. Sports. Cheer. Tumbling. Kick boxing. Boxing. Competitive Ju Jitsu. Marathons."

"That's the way you handle your power." Reaching over, he gently took her hand. Her initial response was to pull back, and when he released her fingers she relaxed and left her hand under his. She smiled slightly at her plate as his fingers gripped her own.

"Yeah." She pushed food around on her plate. "I didn't know that's what it was then. I went to Rome. Went and saw the Remus and Romulus statue under a full moon. A shaman was there. She asked why my brother led my pack."

"Do you want to be Alpha of your pack?" He still held her hand and began to gently rub his thumb on the back of her hand.

"No. Maybe at one point. But no. You're not supposed to be this nice."

He raised her knuckles to his lips. "I'll try to be an asshole next time." She smiled at him. "What about Luna?" She tried to pull her hand back, but he wouldn't let go. "I'm not asking you to let me mark you. I'm just asking a question."

She relaxed a little more. "I was trained to be a Luna. Bred for it, you could say. But to be honest, I would suck at it. Party planning. Luncheons. I like food, but not all the female bullshit that goes with them. Plus, I say shit like 'female bullshit.' Blame it on the Marine Sentence Enhancers."

It was his turn to give a little laugh. "I wouldn't want you any other way." Her heart did a flip flop in her chest as his thumb sent sparks all through her body. "You could have someone else do all the female bullshit. My sister does."

"Still just asking questions?"

"Yes. And planting ideas."

The girl from earlier approached the table with a large paper bag with handles. "Momma says this is for you. There's some lamb in there for the fuzzy one."

"Thanks, Leisl." After she walked away, he asked, "Are you ready?"

"Yeah. It was really good. I don't know what I ate, but it was good."

Pulling out his wallet and leaving two one hundred-dollar bills on the table, he smiled. "I quit ordering a long time ago. I just let her bring me whatever she wants." Standing up, he put his wallet away and offered her a hand. Her own hand felt empty without his. "Ready?"

Smiling, she took his hand and stood up. He broke the connection long enough to pick up the bag and settle it in his other arm. Then the trio left the restaurant, approaching the pickup driver's side first. He opened the back door and set the food on the bench. Teuf decided that was the better place to be and jumped up on the floorboard before laying down facing the food at the other end of the bench.

"Really? This is how I get you in the back seat?" Celeste asked him and he just whined.

Pressing his lips to her temple, Wyatt muttered. "Remind me to buy lamb. Frequently."

She gave a little laugh as he walked her over to the passenger door. She paused before getting in. "I thought chivalry was dead."

"Not in my pack," he said proudly.

The drive back to his town, through it, and towards a secluded cabin was done in a comfortable silence. She had rested her arm on the center console and did not pull away when he took her hand. They drove into a beautiful, wooded area and stopped at a small cabin by a river.

"It's beautiful," she said in awe. "Breathtaking."

"Yes, it is," he replied looking at her.

She looked at him as he raised her hand to his lips again. "I don't think I'm ready for this."

"I'm willing to go slow." He said quietly. "Just promise that you won't run away from me. If you leave me, please tell me."

She nodded. "I'm not worth it," she whispered.

"Yes, you are." He moved some hair behind her ear. "I meant what I said. I don't want you to submit to me. I want you to be my partner. In everything. I've waited 32 years for you. I'm willing to wait until you're ready."

"What if I'm never ready?"

"As long as you stay with me, I'll die a happy man."

"You can't mean that. What about an heir?"

"I certainly do mean it. And I have lots of nieces and nephews."

He slipped his free hand behind her head and brought her to him. He pressed a kiss to her forehead. "I'm willing to wait for you."

Celeste pulled back and looked at him. "Ignoring you would be so much easier if you were more of an asshole."

"I'll work on that for you." He let go of her and sat up straight. "Let's go."

"Where to?" she asked, turning back to him, her door partially open.

"We'll put this up, and then go watch the sunset."

They found a bottle of wine in the bag. Wyatt grabbed some wine glasses out of the cabinet and then found a blanket in a closet before leading her down to the waterfront at the lake. There was a small gazebo on the beach with a double lounger. They sat in silence, wrapped up in the red buffalo print blanket and watched the sunset.

Once the sun was down, they spoke in hushed tones. Not necessarily about anything important. Just getting to know each other. Sitting in silence with her back to his chest, he noticed that her breath was now light and even.

Wrapping her up in his arms and drifted off to sleep.

24 - MOONLIGHT

"Don't move," Wyatt gritted out.

He had woken up a few minutes ago. He was now on his back with her stretched out on top of him. Celeste fit neatly with him. And that was his current problem. It would not take much to slip out of his jeans and into her.

"What?" she asked groggily. Celeste started to sit up, but this caused his shaft to come into contact with her through her thin pants. Her eyes widened as she woke up quickly. "Oh."

Wyatt groaned as he fought for control.

"Do you trust me?" she asked him quietly.

His eyes flew open and met hers. "I trust you. But right now, I don't trust me," he admitted quietly.

"I trust you." She peeled off his shirt.

Celeste changed her position so that she was sitting astride him with his shaft nestled under her. He gave another moan as she began to move against him. Letting go of the blanket, he moved his hands to her thighs. At first, she thought that he was going to make her be still. Instead, he helped her find a rhythm that they both enjoyed.

Keeping one hand on her thigh, he slid the other hand under her shirt. He cupped her breast and pinched her nipple between thumb and forefinger. She gasped and then pulled off her t-shirt and sports bra, tossing them aside. Wyatt cupped her other breast. Celeste leaned into his hands changing her angle and pressure. They both moaned in pleasure.

"Wyatt." Celeste moaned.

"Come on, baby."

With a final cry of his name, she collapsed against him. He wrapped his arms around her and held her close as her breathing returned to normal, and her body quit shaking. He ran his hand down her hair and then watched it fall away from his fingers as he lifted his hand up.

After a moment, Celeste started to move. She slid down his body and began to pull his jeans down. After she pulled them off and were tossed over with her shirt, then slid back up his legs. When she reached her target, she swirled her tongue around the tip. Wyatt groaned and reached for her. She lifted her head and caught his eye.

He knew that she was asking permission. If he said no, she would stop. Without saying anything, he laid his head back and she continued. She licked down his shaft to the base where she sucked a ball into her mouth.

"Oh goddess," Wyatt whispered. Celeste gave a little laugh as she released that one and did the same to the other. She then let that one fall out before running her tongue back up the shaft. Swirling her tongue around the head, she caught some precum with her tongue.

Looking at him again, she held his eyes as he took all of him into her mouth. She adjusted her position, and he felt her push past her gag reflex. In the back of his mind, he knew that he was in her throat. But all he could really think about is how good it felt. She was doing something with her throat muscles as she moved up and down on him, he knew that he would not last long.

"Celeste...."

He pumped his seed into her mouth, and she greedily drank it. When he was through, she released him. She gagged again as he slid past her reflex again.

"Come here." Wyatt held out a hand for her. She slid back up to him and he tucked her at his side. She rested her arm on his chest, and he absently started tracing the tattoos on her arm. "Is this Rory?"

"No, that's Duke. Rory is on the other arm."

"What happened?"

She was quiet for quite a while, and he thought she wasn't going to say anything.

"I was an M.P. for the Marines. One of the K9 officers was an Omega that had a falling out with his Alpha, joined the Corps and became a handler. Duke was set to be terminated because his handler was killed, and he wasn't handling it well. He would snap at everyone, and they were afraid he would turn on his new handler."

"The Omega recognized me as an Alpha. He could get Duke to respond to him. But not enough to save him. He asked me to come talk to him. So, I went. He didn't know that his handler was gone. He kept trying to get out to find him. That's all he wanted. To know what happened."

"I trained as a handler. Duke was my first. On our first deployment, we were going down a road that had been cleared earlier that day. Between convoys they put out new IEDs. Peterson and I were in the lead with the dogs. I was in the back with them. Angel was antsy. Something wasn't right. She was pacing, so I was pacing."

She took a deep breath.

"I was at the back and the explosion threw me clear. By the time they found me I had already healed so they all thought that I just got scraped up, knocked out."

"It was more," he said softly and kissed her temple.

Celeste sat up and placed his hand on her back. His hand felt the scar tissue from being burned. He moved his hand all over her back and felt the rough skin. It didn't completely cover her back, but it covered quite a bit. There were also a few slashes that criss crossed her back.

"That's what started my collection. It was easier to hide the scars under ink than answer questions. I got Rory next. We survived snipers." She turned and pointed to the pucker marks on her shoulder and upper arm. "I went to Andi's pack for a break. Her old pack, before the Council moved her to the Keystone Pack. We went to dinner, and I left Rory by himself. When we got back, his throat had been slit. Autopsy showed that he'd been tranquilized."

He sat up, scooted forward, adjusted the lounger, and then leaned against the raised back. Wyatt then settled Celeste between his and leaned her back against his chest. He wrapped his arms around her, letting her know she was no longer alone. He placed a kiss on her neck, over the spot that he hoped to mark her at. The simple act caused sparks to run through her body and her neck warmed.

"Next came this demonic bastard. He's damn good at his job. He will protect, seek, search, just about whatever I ask, he'll do. He was trained as a defensive K9. But the diva here will detect bombs, arson materials, missing people, cadavers. All of it. Which is why the Corps was not going to let me keep him. But he reverted to his old ways when he was not with me."

Teuf opened his eye from where he lay at their feet and seemed to grin before closing it again.

"Ate a tire."

"Off a bulldozer. And two patrol cars. A couple of magazines, not the paper kind. Training equipment. You know those suits that we wear while training them to bite? He ate one."

Wyatt started laughing. "What you're saying is don't leave him alone with tires."

"He was acting out," she said, debating how much of the next part she should tell.

"Our first tour had us in an outpost. Taliban had a bounty on any K9s and handlers. And an even bigger one on any female soldiers. We got shot at a lot. Tried to kidnap me at least once. Offered to give up a siege they were doing, if they would hand over Teuf and Me."

"I'm sorry that you went through that, mate."

After a moment, she quietly told him, "I'm not certain how I feel about you calling me that."

"Do you feel the same pull?"

"You know that I do."

"Then, when it is just you and I, may I call you mate?"

She thought for a moment. "Only you and I?"

"Only. You. And. I." he said emphasizing each word with a kiss to her neck.

"Will you kiss me?"

"Goddess knows that I want to. I want to do nothing more than turn you around and kiss you. But I'm afraid that if I start with a kiss, I won't stop until you bare my mark." As an emphasis, he very lightly dragged his fangs across the spot he wanted to mark her on. "And I have claimed you every way that I can."

"I'm not ready for that."

"I know. Which is why no matter how much I want to, or how much Demon tells me to, I won't kiss you right now."

"But you plan to?"

"And very thoroughly." He again kissed her neck. "You have no idea how badly I want to give you a hickey."

She laughed at this thought. "It's been a while since I had a hickey."

"High school?"

"Mm-hmmm. Came home from a football game, had my sweater draped around my neck so my parents wouldn't see. My dad would have flipped the fuck out." She gave a small little laugh. "Shit. He's tried to kick me out of the pack, says he wants nothing to do with me, and he'd probably do an honor killing over tonight."

"Your pack still does honor killings?"

"No. But only because it would make him look bad. He's the only one in the family who still won't talk to me. If he knew that they all talked to me, he'd probably go crazy."

"Tried to kick you out?"

"Before I turned 25, my mom and Sirius wouldn't let him."

"And when you turned 25 the authority of Alpha transferred to you."

"I would love to see the look on his face when he found out how much influence I have over pack decisions. Sirius consults me on the big decisions. But the day-to-day decisions are his."

"I guess it's you that I really need to talk to."

"Big decision?"

"Very big. But before I tell you, I need you to promise to listen to me. Listen to everything, before you make any decision."

"Okay. What is it?"

"Promise?"

"Promise. You want a pinky promise?" she asked holding up her pinky.

He gave a little laugh and looped his pinky with hers. "We have to have that discussion in my office."

"Tease."

He kissed her neck. "Yes ma'am."

25 - THE OFFICE

Early the following morning, Celeste listened to the plans and did not say anything. At first Wyatt could feel her anger. But as he got more into the details of what he intended to do, she relaxed. When he was through, she asked some very specific questions. Pointed out some problems. Offered suggestions. And then he sat waiting to find out if the true Alpha of the Silver Lake Pack would support him.

She stood up and sat the papers on his desk and then walked around to stand in front of him.

"Sit on your hands," she commanded.

"What?" he asked, confused.

"Sit on your hands," she repeated.

Still confused, he did as he was told. She placed her hands on his shoulders and then straddled him on his chair. He tilted his head back to look up at her. She brushed her lips across his, before coming back and gently tugged on his bottom lip with her teeth. He opened his mouth, and she deepened the kiss as tongue met tongue. He started to move his hands, he wanted to bury his hands in that wonderful black hair of hers.

"Leave your hands there."

"No fair."

"I'm kissing you. You're not kissing me."

"Technically, we're kissing each other."

"I'm in charge right now." She leaned down and kissed his neck.

"That's just wrong." He lightly nipped at his marking point. "Oh goddess." He sighed out.

"You have my full support. As the true Alpha. And as a woman."

"And as my mate?" he whispered. "Do you support me in this as my mate?"

She kissed him again before whispering against his lips, "Yes."

He smiled. "You have no idea how happy that makes me."

"I'm not ready-" she sat back on his lap, and he moved his hands to his waist.

"I know. I'm not going to ask for anything further. We're on your timeline."

"This would be so much easier if you were an asshole."

"Really?" he asked, moving some hair behind her ear.

"Yeah. Because if you were an asshole, then I would be ready and I would just reject you." She let out a sigh. "There is part of me is screaming for me to run as fast and as hard as I can to get the fuck out of here."

"But?" He cupped her cheek and she leaned into the simple embrace.

"There's another part of me that wants me to submit to you."

"I meant what I said," Wyatt told her again. "I do not want you to submit to me. I want a partner. Someone that I can share my duties, my troubles, my victories with. I want you as my equal."

"I'm a hard person to live with."

"You're a hard person to live without."

"I drink way too much coffee."

"I'll buy a coffee farm."

"And, when the mood strikes, too much whiskey."

"The pack has a brewery."

"I'm addicted to tattoos."

"And I'm addicted to you."

"I'm not getting rid of my dog."

"I'm keeping your dog."

"I have an Alpha personality."

"So do I."

"You're not making this easy."

"The best things in life come from struggles."

There was a knock on the door. Celeste quickly moved off his lap and grabbed a piece of paper off his desk. Stifling a laugh, he called out for the person to enter.

"I'm sorry, Alpha," his Omega assistant said, opening the door slightly. "Alpha Sirius is here to see you."

"Show him in, please."

The Omega nodded and he closed the door.

"Do you like the new football jerseys?" Wyatt asked her with a grin.

"What?" She looked down at the paper that she held. It was part of a fund request for new football jerseys. "Oh." She sat the paper back down.

The door opened and Sirius walked in.

"Oh, good. She's the one that I came to see."

"The idiot called you?" she asked.

"He did. Said that you were here. Was hoping that you would call me."

"I've been a little busy," she supplied. "He knows."

"How much does he know?" Sirius asked his sister.

"That you answer to me."

"That pretty well sums it up," Sirius said. "I thought that we should discuss the Hunt with her."

"That's what we were just talking about," Wyatt admitted.

They fell back into the discussion. And then the two siblings visited for a while, catching up on each other's lives, before Sirius had to leave. Once they were alone in the office again, he watched her for a moment before speaking. Walking around the office, she studied the crammed bookshelves that were filled with pack law books, historical almanacs, and fiction novels.

"We have some veterans groups here," Wyatt said. "Maybe, you can go with me."

"Maybe," she agreed.

"Good. We'll go this afternoon." Wyatt turned around and looked at him. He shrugged his shoulders. "I always go to the Sunday meetings. They have a playtime for the kids while we have a meeting. And there's usually lunch."

She turned and looked at him and then very quietly said, "I'm not ready for us to be out in the open."

"And nothing has to be said about us. You won't be the first veteran I've brought to a meeting."

He pulled her into his lap and nuzzled her neck. "You're the only one that I've ever taken to meet Momma. Or even taken to Momma's. And you're definitely the only one that I've slept with. The only woman that has ever taken me down their throat. That was amazing, by the way."

Pulling back, he met her eyes. "You don't have to talk. Just listen. If you want to share, you can. I've seen your scars. Even the ones you didn't tell me about. If you have that many scars on the outside, I can't even imagine the scars on the inside."

"No one will judge?" she quietly asked.

"We've all been down the same road. We all travel it differently."

"I'm pretty sure that my path goes down some twisted dark road."

"There is even an all-female group that meets on Thursday night."

"Oh, goddess, no. I would rather handle extreme testosterone over estrogen any day."

"Got it. No spa days."

She smiled. "Exactly. I do, however, like a really hot shower and the occasional soak in a tub. And Teuf loves his daily showers."

"With you?"

"With me."

He looked over at the dog asleep on the floor. "Lucky dog."

26 - MESSY TWISTER

Celeste had been to three Sunday meetings. The most that they had gotten out of her was "Celeste, Marines, K9 handler, 10 years, 4 tours Afghanistan." And Wyatt was right; they didn't push, they didn't judge, and most of the questions she got had to do with her tattoos. And they always had coffee. She wasn't sure who made the coffee, but she was certain that she loved them.

Usually, after the meeting they would hang out outside with the families. She and Wyatt had a standing date at Mama's on Sunday nights.

They would go running together in the mornings. Perseus had already asked what was going on between them. She still wasn't ready for the full commitment. Her answer had simply been that they were testing the waters. Keeping their relationship a secret was difficult. There was always someone at the pack house. And the town was small.

Wyatt continued to respect her request to take it slow. He didn't try to kiss her. But he had no problem with her kissing him. He would sit on his hands, and she would straddle him, keeping him from pulling them free. Nothing else had happened since the night at the cabin. Both thought about it.

She was in his office one late May afternoon when the principal of the high school came in.

"I'm sorry, Alpha," the woman was saying as she came through the door.

"It's okay, Mrs. Jones," Wyatt said motioning for her to sit. "What can I do for you?"

The woman looked at Celeste and her colorful arms. "Are you sure? If you have other business…."

"I can leave if you want," Celeste said, starting to straighten from where she leaned against the desk.

"No," Wyatt said, "Stay, please."

He tugged on her hand, and she moved so that she was sitting on the arm of his chair. He rested his arm around her slipping his fingers into her belt loop. She draped her arm across his shoulders. The statement was clear. She would someday be the Luna.

"Reilly had been planning the end of year fun day for the seniors. But, as you know, she met her mate and left. None of us thought about this until today. And it is supposed to be Saturday," Mrs. Jones explained. "I know that this is not usually your duty, but there's also no funds set aside."

"The funds are kept in a separate account," Wyatt explained. "I had assumed someone else had taken over. I do have her contacts for bounce houses and all of that."

"That's good, but will we be able to get what we want in time?"

"They will be here Friday to discuss what we want for next year. We always do the initial contract a year out. We can make changes if we need to. I think everything is set for Saturday."

"Oh!" Mrs. Jones said in surprise. "I didn't realize that you were that involved in the school affairs."

"My sisters do a lot of the Luna duties. But I remember the end of year day fondly. I had lots of fun. I do this one."

"We always have fun at it," Mrs. Jones agreed. "What did your school do, dear?"

"I went to a human school," Celeste said. "We had a party after graduation. But we didn't have a day. At the end of cheer camp, we would have some stuff. The best was messy twister."

"Messy twister?" they both asked.

"Yeah. You take those cheap pie pans and lay them out like a twister mat. Then you put stuff in them. Chocolate sauce. Jell-O. Jelly. Icing. And a water hose to rinse everybody off."

"That actually sounds like fun." Mrs. Jones said, and Wyatt agreed. "Will you take care of it, Miss?"

"Yeah. Would love to," Celeste said excitedly.

"Great," Wyatt said. "The meeting on Friday is at 11."

"I'll be sure to be here. Will you join us, also?" the principal asked, looking at Celeste.

"Ummm…" Celeste looked over at Wyatt.

"Please?" he asked quietly.

"I'll have to cancel my nail and hair appointments," she teased.

"I'd believe you more if you had said an ink appointment."

"That's Monday."

"Alpha, if there is nothing else."

"Yes, thank you Mrs. Jones," Wyatt said and the woman left unnoticed.

"What are you getting now?" Wyatt asked, pulling her into his lap. "And where?"

"Not sure. I dropped off some ideas the other day. I'll see what he came up with and go from there."

"Do you mind helping out with the senior day?"

"Do you mind me getting more ink?"

"Can I put lotion on it?"

"That could probably be arranged."

He slid his hands up her back under her shirt, scars slid under his gentle touch. "If I keep my hands back here, will you kiss me?" he asked with his lips barely away from hers.

Wyatt pulled her closer the instant her lips touched his. Her shirt rose on his arms exposing her back. Celeste shifted but neither was content. Tightening his grip on her, he stood up and sat her on the desk. She wrapped her legs around his waist locking her ankles.

"This is such a bad idea." He moved to nuzzle her neck.

"Probably," she agreed, giving him more access.

There was a knock on the door.

"Do you have another appointment?"

"No. Jones was the last one."

Another knock.

"Are you going to respond?"

"I am. I'm not responding."

There was a more forceful knock.

"WHAT!" Wyatt growled out.

The door opened and one of the warriors walked into the office. "I'm sorry, Alpha. Rodrick was trying to reach you through the mind link."

"I was otherwise occupied," Wyatt said frustrated. "Is there a point?"

"Yes, Alpha," the warrior said, staring at the tattooed back. When he didn't elaborate, Wyatt growled. "Sorry, Alpha. There is a man at the eastern gate asking to speak with you."

"Bring him here."

"He's insisting that you come to him. He said that it's very important that he speaks to you, and you need to be alone. Away from prying eyes and ears."

Wyatt understood. Werewolves had extremely sensitive hearing. He pulled his hands out of Celeste's shirt and straightened it. He then cupped her face and did what he did not trust himself to do. He kissed her. When he lifted his head, his eyes were dark with desire and need.

"You might want to go home tonight. I'm barely hanging on to my promise to you."

She nodded. Celeste considered staying to see what would happen. But the kiss that he gave her before walking out told her that if she was still here when he got back, he would mark and mate her. returned to her brother's house after Wyatt and the warrior left.

27 - GUNNY

The pack vehicle pulled up to the eastern gate and Wyatt saw the man propped up against a Jeep Wrangler. He pulled over to the side and got out of the pickup. As he walked over to the man, he could smell that the dark man was just that. A human. He left Celeste for this???

Wyatt was irritated. And he had a funny feeling it was just going to get worse.

The man stood up and took a few steps toward Wyatt. "Are you the Alpha?"

"I am. Who are you?"

"You have a Marine staying here?"

"I have several Marines here. Who are you?"

"This one has lots of tattoos." Wyatt stopped. "Yeah, you know her."

The man turned and motioned for Wyatt to join him. "Come on. We need to talk."

"Who are you?"

"Get in." He opened the door and stepped up on the running board to look over at the Alpha with one hand on the door and the other hardtop roof. "I don't know how much you know about what happened last year, but we have a tradition."

Wyatt moved to get in the Jeep when one of the warriors started to say something to him.

"Guys, I'm not going to do anything to him, except try to help a friend," the Hispanic man told them. "Guessing that y'all know her too?" he said and then rolled his eyes. "Look, I served with her.",

Wyatt got into the passenger seat and the man slid into the driver's seat. He offered his hand, "Gunny Williams." At the badly concealed look of confusion, he chuckled. "I got my looks from my mother, Imelda."

He nodded, admitting his faulty assumption and accepting the hand. "Alpha Wyatt."

Gunny put the Jeep in gear and turned it around. As he gunned it down the road, he asked, "You know she's lost two dogs, right?"

"Duke and Rory."

"Yes, we also lost Marley on this last tour. Before she renamed him, Teuf was Maximus. Let's face it, that dog is a hellhound."

"Teufelhunden."

"That's it," Gunny said pulling to the side of the road. "Marley and Teuf were littermates. Marley was supposed to be hers. But she took Teuf because their personalities meshed so well. Angel is more hell hound than she is an angel."

Wyatt chuckled. "Mine is named Demon, and yet he's very mild."

"That is an irony," Gunny said. "Our dogs are part of us. Part of our team. An extension of the handler. Jack lost Marley. But we all lost a teammate. Marley took the bullet that should have hit Sles. Sorry, Celeste. She felt guilty."

"That's why she didn't reup," Wyatt assumed.

"Ehh… not exactly. That and the Navy Alpha, I don't know the details of that." He shrugged. "I'm sure that you've seen the tattoos of Duke and Rory. We promised that we would be there when she got Marley. Tradition. Tattoos and alcohol."

"In that order?" Wyatt asked.

"Always, you've got to hydrate." Gunny nodded his head. "Angel shredded the sniper, now she's afraid to let Angel out. It used to be, she'd shift and chase my pups around." He smiled at the memories.

"Your pups?"

"My mate is were. She got kicked out of her pack for mating with me. She's considered rogue, but she's called packless. On the account that I belong to the Marine pack. Not sure what we'll do now that I'm out."

"We have good schools," Wyatt commented with a grin. "And several … We always called them halflings, but I don't know if that's considered," he gave a shrug, "rude."

"We call them halflings too. It probably is derogatory, but they say it proudly."

Wyatt nodded. "I knew several in service that were not accepted by packs. They're accepted here."

Gunny smiled to show his appreciation. "I'll mention it to Sammi."

"On Sundays, we have a picnic, inside during winter. You're more than welcome to bring your family. We have a veteran's groups that meets on Sunday also. Celeste has been coming to the meetings."

"Has she said anything?"

"Name, rank, serial number. Pretty sure she just goes for the coffee."

"Hydrate." Gunny laughed. "I'm certain that her blood type is dark roast and skin color is multi."

Wyatt chuckled. "When I was trying to convince her to date me, she was listing her flaws. Drank too much coffee and whiskey and was addicted to tattoos."

"Pretty accurate. What did you tell her?"

"I'd buy a coffee plantation; the pack has a distillery; and I like her ink."

"Have you seen the putty tat?"

"I guess not."

"Trust me, you would know." Gunny put the Jeep back in gear and then turned back around. "If you ever get her drunk, ask her what she can do with a banana."

"I'm a little scared to ask."

"We were all drunk. I know Marines drink. No way." They both chuckled. "Anyway, we're drunk, and Jack says that they need to go so that he can shove his dick down Jill's throat. And being drunk, and a curious freaky little virgin, Celeste asked how you do that. So, in the middle of a bar in San Francisco, Jill teaches her how to deep throat a banana. She hasn't paid for drinks since."

"The banana trick."

"You've seen the banana trick?"

"Not exactly," Wyatt chuckled. "But I have heard the term."

Gunny gave him a strange look before slamming on his brakes and looking at Wyatt. "Freaky deaky virgin. Must be something special about you."

"She is my mate."

"She never wanted one of those."

"I've been told."

"She'll bolt if she feels trapped."

"We're on her timeline."

"Smart man." Gunny grinned.

"We have been since I first found her scent. It's still the greatest scent in the world."

"When was that?"

"Ten years ago," Wyatt sighed. "I've kept my distance. Tried not to get too close if we were near each other. Even now, she sets the pace."

"You're a better man than me. I would have already thrown her on the bed and had my way with her. Or at least found the putty tat."

"Now, I'm going to have find the putty tat."

"You won't be disappointed," Gunny said as he took off again. "I got to say, I'm impressed with you. Most people flip out with my driving."

"I've been in country. I've ridden with plenty of drivers just like you."

"We don't stop until we get there."

"Exactly," Wyatt said with a grin. "How long were y'all together?"

"Seven years. We did three tours together. I know that she did four and none of them were kind to her. I swear that country had it out for her."

"I've seen the scars."

"If you ain't seen the putty tat, you ain't seen all of them. There's a reason why she wears granny panties, boy shorts, whatever the hell they're called. And you won't ever get her in a swimsuit."

"I'll keep that in mind." Wyatt grinned. "If you're going to be in town on Sunday, you should come join us. I'll let the guards know."

"If we come Sunday, there's going to be about four of us. Jack, Jill, me, and Doc. Jack and Jill were there at the same time, but different units." He slammed on the brakes, stopping just feet away from the gate. "Give me your phone number," he said, grabbing his phone.

Wyatt rattled off the number and then waited for his phone to ring before adding the other man's information to his. They shook hands and Wyatt got out. Gunny started to back up then stopped. He opened the door and put one foot on the running board and leaned on the door.

"Alpha?"

Wyatt turned and looked at him, stopping just outside his pack lands.

"Take care of her."

Wyatt's throat closed as he fought down emotions. He simply nodded and then forced out "Sunday."

Gunny smiled at him. "Sunday."

28 - MORNING WAKE UP

The nightmare came on without warning.

Her time in the Crystal River Pack had been emotional and trying for Celeste. She had told him about the night terrors as they sat by the river. He knew about them personally and knew that the nightmares would soon follow. And they would come with a vengeance.

The terrifying scream trapped in her throat. Or she thought it was. In truth, it woke her brother and his wife. And their neighbors. Her panic flowed through the light connection of the mate link that was just starting to form.

The link was strong enough to wake Demon and Wyatt. Instant fear had the beast taking over their shared body and running on four legs across the town. Wyatt resumed control as they climbed the steps to the wide porch. Standing naked on the wooden planks, he banged on the door until a surprised Viviane opened the door.

Dashing past his youngest sister's friend, he rushed upstairs and towards his mate. "Leave."

The simple command had Perseus walking out of the bedroom and closing the door. Teuf gave a warning growl at the Alpha who held up his hands in surrender.

"I want to help her. She's my mate, my soul."

Wyatt would have sworn that the dog understood the words the man uttered. His growls gave way to whimpers and he moved off the thrashing body. Wyatt moved quickly but carefully and slid under the covers. Gathering her body next to him, he held her close and began to sing whatever songs came to him. He wasn't sure if he had the words right. Or even if the lyrics that he sang all belonged to one song. Or even the same artist.

Honestly, he really didn't care. Slowly, the panic receded. The screams subsided, and the thrashing stopped all together. When she once again slept calmly, Wyatt reached over and scratched Teuf behind his ear.

"You get some sleep, too. Thanks for taking care of her."

The German shepherd settled in next to the Alpha and let out a deep sigh as his eyes closed. Smiling at the dog, Wyatt closed his own eyes and let sleep pull him under.

Wyatt woke up as the sun rose, and Celeste began to stir on top of a very naked Wyatt. He sensed her confusion as she looked around her room at Perseus and Viviane's house. She turned her head towards where Teuf was curled up next to them, with Wyatt's arm around the dog.

"What are you thinking?" he rumbled underneath her cheek.

"Why are you chasing me."

"You're perfect for me."

"No. I'm no good for anyone." With that statement, she got up and walked across the hall to the bathroom. The shower turned on and Wyatt looked at Teuf.

"Not this time, boy."

Teuf laid back down as Wyatt got up. He too walked across the hallway, ignoring the curious look from Perseus as the younger man left for his run. He stepped into the bathroom, closing and locking the door behind him. He then stepped into the shower. Celeste turned around to face him. Before she could say anything, he cupped her face and tilted it up to him.

He kissed her deeply and passionately. By the time he pulled away, they were both breathless and she was clinging to his neck, her toes literally curled. He took her hand and placed it over his heart.

"It's only beating for you. The moon goddess made it just for you. And she made you just for me. I asked you before not to run away from me. Now I'm asking you to stay and trust me."

She reached up and kissed him. He could taste the saltiness of tears. He wasn't sure if they were hers or his. Or both. But he could feel her whole heart in that kiss.

"Trust me. You are my everything. Don't ever think that you're not worth it."

"But-"

"No buts. You are worth it."

"Why?"

"Why are you worth it?" he asked, and she nodded. "Have you not figured it out?" burying his hands in her hair, he attacked her mouth again. When he finally released her mouth, she was pressed against the wall, they were both breathless again and eyes were dark with desire.

"I love you, Celeste."

29 - QUESTIONS

I love you, Celeste.

"What the hell?" Celeste muttered again. She had been asking herself "What the hell?" ever since Wyatt made his declaration yesterday. Today she had a meeting that she had promised to attend. She had avoided him all day yesterday. And had driven Viviane crazy being at the house all day. When she asked if something had happened between them and when Celeste told her about his declaration, she had been completely unfazed. The question was, how do you feel about him? That had been her response.

"What the hell?"

"What's bothering you?" Roderick asked.

She looked up to see the triplets standing in the kitchen like usual. She liked them; she really did. But they weren't her Marines. She really needed Jill. Desperately, she needed what they had dubbed a girlfriend talk. Frequently these talks involved a bottle of whiskey and kicking the other guys out. Gunny's wife, Sammy, would also join them, and if she wasn't pregnant, she'd help them put away a few bottles of whiskey.

Celeste grabbed the one closest to her, she thought it was Roderick, and kissed him. It took a few seconds, but he responded. There were no zings along her spine from whichever triplet this one was. Nor was there the desperate desire for the kiss to never end. It was just… nothing. As quickly as she had started it, she ended it by shoving him away.

Although she had hoped that there would be some reaction, deep down, she knew that there would not be. The kiss had been … nice. But when Wyatt kissed her, the Earth shifted, her insides turned to goo and her brain became mush. it was what she never wanted. A brainless fool who fell all over herself trying to impress her fated mate.

What she had with Wyatt was also exactly what she wanted. To be accepted as she was and not forced into a standard mold of the Perfect Luna.

Muttering to herself she stormed past them and her brother to sit on the stairs and think. But she could hear them. And that made it worse.

"What's wrong with her?" she heard one of the triplets ask.

"Alpha told her that he loves her," Perseus said.

"Oh goddess, he's going to kill me."

"I doubt it."

"No, he's going to smell me on her," the triplet insisted.

"He's more understanding than that," her brother assured the distraught man.

"Than what? I kissed the Luna."

"More like she kissed you."

The Luna. She stood up and went to her room. His scent was still there. She loved that scent. That irritated her even more. Almost as much as being called Luna. Did she want that?

Of course, she did. It came with him. And she wanted him.

"Give it up, sunshine," Angel told her. "You're just as in love as he is."

"Shut up," she growled at the wolf.

"You are. Hell, we are," the wolf taunted back.

"You are no help."

"You want me to be helpful?" her wolf asked, irritated. "Here's my helpful Advice. Go to him."

"How is that helpful?"

"How is what helpful?" Viviane asked from the doorway.

Celeste turned and looked at her sister-in-law. "I'm just so confused."

"Why? Do you have feelings for him?"

"Yes, but-"

"No buts, no justifications and no quantification. Do you have feelings for him?"

Sighing, Celeste said, "Yes, I do."

"Do you love him?"

"Yes."

"Then what are you going to do about it?"

It wasn't a girlfriend talk. But it was damned close. Celeste let out a deep breath and then left. She walked to the pack house the long way. Teuf trailing beside her the whole way. She considered talking to him, but he adored the Alpha. He had been upset that she had avoided him all day yesterday.

"It's because he gives you treats," she blurted out to the dog, causing the two other people near her to look at her oddly. But she knew that wasn't true.

He was a good man. Kind but firm. Lenient, but expected the rules to be followed. Fun but knew when to be serious. And, damn, he was a good kisser.

"Didn't you hope that he would come back to your room last night?" Angel asked.

Yes, she had. She wanted him to come to her and take her. Take away her virginity. Take away all the doubts and fears that she had. And he would.

But she had to ask for it. They were on her schedule. She had all the control. It was up to her. And she knew what she wanted.

By the time she arrived at the pack house, it was nearly time for their meeting. She walked into the office without knocking. She was rewarded with one of his heart stopping smiles. He held his arm out for her, and she went willingly. She had missed this so much yesterday.

Wyatt kissed her deeply. But when he caught himself sliding his hands under her shirt, he stopped and pulled back. This time, she really did not want him to stop.

"What's going on in that beautiful head of yours?"

Celeste just smiled at him, "I'll tell you after the meeting."

He smiled at her and kissed her forehead. There was something different about her today. He just wasn't sure what. He didn't have time to contemplate this, Mrs. Jones arrived, and they moved to the conference room.

30 - CONFESSION

If you would quit taking those pills, I could go to Demon and get this meeting over with. It was an argument that Celeste had often with Angel. The beast wanted to go to her mate. The woman wanted to live her life on her own terms.

Today, Celeste would compromise with her other half. If this meeting for the senior field day ever ended. The conference room was across the hall from Wyatt's office. The outside wall was floor to ceiling windows with a door leading out to the patio on the far side. A long whiteboard lined the opposite wall between the two doors from the hallway.

The wall behind the head of the long wooden mahogany table had a large, imposing wood carving of the pack crest. Celeste guessed that the shield was at least eight feet tall and six feet at its widest point. Above a filled mahogany buffet table against the far wall, were seven variations of the crest.

In the center of the paintings was a modern twist of the crest. A golden wolf with red highlights howled at the crescent moon in the corner. Behind the wolf was a grove of weeping willow trees topped by two clouds drifting across the star-filled sky. The shield and blue banners were on a background that matched the golden color of the wolf.

Celeste smiled at seeing the wall of paintings. This was something that her father would never allow. The crests were rooted deep in tradition and should never be changed.

Wyatt took the seat at the end of the long table and indicated that Celeste should sit to his immediate left. The chair of the Luna. The chair that he had told her previously had been left open, even when his sisters would act in the place of Luna. It was done out of respect for the future Luna. For her.

And now, he was placing her in the seat of honor. She was not merely acting as Luna. She was being treated as Luna. She was, as far as the pack members in the meeting were concerned, the Luna.

The meeting lasted about two hours. But to Celeste, it seemed like forever. When the last attendee had finally left, Wyatt pulled her into his lap.

"You have something that you wanted to talk about?"

"I want you to mark me."

His eyes flicked to the spot on her neck where he would bite her and mark her for all the were-world to know that this was his mate. Swallowing hard, he looked back up to her eyes. "Are you sure?"

She knew why he was questioning her. Ten years ago, she ran away to prevent being marked against her will. Prevent being raped, Having her choices taken away from her.

"Yes. Just… not yet."

"Okay."

"But I do know that I want you too."

"When you're ready," he said softly.

She nodded. "But I want to go upstairs."

"Upstairs?" he croaked out.

"I want you to take me upstairs."

He closed his eyes, and she could feel the internal struggle within him. "Now?"

"Now. Take me upstairs and make love to me," she whispered next to his ear. He contacted his Omega through the mind link and told him to cancel his meetings for the rest of the day. Then he scooped her up and carried her up to his bedroom on the fourth floor.

An Omega maid that was in the room, having just put fresh towels in the bathroom, she looked at her Alpha and the tattooed woman, frozen in place by her surprise and fear.

"Get out." He commanded and she ran for the door. By the time she reached the bottom floor, the entire house staff knew that the Alpha had canceled his appointments and had taken Celeste upstairs. It took a little longer for it to make it around to the whole pack. But by nightfall, even Sirius knew where his sister had spent her afternoon.

Mate. She is our mate. She will forgive us. As long as you don't fuck it up. Demon warned the man that he shared a body and soul with.

"Get out," Wyatt told the Omega as she came out of his bathroom. There was a look of shock on her face but as soon as he said the words, she bolted for the door. Once she was out of the door, he kicked it closed and then pushed the latch on the bottom with his heel locking the door. He did the same for the second French door which was already closed.

With the doors closed and locked, he sat Celeste on the bed and trapped her between his arms as he leaned down and kissed her. Lifting his head slightly, he quietly asked, "You're really here? This isn't some really realistic dream, right?"

She smiled at him and then reached up to kiss him. "I'm here. I'm really here."

"Don't go anywhere," he whispered and she smiled at him.

"I'm not going anywhere," she whispered back.

"Ever?" He sounded so scared, fear laced his words and shone in his eyes.

"Ever. I promise," she said and he visibly relaxed.

Wyatt stood up and went to close and lock the glass French doors leading out to the balcony. He then drew the shades on them and windows next to them. He did the same thing to the doors and windows on the other side of the bed before coming back to her.

"Afraid of peeping Toms?" she teased.

"With as long as the pack has waited for me to take a Luna? Yes. Very much so," he admitted.

"Really?"

"They thought that I would never find you." He laid down next to her, linking their fingers together.

"But you did."

"I did," he smiled at her. "There is something that you need to know before we go any further." Wyatt let out a breath before confessing. "The year that your pack hosted the Hunt…"

"I wasn't there."

He kissed her knuckles. "I went to go meet Sirius in his office, but the instant that I stepped inside the pack house, I could smell my mate. Demon was going crazy screaming mate at me over and over. So, I followed the scent and found your room. I was in your room when Sirius found me. I told him that you were my mate."

"What did he say to that?"

"Asked me what I thought about the Hunt. I still think the same thing, I hate it. And that it should be stopped."

Celeste smiled at him and then reached over and touched his cheek. He turned and pressed a kiss to her palm.

"He said that you would like that answer."

"I do," she confirmed.

"I have something that I need to show you," he said rolling off the bed walking around to the other side of the bed. He held out his hand and she took it. Wyatt led her into his closet and opened the top drawer of the built-in cabinet. It was filled with Ziploc bags that had cloth in them.

She picked one out of the drawer and looked at it. She looked up at him and he nodded. Carefully, she opened the bag and pulled out the T-shirt. Unfolding it, she recognized it as one of her missing shirts.

"Are all of these mine?" she asked, not sure how she felt about it.

"Yes. They have your scent on them."

"How did you get them?"

"Sirius. Someone would get a shirt and get it to him. Then he would mail it to me."

"I thought that I smelled you sometimes," she said softly.

"I tried to stay away. To give you time and space. But I had to see you."

"New Orleans?"

"Yes. But I knew that if you came to me then, you would end up regretting it. So… I left."

She stood there processing everything. Her silence made him nervous.

"Which one is your favorite?" Celeste finally asked.

He led her back to the bed and pulled back the covers. From under his pillow, he pulled out the blue shirt that Sirius gave him ten years ago. "It was the first one I got. I've slept with it ever since."

She looked at the school cheer team t-shirt that had been one of her favorites in high school. It was a few sizes too big so that she could wear it with leggings. She took the shirt from him and walked into the bathroom. So much had changed since the last time she had worn this shirt. It had been almost ten years exactly.

And the man that she loved had kept it close to him all that time. Celeste sat it down on the counter and then looked in the mirror. Was she really going to do this? She picked up the shirt again and smelled it. Her scent was very faint on it. But his scent was strong. She sat it back down and then stripped off her clothes and pulled the shirt on.

31 - MARKED

I want to be marked, Bitch. Angel told Celeste as she looked in the mirror. Smirking at her beast, a decision was made and she placed her old T-shirt on the counter. Then she quickly stripped out of her clothes and pulled the shirt on before giving herself a pep talk in the mirror.

A few minutes later, she stepped out of the bathroom and Wyatt was sitting on the bed, his head hung low with elbows resting on his legs. He looked so dejected. She walked over and stood in front of him. Celeste put her hands on his shoulders, and he looked up at her.

The smile came slowly as he realized that she wasn't upset. He reached out and grabbed her legs pulling her between his. Sliding his hands up, he discovered that she had nothing underneath.

"Definitely my favorite," he murmured as he pulled her down for a kiss. He then stood up and lifted her with his hands' on her hips. She wrapped her legs around his waist as he turned around and laid them down on the bed.

"First, I'm going to explore all of your tattoos." He told her as he slipped the shirt off. Starting with the tattoo of the dragon on her right collarbone, he trailed his fingers along, following with kisses.

"You realize we'll be here for a while." She pointed out as he traced the tribal band above Duke.

"That's the plan." He said moving to the compass rose on her outer elbow. He then followed the Celtic cross to where Semper Fidelis wrapped around her wrist. "I'll come back for the rest."

Wyatt moved to the Marine Corps emblem on her hip. Next to it was the unit patch. He then followed pad tracks to the junction of her legs. She was clean shaven and there was Tweety Bird declaring that he thought he saw a putty tat.

"Nice putty tat." He laughed as he moved lower, opening her up with his fingers before his tongue began to torture her. He sucked on her clit and then drove his tongue deep inside her. He eventually returned to her clit and slipped a finger inside her.

Moaning, Celeste arched against him. Just before she went over the edge, he pulled back and removed his finger. She whimpered with a complaint. He simply blew on her wet core.

"Not yet my love." He warned as she settled down. But just like he had stopped, when her breath was almost back to normal, his mouth returned, and he slipped two fingers inside her. Again, just as she was at the crest, he pulled away and removed his fingers. Her complaint was louder and more desperate this time.

"Wyatt." She moaned as she reached for him. He went to her willingly, meeting her lips with his. Tasting herself made her want him more. Buttons flew everywhere as she ripped open his shirt. His hands got caught on the buttons at his wrists. She extended her claws and ripped his arms free.

They released each other only long enough to remove his white undershirt. Then they were skin to skin and mouth to mouth. He toed off his shoes as he pressed her back into the bed. She reached for his belt; he stopped her.

"Not yet."

Celeste objected as his mouth left hers. He trailed little nips along her jaw and down her neck to where he would mark her. In the heat and passion of the moment, he knew that he could mark her, and she would not object. Right now. But she would be mad at him later. So instead, he marked her with a hickey. The pressure and tenderness of the spot had her arching against him again.

Wyatt grabbed her hand and put it between them and pressed her fingers inside her. "Come for me." He demanded before returning to her neck. This time as she brought herself to orgasm, he moved back down back between her legs. He watched her fingers pumping in and out and against her clit.

"That's it, baby." He encouraged her by sliding his own fingers back into her. As he began to match her movements, he slid a third finger inside her. That pushed her over and her walls began to convulse around their finger as juices flowed out.

"You smell so good." He said as he pulled her hand away and began to suck on her fingers. "You taste good too."

"Do I?" she challenged with a grin.

"You do." He told her around her fingers. He removed his own fingers from her and offered them. She greedily sucked and licked her juices off him. This time when she reached for his belt, he didn't stop her. He stood and helped to shed his pants and boxers.

She quickly took him into her mouth. This time it was his turn to moan.

"I won't last long if you keep that up." He warned her as she pumped her mouth and hand on his shaft.

"Don't want that." She said looking up at him.

"No, we don't." He agreed as he knelt before her. He cupped one breast and took the other into his mouth. "Do it again."

"Do what?" she asked as her head fell back in pleasure.

“Make yourself come for me.”

“But that’s not-"

“I know what you want.” He admitted changing from one breast to the other. “But you are so tight. I don’t want to hurt you.”

Smiling at him and his thoughtfulness, she moved her fingers back down and began to move them against her clit again. He sat back on his heels and watched her again. Then he slid his fingers in again and helped her reach another climax. This time as she reached her climax, he pulled his fingers out. She complained at the loss.

Wyatt gave a little laugh as he placed his arms under her legs and grabbed her hips. Moving her further onto the bed and laying her back. At the same time, he crawled up onto the bed. He paused, watching her again. Knowing that he was looking at her pushed her closer. As she started to orgasm, he moved her hand and caught both above her head and positioned himself.

He pushed into her as her body was still racked with pleasure. She was still tight, and her body resisted. But then, she started to come again, and her body took him in. He pierced her innocence, and she gave a cry of surprise and he stopped.

Celeste arched into him trying to take in the rest of him. When he would not budge, she wrapped her legs around his waist and pulled herself onto him. He cupped her face and kissed her tenderly. He started moving in her, small gentle strokes. They built up in pressure and speed and soon Celeste was crying out for him as she went over the edge.

"Can you handle a little longer?" he asked her quietly. She grinned at him and nodded before pulling him down for a kiss. He started moving in her again and this time went a bit faster and harder. Both of their grunts and moans echoed in the room.

As they both came together, Celeste pulled him down to her and sank her fangs into his neck, marking him as hers. Hers and only hers.

Wyatt resisted the urge to do the same. He was glad that he now bore her mark. Soon, she would bear more than just a hickey. Soon she would bear his mark. And then, hopefully, his pup.

They lay there for several minutes, catching their breath and enjoying being in each other's arms. Slowly, Wyatt moved off and out of her. She objected to the loss, and he merely chuckled as he gathered her into his arms and turned them so that they lay with their heads on pillow. She now lay with her back to his chest. She tried to turn, wanting him back in her arms.

Sensing what she wanted; he stopped her movements by laying his leg over hers. She pouted and he kissed her hair. "You'll be sore if I'm in you too much."

"I've been sore before."

"Not like that, mate."

Mate. That didn't bother her as much now that she had marked him. She marked him. Her body stiffened.

"What's wrong, mate?"

"I marked you." Celeste whispered, guilt in her voice. "Without your consent."

He turned her so that she was laying on her back. Then he leaned over and kissed her. Gently, tenderly at first. But it soon became demanding and possessive. From her. He raised his head and smiled down at her. "You've had my consent from the very first day I caught your scent." He kissed her shoulder, where the pucker mark from a bullet was. "I've had ten years to get to know you. Ten years to fall in love with you. Ten years to wait for you. You've had a month."

"Why couldn't you have been an asshole?" Celeste asked touching his cheek.

Wyatt smiled at her. "I assure you, mate of mine, I can be."

"But not to me."

"But not to you," he agreed. "You are my mate. I will always cherish you. Protect you. Honor you. Love you. Obey you." He kissed her between each promise that he made. "And have you walk beside me, for the rest of our days."

"Obey?" she asked huskily.

"But also protect," he replied caressing her cheek. "I will make love to you again. Today. But you need time before I am back inside you."

She knew that he was probably right. But that did not mean that she wanted him any less. "When?"

Grinning at her, he huskily replied, "After our bath."

32 - BUBBLE BATH

"Our bath?" she replied, emphasizing the first word.

"Oh, yes. Our bath." He emphasized 'our' just as she had. He then kissed her before getting off the bed and going into the bathroom. Soon she heard water running. Wyatt then came out and went into his closet. Then he came back to the bed wearing shorts. Kissing her, he teased, "Don't go anywhere."

"Not this time," she teased back.

He got back off the bed and walked to the door. He unlocked the door and opened it to find Teuf curled up in the hall. "Are you looking for someone?" The dog stretched and went to get on the bed.

Celeste watched as Wyatt closed the door behind him. She buried her face in the shepherd's collar of fur. She did not regret what she had done. Nor did she regret telling him that she wanted to be marked. To be honest, she did not even regret marking him. No, she had no regrets. And as she thought about it, she knew the only time that seemed appropriate for her to be marked.

"I know what to do, Teuf."

Teuf simply turned and licked her face. She laughed at him and rubbed his belly when he exposed it. "Pathetic."

"Him or me?" Wyatt asked as he came back into the room carrying a tray.

"Him." She said as he kicked the door closed and locked it again. "Maybe you too if you're locking me in here."

"Locking the world out," Wyatt admitted as he took the tray to the bathroom.

"You must be lucky," Celeste told Teuf as she booped his snout.

"He's the only other male that I'll allow in our bed," he said helping her to stand up. "For now."

"For now?" she asked, following him into the bathroom.

"Mmmmm-hmmm," he said stopping next to the giant bathtub filling up with hot water and bubbles. "Someday, when you're ready, I'm hoping to have a son. But…" he kissed her forehead, "I would love a stubborn, hard-headed, beautiful, wonderful daughter, just like her mother."

"I'm barely ready to be marked. Much less, think about pups," she Admitted.

"I know," he told her. "When you're ready."

"You really should have been an asshole."

He chuckled. "I could be. I could refuse to use protection when you come into heat."

"Oh goddess, I didn't think about that," she admitted.

"I did. But I don't smell your heat."

"No, it's closer to the end of the month," she stated.

"That gives me time to get condoms," he said stepping into the tub and then helping her in. He sat down and then settled her between his legs resting her back against his chest. He handed her a glass of wine. "I brought whiskey if you would rather have that."

She sipped the rose wine and found it surprisingly sweet. "I like this one."

"I'm glad." He kissed her hickey.

"I know when I want you to mark me," she whispered.

"Okay. Now would be good." Wyatt continued to kiss her neck.

She gave a light laugh. "I want to do the Luna ceremony the night of the non-hunt."

He turned her face and leaned around so that he met her eyes. "Are you sure?"

"I am." She kissed him. "I love you. And you have been so patient and kind and not an asshole."

"I promise to be an asshole at some point for you."

"Just once."

He smiled at her. "Just once. But I want something from you."

"You get me, you got my virginity, what more do you want?"

"I want to tell our story at the Hunt."

"That I ran away?"

"Yes. I want people to understand why I refuse to hold a Hunt. And you are part of that."

She turned around, putting her hands on his shoulders and straddled him, positioning herself above him. She held his eyes captive as she lowered herself onto him. He shifted and wrapped her legs around him. Guiding her, they found a gentle rhythm that had the water splashing a little over the edge.

They continued to keep eye contact until her head began to fall back and her eyes began to close on their own. Wyatt reached up and placed his hands on her upper back, supporting her and pulling her down even further. Her walls began to pulse around him pulling him into his own release.

Celeste leaned forward and wrapped her arms around his neck holding him close as they both settled back down to earth. Wrapping his arms around her, he held her close breathing in the new scent of them mixed.

"If you can be okay with me talking to Jill about our sex life, I have no problems with you telling everyone about me running away, only to end up running to you."

He chuckled. "You okay with me teasing your brothers?"

"Fuck yeah. You see how Pers wigged out at the thought of me knowing about sex?" she replied with a grin against his neck. "Going back to the house is going to be fun."

"Why do you need to go back."

"Well, my stuff is there. And I need to make Pers wig out. And the stuff for messy twister."

"Mmmmm." He tugged on her earlobe with his teeth. "How much chocolate syrup did you get?"

33 - GRADUATION

There was a loud knock on the locked bedroom door. When it went unanswered, the person in the hall knocked again before calling out, "Alpha?"

"What?" Wyatt growled at being awakened, curled around Celeste.

Burying his face in her hair, he inhaled her scent and could feel the anger dissipating. He had always thought that his father must have had issues with how quickly his mood would change from angry to calm. Now that he had his mate in his arms, he understood the calming effect of the mate connection.

"Sorry to disturb you, sir, but you have an appointment in an hour," Terry reminded him through the door.

"Is it something Stephen can handle?" he asked, tracing the outline of the tattoo on her hip.

"No, sir, it's graduation."

"Crap. I forgot. You have anything to wear for a graduation ceremony?" he asked kissing her shoulder.

"Not really. Don't exactly have a Luna wardrobe. "Well, unless they're graduating from topless dancing school." She laughed at his arched eyebrow. "What? We were always equal opportunity. Topless. Male nude. Gay bar. Depended on the mood and who was picking."

"What would you pick?"

"Usually, topless. I'd get one lap dance, and then I had guys buying me drinks, sending me more lap dances. More drinks. It's a vicious cycle."

"Alpha?" Terry called from the other side of the door. .

"Very well. Miss Wynne thought that Miss Celeste might not have anything to wear. What do you want me to do with her dress?"

"Please tell me he did not say dress," Celeste moaned.

"He did." He kissed her temple before getting out of bed and going to the door. Teuf trotted in and headed for the bed as soon as the door opened. Wyatt accepted the dress bag and shopping bag from his Omega.

"Miss Wynne offered to do her hair and makeup. If she would like."

Wyatt turned and looked at Celeste. She nodded her head. "Please."

"About fifteen minutes?" Wyatt asked her.

"Yeah." She got out of bed and came to get the dress. She opened the bag and found herself looking at a navy-blue strapless dress with a silver cardigan. "It's pretty."

Wyatt noticed that Terry was gawking at all her tattoos. Chuckling he pushed the door closed. Looking inside the shopping bag he let out a whistle. "My sister thought of everything." He pulled a garter belt out.

"She thinks I'm going to wear that?" Celeste asked, looking at the black lace.

"Oh, yes," he said, his voice husky and eyes dark. "I'm planning on taking it off later."

"Is that all you think about?" Celeste teased.

"It is when you're naked in front of me."

"No time, Alpha," she pointed out.

"There will be when we get home, Luna." He handed her the shopping bag. "I really like the way that sounds. And Luna." Wyatt pulled her close, his erection pressed against her stomach.

"Still don't have time." Celeste said, wrapping her arms around his neck and meeting his kiss.

"You ever hear of a quickie?" he suggested.

"I have, and it's not something I want to walk in on," Wynne said, coming through the door. "Go get dressed. I need to make your Luna look gorgeous."

"You could knock," Wyatt called after his sister as she went into the bathroom. Then leaned down and kissed Celeste. "She loves planning things. If you want someone to help plan the ceremony."

"Repeat that last sentence but remove the word help," Celeste said.

"Wyatt!" Wynne called from the bathroom. "Was there a hippo in the bathtub?"

"No," Celeste answered, walking around him and heading towards the bathroom, "we had sex in a bubble bath."

"Ew!" Wynne cried and Celeste laughed as he walked into his closet. He could hear them talking and laughing. Even though he couldn't quite understand what they were saying. He was glad that they were getting along. Almost as happy as he was that she wanted him to mark her.

His fingers brushed against her mark on his neck as he straightened his collar. If he could go without the tie, he would. Hell, he'd go shirtless just to show off the mark. Grabbing the tie, he walked out of the closet and into the bathroom.

Celeste was wearing the dress and sitting on the stool his mother had once used, facing away from the mirror. Her makeup was light but somehow her eyes sparkled. She looked up at him and his stomach dropped to his feet and his heart forgot to beat.

"Hello, beautiful."

"Leave her clothes on," Wynne said as she clipped the barrette and then smoothed down the black hair.

Behind him, the bedroom door opened and he detected the scents of his parents, Jonathan and Elizabeth, as they entered his chambers. He knew the instant that his sister scented their parents and he moved out of the way for her to pass.

"Why is there a dog on your bed?" Elizabeth asked, walking into his son's room.

"Hey, mom," Wynne said as she went to hug her mom. "I didn't think that you were going to be here till next week."

"We decided not to miss graduation," she hugged her youngest daughter. "Now why is there a dog on the bed?"

"Good question," Jonathan asked, walking in.

"That's Teuf," Wynne said, walking over to the bed. "Come here." Teuf crawled over to her and sat still as she put a bow tie on him. "Oh! You're so handsome."

"Quit encouraging the diva" Celeste said, stepping out of the bathroom. "Teuf. Vest." He jumped off the bed and ran out the door.

Wyatt stepped up behind her and rubbed his hands up and down her bare arms. "Mom, dad." He felt her stiffen under their scrutiny. "This is Celeste Moore-"

"True Alpha of the Silver Lake Pack," Jonathan finished.

"What?" the other two women said in surprise.

"Yes, Alpha Jonathan," she answered, relaxing and smiling at him.

"How do you know that?" Elizabeth asked her husband.

"Silver eyes," he said, offering her a hug. "The real question is, why is my son marked, but you're not."

"Because he has more control than I do," Celeste admitted as she accepted the hug. She sighed as she sank into a father's hug. Tears filled her eyes when he kissed the top of her head.

"Your father was wrong for chasing you away. And even more wrong for keeping you away." The older Alpha told her. "Anytime you need a dad hug, you let me know."

"Thank you," she croaked out trying not to cry. Teuf nudged her leg. Wyatt knelt and put his vest on.

"We need to go," Elizabeth pointed out softly.

"They won't start without their Alphas," Her husband said as he let the black-haired woman step out of his embrace.

"You two need to get there," Celeste told him.

"Not me, dear," Jonathan said, offering his arm to his wife. "My son and his very colorful mate."

Jonathan was right, when they arrived at the football Stadium, next to the Alpha's chair, was another. It was not as large as the one for Wyatt. But it also was not as small as a Luna's chair. She thought it was like sitting on a throne.

When they had first arrived, Wyatt was pulled away for a moment and it was still warm in the sun. She took off her cardigan. She could feel the eyes on her. Not that it bothered her. She had been stared at for most of her life. If not for her silver eyes. Then for being Alpha's daughter. Or one of the few females competing in martial arts and boxing. And then she ran away. Of course, there were also the many tattoos.

She was stared at for a completely different reason when Alpha Wyatt stepped over to her and kissed her. And it was not a 'nice to see you' kiss. It was more of I cannot wait to see a whole lot more of you later type of kiss. Then he took her hand and led her to the dais. She sat next to him and the only time that he released her hand was when he helped her put her cardigan back on.

34 - IT CAN WAIT

Most of the Crystal River pack was very welcoming. There were, of course, a few females who still vied for the attention of their Alpha. But he now had his mate, his Luna, the other half of his soul.

After the graduation ceremony, there was a small get together. But most of the fun would be the following day at the pack picnic. As the seniors ran off to run in the woods, the rest of the pack wandered back to their homes. All were excited for the festivities the following day. It was the weekend before Memorial Day, but it marked the beginning of summer for the pack. Since Wyatt had come home to the pack, he had made several changes, and the summer weekend activities were some of the favorites.

Beginning with the senior graduation picnic and ending with the Labor Day picnic, the summer was filled with activities. Outdoor movies. Picnics. Games. Friendly rivalries between the Crystal Pass police and fire departments and those in their sister city of Crystal Springs.

The territory of the Crystal River Pack encompassed both cities and some outlying land surrounding them. Most pack members lived in Crystal Pass, but there were also members in Crystal Springs. There were also several farms and smaller towns in the large swath of land that belonged to the pack.

Suddenly, the large pack territory seemed to be miniscule as the talk of the Alpha finally finding his mate suddenly overshadowed graduation and celebration.

When the maid had dashed out of the master suite, she had not been silent. It did not take long for the entire staff to know that the Alpha had taken a woman to his chambers. Never before had Wyatt done such a thing. Sure, he had bedded them in his youth, seeking his release from time to time. But never in his childhood home, and certainly never in his bed.

It had taken only minutes for word to spread through the pack. They all knew what this meant. They finally had a Luna. Mrs. Jones confirmed everything when she said that the woman had sat in the Luna's seat during their meeting.

Wynne excitedly showed up at Viviane and Perseus' house where they celebrated before going to find clothes and accessories for Celeste. Then Viviane returned home and gathered up some of Celeste's clothes and what Teuf needed for a few days. After the graduation ceremony, Celeste and Wyatt collected her things from her brother's house. Perseus hugged her telling her that he was glad she found happiness. And then he tried to find a hole to die in when she told him that the sex was good too.

Wyatt did not keep his word about removing the garter belt and thigh highs. In fact, when they finally fell asleep, that was the only thing that she was wearing. And in the morning, when she got up out of bed, the shower had to be postponed.

"You need lots of these in your wardrobe," Wyatt said as he finally removed them, with his teeth.

"Do I need anything else?" she asked as he came back up to remove the other leg.

"Not for me, you don't," he swiftly undid the clasps and then pulled that one down also.

"Alpha?" Terry said at the door after knocking.

"What now?" he growled out as he pulled Celeste to him.

Celeste placed a hand on either side of his face and smiled at him. He smiled back at her.

"Your father-" Terry started.

"Is he dying?"

"No, sir."

"Is anyone dying?"

"N-no sir."

"Is anyone going to die in the next thirty minutes?"

"No, Alpha."

"Forty-five?" Celeste interjected.

"No, Luna."

"Then tell my father that I will be with him shortly." Wyatt said as he wrapped her legs around his waist.

Terry left when he started hearing the bed move. A few minutes later, the door burst open, and Jonathan walked into the bedroom.

"You're right, it can wait," he told his son and then left, locking the door behind him.

35 - MR. CELESTE

"Gunny's phone, Mrs. Gunny speaking," was the greeting that Wyatt got when he called the number in his phone listed as Gunny.

Chuckling, Wyatt replied, "Mrs. Gunny, I guess I'm Mr. Celeste."

"Oh! Alpha Wyatt!" the Hawaiian accent was more pronounced now that she was embarrassed. "I am so-"

"It's fine, Sammi." He laughed. "Do you mind if I ask where you are at?"

"Crystal Springs, sir."

"That's right down the road from us. We're having, I guess you could call it a pack picnic. We do it every year for our graduating seniors. Since, you're so close, why don't you come out?"

"All of us?" she asked, sounding surprised.

"Why not?"

"Doc, Jack, and Jill are here to," she said and then added, "Jill is werecat."

"I served with a few. You're all welcome to come. Are your pups with you?"

"Yes. Gunny is trying to get them in the tub."

"Tell him not to worry about that. By the end of the day, they'll be too tired to fight the tub."

"Okay. Thank you, Alpha Wyatt."

"You're welcome. Will you be in the Jeep?"

"Jill likes to drive the jeep. And with the pups, the minivan is better for us."

"I'll let the patrol know. Come in through the east gate and follow that road to the center of town. Turn right at the third stop sign and follow that out to the training grounds."

When Wyatt had given the directions, he was grateful that the town was laid out in a grid pattern. He had been to several pack lands where the streets curved and twisted, and you would have to take a half dozen turns to get where you wanted. There were four main roads in Crystal Pass, and from any one of them, you could get anywhere in town.

He was thinking about this as he was discreetly trying to watch for Gunny. Currently, he stood across from Celeste talking with his parents and sister about the Hunt and Luna ceremony. He didn't see them at first, but he caught the distinct smell of werecat. Male werecat.

He saw two kids, a boy and a girl, before he saw Gunny. Gunny put his finger to his lips as Wyatt started to say something. He heard the pop of a cap being removed from markers as giggles escaped from the two kids.

"Fee fie foe fum, who's a ticklish son of a gun?" Celeste asked with a smile. The two giggling kids took off running. "I'll be right back," she said and then took off running after them.

Gunny walked up with a female wolf who picked up the discarded markers.

"Gunny," Wyatt said with a grin.

"Alpha. Thanks for inviting us," Gunny said extending a hand which Wyatt grasped.

"Oh." The woman exposed her neck in submission. Her eyes widened as he knelt in front of her.

"Mrs. Gunny?"

"Mr. Celeste?"

Wyatt nodded and helped her up as the little girl squealed. They looked over and saw that Celeste had her in her arms and was acting like she was gnawing on her throat, complete with playful growls. The little boy stood close by grinning. The giggling girl was placed back on her feet with a playful swat to her butt. Celeste eyed the little boy who took off running again, Celeste hot after him.

"Come here you little halfling!" she yelled as he ran back towards his parents. She scooped him up before he got there and did the same as she had to his twin sister.

"The twins adore her," Sammi said with a sigh, resting a hand on her growing belly. "Alpha Wyatt, can I ask you a question?"

"Sure, ask anything," he said with a grin.

"Do you think it was wise to get the five pervs back together?"

"Hey!" the three men with her objected.

"We resemble that remark!" the older man said.

"Yes, Doc, I know you do." Sammi shook her head.

"Do you know what my wife called us?" Gunny asked, handing the toddler over to Sammi.

She bent over and gnawed on the little girls' belly as she squealed. "Pervs?" she guessed standing back up as the little girl continued to giggle. Celeste wiped away a fake tear before giving Sammi a loud snacking kiss on her cheek. "You always say the sweetest things."

"Still fucked in the head I see." Sammi laughed as she sat the toddler down who immediately latched onto Teuf.

"Is Teuf okay with the baby?" Elizabeth asked.

"He's a sucker for pups," Celeste said as he bathed the girl's face in kisses.

"It's not like she gets fucked any other way," Jack said dryly.

"Speaking of which, what is my virginity pool up to?" Celeste asked offhand.

"Virginity pool?" Jonathan asked with a cocked eyebrow.

"Why?" Gunny asked and she simply shrugged her shoulders. The three men and Sammi all yelled for Jill. With a laugh, Celeste took off running.

"What?" A man asked as he stepped over to them still watching a good-looking warrior walk by. "Damn. Why couldn't I have been a dog?"

"Quit thinking with your dick and go get your girlfriend," Jack told him.

"Grumpy," Jill said as he turned and saw her waving at him from the far side of the field. Grinning, he took off after her.

"That's Jill?" Wyatt asked a little confused.

"You thought Jill was a girl," Sammi observed.

"Like he's not?" Doc asked rolling his eyes.

"He's my partner. You know, Jack and Jill. It fits him better than Matthew." Jack explained to the confused-looking family. Elizabeth grinned and gave a small laugh.

"Be a good dog, and I'll give you a bone!" Jill yelled.

"Don't make me get a laser pointer!" she taunted back as she made a wide circle around Wyatt. Jill cut through the group and grabbed her around her waist. He buried his face in her neck and inhaled. He then quickly sat her down and stepped away with his hands up.

"She's mated.=," Jill said. "She's not marked, but she's mated." He sniffed the air and then met Wyatt's eyes. "To you. Wonder Pup." He stepped closer to the Alpha and smelled him and saw the marks on his neck. He then turned to Celeste. "Girlfriend, I need details. Leave nothing out."

"Cat, mate." She pointed to Wyatt and then to his parents, "mate's parents."

"Fine, I still need details, girlfriend!" he said, starting to pull her away.

"Bathtub was involved at some point." Wynne helpfully added seeing her brother squirm in front of their parents.

"I like you, little girlfriend," Jill said, grabbing Wynne's hand.

"What the hell?" Celeste demanded. "She never got accused of being your girlfriend."

Jill grinned at his old friend. "If my dad was pissed at me showing up with a wolf, could you imagine how pissed he'd be if I showed up with a Donskoi?"

Celeste's eyes widened before she started laughing. "You could have a harem."

"There are definite possibilities with that. But for now, we have more important things than pissing off my father. Pretend it's not your brother, we need details." Wynne shrugged and allowed herself to be pulled away. "We're an even number again!"

"That girl does not need to hang out with y'all," Sammi advised.

"Why not?" Doc asked.

"Hey!" Jack yelled at the trio. "When?"

Among the many other things that the group of friends were known for, the bets made among them were notorious. The most famous bet ended up with Celeste and Jill getting now infamous tattoos. The longest running bet was Celeste's virginity. Once they had learned that she was a virgin, they had started placing bets concerning when and with whom she would lose it.

The buy in for a date was a set price, $500 per day. The same cost for the name of her partner. Over the years, other Marines and a few soldiers and sailors had bought dates and put their names down. After using all their skills, panty melting smiles and best lines, they were a little poorer and the pot had grown.

"Yesterday," Celeste called back as Jack was getting out his phone and pulling up the app.

"Who had yesterday?" Gunny asked.

"Alpha Wyatt," Jack said. "That's not fair."

"No," Sammi pointed out, "the rules stated that she could not buy a date. There was nothing saying that the other party involved could not. Sorry, pervs, pay up."

Looking at each other, there were several grumblings of "Hydrate" before the little self-made family grinned at each other.

"I need your banking information," Jack grumbled.

"Can't just do cash?" Wyatt asked.

"I don't carry around $24,000 cash," Jack said.

"She said five hundred," Wyatt objected.

"That was the buy in," Doc corrected. "What am I at?"

Jack scrolled for a second and then clicked on a few things on his phone screen, finally pulling up the information that he needed. "Eighty."

Grinning, Doc said, "Twenty more and I'll answer."

"Twenty dollars?" Jonathan asked.

"Thousand," the three answered.

"Put my winnings on his," Wyatt said.

"Alright." Jack did a few things on his phone and then looked up at Wyatt. "Gay, straight or bi?"

Wyatt barely caught Doc holding three fingers against his opposite bicep as he crossed his arms. "Bi." Wyatt answered and Doc gave a slight nod.

"Alright. You're now over a hundred. Answer," Jack demanded.

Doc grinned at him before walking over and kissing Jack. "Bi."

"Woohoo!" Sammi cried out.

"Obviously, my wife picked that." Gunny laughed. "Who else?"

"Alpha, Sammi, Jill, and Sles," Jack said.

"That puts me back on top!" Sammi grinned. "I like being on top."

"I know," Gunny said mischievously.

"Not like that!" She smacked her husband playfully.

36 - BULLIES

The group that included Alpha Wyatt, his parents, Gunny and his wife with the youngest pup asleep against his chest, Doc, and Jack stood in almost the same place that they had been in when Jill dragged Celeste and Wynne to the tree line for a "girlfriend talk." They had shifted slightly when a group of pups ran through the area. With all the pups running around, they almost missed the sad little girl who returned to her parents with a cheerful girl following behind her.

"Momma," the little girl said with tears in her voice.

"What's the matter, baby?" Sammi asked, all playfulness gone.

"Where's aunt Sles?" she asked quietly.

The little girl who stood behind her smiled smugly.

“She's with Aunt Jill. Did you call her?” Her mother tried to soothe her.

“I’m not strong enough,” she muttered.

“I told you,” the other little smirked.

Wyatt started to say something but stopped when he saw Celeste approaching and shook her head telling him to remain silent. Squatting down behind the little girl, clinging to her mother’s legs, she asked, “Not strong enough for what, halfling?”

“To call you,” she murmured.

“Bella, turn around and look at me,” she said, sitting on the ground as slowly the girl turned. “You weren’t by the big bounce house, which is where you called me from with the mind link. It took me a minute to find you. I’m guessing that someone is saying that you’re not a real wolf?”

“She’s not.” the other little girl sneered at Bella. “She’s just a half breed.”

Since their father was human, they had been subjected to bullying and harassment by people who believed in pure blood. Where her brother dismissed it and let it roll off his back, Bella was a more sensitive child. Celeste knew that as they got older, it would get worse for Bella.

It was just another double standard in their world. A male could mate with whoever he wanted. But a female needed to be of pure blood and mate with another wolf.

Bella nodded and Celeste caught the little eye movement towards the other little girl. “You know what you do?” She shook her head no. “You tell them to go piss off.”

Gunny smacked the back of her head, but Celeste ignored him.

Bella blushed and laughed. “I can’t say that.”

“Sure, you can. It’s simple. Puh-iss. Ahh-ffff. Put it all together. Piss off.”

The other little girl gaped at her. “I’m going to tell my daddy!”

“Please do.” Celeste told her. “Tell him I’ll be right here.”

The other little girl ran off in a huff.

“Not trying to tell you how to be a Luna,” Elizabeth said, “but maybe not the best way.”

“Probably not.” Celeste agreed, standing up with Bella in her arms.

“That’s the Morrison girl, isn’t it?” Jonathan asked Wyatt.

“Miranda, the youngest,” he confirmed. “They’re all bullies.” He sighed. “Their oldest was kicked out of school for picking on some of the kids from the orphanage. She's attending school over in Crystal Springs, now."

"Who told my daughter to piss off?" Thomas Morrison asked storming up to the group.

Feeling Wyatt step forward, she held a hand up to him and then placed Bella in Jonathan's arms. "I did," Celeste admitted. "Maybe you should ask her why."

"Okay, for the benefit of the Alpha, I will. Miranda, why did this bitch tell you that?"

Celeste held up her hand again to Wyatt, silently asking that he let her handle the situation, and Jill stepped in front of him. Demon growled low in his throat and Jill just turned and chuffed at him. Under other circumstances, Celeste would have been amused at the realization that Jill was a tiger.

"She didn't like the way I talked about that half breed." The little girl said.

This time, Celeste held her hand up to Sammi with her claws out. Sammi saw the black claws in front of her and stepped back. Angel was close to the surface and fighting against the wolf's bane suppressant that Celeste had taken that day.

"I'm working very hard at keeping my wolf in check right now," Celeste warned. "Because of that, I'm going to advise that you consider your next words very carefully."

"Or what, you little whore?" he taunted.

The other three Marines and Sammi stepped in front of the Alpha family and started pushing them back.

"Not the words that I would have advised," Celeste said. "Now, I think you and your daughter need a lesson in kindness and common courtesy."

"Not from the likes of you," he said as he was starting to shift.

"I do not advise that," Celeste gave a final warning as he completed his shift. "This is not something that you want to do," she warned as he growled at her.

The brown werewolf swiped his paw at her. With snapping and popping of bones, Wyatt quickly shifted, ripping his clothes to shreds. Jumping in front of Celeste, his black and silver wolf looked down at the smaller wolf from his imposing height. The Beta wolf, which was large, barely came to his shoulders. Demon bared his teeth and the smaller wolf lay down in submission, whimpering as he rolled over onto his back.

"Teuf!" Celeste called out. "Bag!"

The dog ran to her pickup, jumped into the back, grabbed a gym bag, and ran over to his mistress. Jill took the bag and tossed it towards where Demon sat on his haunches. Jill scratched Teuf behind his ear before telling him that he was a good boy.

"No, Teuf," Celeste shook her head as he bared his teeth and approached Thomas, who had shifted into his brown wolf. Demon looked at him and snapped, sending him whimpering back to his mistress.

"Thomas, I think that you need to shift back," Jonathan suggested. Still whimpering, he belly-crawled into the tree line before shifting and waiting for his wife to bring him some new clothes to replace those torn in the transformation to his were form.

"Demon," Elizabeth said softly. "The pup is safe."

Demon turned and went to Jonathan who was still holding Bella in his arms. He nudged the little girl who turned and pet his head.

"I'm good, Alpha."

Demon sat down and shifted back. Standing, he picked up the bag that Jill had tossed at him. Jill and his fellow Marines created a barrier to provide Wyatt some privacy.

"Miranda," Celeste said, squatting down in front of her. "Look at me, love." Celeste took the girl's hand and tugged her gently until the girl met her eyes. Pushing Angel to the back of her mind, Celeste moved from an aggressive protector to a gentle guardian. "Does it scare you when your dad does that?"

She nodded.

Celeste knew that the little girl would be too young to understand the urge to submit to an Alpha. She was gentle with the little girl, exactly as she would be with Bella or any of her many nieces. "I can tell. Does he get angry a lot?"

Again, the little girl nodded.

"Does he ever hurt you, when he gets angry?"

"Not me," Miranda whispered. Just as she said that there was a cry from inside the woods where Thomas had gone. Teuf faced that direction, baring his teeth with his hackles up.

"Protect," Celeste told him, and he bolted for the tree line. They could hear him barking and snarling and soon he was forcing the half-dressed man out of the trees. "Miranda, does your dad hurt your mom?"

"Sometimes," she whispered with tears on her cheeks.

"Go get your mom and bring her here, my friend, Doc, is going to go with you." She recognized the look of fear on the little face. "Teuf won't hurt you. He will come back with you and your mom, but he won't hurt you."

Miranda nodded accepting Doc's extended hand and they walked towards where her mother was still hiding in the trees.

"How did you know?" Elizabeth asked.

"The way she looked when she said she was going to get her dad. And how she didn't know how to react when I was not scared of her dad," Celeste said standing up. "Silver Lake Pack is known for its violence and male chauvinism. You start recognizing it pretty easily."

"Your father?" Wyatt asked.

"Not physical. But us girls knew that we were to grow up, do the Hunt, have a good match, and make babies. I refused to comply." She walked over to Wyatt and slipped her arms around his neck. "And now look, helping to host a non-hunt and partially mated to a good match."

He smiled and leaned over to kiss her.

"And the babies?" Elizabeth asked hopefully.

"Yeah… That would be a no." Celeste turned her attention from the mother to the son. "You get me pregnant in my next heat, and I will kill you,"

"Dully noted," he said resting his forehead on hers.

"Miss Cel… Cel…," Miranda said struggling with the name.

"Sles. You can call me Sles," Celeste said, squatting down in front of the girl.

"My mommy doesn't want to come out. She's scared of what he'll do."

"My dog?" she asked, and the little girl shook her head. Picking up the little girl she stood up and Miranda laid her head on her shoulder.

Celeste closed her eyes and took a deep breath. "Teuf." She whispered. "Bring her to me."

"Can he really hear her when she whispers?" Jonathan asked. The Marines and Sammi just smiled at him. Gunny pointed to the trees where Teuf was using his body to force a woman towards the group. He never took his eyes off the man.

"Mommy!" Miranda said, reaching for her mother.

Celeste let Miranda go and inspected the woman's face. "Is there somewhere that they can stay?" she asked Wyatt quietly.

"Their house. I have warriors coming to get him," Jonathan replied.

"That damn dog!" Thomas screamed coming towards them.

Teuf sat down in front of his mistress and looked up at her. "Are you sure?" Celeste suddenly asked and then grinned. "Since it looks like we'll be here a while, they're bound to find out sooner or later." Looking down at the dog, scratching behind his ear, she said, "I'll ask."

Hearing the heel hound's thoughts in her head had become so normal for Celeste that she never even thought about it anymore. She held conversations with him and her Marines and found family knew when she was talking with him, and she often forgot that others were not used to hearing one-sided conversations.

"Thomas!" Celeste called out. "Would your wolf like to take on my hound?"

"Does that mean what I think it means?" Sammi asked excitedly.

"Only one reason she calls him a hound," Gunny confirmed.

"Are you sure about that?" Wyatt asked. Celeste was amused at his concern for her German shepherd.

"He's sure," Celeste answered as Thomas answered that he did.

"If you're sure," Wyatt said. "They have an area set up for sparring."

"Excellent," Celeste grinned and followed him over to the small sparring area. Once they were there, Teuf trotted to the far side of the square. Celeste stopped in the middle and turned to look at Thomas as he stripped off his shirt.

"Wait until he's in the center before you shift," Celeste told him and started to turn to go to her dog.

"Afraid I'll hurt your dog?" he called back.

"I want you to know what you're up against… in case you change your mind." She removed Teuf's vest then kissed the top of his head. "Teufelhunden, don't hurt him too bad." Giving him one more scratch behind the ear, she stood up. As she took the few steps to where her Marine family stood, the dog began his ritual to initiate the shift from dog to hound.

"Body shake," Jack said as Teuf shook out his body.

"Upward dog," Gunny said as the dog stretched out his back legs.

"Downward dog," Jill said as he lowered his head between his paws before standing back up.

"Head shake," Doc added as the dog's head shook.

"Shoulder roll," Celeste completed as Teuf rolled his shoulders before he did his own shift.

"I love watching him shift." Sammi said as clapped her hands excitedly.

"Watching him… what?" Jonathan asked, his voice trailing off as he watched the dog transform in front of them.

The brown fur darkened to black, and his body tripled in size. His snout elongated and teeth extended. When he breathed out, light smoke showed in the red glow of his eyes.

"That's a fucking hell hound!" Thomas screamed.

"Teufelhunden," Wyatt said with a little laugh.

"Not once have I ever denied that. His full name literally translates into Hell Hound." Celeste pointed out. "Does your wolf still want to take him on?"

"Are you fucking crazy?" he screamed back.

"I have been accused of that. After all, I have a hell hound as a pet."

Teuf huffed.

"Sorry," Celeste corrected, "companion. Diva."

"You talk to that thing?" Thomas yelled.

"I do," she said as they both began to stalk towards him. "Keep that image in mind the next time you decide to hit your wife. Or your daughter." They stopped in front of him and Teuf gave a low guttural growl. He looked down towards Teuf and was caught in her gaze as her silver eyes glowed as Angel rose to the surface.

"How… how do you know?" he stammered.

"He can see into your soul, and I see what he sees." She looked towards the warriors. "You can have him now." She looked over her shoulder at Teuf and nodded. He shook hard and returned to his normal self.

"Can you really see into his soul?" Wynne asked quietly when Celeste got back over by them.

"No. But he doesn't need to know that."

37 - FREE TATTOOS

The sun was going down and the day's festivities were winding down. Messy twister had been a hit. In fact, it was such a hit that it was set up by the bonfire. Celeste had done a round of twister with some of the cheerleaders and Wyatt decided that she needed a shower. Stephen laughed at him when Wyatt put her over his shoulder and grabbed one of the bottles of chocolate syrup.

They did get in the shower. And eventually, the water even got turned on. Wyatt now found himself in the tattoo parlor while his mate and the artist discussed what she wanted. And apparently, he knew how to do a tattoo with ashes in the ink.

Like the other veterans from his pack that had gone, he was a little surprised to find out that ashes from Duke and Rory were in their tattoos. And now she was getting Marley done the same way. Celeste was wearing a halter top that showed off her back piece.

The Silver Lake Pack Crest was on her right shoulder blade, the Marine Corps Pack Crest in the center and she had already talked to the artist about putting his Crest on the left. Beneath that were Angel wings with a silver and black wolf between them. He assumed this was in tribute to Angel.

He knew the two crests on her back well. Silver Lake from dealing with Sirius at the neighboring pack; seeing it on official documents, the jackets for formal meetings and the tattoos on the pack members. And the Marine Corps from his time being embedded with them. As the Marine Doc, he had considered getting their crest tattooed on him. Tracing it with his finger, he considered it again.

In the shape of a military shield with a background of deep, midnight blue with a full silver moon partially veiled by a stylized American flag. In the center stood a formidable werewolf in a vigilant pose, its fur a combination of military green and silver, golden eyes glowed with determination. The werewolf held an M16 across his chest, teeth bared. Across the top in Marine red was a banner in bold gold letters with the pack motto. Semper Fidelis Lupus – Always Faithful Wolf. On either side of the shield, there were olive branches and arrows, paw prints linking the two. At the very bottom was the golden Eagle Globe and Anchor of the United States Marine Corps.

On her lower back was Irish Claddagh done in Irish knots. Between the Claddagh and wings was an outline of a wolf howling at the moon. Inside the wolf was a scene from the outlook over Silver Lake where she had always gone to think as a girl. There were six smaller wolf outlines on either side of the big one. Each was a different color with two letters on them, one for each of her siblings. And even though she was no longer close with her father, on her left side was a mated pair of wolves for her parents.

Behind all of it and linking it all together was an intricate blue Celtic knot. During his explorations of her tattoos, and he still had plenty to explore, he noticed that there was always a background tattoo linking everything together. Not a solid color as many people did, but a light background.

Currently, she was laying on her left side as Marley was being added to her right side. The others were picking out what they wanted to get. But Cole was spending more time paying attention to what Wynne was looking at than the book in front of him.

"I don't know what to get." Wynne finally declared.

"Rules!" Jill called out from the chair he was in. "Sles, tell her the rules!"

"Rule number one, it's your body, to hell with everybody else." Celeste said.

"Coming from the walking coloring book!" Doc teased.

"Rule number two, get them somewhere that, if needed, they can be covered up."

"Marine Corps regulations are the only reason she does not have her legs finished." Jack pointed out.

"True story. Rule number three, make sure it means something to you. Don't get the latest trendy tattoo because everyone else has it. It's your body, your ink, and you're living with it for the rest of your life."

"Banana!" Jack, Doc and Gunny called out.

"Banana has a meaning!" Jill objected, and then proudly added "Not everyone can deepthroat a twelve-inch banana."

"I learned from my best girlfriend." Celeste called back and blew Jill a kiss.

"Jack quit looking at me like that." Jill said as he met his mates' lust filled eyes. He then turned and looked at Wyatt. "I've seen what you're packing. You better be glad she can." Wyatt looked away uncomfortably. "Oh, girlfriend, you left out a detail."

"Did not."

"Ummm, girlfriend, from the way your man is acting, you sure as hell did."

"No, sir. You asked about what happened when I lost my virginity. Not what happened before."

"Are we going to talk about my sister's sex life all night?" Perseus asked.

"No, we'll get to yours at some point." Celeste told him.

"How do you do it?" Wynne asked and all eyes fell on her.

"Sex?" Cole asked with wide eyes.

She looked at Celeste with bright red cheeks. "Deep throat." She squeaked out.

"Just got to get past the gag reflex." Jill and Celeste said.

"I would offer to teach you," Jill said, "but freaky deaky over there can peel the damn thing."

The artist working on Celeste stopped and looked at her. "You can peel a banana?" she nodded her head. "With your throat?" she nodded again. "You do that, and your tattoo is free."

"Someone go get me a banana." Celeste said.

The shop owner was finishing up on Gunny and said, "If you can do that, all the tattoos are free."

"I'll go get you one, freaky deaky." Gunny told her as his arm was being covered by ointment. "Wyatt, do you see why my wife calls us the pervs?"

"And we haven't even had alcohol yet!" Doc pointed out.

"HYDRATE!" The group of Marines called out and then they all laughed.

"Or a lap dance!" Celeste added. "I haven't had a lap dance since California."

"Oddly enough, we haven't had a night of free alcohol since you left California." Jack said as his tattoo was being finished. "Problem is, I don't know if your man is going to let us hang out with you after tonight. He might revoke his invitation for Sammi and the kids to stay."

"No, I was warned about you guys." Wyatt said laughing. "I didn't believe Sirius when he told me, or you, Perseus. And I was a little distracted when Celeste was warning me earlier."

"Girlfriend, what were you doing?" Jill asked.

"I was just sitting there." She said innocently.

"On his cock!" Jill, Gunny and Doc said.

"Oh, you know the position?" Celeste laughed.

"I do." Jill said.

"We know!" Gunny said. "You two were the only ones getting laid while we were in country."

"I'm sure we weren't the only ones in the entire country getting laid." Jack said coming back in.

"They weren't. Were they Doc?" Celeste said.

"That's an advantage that I have." He admitted. "It's like flipping a coin."

"Give head or chase tail?" Celeste offered.

Wynne walked over to where Celeste was with a page of tattoos. She pointed to a cluster of lilies. Her wolf had liked it since her name was Lily. "Where should I get this?"

"Either on the forearm, thigh or upper arm." Celeste suggested. "Especially until you know how much you like getting tattoos. The meatier, the less it hurts."

"And the more it hurts," Jill started and then all four finished, "the wetter Sles gets."

"Guilty." Celeste admitted.

"Wyatt, how do you feel about inflicting a little pain?" Gunny asked.

"Now I know why you're addicted to tattoos." Wyatt said, walking over and looking down at her. I can smell you getting wet. He told her through the mind link.

Then we might have to stop somewhere so that you can do something about it. She replied.

"We always had our suspicions, but puddy tat confirmed it." Jack said.

"I like puddy tat." He leaned down and kissed her before getting in the chair next to her.

"I like you liking puddy tat." She said huskily.

With a knowing smile he replied, "I know."

"She tell you about getting puddy tat?" Jill asked.

"I'm guessing that she's still a screamer?" Jack asked.

"I think I need to hear about puddy tat." Wyatt told his mate and she just grinned while he looked at her in a questioning way, while the rest of the room looked at her.

"I know the answer to that." Jill said smugly.

"Yes, you do." She admitted.

"And so do you." Jill confirmed looking at Wyatt.

"I think I need to know about puddy tat." The artist said. "What kind of a tattoo does that?"

"More of a where." Celeste said and tapped her arm, the agreed upon signal for needing a break. She rolled to her back and then undid her pants. Pulling them open wide and pushing them down a little bit, she lifted her hips to give him a better view of the tattoo.

Really?

They'll see it when I shift.

I was thinking more about the intoxicating aroma. Are you wearing panties?

Fewer things for you to take off. She fixed her jeans and then rolled back to her side and looked at her mate. Besides, I like the feel of my jeans rubbing against my clit. Makes me think of what you've done to it.

There was a low growl coming from his chest. We may not make it to the bar if you keep that up.

Then you won't get to see me get a lap dance. A nearly naked woman pressed up against me, tit to tit. Her clit only inches away from mine. And then I'm going to hug her and with my scent on her, she's going to go dance for you.

Wyatt motioned for the artist working on his chest to stop and then he stood up and took a few steps to where his mate lay, her tattoo freshly finished. He leaned down and trapped her between his arms and kissed her.

"You're on the verge of starting something you may not be able to finish." He warned her quietly.

She grinned at him. "I need your keys."

"Why?"

"So, I can go get a hotel room." She said, running her hand down his bare chest. "Because after I do the banana trick when I get back, we're going to be late getting to the bar."

The growl was back, and his fangs extended just a little. Just enough to draw a little blood with the next kiss. He could smell her arousal intensify with the light pain. He handed her the keys and told her to get the penthouse suite. She smiled and rolled off the table only to find herself hard against him and he was hard against her. Celeste reached up and pulled him down to her for a very passionate kiss.

"Get a room." Doc teased.

"That's where I'm headed to." She said, breaking off the kiss. Turning to the artist she asked, "Can you be done with him by the time I get back? I have some plans for him."

"I'm sure you do." He said laughing as Wyatt smacked her ass before sitting back in his chair. "How long have you two been together?"

"I guess you could say ten years." Wyatt said smiling watching her leave. He saw the questioning looks on his packs faces but missed the proud grin of his mate's as he added, "There hasn't been anyone else for me since then."

38 - BANANA TRICK

It only took her about 15 minutes to reserve the room and get back. By then Wyatt was nearly done with his tattoo. As it was finished up Celeste cut the top off the banana and bent the peel back about half an inch all the way around. She gave it a little squeeze at the bottom to break it loose.

Looking over, she watched as the ointment was being put on Wyatt's tattoo. "Okay, boys, straight up, on the knees or freaky deaky?"

All four of her Marines called out "Freaky deaky!"

"What's the difference?" someone asked.

"Straight up is standing up, which is the hardest for peeling. But also, how I learned."

"In the middle of a gay bar in San Francisco." Jill added.

"I've never had so many gay men buy me drinks before. Thank you, teacher." Celeste said, looking at Jill. "Knees is obviously on my knees."

"And freaky deaky?" Cole asked and she just smiled at him.

"You need an assistant?" Jill asked walking over to where she was standing. "Unless you're planning on landing in his lap, you need a little more room." He said, taking the banana from her.

"Yeah, yeah." She said taking two good sized steps forward. She then bent over backwards until her hands hit the floor just about where she had just been. Adjusting her stance so she could balance on one hand, Celeste never broke eye contact with Wyatt.

Once in a good position, Jill handed her the banana and sat down on the floor. She swirled her tongue around the bottom of the banana and Wyatt squirmed remembering how that felt. She smiled at him before moving so that her mouth and throat were in a straight line.

They all watched as the banana slowly disappeared. She gagged a little, but then continued until only about an inch was outside of her mouth. She let go of it and they could see her throat muscles moving. Wyatt squirmed again remembering that night by the lake.

Slowly at first, the banana slid out of its peel. It picked up some speed and then fell out of her mouth and into her hand. She handed it to Jill before removing the peel, again gagging just a bit. Jill took that also before Celeste again adjusted her hands.

She rose on her toes and then brought her right leg up and over before straightening her legs out flat in opposite directions. Then she put her right foot on the floor and then brought her left foot over also. She had just started standing when she found herself on Wyatt's shoulder.

"We'll see you at the bar." He said walking out the door.

"I don't think they'll make it to the bar." Wynne said.

"They will." Jill said. "There's a reason she earned the name freaky deaky virgin."

"Besides," Doc chuckled, "hydration is very important."

"Get rid of that." Jack warned his mate watching the other man slide his lips around the pale banana.

He pulled it out of his mouth and made a light popping sound with it. "Why?"

"Matthew." Jack warned.

Jill dropped the banana and peel into the offered trashcan before walking over and putting his hands on Jack's waist and kissed him. "Jackson."

Jack put his arms on Jill's shoulders and pulled him back in for another kiss. "Behave, mate."

"You like it better when I don't behave." He pointed out. "Besides, we already have a hotel room."

"I'm not throwing you over my shoulder." Jack teased his mate, who was beefier than himself. Jill grinned and placed Jack on his shoulder before heading for the door. Smacking Jill's ass, he looked at Doc, "We'll see you at the bar."

Doc looked at Gunny laughing.

"It's just you and me, until you decide which way you're going tonight." Gunny told him. "I've got a little longer until my mate becomes a total horndog. Until then," he looked at his hand, "it's just me and an old friend because I am banned from being about three feet from her."

"It's not like you can get her any more pregnant." Wynne said before she blushed beet red.

"You're going to fit in real well with us pervs." Doc laughed.

"I don't think so." Cole objected.

"Then I advise that you do something about it." Gunny suggested. "Because she is an unmarked, unclaimed female of age and she can choose who she hangs out with."

"She's Wyatt's sister." Cole pointed out.

"And if I can figure it out, he already knows." Gunny pointed out. "Who was it that invited you tonight?"

"Wyatt." Cole admitted and Gunny cocked an eyebrow at him. "Oh." The full implication hit him. "OH!"

"You'll have to forgive him little girl," Doc teased Wynne, "he's not thinking with the head on his shoulders."

She bit her lip and trailed her eyes down to the large bulge in his pants. "I know."

"Yeah, I say we keep her." Doc said and Gunny agreed.

The Hispanic man offered the former medic a high-five. "Hydrate."

"Hell, yeah." Doc replied.

39 - SEEING STARRS

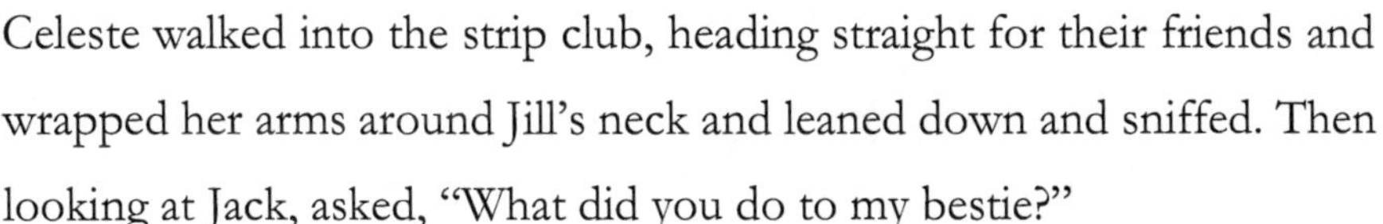

Celeste walked into the strip club, heading straight for their friends and wrapped her arms around Jill's neck and leaned down and sniffed. Then looking at Jack, asked, "What did you do to my bestie?"

"You should ask your bestie what he did to me, " Jack corrected, flagging down their waitress.

"Good boy, " Celeste said, kissing her bestie's cheek.

"And you?" Jill asked. "What all did you do to your man?"

"Not near as much as I plan to, " she replied. "Do we have a tab yet?"

"Good girl." Jill kissed her cheek. "Yeah, Doc had his card. It's on him tonight."

"Corona, a bottle of Jameson, Absolut Lime, and Johnny Walker, either blue or black."

"Bottles?" the waitress asked with eyes wide.

"Yes, can I get a bucket of Corona?"

"Get me a bucket!" Gunny called as he tipped a well-endowed dancer.

"And a bucket of his Bud Light, " Celeste added. "Anybody else? It's on Doc tonight."

"Did you put your winnings on the card?" Jill asked and when Celeste nodded, he laughed. "Me too!"

"Hello! " Celeste murmured.

"She's picked one!" Doc called. "Brunette in red lace, " he said, not looking in the direction that Celeste was facing.

"Oh, Doc, you know my type!" she laughed and then with a finger on the waitresses' chin, turned her face to where the dancer in question was. "What's her name?"

"Starr, " the waitress said.

"It's destiny, Celeste, " Wynne teased.

"Hell, yeah, " Celeste agreed as Wyatt pulled her into his lap. "Just bring buckets of all the different beers they have. And have Starr come see me, please."

"You batting for both teams, now?" Sirius asked as he pulled up a chair next to his sister.

"Hope you don't mind," Perseus gave a small smile. "I called him."

"You're good." Celeste smiled at her younger brother and then the older one. "And no, it just became tradition. There's lots of bars around the bases, the strip bars are just more fun."

"And you getting the first lap dance?" her brother asked.

"Drunk men watching a woman get a lap dance buy a lot of drinks."

"Sles, the bartender is coming over, " Jill said.

"Hi, I'm Scott, I'm the bartender. Amelia gave me a big order and I just wanted to make sure that you are aware of how much the bill would be, " he said looking at the men.

"Scott, you see that pretty lady there with the pretty silver eyes and more tattoos than her man knows what to do with?" Gunny asked from the far side of the group.

"He's figuring out what to do with them." Celeste said and Wyatt was caught tracing the triquetra knot on her left shoulder.

"What? There's a lot of ink to explore on her body, " he said guiltily. "And she keeps adding."

"Anyway, " Gunny said, shaking his head. "She's in charge. LT."

"You were an officer?" Will asked.

"Yup. I had a field commission and was allowed to keep it, " she confirmed.

"Catch, " Jack said, tossing her his phone. "Bank account is pulling up."

"Thank you, " She looked at the screen. "If we drink more than $100,000 in alcohol tonight, forget the bill, call an ambulance."

"Do we really have that much in the alcohol fund?" Jill asked and Celeste handed over the phone. "Oh, Sammi put her winnings in here too. Plus, we had that year where we couldn't do shit."

"Scott," Celeste said to the bartender, who was still standing there with his mouth wide open. "I am a very good tipper, but only if you bring me alcohol."

"Scott, how much is your rent?" Jack asked.

"What?" he asked.

"How much is your rent?" Jack repeated.

"$750."

"Keep her happy, and you'll go home with at least twice that in her tip tonight." Jill told him.

"I may have to change my fantasy so that you get a lap dance." Will joked and Wyatt growled as several buckets of beer and multiple bottles of liquor and shot glasses were placed on the collection of tables by the waitresses.

"Chill. I'm the one that started that bullshit, " Celeste said kissing her mate. The Marines all grabbed fresh beers and clinked them all together, giving their typical salute. "Hydrate."

I don't like knowing that one of my wolves is thinking about you like that. Wyatt said through the mate link.

And you're going to tell me that when you were his age, you didn't think about another man's mate?

Wyatt glared at her, and she smiled at him knowing she was right.

Doesn't mean that I have to like it.

You're the only one that I'm doing anything with. Have ever done anything with.

You sure know a lot for having never done anything. Was that really the first blow job that you ever did?

She blushed as she looked away, he gently turned her face back to look at him. Yes. I pushed the limits, but no one ever made it past first base.

Why? He asked her and she looked away. Grabbing her chin, he forced her to look at him. Why?

You. She sighed and took his hand, linking their fingers together. The first time that I caught your scent was when I graduated from boot camp. Goddess, you smell awesome. I had to fight with myself not to go find you. Angel, she had other ideas. And she could reach out to Demon. Demon told her that you both would wait for us until we were both ready.

He reached over and caressed her cheek. I saw your head pop up and you looked for me. But you had run away, so I knew you weren't ready for a mate. You were a Marine. I was in the Navy. Goddess knows that would not have worked well.

I'm lucky you're my mate. She smiled at him.

Even though I'm not an asshole?

Yes. It finally clicked that Jill was calling her name. "What?" she snapped.

"Chill out, girlfriend. Your Starr is here."

"Sorry, Jill, " Celeste said.

Jill just smiled at her as the two Marines had a silent conversation through looks and subtle gestures that came from being in combat together. Celeste conveyed that she was fine and did not need to be rescued.

Turning her attention to Starr, Celeste smiled at the dancer. "Sorry about that."

"No, if I had a man that looked at me like that, I'd ignore the world too, " Starr admitted as Celeste moved to the empty chair next to Wyatt. The chair that Sirius had been in and she looked around to find both of her brothers at the bar with their backs to the table.

Celeste grinned. "I think I'm going to like you. By tradition, I get the first dance. Tonight, he gets second." She pointed at Wyatt and then motioned for the girl to sit in her lap. Once she was settled, Celeste moved some of Starr's curly hair behind her ear and whispered so low that even straining, the werewolves could not hear what she said over the music. The dancer smiled and nodded, eyeing Wyatt.

The next song started, and Starr started moving on her lap before slowly sliding off and onto her knees in front of Celeste. Every eye in the building seemed to be trained on them. Not even halfway through the song, the first drink arrived. She never took her red lace dress off, which meant that she could rub against Celeste and not worry about breaking any rules or laws.

You told her to do that, didn't you?

Do what? Celeste asked as she looked over at Wyatt whose eyes were dark with desire.

Get your scent all over her.

Grinning at her mate, she turned her attention back to Starr who was climbing back into her lap and straddled her legs. She rubbed her chest against Celeste, the whole time, they were both watching Wyatt who was entranced by his mate getting a lap dance. Placing her hands on the back of the chair, Starr raised herself up, keeping as much of her body on Celeste as possible. When the song ended, she leaned down and kissed Celeste on the lips causing Wyatt to growl. It was not a possessive growl, more of a growl of desire. Both women looked at him and grinned.

"You're going to be paying for that later." He growled out.

"That is the plan." She admitted as Starr moved off her lap and moved over to Wyatt as the next song started.

Immediately, he could smell his mate on the other woman. Closing his eyes, he took a deep breath which only made it worse.

You are a cruel, cruel woman.

Am I?

You do know it's dangerous to lead on an Alpha without satisfying him?

Or her. Remember, I'm also an Alpha.

Starr moved off his lap and he opened his eyes just as she removed the red lace dress. He groaned and looked at his mate.

I'm not looking at her.

You can.

No. Only you.

Can you still smell me on her?

Goddess, yes. And I can smell you from over there.

Celeste smiled at him. The song is nearly over. Look at her, she has something for you from me.

Confused, he looked back at her to find that she had put her dress back on. She leaned down and kissed him on his lips. "From your wife." She whispered.

He smiled at her as she stepped away. Celeste stood up and pulled money out of her pocket. She removed the rubber band from the large stack of bills and peeled off three $20 and tucked them between Starr's tits. The rest she tossed onto the closest table to her.

"Okay, gentlemen, catch or release?" Celeste asked as Wyatt pulled her into his lap.

"Catch!" her guys said.

"Translation, do you want to keep her with us, or let her go back on stage?" Gunny asked the rest of the group. They also agreed to keep her with them. "Hey, Sles, never mind, you're a little busy."

Celeste was on Wyatt's lap with her arms around his neck while he had one arm around her waist while the other hand was buried deep in her hair as he devoured her mouth with his.

"I would tell them to get a room, but they already have one." Perseus said dryly as he and Sirius returned to the tables and the others laughed.

"Amelia, we need to buy Starr off stage." Jack told the waitress that had been convinced to sit in Doc's lap.

"How many rotations?" she asked.

"At least the next two hours." Jill said. "And our baby girl there has her eyes on the blonde on stage four, so I think we need her too."

Wynne blushed a deep red and tried to hide her face.

"I really don't think so." Cole said uncomfortably.

Wyatt broke away from Celeste, who laid her head on his shoulder. "I'm going to forget for a moment that she's my sister and tell you, let your mate get a lap dance."

"Told you that he knew." Gunny grinned.

"I'm not an idiot." Wyatt pointed out as Celeste nipped her mark on his neck. "Stop that or you're not going to finish your beers and we're going to leave right now."

She grabbed another beer from her bucket and pushed the lime down with her thumb. "I'll be good."

"Just for now." Wyatt said, kissing her temple before taking a swig of her beer.

"Trying to get me through my beers faster?" she asked.

"Maybe." He grinned.

40 - PRIVATE DANCE

They had arrived back at the hotel and Gunny headed straight for his wife. Teuf followed him and slept in the room with the pups. Wyatt and Celeste took the elevator up to the penthouse. Wyatt handed over the black bag and told her that he was dying to see her in the outfit. She stepped out of the bathroom wearing the skimpy blue dress and carrying the black 3-inch heels.

"You got to put the shoes on too." He told her as he sat in the chair by the balcony.

"Why?" she asked, walking to him.

"Because my freaky deaky mate, I want a lap dance from you."

"Oh." She said quietly as he pulled her into his lap.

"I'm going to assume that you've had enough of them that you would know what you're doing." He brushed a finger across her cheek. "I've been thinking about it ever since you got it."

"I didn't put the panties on." She Admitted.

"I won't object." He told her. "Will you give me a lap dance?"

"Take your shirt off." Celeste demanded as she stood up.

He removed his shirt as she slipped the shoes on. He had already put some music on through the smart TV. She started dancing, much the same way that Starr had done earlier. Between them, there were a lot of light caresses and kisses. He tried to remove her dress, but she told him no.

The first song ended, and another began. The touches and kisses became more urgent. More demanding. This time when he tried to remove the dress, she helped him. Now, wearing only the blue garter and black heels, she straddled his lap.

The dance ended as he caught her nipple in his mouth. She gasped when she felt his fingers gently opening her and teasing her clit. After a bit of teasing, he slipped a finger inside as he moved to the other breast. He slipped two more fingers inside her and pumped them in and out.

She had her hands on his shoulders for balance and he had his other arm wrapped around her waist. Releasing her breast, he leaned his head back and looked up at her. She had her head thrown back and her straight black hair was tickling his arm.

"Celeste, baby." Wyatt said huskily. "Look at me."

It took a little more coaxing, but she finally looked at him. He could tell that she was approaching an orgasm. As she got closer, her eyes began to close.

"Keep your eyes open. Watch me. Let me see you come."

She did as he asked and somehow the act of watching each other seemed to intensify the orgasm. She didn't close her eyes, or look away, but she cried out for him as her walls milked his fingers and her juices flowed out over his hand.

He removed his fingers and she sat on his lap. Wyatt brought his fingers to his mouth and sucked her juices off it. When he started to pull that one out and replace it with the second one, she caught his wrist and brought the fingers to her mouth. Celeste took the last two fingers into her mouth and sucked her own juices off him.

When she finally released them, he buried his hand in her hair and kissed her. Keeping his arm around her waist and hand in her hair, he stood up. She immediately wrapped her legs around his waist and arms around his neck. Taking a few steps, they reached the bed, and he laid her down. She expected him to slide into her and was prepared for that.

Instead, he unwrapped her legs and grabbed onto the heels of her shoes. Wyatt held her legs where he wanted them as he got down on his knees. Keeping her feet, and therefore her legs, where he wanted, he began to tease her with his mouth. Soon, she was squirming and moaning for him. She would cry out for him as she grabbed his head with her hands.

With his hair firmly in her fists, she wasn't certain if she had intended to push him away or keep him there. But she bucked against him as she crested again and pulled him even more into her. He gave a little chuckle but never stopped his assault. Celeste wasn't sure how he could still breathe, but air didn't seem to be important now. Just her pussy and his tongue.

She wasn't sure how long he was between her legs, but she knew that it was a while. She reached a point where she had to let go of his head because her arms were heavy, and they fell to the bed.

"Wyatt." She whispered. "I can't…"

Slowly he pulled away from her. As he stood up, he removed his pants. He again grabbed the heels and held her legs far apart as he pushed into her. He went antagonizing slowly as he pushed past her now tender clit. Every inch seemed to have doubled.

As he pushed his way home, she arched against him, giving into the orgasm. He began moving in her before it ended, causing it to be extended and her to cry out for him.

"Da-Wyatt…"

"It's okay, baby. Just give into what your body wants."

She reached for him, and he let go of her shoes allowing her legs to wrap around him. Wyatt leaned down and gathered her to him as their mouths found each other. She wrapped her arms around his neck, and he straightened up causing her to slide onto him a little deeper. He then stepped out of his jeans and towards the nearest wall. Pressing her back to the wall, he braced himself with his forearms on either side of her as he began to pound into her again.

"Oh, goddess," he said against her lips. "I'm not going to last much longer."

Celeste grabbed his head and forced him back enough that she could see his eyes. "Come for me." He growled as his own words taunted him. His canines extended and he tried to go for her neck. Instead, she held his head a little tighter. "Look at me. Watch me."

Growling, he did as he was told and they both watched as the other eyes glazed over and gave into their orgasms, heightened by watching each other. She let go of his head and he buried his face in her neck, breathing in her scent to calm himself. He lightly scraped his fangs across her marking spot causing a shiver to course through her.

"I'm sorry," Wyatt said kissing the same spot.

"For what?" she asked, holding his head to her neck.

"I nearly marked you. And I know that you're not ready."

Celeste pulled his head back and kissed him before meeting his eyes. "I would not have objected. I am ready. The reason that I want to wait has nothing to do with not being ready."

He looked at her in confusion. "I don't understand."

"The solstice will be ten years since you first found me. Ten years since I made the decision to run away from my father and the Hunt. And you," she gave him a little kiss. "I want my dad to see you mark me. To see me give you my permission to do so. To know that, just because the moon goddess made us for each other, we are together because we love each other. That we choose to be together."

She caressed his neck and cheek. "That I made the choice. And that you waited."

"And it wasn't forced onto you," he finished with understanding.

She smiled and nodded, "Yes."

He returned her smile. "I really do love you."

"I know. And I love you too."

41 - VIP LOUNGE

The blonde dancer came over and gave Wynne a lap dance. This time, both Sirius and Perseus watched. By the end of the song, they both understood the allure of watching a woman get a lap dance.

"Celeste," Sirius leaned over and spoke loudly. "I've got to go soon, but we need to talk."

She nodded and kissed Wyatt before standing up and grabbing a few of the twenties and a couple of beers off the table. Almost as an afterthought, she grabbed the bottle of lime-flavored vodka. With a wave of her hand, she motioned for them to follow her.

Both brothers fell in line behind her as she climbed the stairs to the VIP area. She tipped the bouncer and said something next to his ear, he unlatched the velvet rope and pointed to his right. The three siblings walked past several tables where men were getting lap dances and possibly other services. Sirius refused to actually look and see if his suspicions were correct.

The further they walked, the quieter the music got and soon it was just a low thump of base and a dull roar of music. At the end of the balcony, Celeste sat at a booth with a small round table in the center of the semicircle bench.

"What's on your mind?" she asked as she sat her drinks on the table.

"Pers has a few concerns, and I'm agreeing with him." Sirius admitted. "I know that you were never trained as an Alpha -"

"Stop." she sighed and leaned back against the pleather and tucked her foot up under her. "The reason that I got a field commission and became an officer is because I was trained as an Alpha. The Elders insisted on it."

Pausing to take a deep drink of her vodka, she closed her eyes briefly and Sirius wondered if he was wrong about her.

"Before I turned twenty-five, I was called before the High Council. I was ordered to Rome to go before the three Elders, the Divine Oracle, the High Priestess and the Divine Healer. They wanted to make sure that when I turned twenty-five and ascended to my position, I was not going to throw Silver Lake into chaos."

"Why would they think that you would do that?" Perseus asked.

"Because she had every right to do it." Sirius nodded in understanding.

"And because I threatened to do just that." she admitted. "It was how I got them to open the investigation into Aria's death." she looked at her older brother. "You were at the trial. You saw what I saw. What everyone else saw. You saw what happened to our sister."

"What happened?" Perseus asked quietly and both his older siblings shook their heads.

"It's sealed. Anyone involved in the trial itself cannot discuss it without explicit permission." Sirius explained.

"We can't discuss anything that was presented in the trial. I have more files, documents, pictures, videos… things that neither of you ever need to see."

She looked away and swallowed hard a few times. When she looked back at her brothers, Sirius saw the pain and anguish in her eyes.

"I knew the consequences of pissing off dad and leaving the pack. I thought that I knew the consequences of going to the Marines." She took a deep breath and when she spoke again, her voice was soft and filled with emotions and tears. "I did not know the consequences of combat. Or the consequences of forcing the investigation into Mesa Verde after Aria's death."

"Even with the nightmares, the drinking," she motioned to her found family below, "the strange traditions and having other Alpha's dismiss me, I would do it again. Every bit of it. From running away, to angering the High Council and everything in between. I would do it again."

"You're not the sister that I remember." Perseus said. "I remember the girl who smiled easily and protected us younger kids."

"She's still here, Pers." Celeste gave a sad smile. "She just had to grow up."

"I'm going to make a suggestion." Sirius told her. "I want you to tone down the craziness. You have a lot going on. A lot of eyes on you. And you're going to have even more."

Celeste nodded. "It's like a last hurrah. We're all reaching the end of our contracts. I think Sammi is ready for Gunny to get out." Smiling, she looked down at her closest friends. "Jack and jill fell in love with a little girl from the orphanage earlier today. Jill's always wanted kids and Jack will give him anything he wants."

"What about Doc?" Perseus asked.

"I think he has a few more years. But we all wanted to find a place to be close to each other afterwards." Sirius reached over and brushed the tear off her cheek. "Jill was cast out of her Pride and Sammi her pack. We came together all needing a family, We made one."

Sirius nodded in understanding as she emptied her beer bottle. "Do you often drink this much?"

"No, just when I know that the nightmares are going to be bad. The tattoo that I got tonight is for a K9 that gave her life for me. Protecting me. The memories are right there, just under the surface." she tapped her head. "You see the five of us having fun, getting drunk, being a little too perverted."

She shook her head. "We're trying to make peace with our demons."

42 - NEW FAMILY

It had been a week and a half since the night at the strip club. Celeste was assuming more roles of a Luna under her mothers-in-law's guidance. True to what Wyatt had predicted, his sisters stepped up to take over what Celeste had dubbed the female bullshit. Wynne loved being able to plan the upcoming special events - The Hunt and all the formal dinners that went with it, the mating ceremony which would also include the Luna Ceremony.

But Celeste did enjoy the other duties of her job. She loved spending time with the children at the orphanage and the schools. The work with the city council and mayor's office always was a challenge. Especially coordinating events between the two cities within the pack lands. Crystal Pass was the main werewolf city and Crystal Springs was the main pila town. A few smaller villages and townships rounded out the Crystal River Pack.

And then there was the charity work and her favorite - working with fellow veterans. She couldn't say that her nightmares were gone. Nor could she say that she was friends with her demons. But she was getting there. Working with others who had also seen some of the same horrors that she had, helped lessen the burden.

There was also keeping up good relations with the surrounding packs. Her birth pack was just across the state border to the South, just north of Baltimore. Crystal River was closer to Philadelphia and a smaller pack, Little Ridge, had a thin strip of territory between the two.

Wynne had moved in with Cole and his mother. At first, she wasn't sure about moving in with a man who still lived with his mother. But when he told her that they had lost his father and he was the last of her children still in the pack, her heart went out to her and her mate's dedication to family.

Celeste was thinking about this as she walked through the former Gamma's house for the new family that was moving into the pack. Wyatt hadn't told her much about them. She knew that they had been in the military, something that not many packs agreed with. The original pack the family was in did not, and they had been kicked out. This happened so often that every branch of the military had its own pack. She herself had belonged to the one in the Marine Corps.

Although she understood why so many packs discouraged service, she also understood that the freedoms they had come at a cost. With every were or shifter that served alongside pila service members, there was a bigger chance of their secret being told. Their world being exposed. And yet, without the were-community it would be safe to say that there would be no America today.

The military had been how she had met Jill. He had not met Jack yet and was still going by his given name, Matthew. When he had come out as gay, his pride had kicked him out. The Corps did not have many werecats, so the pack accepted them. Jill had been the first MP Celeste met. They became good friends quickly. He had been kicked out of his pride for who he was. And she had left her pack because of who she was.

The rest of their crew had come along one at a time. She had been stationed in Hawaii with Gunny when he met Sammi. The Kilauea Pack did not approve of her mating with a human. No matter how much she objected to the Alpha refusing to accept her mate, nothing worked. Not even when she reminded him that her mate was made just for her by the moon goddess herself. The Alpha told her to pick one or the other. He was surprised when she chose the human. The Corps pack welcomed her with open arms.

The next time she had seen Matthew, he had met Jack, and they were inseparable. They had been at Moby's in San Francisco when Moby referred to them as Jack and Jill. That night, Jill was born.

Doc came along during her second deployment to Afghanistan. At the time, he was an army medic coming to the end of his tour. The next time she saw him, he was in a navy uniform and embedded with her unit. She had Rory at the time that she went to go visit her sister Andi. She would later regret that trip. Absently, she gently touched the tattoo of Rory on her side.

Shortly after her return, she was assigned Marley. But she was pulled towards Max. She couldn't explain it, but she felt like they belonged together. She was told that he was to be put down because he could not be controlled. She spoke with the Alpha on base, a full bird colonel. He pulled a few strings, and she got Max.

She had always been able to talk with the dogs. That's what made her such a good handler. With Duke and Rory, it had been simple conversations. But Max, he was different. And one night, on a run, when a group of drunk men tried to attack her, Max showed his true form. She had only seen one hellhound before. But there was no doubt, he was a hell hound.

Currently, Teuf lay on his back in the living room on the sun-soaked tile. She wasn't sure why she had walked down memory lane. But as she again checked the refrigerator, Celeste couldn't help but hope that the new family would find peace here. Just as she had.

She walked upstairs to check the bedrooms and bathrooms and opened the windows to let the empty house air out. The family moving in had five children. There were six bedrooms upstairs and three bathrooms. Not including the master suite and two powder rooms downstairs. There was also a home office, game room, and open floor plan with the living/dining room and kitchen. Wyatt also had a fort and wooden playset built in the backyard. It wasn't unusual for families with young kids to get them. But she thought that it seemed strange that a new family would get such a large house.

And so close to the Alpha.

He had not mentioned bringing in a new Gamma. But he did say something about getting a new head of security for the newly formed Human Relations department. Not to be confused with a corporate based HR department. This department would work with the local pila governments to offer up friendly relations while keeping the pack safely hidden away.

Looking out the bedroom window, she could see their balcony. Now that there would be kids who could see that, she would have to tell Wyatt that there would be no more trysts on the balcony. Suddenly she wondered if the Beta or former Gamma had seen them. She was contemplating this when she heard the door downstairs open.

Celeste went and checked her appearance in the bathroom mirror. She didn't wear fancy dresses like her mother-in-law did. But since she was performing Luna duties, she dressed nicer than shorts and t-shirt. Today she wore gray slacks and a black blazer over a blue silk tank top. And of course, Wyatt's new favorite, her three-inch heels.

It had taken her a few days to learn how to walk in them. But she quickly discovered that he was an absolute sucker for her in high heels. She touched up her lip gloss before walking out and heading downstairs. On her way down, listening to the click clack of her heels on the wooden stairs, she thought about the heels she had bought earlier today.

If three-inch heels got him riled up, imagine what six-inch heels would do.

"Good afternoon," Celeste said, stepping off the bottom step. "I was just opening up the house- SAMMI!"

"Hello Luna," Sammi said, smiling at her. "Hope you don't mind, Gunny wanted to surprise you."

Celeste embraced her friend's wife. "You look like you're about to pop!"

"About another month and they'll be here," she said as the twins came through the door. "I desperately need a toilet."

"Right this way," she said, leading her to the closest powder room. "Already made sure there's toilet paper."

"Best Luna ever!" the pregnant woman declared closing the door behind her.

"Aunt Sles!" Marcus called running towards her. "Is this really our new house?"

"It really is," Celeste said, hugging him and then Bella. "You're an asshole, you know that right?" she grinned as her mate entered the house behind her friend and fellow Marine.

"You kept complaining that I wasn't one." Wyatt said, wrapping an arm around her shoulders. "Now, you complain that I am one."

"Aren't you looking all Luna like?" Gunny asked, walking in carrying Michelle. "Walking around in heels and everything."

Wyatt looked at the shoes his mate was wearing. "Are those…?"

Smiling, Celeste simply said, "They are."

A deep growl rumbled in his chest and Demon pushed for control. They struggled for a moment before Wyatt was in control again.

"Alpha," Sammi said, coming back into the living room.

"Sammi," he said, offering her a light hug. "Do you know when your furniture will be here?"

"Supposed to be tomorrow. We'll spend the night at the hotel," Gunny said.

"Nonsense," Wyatt said. "You can stay at the pack house until you're settled."

"I don't want us to be an imposition," Sammi said.

"That's why we have a pack house," Celeste said.

"And no bars for those two this time," Wyatt said with a grin.

"No, no bars." Gunny agreed. "When did you want me to start on the new position?"

"Gunny?" Celeste asked, looking up at her mate in his black suit. "You chose Gunny for your new head of Human Relations?"

Grinning down at her he nodded. "Who better than a human mated to a wolf?"

43 - PORTRAITS

Malachi walked towards the pack house only hours before they were scheduled to leave for the Crystal River pack in Pennsylvania. Their packs were practically neighbors with only a small pack, Little Ridge, between them. Crystal River was a larger pack that was founded around the same time. Both larger packs had founding fathers of the United States and signers of the Declaration and Constitution.

As he thought about this, he detoured to the building that held their council chambers. Walking down the long hall, he looked at all the formal portraits of the previous Alphas and their Lunas. Starting with the first Alpha, sent by King James, the first, not the second. He and his warriors were sent to help protect the new colonies.

The fashions and hairstyles changed through the generations. Ruffled shirts and colorful waistcoats gave way to three-piece suits and ties. Ball gowns became skirt suits. The Alphas all sat in the same throne-like chair with the Luna behind him and slightly to the right. Her right hand rested on his shoulder showing the Luna ring.

He stopped between the portraits of him and Aislinn and Sirius and Laura and noticed that the Alphas had the same coloring. Hair that was black as night. Eyes that were the silver of a full moon. That was until the Alpha angered the moon goddess, and she took her blessing away. His father, he and now his son, all shared the same coloring as the rest of the family. No markings. No chosen Alpha.

As was tradition, they had sat for the portrait shortly after the Luna Ceremony. Nearly forty years and thirteen children ago. Aislinn was slim and beautiful in the outfit that his mother had picked for her. A deep emerald, green shift dress to compliment her bright auburn hair.

He always loved this portrait of them. They had only known each other for a month, but he knew that she was his heart and soul. He could not imagine his life without her. They had just clicked.

Glancing at the portrait of his son, Malachi shook his head. As with so many things, Sirius threw tradition out the window. Laura was seated in the chair in a skin-tight blue halter dress that ended well above her knee. One foot was tucked up under her and she was turned to look up at her husband.

Sirius was looking down at her with absolute love and adoration in his eyes. His hand was cupping her neck as if he was about to kiss her. Her hand was on his wrist showing off the wedding ring instead of the Luna ring. You could only see part of her face, but his look was mirrored in hers.

Looking back at the portrait of him and Aislinn, he really looked at his wife. He wanted to see that same look in her face. In her eyes.

The artist had captured them perfectly. And for the first time, he saw the fear in her eyes. She had been so timid when they had mated. He saw more of a doe than a wolf in her. Once again, he saw the timidness, the fear, the uncertainty.

Walking back down the hall, he paid attention to the women this time. They looked more like Aislinn than Laura. Fearful. Worried. Concerned.

The men all looked like conquerors showing off their prizes. Isn't that what they were? Malachi thought as he walked out of the building and crossed to the pack house. He and Aislinn had moved out a few years ago and into the house that had been his mother's house until her death.

His father, Grant, had broken the mate bond and left his wife of thirty years for a much younger woman. Less than a month later, Grant had been killed by rogues and Bridget did not seem surprised or even upset. Grant had not been an easy man to live with. There was no living up to his expectations. He could only imagine what it would be like to be married to him.

Leaving the building he again headed for the packhouse. Once inside, he bypassed the office on the bottom floor and headed for the family living spaces. Now that he had seen their portrait in a new light, he wanted to look at something else.

Turning to his right, we went down the corridor that was now used for visiting family members. The pictures here were formal. Once again, the Alpha sat on his throne and his wife stood behind him. Children sat at his feet. Again, the Alpha looked like the conqueror surrounded by his prizes.

Reaching the end of the ivory hall with reclaimed wood floors, he turned around and walked back towards the other corridor. Reaching where the pictures of his family were, he watched as his family grew. One child, twins, another baby, then another. Thirteen children, including two sets of twins, in just over eighteen years.

The pictures were carefully staged. Outfits coordinated. He remembered Celeste once described the pictures as a generic portrait studio for werewolves.

Looking at them for the first time, actually taking the time and looking, he saw how many of his children were miserable. Did he ever really listen to them? Reaching out, he touched the last picture that Celeste was in. It had been taken less than a month before she ran away.

She already knew what she was going to do.

Her family's hearts would be broken, and she didn't care.

Going down the opposite corridor, he looked at the pictures of Sirius and his growing family. These were not staged. They were candid shots. The frames were not uniform. Some were collage style frames. Others marked special occasions. First Mother's Day. First birthdays. There were even a few of the larger pictures that had smaller pictures tucked into the corners of the frame.

Stopping and looking at ones taken when the newest baby was born, he saw concerned parents in the NICU unit of the pack hospital. There were pictures of Laura after she gave birth to each of the pups. She wasn't worried about how she looked. Her hair was not styled, there was no makeup, and she wore a standard hospital gown.

This was the pack Luna at her most vulnerable. And she was okay with people seeing her like this. Seeing her weak. And that somehow made her stronger.

He noticed that there were also pictures of Sirius with his siblings. Aurora and Danika at various plays over the years. Aurora when she performed as part of the chorus for Wicked on Broadway. Another picture from when she was a chorus member and backup in Hamilton.

Sky and Joseph with their pups when they had last visited. Perseus and Viviane at their mating ceremony the year before.

Andromeda and several other Council investigators at a meeting at the Bay City Pack.

A picture of Portia on Sirius' back as they both smiled at the camera. She looked so happy in this picture. Glancing down the long hallway, his mind pulled up the picture of the family taken at the beginning of the month. Fear was etched all over her face. And hatred burned in her eyes.

But here, taken recently and tucked into an upper corner of a larger picture, she looked happy and worry free. He knew it was recent because of the nose ring that she had gotten the day after she graduated high school. He wondered what her mate would think about it.

That brought back the memory of Celeste accusing him of selling her to a stranger. He's your mate. Aislinn had argued. Had she met her mate now? Was there still a chance for her to meet him?

An unknown picture caught his attention: Celeste when she graduated from bootcamp.

Anger and resolve coursed through him. He would think no more of this. Portia's future was his responsibility. She would do the Hunt.

44 - ARRIVALS

The first of the packs had arrived and the rest would arrive the next day for the Hunt, or, non-hunt, on Friday. They had a nice dinner with the Alphas who had arrived. Wyatt had been a little disappointed when Celeste came down in a dress that covered all her tattoos. Those beautiful, colorful tattoos, that he was slowly and methodically exploring and memorizing, were part of her. Part of his mate. Part of his Luna.

He never wanted to see them hidden.

By the time everyone had left, it was nine, he had told Celeste that he was going to go to work in his office. She had told him that he could have one hour. If he was not in their bed in an hour, she would come to get him. Now, just shy of an hour later, he had no idea what he was in for.

Down the hall, his mate soaked in the large tub. She scrubbed off the layers of makeup that Wynne had put on her. Wyatt had told her that she looked beautiful, and he meant it. But she knew that he preferred no makeup. Then she shaved and scrubbed her body before washing her hair. She slathered her body with lotion and then spritzed his favorite perfume on her pressure points.

She walked into the bedroom naked and Teuf looked up at her. If dogs could roll their eyes, she was pretty sure that he did when he looked at her. Celeste went into Wyatt's closet and picked out one of his long-sleeved white dress shirts. She completely unbuttoned it before pulling it on. She left it unbuttoned and rolled the sleeves above her wrists.

Celeste left his closet and went into hers. She put on the platinum, diamond and sapphire teardrop earrings and necklace that Wyatt gave her. She had woken up in an empty bed, with the box on his pillow. There had also been a note telling her that he hated that he would not be there when she woke up. He couldn't guarantee that he would always be there, but he would as much as possible.

It had also been the day that she had gone with Elizabeth, Wynne and Viviane. Shopping. If there was anything in the world worse than shopping with a woman, it was shopping with three. He never admitted it, but she was pretty sure that was another reason he wasn't there. She had agreed to go shopping with Viviane. Viviane invited Wynne, who invited her mother.

They had left at nine that morning and got home after a late dinner around ten that night. The following morning, Wyatt was nibbling on her neck, telling her there were other things that he wanted to nibble on, when Teuf went to the door excited. A moment later, Elizabeth walked in, telling her son to leave the poor girl alone. He had a pack to run, and she had an appointment with the dressmakers.

Wyatt buried his face in her neck and declared that he was changing the locks to the bedroom.

She got the box off the shelf and sat on the bed to put on the stilettos. Her original plan had been to wear the new shoes the night she had gotten them. But Sammi and Gunny had arrived. And she discovered that she needed to practice walking in them. And now, a week later, she was confident in herself. Teuf cocked his head at her.

"You don't have to sleep in here tonight," Celeste reminded him.

He got up and went to the door.

Celeste opened the door and turned to the right to go to Wyatt's office. Teuf continued down the stairs. If she had to guess, he would go to Elizabeth's house.

Celeste stepped into the doorway and saw Wyatt working on the computer. He had his glasses on and dear goddess, she had never found the nerd look sexy before. But looking at him in his glasses, she felt her jaw hit the floor and her tongue roll out of her mouth.

"Your hour is up."

Wyatt turned and lost his voice; his jaw was working up and down with no sound coming out. He finally just motioned for her to come to him. She glided around the desk and his eyes traveled down to the shoes. He was transfixed on sapphire blue shoes with metal stiletto heels. Celeste stopped just in front of him, and he reached out and opened his shirt.

Sliding his arms around her he let out a growl, discovering nothing underneath. He pressed a kiss to her abdomen before picking her up and setting her on the desk. Moving her hair behind her ears, he saw the earrings that he had picked out for her. He then traced the necklace with his fingertip.

"Do you know when I got this?" he whispered and shook her head no. "Your nineteenth birthday." He kissed her neck, lightly nipping her marking spot. "I was in Paris and got an email from Sirius. When I found out it was your birthday, I really started missing you. I was there with some from the Navy and Marine packs. Dahlia saw that I was upset and told me that I should go find something for your birthday."

"How would you have gotten it to me?"

"As she said, that wasn't the point." He smiled at her, and she could see all his love and pain in his eyes. "Every year on November tenth, I would buy you a present and have cake, red velvet, and if I couldn't find that, buttermilk pie." She smiled at him knowing so much about her. "If possible, I would go to a birthday ball. Some of the pack members knew that I knew who you were. I would never tell them, and believe me, they asked."

"The only thing that they knew was that you were in the Marines and that I would sometimes be able to see you from afar. Well, they knew your rank. So, whatever your rank, you were PFC Luna. SGT Luna. WO Luna. And last year, when I was talking to one of them, they asked how you were doing, and I bragged about your promotion. I just wish I could have celebrated with you."

"I'm sorry," Celeste whispered with tears filling her eyes.

"For what, my love?" he asked, wiping away a tear with his thumb.

She leaned into the hand that cupped her cheek. "If I had just done the Hunt, we would have met ten years ago, and I wouldn't have hurt you so much. We could have spent all these years together. I should have just done the Hunt."

"My grandmother used to say that could've, would've, and should've ruined your life." He kissed her gently. "Had you done the Hunt there is no way to guarantee that I would have been there. I wasn't planning on going. I hadn't been since my first Hunt. My sister was nearly raped at it. I happened to hear her scream and went to her. I had no intention of going and did not want to go. My other sister, Wenona, was scared to go because of what happened to Whitney. She made herself sick, with help from her favorite brother."

Celeste smiled, "She only has one brother."

"Narrows down the competition." He grinned back. "It made her way sicker than we had expected and mom and dad stayed and made me go. I didn't participate. I went to a meeting with Sirius. But when I walked into the pack house, there was this most alluring smell. And I had to find the source. Guess where I found it."

"My room."

Wyatt nodded. "Your room. Your room with all of your sports and cheer trophies. And two sets of black belts. And a junior state golden gloves plaque. And kickboxing gloves. And cookie monster. Why don't you have a tattoo of cookie monster?"

"I'll get one." She sniffled with a smile.

"Good. And, if we had met at the Hunt, I might not hate it as much. I might not be spearheading the movement to end the Hunt. And more importantly, you wouldn't be the you that you are. You wouldn't have all these tattoos that I love so much. I hated that you covered them up. Don't ever do that again."

"One more time. And then never again." She agreed and he frowned. "I already have the dress for the Alpha dinner tomorrow."

"Never again after that?"

"Never" she agreed.

"I know that you can't promise me never, never; just like I can't promise to be there every morning when you wake up, but I'll accept never again if possible." He kissed her with his promise.

"I promise," she said against his lips before kissing him again.

"Does your Luna dress cover them up?"

She smiled shaking her head. "No. In fact, it shows off a lot of them."

"My favorites?"

"Not puddy tat," she said with a laugh. "My back. It's sleeveless. The top part of the front is sheer."

"My little dragon friend?" Wyatt asked, moving the shirt and trailing kisses along the dragon on her collarbone.

"Yes," she said, leaning her head back to give him better access.

"Good," Wyatt said as he reached down and took off one shoe, and then the other. "We're going to save those for a special occasion."

"Special occasion?" Celeste asked as he picked her up and she wrapped her legs around his waist.

"Very special" he said, carrying her to the bedroom. "Tuesday sounds pretty special."

"Tuesday? What's so special about Tuesday?"

"If you're there?" he said, laying her on the bed. "Everything. But this Tuesday, all this crap will be over. All the extra people will be gone. And even more importantly," he explained, stripping off his clothes, "Stephen has agreed to take over my duties for the day, so I can keep you in bed all day. And it's the day after the locks are being changed on all our bedroom doors."

"You really are changing the locks?" she laughed as he crawled back over her and began to suck on her neck.

"Goddess, yes." He answered. "I don't plan on having any more interruptions until we have a pup that needs your attention. Speaking of which, when is your heat?"

"Next week," she said as he reached for something in the bedside table. "I saw the doctor earlier today."

He came back to her with a box of condoms. "Back up." He kissed her before moving down to her nipples. "The responsibility shouldn't be all yours."

She grabbed his head and brought him back to her mouth. "I love you. And I'm really glad that you're not an asshole."

He smiled down at her. "I love you too. And I'm glad that I'm not an asshole. But my freaky deaky mate, I want to watch you ride me while you're wearing my shirt." He kissed her and rolled them over so that she was on top.

Motioning to the box of condoms, Celeste asked, "Do we need one of those?"

"Not yet. Grab the headboard." She did as he commanded, and he pulled her up and settled her knees on either side of his head. "Ride me here first." He told her as he pulled her hips down and raised his head. Wyatt guided her rhythm at first, but then she took over. He enjoyed the sight of her above him almost as much as she enjoyed the position.

After several orgasms, he fumbled around for the condoms and got one on. Wyatt brought her almost to the point of release and then moved her from his face to his cock.

"Wyatt!" Celeste cried out as she slid onto him and found the release just recently denied.

"That's it, baby," he said, watching her find a good rhythm. "That's it, Celeste, ride me, my love."

With every downward push, she took more of him into her until he was completely inside her and she could feel him brushing against her cervix.

"Oh, goddess, Wyatt."

"I know." He fought for control but lost it with her next orgasm and joined her. "Oh, goddess, Celeste." He agreed as she collapsed on him, both of their bodies still pulsating. Wrapping his arms around her, he Admitted, "I was supposed to last longer with the condom."

She chuckled. "With the condom may have been the fastest that you came."

Kissing her temple, he also chuckled. "I think you're right. Get some sleep and we'll try again."

"Are you telling me that you're also not ready for an immediate round two?"

"Exactly, my mate." He rolled them to their side, pulling out of her. He removed the condom and dropped it in the trash can. She snuggled up to him and rested her head on his chest.

"Wyatt."

"Yes, love."

"I'm nervous about seeing my father."

"I'll be with you the whole time."

"I love you, Wyatt."

"I love you too, Celeste."

"After my heat…"

She stopped and he thought that she had fallen asleep. But then she rose up and looked down at him. She bit her lip with uncertainty. He reached up and caressed her cheek.

"What do you want after your heat?" he prodded gently.

"Angel wants to mate with Demon. To be honest, she wants to during our heat."

"But we aren't ready for a pup, yet."

"You aren't either?"

"I've spent ten years waiting for you. I want more time with you before I give you a pup." He brought her down for a kiss. "Don't get me wrong, I want a pup with you. I want several pups. As many as you will give me. If you want, we can kick everyone out of the pack house and put a pup in every room. I would not advise it, there's about fifty rooms."

She laughed. "I want a big family, but not that big."

"Good. I love you, mate."

"I love you too." She smiled at him. "Will you give me a pup before my birthday?"

"I'll give you a pup anytime you want." He pulled her down for another kiss. "Every time you want."

"Good." She lay back down, and he kept his hand in her hair, his thumb gently caressing her cheek as they fell asleep.

45 - MOTHERS

"Why are you two not up yet?" Elizabeth asked as she burst into the master bedroom.

"Monday," Wyatt growled and Celeste giggled.

"Don't worry about Teuf. He already had two showers this morning," Elizabeth said as the dog in question got on the bed and laid down. His head popped up at the word showers.

"He may have already had two," Celeste told her. "But he just heard the word again."

"Then I'll take him with me. But you two need to get up," Elizabeth said again approaching the bed where her son lay wrapped up around his mate. "You have Alpha's waiting on you in the dining room. And more arriving soon."

"I blame it on your son," Celeste teased. "I used to get up at four."

"We were up at four," Wyatt reminded her and tugged on her earlobe with his teeth.

Elizabeth smacked the back of his head. "Maybe if you would let the poor girl sleep, you two would be up at a decent hour."

"I like the idea of an indecent hour,," Wyatt said, nibbling on Celeste's neck.

"Elizabeth, leave the kids alone," Jonathan said walking into the room. "Don't you remember how we were when we were first mated?"

"Monday," Wyatt muttered again.

"You were twenty," Elizabeth argued. "He's 32."

"I'm now 56, and you weren't complaining about my age this morning," her mate countered.

"Tap that ass!" Celeste called out while Wyatt made gagging noises.

"Please, don't ever say that to my parents ever again," Whitney said, joining her parents.

"Agreed." Wynne said.

"How the hell do you think you all got here?" Celeste asked.

The girls made gagging noises as Wyatt rolled to his back. "Thanks for ruining any plans for a morning quickie," he grumbled.

"Tuesday,," Celeste said and heard him groan as his sisters complained about the suddenly pitched tent under the sheet. "Teuf, go with Wynne,," Celeste said, throwing off the sheet and standing up and stretching. Wyatt looked over and growled at her and she simply smiled seductively over her shoulder at him.

"USDA prime grade A." Whitney said reading one of her tattoos.

"Yes, she is,," Wyatt said looking over at his mate.

"Come take a shower with me," she said looking at Wyatt as she walked around the bed towards the bathroom. Pointing at Teuf as he started to get up, he added, "Not you, Fuzzball."

Teuf whined as he laid back down. Wyatt threw off the sheet and followed Celeste into the bathroom. "Just in case you guys are planning on staying in here, she is a screamer,," Wyatt said as he heard the shower turn on.

"Are you going to get in here and fuck me, or not?" Celeste yelled from the bathroom.

"I'm coming," he said, walking towards the bathroom.

"Already?" she called back. "Without me?"

The four people still standing in the bedroom looked at each uncomfortably as Wyatt walked back into the bedroom and started shifting sheets around until he found the roll of condoms. "Promised her no pups yet," he told them as he went back to the bathroom.

Celeste giggled from inside the bathroom, and they heard him saying something as the shower door closed. Whitney and Wynne both plugged their ears and dashed out the door. Teuf hopped off the bed and followed Wynne. Elizabeth stared wide eyed as a loud moan came from the bathroom.

"You wanted them out of bed," Jonathan grinned. "They are now out of bed."

Their son's name was moaned from inside the bathroom. Elizabeth blushed and Jonathan chuckled.

"I can't believe they're doing that knowing that we are out here," she told her husband.

"Then I guess it's time for us to leave," Jonathan said, walking towards the door and holding his hand out for her. "Come along, my Luna."

She gave a little growl as she followed her mate out into the hall. Just before they reached the elevator, there was a scream of pleasure that came from the bedroom. Just as they heard the scream, the elevator door opened, and Stephen stood there.

"Glad to hear that they're up," he said as the former Alpha and Luna stepped onto the elevator and the doors closed behind them. "They usually shut the door though."

"That may be our fault," Jonathan chuckled.

"Oh, goddess," Elizabeth said, blushing again. "You don't think any of the guests can hear them, do you?"

"Fifth floor is completely soundproof," Stephen told her as he was handing Jonathan a clipboard. "These are the cabin assignments. We're working off tablets, but this is the hardcopy."

"Thanks," Jonathan said. "Yes, dear, even for our sensitive hearing."

The elevator doors opened to the hustle and bustle of the Crystal River Pack and all their guests that have arrived. Sirius approached the elevator with his father.

"It's about time," Malachi snarled. "Where is Alpha Wyatt?"

"He's in the shower and will be down shortly," Stephen soothed.

"He was up late taking care of something that popped up," Jonathan added. Elizabeth started to add a snide comment and Sirius shook his head slightly. She thought that this was odd and asked her mate.

Why are you just not telling him that he is upstairs with his mate?

Malachi is her father.

So, he would understand-

He disowned her. He has tried to get her kicked out of the pack.

Why?

Jonathan excused both himself and his mate before leading her away from the other two men.

That is not my story to tell, my Luna.

I want to know what she did that would make her father disown her.

And you will get all the details tomorrow. Like everyone else.

I'm not everyone else. I'm his mother.

And they are handling it how they choose to. He kissed her on her temple. "Go, my Luna. We both have duties to attend to."

I'm very upset with you.

I'm sure you are. He smiled as he walked away to help settle all the new packs into cabins.

"Luna." A Beta female from another pack approached her. "I was hoping to introduce my daughter to your son," she said, gesturing to a beautiful young woman next to her.

Why is she-

Very few, outside of our pack, know that he has found his mate. Jonathon explained from where he stood speaking to the Alpha from the Crescent City Pack. That is how they both wish for it to be right now. Honor their wishes. Introduce the girl to him.

"Why yes," Elizabeth said smiling. "And how old are you, child?"

"Seventeen, Luna," The girl practically purred.

She's a baby being thrown at a man nearly twice her age!

And my darling Luna, Jonathan turned and smiled at her, you now see why our son does not like the Hunt.

"Yes, you do know that my son is in his thirties?"

"And has not found his mate," the mother said. "Obviously, he is still up for grabs. With respect, Luna."

"Yes. Yes. There he is now." Elizabeth waved at her son and mind linked him at the same time. You better have a good reason for not acknowledging your mate.

Believe me, mother, I do.

"Wyatt, this is Beta…"

"Audrey. Of the Burnt Ashes Pack." She motioned to her daughter. "And this is my daughter, Starr."

"Starr," he grinned. "That's one of my favorite names."

I don't think that she'll give me a lap dance. Celeste told him through the mate link.

I wouldn't want this child doing that. He replied to her discreetly watching as some of his warriors snuck her out of the pack house. I might have to get the brunette with a red lace dress to give you another one.

Maybe she can give me one while I'm on your lap.

Wyatt fought hard against the image that was trying to fill his mind and the growl that wanted to come out. I'm uncovering your tattoos later.

I'm counting on it.

"Wyatt, Beta Audrey just asked about your time in the service," Elizabeth said, bringing him back to their conversation.

"Sorry, mother," he kissed her temple. "Maybe we can discuss it after the Hunt? Please excuse me, I need to go see about something."

Keep your dick out of her! His mother berated him.

I do have other duties.

46 - THE ALPHA DINNER

The formal dining room reception area was full of Alphas and Lunas. They milled around, rubbing elbows and trying to outdo each other. Currently, Wyatt was talking with Sirius, Laura and the female Alpha of the Autumn Hills pack, Amber.

Wynne had brought Teuf with her when she had come to do Celeste's hair and makeup. She had told him that from the way dog and handler acted, they had been separated for years and not just hours. He had seen Wynne leave twenty minutes ago. Where was his mate?

And then, he felt her. She wasn't quite in the dining room yet. But he knew that she was close. And as she approached, he began to get lost in her scent.

The far end of the room grew quiet, and the silence slowly spread across the room. Wyatt thought that he knew what everyone was looking at. Teuf. But when he turned to the woman causing the click clack to echo across the hall, he discovered that no one even cared about the dog.

No. They weren't looking at the dog. Instead, they were looking at the woman in the sapphire and silver dress. It had long sleeves with an intricate pattern stitched in sparkling silver thread. Obviously, it was not actually silver, but the effect was the same as it shimmered, shined and accentuated her silver eyes.

The mandarin collar was silver with the same pattern, but sapphire blue. There was a matching sash of silver between the top and skirt. The fitted bodice and the skirt were a solid blue with stitching only along the bottom.

Her hair was done in a French twist with a few tender curls in strategic spots. He was drooling all right. Just as every other man in the room was. Possibly even some of the women. He caught her eyes and noticed that his sister had done something to really make her silver eyes pop. Whatever it was, he hoped she would do it again tomorrow night.

Did I ever say thank you for my birthday present?

When she asked that through the mate link, he realized that she was wearing the jewelry again.

You are thanking me right now.

Are you drooling?

Drowning. That dress is… is… oh goddess.

What? Nothing about my shoes?

He glanced down and there were the stilettos.

If you kill me tonight, you won't be marked tomorrow.

It's a good thing that I know CPR.

Don't think that I could even spell that right now.

Let me help. Charlie. Papa. Romeo.

Got it. Fuck. Me. Now.

Close.

"Poor Teuf," General Abernathy said, approaching the dog and kneeling to pet him. "She put you in a bow tie."

"He still knows he's beautiful," Celeste said, turning to where Teuf sat, getting attention. When she turned, Wyatt saw the line on the back of stockings. He had told her that the old-style stockings with the seam going up the back, had to be the sexiest thing on earth.

"I'm pretty sure your sister is trying to kill me," Wyatt muttered to Sirius.

"I'm pretty sure that she just became a mass murderer of men," came the soft reply before he approached his sister. "Celeste."

"Sirius." She smiled and accepted the light kiss on the cheek.

The general stood up and offered his hand. "You must be the brother of Alpha Celeste."

"I am," he said, accepting the Marines hand. "Sirius, acting Alpha of the Silver Lake pack. This is my wife, Laura. I'm assuming that you two served together."

"Alpha James. I am over the Pendleton division of the Corps pack. And matchmaker to these too."

"Please don't insult my date," she teased.

"I would never insult a fellow Marine." The general replied.

Conversations slowly began to pick up again around the room. Wyatt looked and saw the three guards assigned to her had practically disappeared into their surroundings. He was glad that his pack already loved his mate. Most already called her Luna. A few even Addressed her as Alpha. Either was fine. And both were correct.

Wyatt nodded to the Omega at the door and the doors were opened to the formal dining room.

"Alpha Wyatt," The Omega called. "Your meal is ready."

"Ladies and gentlemen, shall we?" Wyatt called. "Alpha Celeste, may I have a moment?" and just like that, he had her elbow in his hand and guided her to a seat next to her. Whitney sat in the Luna spot. She quickly moved, making the excuse that the two Alphas had business to discuss.

"Alpha Celeste," Alpha Victor, a new and young Alpha, said with lust in his eyes. "You look good enough to eat."

Should I tell him that you are good to eat?

Perhaps you can show me how good later?

Absolutely.

"Thank you, Alpha," Celeste said, with a smile as the first course was served.

Will you dance for me tonight? In that dress? Wyatt asked through the mind link as the salad plates were taken away and the main course of steak was served.

No. But I have something else for that.

Are you trying to kill me?

No. Just tease. She replied while listening to the Alpha on the other side of her.

What do you have on under that?

A garter belt.

What else?

Lotion. Celeste smiled at him as chocolate and raspberry mousse was placed in front of her.

Dear goddess, I offer myself as a sacrifice to you, let my bed be your temple and my mate, your priestess.

I'll hold you to that.

As long as you hold me to your body.

47 - EARLY MORNING MEETING

The night had been an early one. The morning, even earlier. Celeste had dressed for the early morning meeting in one of her outfits that she had dubbed the Luna outfit. Since the morning air was still cool, she wore a light, long sleeve black sweater and blue slacks. And of course, her now signature high heels.

Wyatt was dressed in slacks and a black button up shirt. He wore no tie, and the top few buttons were undone and he knew that her mark could be seen.

She had been sitting in his lap, but having decided that she needed coffee, was at the coffee bar in the first-floor office when the Alpha and Luna of the Mountain Crest pack were escorted in. The guards that brought them took up positions on either side of the door.

The Alpha saw her at the coffee bar and assumed that she was an assistant.

"Hey, girl, fix me a mocha," Alpha John called over to her. "Dear, do you want anything?"

"I'll take a mocha also," Luna Tina said as Stephen, Ellie and Savannah entered the room.

I can only make black coffee.

And my freaky deaky Luna, if they are smart, they will be grateful for whatever you give them.

"We were wondering where our daughter had spent the night," Tina said with a knowing smile.

Yeah, right.

Behave, my Luna.

Celeste stacked the four disposable cups and walked back to the desk. She handed the cups over to the guest couple. John took a drink of his and then opened it up to look at black coffee.

"I think you gave me the wrong cup. This is black."

"They all are," Celeste said, taking a drink of hers.

John glared at her before he started to throw the coffee at her.

"I would not advise that action if you want to walk out of this room," Wyatt growled.

"You need a better assistant. I had heard that you were too lenient with your Omegas. They need better discipline." John scoffed. "Such disrespect to an Alpha."

"Last warning, Mr. Fields," Wyatt said as his eyes turned black. "She is not my assistant nor an Omega."

"It's Alpha," Tina corrected.

"Alpha is a title that is earned," Wyatt corrected. "Anyone who whores their child out does not deserve it."

"She did spend the night with you in your bed," John smirked.

"She did not!" Wyatt said. "Child, where did you spend the night?"

"In the guest room of Beta Stephen's house," Savannah said quietly.

"Once we tell people she spent the night with you, you'll have to take her as a mate," Tina said proudly.

"No. What is going to happen is that you two will be confined to your cabin again. Once the Hunt has started, I will ask for the Council to convene. And do you know what I'm going to tell them?"

John stood angrily and was about to speak but thought better of it.

Wyatt stood up to his full height. "Care to make any kind of a guess?"

They both squirmed nervously under his cold glare.

"You know that the Council has a record of all births, right?" Wyatt asked harshly and John sat down, pale and weak. "And do you know what I found when I looked up your daughter? Your only child?"

Tina swallowed hard and avoided his gaze as guilt filled her face.

"Fifteen!" Wyatt yelled and the couple in front of him flinched.

"Which one of you had the idea?" Neither spoke. "You either tell me which one of you came up with this idea, or you will both go to my dungeon."

They both cast their eyes down silently.

"Tell me now!" he commanded with authority in his voice. Since they were guests on his pack lands, they had no option but to obey.

"We both came up with it," Tina admitted.

"Why?" Wyatt continued to use his Alpha command on her.

"To hide her pregnancy," she was compelled to answer.

"Child, who is the father?" Wyatt asked her gently and she pointed to her father. "No, child, not your father. Who is the father of the baby?"

With tears streaming down her face, she continued to point at him and nodded her head. Before anyone could react, Wyatt was around the desk and beating the man. Celeste rushed over and put her hand on his arm.

"Not like this, my love," she said softly. He dropped the other man and pulled her into his arms. Wyatt buried his face in her neck and took deep calming breaths. "That's it. Calm down, baby."

After a few minutes of her soothing him, Wyatt looked down at her and kissed her. "I love you."

"I love you, too," she smiled back at him.

He turned his attention to the girl's mother. "How long have you known about this?"

"About a year," the woman sobbed.

Celeste punched her in the face knocking her out. As she prepared to swing again, Wyatt stopped her and returned her words to her, "Not like this, my love."

She smiled at him and then buried her face in his chest.

"Take them to the dungeons. Keep them separate. Ellie, take the girl to the hospital please."

Ellie nodded and gathered up the girl. Wyatt motioned for one of the guards and he stepped forward and scooped her up in his arms.

"I'll follow you," the guard told her. She nodded and started to walk out of the office. Four other guards approached to escort them.

"I don't like it when you're an asshole," Celeste told her mate, looking up at him.

"I don't either," Wyatt admitted.

"He didn't even go full on asshole," Stephen said as the couple was taken out of the office. "Do you want to have a doctor check on them?"

"No, I really don't," Wyatt admitted. "Wait a few hours. Then let them be treated."

Stephen gave a light laugh. "I understand. Just an FYI here, Ellie has become quite attached to the girl. Very protective."

"I expect no less from your better half," Wyatt admitted. He then looked down at Celeste. "Have I told you lately how much I like you in heels?"

She smiled. "I don't feel so short in them. Which is saying something because I'm not very short "

"When you're over six and a half feet, just about everyone is short."

"I'm not wearing 12-inch heels just so I can be eye level with you."

Wyatt tightened his grip on her waist and lifted her up so that they were eye level. Instinctively, she wrapped her arms around his neck. "I like it when you are eye level like this." He placed a gentle fist under her chin and rubbed his thumb along her jawline. "When we go to bed tonight, you will be my Luna. And you will have my mark. But I'm still going to give you hickeys."

The grin and promise of hickeys had the desired effect. He took a deep breath taking in her aroused scent. Celeste grinned back before kissing him.

"You're horrible," she told him.

"Complaining?" he asked with a teasing kiss.

"Never," she gave him her own teasing kiss.

"Alpha?" came from the doorway.

He sighed and rested his forehead on hers. "Yes?"

"Your mother is here to see the Luna," Anna told them. "She is upset that she cannot go to your floor."

"I promise, that is only temporary," Wyatt said. "Have her wait in the Luna's office."

"Yes, Alpha." She pulled the door closed behind her.

"I have an office?"

"Technically, you have three. This one. The Luna office is on the second floor. And your private office is on our floor." He grinned at her. "I had the Luna office redecorated. Your private office is all you."

48 - LUNA OFFICE

Wyatt took Celeste up to the Luna office on the second floor. It still smelled faintly of fresh paint. It was a beautiful shade of pale blue with sapphire blue accents. The built-in shelves on the far wall held a small library, a lot of pictures of her family, a few little nick knacks and a cookie monster cookie jar. Upon opening the jar, she had found fresh oatmeal raisin cookies, individually wrapped.

The large desk in the middle of the room was a grand cherry wood antique. It matched the built-in and other furnishings. On the wall beside the French doors, was large flat screen TV. Underneath it was a cabinet with four doors and drawers. When she looked, it was empty. She had no idea what she would fill it with.

There were double doors leading into another room on each side of the room. The doors on her left led into a private full bathroom. Complete with a large shower, toilet, sink and vanity with a matching chair. This was also done in blue with grey accents. Inside the attached closet were two sets of clothes with shoes and accessories, and all the linens a small Army would need to bathe.

Elizabeth told her that the vanity was already stocked with her preferred makeup and hair essentials. When she opened the drawer she found her tattoo lotion, chap stick, mascara and lip gloss. The other drawer held a brush, comb and a few dozen hair ties. Her mother-in-law told her she was the easiest of all the girls to buy makeup for.

She had then gone to the other side and through those doors and found a large sitting room. Cherry wood shelves were built in here also and the colors matched that of her office. But instead of a desk, there were two matching dark gray couches facing one another with a cherry wood coffee table in between. Both had several throw pillows in various shades of blue and light gray throw blankets on the back.

Towards the French doors leading to the balcony, was a round cherry table with four matching chairs surrounding it. On the side opposite the built-in shelves was a wet bar with glass decanters with platinum medallions hanging around the neck. Looking at the medallions, she found they were filled with her favorite whiskeys and other liquors. There was a shelf above with barware and stemware hanging below. There was also a small refrigerator, a wine refrigerator and her favorite item in the whole suite.

Keurig.

The whole office suite had been decorated with her personal preferences in mind. From the colors to the drinks to her favorite cookies. She was a little overwhelmed. The Luna at the Silver Lake Pack had a small desk in the back corner of the Alpha office. And here, she had three rooms just for her.

Just as she was about to hug her mate, the doors on the opposite side of her office opened and Anna stepped inside. She walked over and asked if there was anything that needed to be changed or updated. Celeste could think of nothing. Curiously, she stepped through the door and found herself in an office for her assistant, Anna.

The young Omega was several inches shorter than herself and a little softer with a slight pudge. Her dark shoulder length curly blonde hair and bright green almond shaped eyes almost seemed to contrast her light caramel colored skin. She wore a grey skirt, pink sweater, and black kitten heels. Her kind eyes instantly caused Celeste to like her.

Anna apologized that her office had not been updated to match the Luna office yet. Anna stared at her in surprise when Celeste told her that it was her own office and if Anna wanted to paint it neon green with purple polka dots and yellow triangles, she could. Quietly, the Omega said that she liked pink. Celeste told her to pick the color and it would be repainted.

Without thinking, the woman hugged her new Luna. Celeste wrapped her arms around her and hugged her back. Realizing what she had done, Anna stepped back with wide eyes. She began to apologize for her outburst, but Celeste held up her hand to stop her. The new Luna pointed out that they would be spending a lot of time together, it would be better if they were friends rather than just employer and employee.

Both Elizabeth and Anna gaped at her, and Wyatt beamed with pride, when Celeste stated that she had plans for Tuesday but would love to spend Monday with her so they could get to know each other. She said that she was open to any activity, except for shopping. Since she had told Wyatt that she wanted to be his mate and Luna, she had been shopping more than in the rest of her 28 years put together.

Anna gave a small laugh and stated that she would love to go to the local natural science and history museum in the human town. They currently had a dinosaur exhibit that her seven-year-old daughter would love to see pictures of.

Celeste had adamantly said no. If Anna was going because her daughter wanted to see the dinosaur exhibit, she should be there also. Again, Wyatt beamed with pride and Anna felt her eyes fill with tears. She asked if she could call her daughter to tell her. Smiling, the new Luna hugged her and suggested that she take the day off and they would start on Monday.

Anna burst into tears and Celeste asked Wyatt if she could have a driver take her home. He smiled and said that a car would be out front in just a few minutes. After Anna left, Elizabeth handed over a leather-bound journal explaining that since the late 1600s, the Luna of the Crystal River Pack kept a journal of important events beginning with their Luna ceremony. She then kissed Celeste and Wyatt on their cheeks and left.

Wyatt took her back into her office and showed her the bed for Teuf. There was a matching one in the sitting room at the end of one of the couches. He then had her sit at her desk. She looked across the large desk and smiled at the two blue upholstered high back chairs facing her. Then curiously, she began opening drawers and, in the large center drawer, she found a jewelry box.

Inside she found another platinum, sapphire and diamond jewelry set. Along with earrings and a necklace, there was also a matching bracelet. Wyatt kissed her temple and told her that his mother had said that it would go well with her Luna dress. And he was right. It would look beautiful with her dress.

If they didn't have to change and go to the non-hunt, she would take him upstairs and put on this jewelry and nothing else. He heard her thought and groaned begging her for that image to become real. Her response was Tuesday. He then informed her that if she planned on wearing nothing but jewelry and stilettos on Tuesday, they should go ahead and clear both schedules for Wednesday also.

Before she contemplated if this was a possibility, Wyatt suggested that they go get changed, it was now approaching time for them to open the non-hunt. It took just about all of her willpower not to jump him. She was pretty sure that the next few days would be hell. She woke early this morning, much to her mate's delight, desperate for his body. She was going into her heat and last month was difficult being close to him. This month being in the same bed would be worse.

49 - ESCAPE

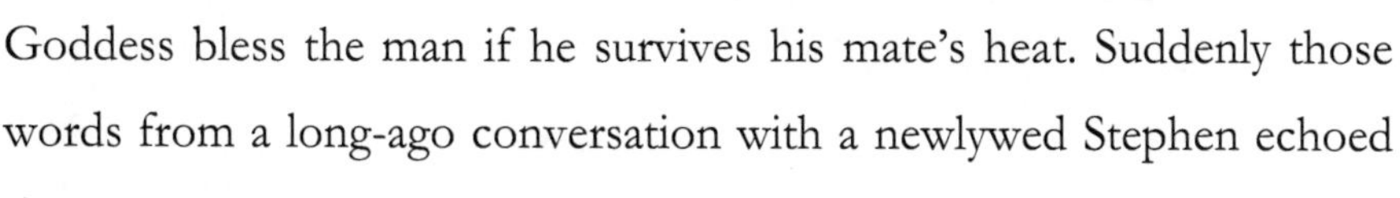

Goddess bless the man if he survives his mate's heat. Suddenly those words from a long-ago conversation with a newlywed Stephen echoed through his mind as Wyatt led Celeste to their floor.

Once they were back in their bedroom, she was able to convince him for a quick round. Not that it took much convincing. Especially once he realized that she was going into heat. Her scent was amplified and there was little he could do to resist her except gather his clothes and go get ready on the fourth floor.

The fifth floor was theirs and theirs alone. They each had a personal office. Their chambers. There was a nursery attached to the bedroom. A media room, they had fallen asleep in there the other night watching one of her favorite movies, Heartbreak Ridge. There was also a fully stocked kitchen, a dining room and a living room that all flowed together.

And the only way up to their floor was the elevator and the staircase at the other end of the wing which ended on fourth floor. When they came along, and were old enough, this would be for their pups. His grandfather had seventeen children. There were twenty bedrooms and bathrooms on this floor.

He stepped into the first bedroom and headed for the shower. It's a good thing that once they opened the non-hunt, he would not see her again until the ceremony. Otherwise, he would bring her back to their chambers and not let her out until her heat was over. Demon would prefer to keep her there until she had a pup inside her.

At least one pup.

This was one of the times that he wished that he was not quite so honorable. He had given his word that he would wait until she was ready for pups. But damn, smelling her while she is in heat, made it difficult. Once he had a shower and went to get dressed, he discovered that her scent was all over the clothes he had grabbed.

Stephen, where are you?

About to leave the pack house.

I need a favor. Huge favor. I need you to grab me some clothes out of my office closet and bring them to me.

Do you not have enough in your walk-in closet?

I'm not in the room.

Where are you?

First room on the right on the fourth floor.

She already kicked you out of your own bedroom.

Quit laughing. Or else you can take care of the Hunt.

Pants or jeans or shorts?

Jeans or shorts. Something casual.

On my way up.

What did you do to get kicked out?

She's going into heat. If you would rather, I can go take care of that…

Oh damn. And you were able to walk away?

It took a lot of willpower. And putting her in the shower.

Your willpower or hers?

Mine. Do you and Ellie still have handcuffs?

Yeah. Want to borrow them?

I'm going to suggest that you not give her any ideas. Or you will be running the pack until she's done with me. And I recover.

There was a knock on the door before Stephen walked in grinning.

"Shut up," Wyatt growled with a grin as he took the clothes.

"Happy ten-year anniversary." Stephen laughed as his Alpha pulled on jeans. "If you survive tonight, I'll congratulate you tomorrow for getting mated."

"At least it's only the first day," Wyatt said, sitting down to pull on his tennis shoes.

"I'll say a prayer for you Sunday." He laughed pointing out when she would be at the height of her heat.

"Like I said, I can go back upstairs, and you can go take care of the Hunt."

"As much as I love my brother from another mother, the Hunt is all yours."

"Non-hunt," Wyatt corrected, standing up and pulling on his Navy t-shirt.

"Just so you know, the Omegas really love your Luna now." Stephen closed the door behind them.

"Because of Monday?" Wyatt asked as he pushed the down button for the elevator.

Stephen smiled as the door opened. “And she hugged an Omega.”

“I really don’t deserve her,” Wyatt admitted as they stepped inside. “First floor, Jake.”

The warrior assigned to the elevator nodded and pushed the button. They both smiled at Jake and noticed that he stood for them, keeping the stool behind him hidden by his large size. Wyatt discreetly looked at the man’s leg, knowing that having a prosthetic must make it hard for him to stand for long periods of time.

“Have there been any more attempts to get up to the Alpha floors?” Stephen asked.

“Yes. Three mothers. Two maidens. And your mother,” Jake said as the elevator stopped on the second floor.

Gunny stood there holding his tablet, making sure that everything was still on schedule. “Alpha. Beta Stephen,” he said, stepping into the elevator. “Is Luna Elizabeth still upset?”

“Not since I told her that a fifteen-year-old girl dropped her clothes in front of me.”

“How did they even think that you would believe she was 17?” Gunny asked.

“Alpha?” Jake said as they reached the first floor. “I would love twenty minutes alone with her father.”

"If I were to give all my warriors asking for some time, you would each get about 90 seconds," Wyatt said.

Jake looked his Alpha dead in the eye. "I'll take it."

Wyatt clapped the warrior on the back. "I know the feeling."

As the three men stepped out of the elevator, Wyatt mind linked with Jake.

Let me know when the Luna is heading out.

Yes, Alpha. The triplets went up just before Beta Stephen.

Thanks Jake.

Alpha, we really do love her. I'm glad she's my Luna.

Me too, Jake.

50 - NO HUNTING ALLOWED

Celeste walked with the triplets down to the training grounds. With all the activities and people around, her discrete guards had been replaced with the large triplets that stood out among a crowd. All three wore khaki cargo pants and Polo shirts with the pack crest on the left breast. She thought that the only thing missing was SECURITY across the back of their shirts.

Teuf sniffed the air and occasionally looked back at them. She could smell the treats that were set up around the edges. She knew that she could tell him to go ahead, and he would be safe. The pack loved him now. The other pack's opinions were questionable.

She watched as his ears twitch and his snout turned. Suddenly, the whole group was changing directions. Within a few minutes, they were standing where burritos were being sold.

"Good morning, Estelle," Celeste said to the ten-year-old. "Can I get four burritos and a couple of pieces of sausage?"

"Yes, Luna. Mom set aside some sausage and ham for Sir Teuf," she said, handing over a bag that had Toof written on it. "Do you want sausage, ham or bacon?"

The triplets all took sausage and Celeste took bacon.

"How much?" Celeste asked.

"No cost, for you, Luna," Maria called from the outdoor griddle she had set up.

She nodded and placed a twenty in the tip jar. A few stalls later, she found coffee. Again, they refused to take her money. Again, she put money in the tip jar. The hunters were led out and the crowd erupted in excited applause.

"Think they'll be just as excited when the maidens come out," Ronald said with a little laugh.

"Probably not," Celeste said as she caught sight of her parents. "Guys, my parents are over there. Can I have some space?"

"Yes, Luna." They all spread out, giving her some privacy. But one was always close enough to hear if she called for help. And they all had always her in their sights. Stepping over to her parents she gave Teuf the rest of her breakfast. When she stopped, he laid down to eat.

"Mom," Celeste said nervously. "Dad."

Her mom turned and embraced her while Malachi just stared at her tattooed arms. She felt his eyes on her neck, looking for a mark that was not yet there.

"Are you here to do the Hunt?" he finally asked.

"No," Celeste said as the maidens were brought in on the opposite side from the hunters.

"Well, I don't see you being marked," her father said. "At least not by a mate. But I see that you've got yourself marked up like a tramp." He stepped towards her and sniffed. "Not marked. Not a virgin." He grabbed his wife and walked a few feet away.

"Ma'am?" one of the triplets asked, stepping closer to her.

"I'm fine, Rodger," she replied with a smile, and he nodded and stepped back again.

Celeste looked towards the stage and caught Wyatt's eye as he went up the steps.

Are you okay, my love?

It went about how I expected.

I'm sorry, baby.

Teuf nudged her leg and she absently started scratching his head.

"Good morning," Wyatt said into the microphone, getting everyone's attention. "I'm sure that by now, you've noticed that we're doing things a little differently. Gentlemen, I feel like I need to remind you about our duties as mates. The moon goddess makes our mates for us. She makes them perfect for us. And our duty is to take care of and treasure this gift. We are to protect, guide and love our mates."

Wyatt paused, looking out over the confused crowd. This was not the history filled go get them speech that they always heard before the opening of the Hunt.

"I'm sure that you're wondering why I'm telling you this."

"Maybe we should get advice from someone with a mate," one of the men called out. There were some sentiments of agreement and nervous laughter from the crowd. Wyatt nodded and grinned.

"A few months ago, I would have agreed with you. But let me tell you something that for years, very few people knew until recently. Several years ago, I found my mate." There was a ripple of confusion that moved through the crowd.

Stephen stopped next to Celeste. "Are you okay, Luna?" he asked softly.

"Actually, I am," she said with a smile. "I really am. Thank you, Stephen." She smiled at Wyatt and caught his wink.

"Before I tell you about my wonderful, beautiful, colorful mate," pack members gave a little laugh and Celeste put her hands in her back pockets, "I need to tell you about my sister, Whitney. She went on three Hunts. Her last one was the only one that I've ever participated in. I could not smell my mate. Somehow, I always knew that she was not there. But I was in the heat of the Hunt, the thrill of it. Those who have hunted before, you know what I'm talking about."

"And then I heard my sister cry out for help." Wyatt took a deep breath and looked up at the sky. When he spoke again, his voice cracked with emotion. "Gentlemen, if you have ever heard your sister, mother or another woman that you care for cry out in fear," Whitney stepped up onto the stage and went to him wrapping her arms around his waist, he put his arm around her, "it is the worst sound that you will ever hear."

You're doing good, my love, keep going.

I love you, my Luna.

"When I got to my sister, her mate was about to rape her." Murmurs echoed through the crowd. "Being a responsible and logical 17-year-old male, I handled it in a very mature manner. I beat him senseless. So much so that he had to report to the medical tent."

"I deserved it!" Nathaniel yelled from beside his assigned maiden.

"You did. But you've made up for it since then. That year, there were two other maidens that were raped. One of which would eventually take her own life. That was fourteen years ago. Including those two, in the past fourteen years, one-hundred and seventy-three maidens have been raped. One-hundred and seventy-three, gentlemen." Wyatt paused, allowing it to sink in. "One-hundred and seventy-three."

He looked over at where the Maidens stood. "One-hundred and seventy-three daughters. Sisters. We need to do better. We must do better. We will do better. And that starts today."

Wyatt kissed the top of his sister's head. She smiled at him and then went back to where their parents were watching her kids.

"Now, for those wanting to know about my mate. Yes, I found her at what would have been her first Hunt. Would have been because she was not there. She feared the Hunt so much, she ran away. And she didn't just run away, she RAN. AWAY." Wyatt smiled at her. "The other day, she told me that if she had just been at the Hunt, we would have had ten years together. But I would not want her any other way than how she is. And if she had not spent 10 years in the Marines, she would not be the woman she is today."

Malachi turned and looked at his daughter in surprise.

"Luna, go to your mate," Stephen said, loud enough for her father to hear him. Smiling at Wyatt she made her way around to the stage.

Wyatt watched her as she came to him. Teuf followed. "For ten years, I watched her. Sounds a little creepy, I know. Not quite two months ago, she came to my pack when she got out of the Marines. She came here, because she was no longer welcome in her own pack."

As Celeste started to go up the stairs, he held his arm out to her and she snuggled in next to him, as she wrapped her arms around him, he held her close. With his free hand, he lifted her chin as he looked down at her. Standing on her toes, she met his kiss. Even after he lifted his head, he continued to hold her close, one hand at her waist and the other on her tattooed arm.

"As I said earlier, things will be different. We are having a non-hunt today. And I see some of you are getting a little antsy. Gentlemen, you will find that all the ladies have escorts with them. They are all mated warriors. And they will stay with her until she dismisses them. There are activities set up all over town."

"Instead of hunting your mate, you are going to have to do something that is even harder. You are going to have to win her. Ladies, make them earn your affection. That victory will be so much sweeter. Yes, mother, I see you." He smiled at where Elizabeth now stood with Jill, Sammi and a few other women ready for a day of final preparations for the mating ceremony that night. "You girls have appointments. I'm handing you over to the girls, and I will see you tonight."

He lifted her with one arm around her waist and she moved her arms around his neck. They exchanged another light kiss. He then sat her down and she was still looking up at him when a large hand reached across her shoulder and tapped him on his.

"Are you done with my girlfriend?" Jill asked.

"I'm never going to be done with your girlfriend." Wyatt rested his forehead on hers as tears filled her eyes. "Please don't take my mother to any strip bars."

"Not today," Celeste promised. "I have a very important date tonight."

"Yes, you do," Jill said as he pulled her away and tossed her onto his shoulder. "Come on, girlfriend, we have a ceremony to get you ready for." He looked over at Wynne, "Come on, little girlfriend. You have no idea how long I've waited for this."

Celeste knew that if there was anyone more excited for the ceremony tonight, it was Jill. He loved reminding her that for ten years she had sworn that she did not want a mate. And yet for ten years, she treasured every letter and gift that she received from Wonderpup.

Celeste could feel Wyatt watching her as Jill carried her off the stage with the other women following. She lifted her head and watched as he turned back to the microphone. "Tonight, at eight, back here, that lovely lady who has been kidnapped by her best friend will become my Luna. You are all invited to join us. Please, everyone, go have fun. Unless my mother has recruited you to help set up for tonight."

51 - WEREWOLF COUNCIL

Wyatt was on his way to the conference room on the bottom floor of the pack house. As he came around the corner, Gunny was waiting for him where he had asked for the Marine to meet him.

"Are you ready for this?" Gunny asked as he typed something on the tablet.

"Dealing with a bastard who impregnated his own child? The Luna ceremony? My mate's father? The Council in general? Or walking into a Council meeting with a..." He paused and looked around him before putting a hand to the side of his mouth and whispering "human?"

Gunny gave a little laugh at the dramatics.

"I'm sorry, you'll have to be a little more specific."

"Let's just say, today."

"All of the parts individually, I'm good. Did I mention the non-hunt? Or the Alphas that have complained?" Wyatt opened the door and held it open and as Gunny walked by, he whispered, "With it all one day, I need one of your bar tabs."

Gunny chuckled. "You want the card?"

"I better not." Wyatt shut the door behind him and pointed to an empty chair against the wall behind his own chair. "Ladies, Gentlemen, Elders. Thank you for coming."

"What is he doing here?" Malachi asked, emphasizing he.

"I'm sorry, Alpha Malachi, there are several men in here," Wyatt said, sitting down. "Please be more specific."

"The human," another older Alpha sneered.

"Gunny? He's the head of security for the human town. It is still on my pack lands. Everyone living, or currently staying, in my territory is under my protection. This includes every one of you and your pack members. Forgive me for taking my responsibilities seriously."

There was a silence in the room as the ones objecting were put in their place.

"Are you not afraid of him exposing the were-community o the rest of the world?" Sirius asked and Wyatt knew he asked because others were wondering. He himself already knew the answer.

"And put his wife and pups in danger? No. That I do not fear."

"Is he mated to Kiana?" Alpha Palaui asked.

"I do not know what that is," Wyatt said honestly.

"Alpha," Gunny said, "Sammi's given name is Kiana. But that name only brings her pain as she was forced from her pack, because the moon goddess deemed this mere human worthy of such a gift."

"You took in a rogue?" another Alpha said with a sneer.

"My pack is welcome to all. Marines. Spouses. Pups," Alpha James said with a growl. "Whether they come to us from a loving pack." The Marine general looked at Malachi. "Or the pathetic ones that will abandon their children for making their own choices."

Malachi stood up with his claws and fangs extending, taking the insult that was thrown at him.

"Malachi, sit down," Elder Alpha Marcus said exerting his authority. "You are here only as a courtesy."

His attention turned to the older man. "The title is Alpha."

"And mine is Elder Alpha. You have not held the title of Alpha since you gave control over to your son. And he has done a great job of running the pack while his sister was away serving her country."

Malachi got angrier. The Elder Alpha stood up, pushing out his authority over causing the other Alphas and Lunas in the room to offer their necks in submission. Malachi himself sat down under the pressure of such power. The Elder Alpha sat back down and turned to the Senior Elder Alpha Davis.

"Sirius, since we are discussing your sister, what are her plans for running the pack?" The senior asked.

"Senior Alpha Davis, what we have discussed, and with the approval of the Council, is that I will continue to run the Silver Lake Pack. Any major decisions are still hers to make. And when my youngest is old enough, she will begin to train to be Alpha of the pack." Sirius said and could feel the heat and anger coming from his father.

"How long has this been going on?" Malachi demanded of his son.

"Since the true Alpha, chosen and marked by the moon goddess, turned 25. Olivia also bears the markings. Therefore, I think it only right to train her as the next Alpha."

The senior members of the Council looked at each, having a silent discussion amongst themselves.

"We have no problem with this plan." Marcus said. "I assume that the reason you are here is because she is busy getting ready for her Luna ceremony?"

"Yes, Alpha Marcus." Sirius confirmed.

"Very well, let us move on."

"Begging your pardon, Elder Alpha Marcus," Wyatt said, "there is one more issue concerning my Luna that I would like to clear up with her father." He waited for the nod telling him to proceed. "Malachi, ten years ago I found my mate while on your lands in your house during the Hunt. She ran away from the fear of the Hunt and your reluctance to change. Tonight, ten years to the day, from when I learned who she was, she will become my Luna. Will you present her?"

"No. She abandoned me," Malachi said.

"She believed she was saving herself," Sirius corrected. "You abandoned her, and my other sisters, a long time ago. I would be honored, to present her."

"As would I." Alpha James added.

"I was going to offer to present her, but I am sure that either of these will do a fine job," Marcus offered.

Anger radiated off Wyatt and it was all aimed at one man in the room. Those around him shifted uncomfortably. His glare did not falter when Gunny clapped his hand on Wyatt's shoulder. And when the cellphone that Gunny held in front of him began to ring, he barely glanced at the screen. Then did a double take as he saw the puddy tat tattoo as the picture with Celeste above her number.

"Hello, my love."

"Since Gunny messaged me to call him, and you're answering, it is not going well," Came from the other end of the line with a familiar buzzing sound.

Grinning, Wyatt asked "Where are you? Don't lie, I know the sound of a tattoo gun."

"Then why did you ask?" He could hear the grin in her voice.

"Is cookie monster really part of getting ready?"

"No, but the other one is," she replied. "My mother got a rose."

"You're a very bad influence. I love that," he loved hearing her laugh. "Your father will not present you."

She was silent for a moment and then she quietly told him, "If he can't support me, I don't want him there." The laughter had been replaced by pain.

"Ever?" Wyatt asked softly.

"Ever," Celeste confirmed.

"I'm sorry, my love."

"It's okay. It's not you."

"It's not you either, baby. It's his issue, not yours."

"I love you, Wyatt."

"Love you, too, Sles." He heard the call disconnect and suddenly felt empty. Handing the phone back to Gunny, he admitted, "I don't know if I like you having that picture of her."

"Oddly enough, that's the same thing my wife says. It's changing tonight," He admitted.

"Thank you." Wyatt then turned his attention back to Malachi. "Can you support your daughter, as my Luna? And as the Alpha of the Silver Lake Pack?"

"Maybe as your Luna."

"Can you support my Luna completely without question?"

"Not without question," Malachi sneered. "Have you seen her?"

"I have. I have seen every one of her tattoos. Gunny, make sure that he is off pack lands within the hour."

"Yes, Alpha," Gunny said standing up and walking towards Malachi.

"Really? Going to make the human do your dirty work."

"Half hour," Wyatt said coldly.

"I'd rather be home anyway," Malachi said standing up.

"And where is that going to be?" Sirius asked, before his father could say anything else, he added, "You will not step foot on Silver Lake lands until I have a chance to speak with the Alpha. I do not plan to broach any conversation other than to congratulate her on being mated to Alpha Wyatt."

"Malachi," Senior Elder Davis advised, "I suggest that you throw yourself on the mercy of another Alpha."

Malachi looked around at the other Alphas and Lunas who all indicated one way or another that their lands were not open to him. He finally looked at Sirius, "Why?"

"Seriously? You want to know why?" Sirius stood up and faced his father. "You allowed two of my sisters to be raped and then you simply handed them over to the men who had abused them."

"It was their mates!" Malachi countered.

"Yes, their mates. Aria was beaten and raped by her mate. And every time she came home or called begging to come home or get help, you sent her back to him. Did you know that he forced her to have sex with other people? Notice that I said people? Not men. Did you even listen to her when she told you that she was pregnant? That she didn't know who the father was. She begged to stay with you and mom. At least until she had the pup. And you sent her back."

"She died just a few days before Sky did her Hunt. Then, after hearing horror stories and burying her sister, she was raped by her mate. It was two years before you would even listen to her. And why? Because Celeste left. You always said that of all your girls, Celeste would be the one to take on the world. And win."

"Guess what? She did take on the world. And not only did she win, but she also made it a better place. Did you know that the only reason that Portia did not run away herself is because both Alpha Wyatt and I guaranteed her that she would not be in any type of danger? Not you. Not her father. Not the man who is supposed to protect her from the world."

"But do you know how you really failed your daughters? When we hosted the Hunt and Celeste left, what was your biggest concern? How badly you would look that your daughter was not there. The reason why did not bother you. Your reputation was more important than your daughters. Look at where you are now. Your daughter, who ran away from you, receives more respect in this room than you do. For over a month, this pack has called her their Luna. And you, Alpha, are barely above a rogue."

Malachi looked around and discovered that what his son said was true. His reputation was in tatters. He was one step away from being a rogue. He currently was an outcast. And his wayward daughter was highly respected. He should have chosen his words carefully. He should have thought about what he would say. But anger and embarrassment ruled him now.

"Maybe the slut is not as bad as I think."

At the word "slut," Wyatt stood up and Gunny caught his eye. Though they did not have the mind link, the two veterans had a good understanding. Wyatt gave a small nod and Gunny acknowledged it.

Then he grabbed Malachi by the head and smashed his face hard into his raised knee. While he was still stunned, handcuffs were put on his wrists behind his back. He then raised the werewolf arms high forcing his head onto the conference table.

With the prefilled syringe, he injected Malachi with a dose of wolves' bane, Gunny warned, "Don't ever call my Luna a slut again."

"May I make a suggestion, Alpha Wyatt?" the general grinned. "Since he does not know Celeste as some of the rest of us do, perhaps, he should spend some time getting to know his daughter again. If not from herself, possibly with someone she served with?"

"Just not that human," Malachi said.

Wyatt smiled from the general to Gunny. "Is Jack at the house?"

"If not, I know where to find him." Gunny said, leading the man out of the room.

Once the door closed Wyatt and James began laughing.

"Jack?" Sirius asked with a grin. "As in gay human, Jack?"

"The very same," James confirmed.

"Actually," Wyatt clarified, "the gay human that's mated to a werecat."

52 - INK AND LACE

Celeste had not intended to get the Cookie Monster tattoo; just the Crystal River Pack crest. But she had heard something in Wyatt's voice when he had asked if getting it was important for the Luna ceremony. Maybe not for that, but for them to be mated. She had promised. It was a silly promise. But one that she intended to keep.

And she needed something to help her get over the hurt her dad had inflicted. She did the one thing that she was good at with her father. She rebelled. When Corky was done with the Crest and it had been treated and covered, she asked if he would do one more, just a little one.

"Anything that you want," he said as he set up for her next tattoo.

"You're just going to roll over and do anything she wants?" Whitney asked from where she sat near the door, still surprised to find that her sister had a tattoo.

"Yes ma'am," he said, accepting the pattern from his apprentice. "She has some nice artwork here. And some very expensive pieces. The fact that she is letting me do three pieces within a month tells me that she approves of my work. Since she's wanting to finish out the sleeves on her legs, she will probably be one of my top patrons. What she wants, she gets."

"What can I say?" Celeste teased. "Tattoo artists love me. And my money."

"Personality helps too," Michael added from where he put finishing touches on the rose on Aislinn.

About 45 minutes later, they headed to the dress shop. It was the first time that most of them had seen the dress. It was a stunner. She stepped out in the middle of the room in the white and sapphire blue dress. Originally, the blue accents were going to be a lighter shade. But when Wyatt had given her the first set of jewelry and he loved the sapphire on her, she had asked if it could be changed.

The sheer white neckline was shallow and ran from one shoulder to the other, a fine line of sparkling crystals running across it. The occasional crystals on the sheer overlay covered the whole dress giving just a slight sparkle when she moved. White silk created a sweetheart top of the bodice which flowed into a long form fitting sheath that without the high slit on the left side would have made it impossible to walk. The overlay changed at the waist, small tucks made it flow out allowing for movement and still covering everything, including her open leg.

Starting just below the waist the overlay also began to transition with an ombre tone ending in sapphire blue. The crystals also changed with the material. The silk remained white except for a thin strip of sapphire blue at the waist. Sapphire blue shoes peeked out from under the dress.

Viviane held out a hand to help her step up onto the small round platform in the center of the viewing room. As she stepped up, the stilettos that she wore were exposed. As was the sapphire and white garter.

"How tall are those heels?" Laura asked.

"Six inches" Celeste admitted. "He's a foot taller than me. I need something to help me out."

"Show them the back," Wynne half-whispered.

Smiling, Celeste turned around and showed her exposed back. The small half inch sheer strips that went around her shoulders had the same crystals on both edges as they barely went to her back before attaching to the side of the dress. The sides of the dress were just off her back and plunged down deep. At her waist it began to gently curve in before ending just below her wolf. Her entire back was exposed showing the intricate back piece. Including the new Crest showing all three packs that she had lived in.

"What are these little loops?" her mom asked, tugging on a white eyelet that was barely visible in the edges.

"Fine platinum chains that will hang down her back," Elizabeth explained. "The shorter ones have sapphire hearts in the center and help keep the dress on. The longer ones swoop down and hang loose."

Celeste looked at her with tears in her eyes. "He gave me the jewelry," she said softly.

"He insisted that you needed more sapphires," his mother grinned. "And he needed more oxford shirts."

If she had been anyone else, she probably would have blushed. Instead, she grinned back. "I discovered that high stilettos, jewelry and one of his shirts renders him speechless."

"I'll have to try that with his father," Elizabeth said and had her daughters cringing.

"Not something that I want to think about mom," Wenona said and Whitney agreed.

"How do you think that you got here?" Celeste asked them as she met their eyes in the mirror.

"How do you think that you got here?" Dionne countered.

"Since there's thirteen of us, I'm pretty sure that my parents have fucked thirteen times," Celeste answered. "Possibly more."

Sky looked at her like she was about to lose her lunch. "I'm pregnant. Don't make me think about my parents having sex."

"So, I'm guessing that you mail ordered all your pups?" Celeste asked as she stepped down to go change.

"Well, no, but…." Sky said blushing.

Sammi could see where this was going and started shaking her head while advising, "Don't ask."

"And you're just going to tell us that you two have broken in the entire top floor?" Whitney laughed.

"Except the nursery. Felt a little weird fucking in there," She admitted from inside the changing room. "Recently discovered that we accidentally made a porn in the hallway."

"How did you do that?" Andi asked.

"Security cameras," Celeste laughed.

"I'm changing the subject," Whitney said. "What is my brother's favorite tattoo?"

Sammi and Wynne looked at each other. "Puddy tat." They both said and then started laughing.

"I think you're probably right." Celeste agreed from the other side of the door.

"What's puddy tat?" Elizabeth asked.

A very naked Celeste stepped out of the changing room and pointed to her crotch. "I taught I taw a puddy tat." Laughing at their shocked faces, she pulled her t-shirt back on and grabbed her shorts.

"You really do have tattoos everywhere," Wenona said, shaking her head.

"I don't have any internal ones," Celeste said, fastening her shorts.

"They can do that?" Aislinn asked.

"Doesn't Jill have one?" Wynne asked.

"Yes," Jill said, speaking for the first time.

"You're a guy," the shop assistant said.

"My husband sure hopes I am." He teased with a wink and a grin.

"You're gay?" several said at once.

"Not me. But I'm pretty certain my husband is," he quipped.

"Dear," Sammi said, shifting to look at him, "you're the one with the tattoo reading 'Place dick here,' are you sure it's Jack that's the gay one in the relationship?"

"She makes a good point," Wynne teased.

"You hush up, little girlfriend."

"I'm already being replaced," Celeste winked at Wynne.

Jill walked over and wrapped her up in his arms and kissed the top of her head. "You'll always be my girlfriend, and my favorite dog." He looked over at Teuf who whined. "Well, aren't you two a package deal? She's my favorite so by default, you are too."

Teuf seemed to agree and curled back up.

"And you are our favorite cat."

53 - PRECIOUS MOMENTS

Jack looked at the man sitting across from him at the picnic table. He was uncomfortable around Jack and that made the human grin just a little more. Celeste's father had been thoroughly chastised, first by his son and then by Gunny. So, he decided that he would take a different approach.

Malachi slowly drank his tea, still partially numb from the injection. Jack had seen this reaction before and knew that he should wait until the fog began to clear. He logged into the cloud storage that Celeste used for pictures. They all had access to just about everything for each other. While in service, they had formed a little family. They were each some kind of outcast and found comradery with each other.

Pulling up pictures from her boot camp, he sat the tablet in front of the man.

"Did you know that she graduated top of her class?" Jack asked slowly scrolling through the pictures. "Not just boot, but her MOS training. And then, when she trained as a handler. She's damn good at what she does. Or, I should say, did. But, from what I hear, and see, she's one hell of a Luna."

Jack was glad when Malachi took over scrolling. Even happier when he went back a few pictures.

"That's not the one that's with her," Malachi said pointing at a picture of Celeste carrying Rory on her shoulders.

"No," the Marine confirmed. "That's Rory. She was a shepherd Malinois mix. She survived Afghanistan, only to be poisoned and have her throat slit by a wolf. Someone much like yourself that refused to accept Sles for who she is. He might as well have killed her. Much like you."

"I never meant to hurt her."

"Don't we all say shit like that when we find out we're wrong? You refused to help your other daughters. You would not listen to her. You were more concerned with what other people thought about you, than the hell that your daughters were living in."

Jack reached over and pulled up the hidden file. He put in the password without even having to see the keyboard that popped up on the bottom of the screen.

Malachi was suddenly confronted with the abuse his other daughter had suffered. There were Advantages to being a well-respected Alpha and getting police reports and pictures of Aria was one. He covered his mouth as he saw his daughter with her body covered in black and blue bruises, cuts, scrapes and burns. Jack zoomed in on a picture and focused it on her wrist.

"Silver bonds. They would use them to restrain her while she was raped. Her husband was the Beta of the Mesa Verde pack in Mexico. The Alpha sad females as toys for himself and his pack. The pack police department could do nothing. They were ordered to destroy all the evidence. Instead, the chief reached out to Sles. This is the reason why the Council stepped in and removed the leadership."

"At least something good came of your daughter's murder."

"She killed herself," Malachi said quietly.

He flew through the pictures until he reached the one of Aria's body that was still chained to the table in the dungeon. Her arms were stretched above her, feet splayed on either side of the table, ankles in silver cuffs with short chains attached to the table.

"You could say that she killed herself. She took a lethal dose of silver and wolves' bane. She may have survived them both with treatment. But not the beating that she took with them both in her system. She couldn't take it anymore. You refused to help her. She did the only thing she thought she could."

"Sles appealed to the Council until they agreed to investigate. Luckily for them, Alpha Miguel liked to watch videos of what had been done to the women while he had sex with children. I'll be nice and I won't play any of the videos. Unfortunately, Sles had to watch some when she testified."

Malachi bolted for the nearby trashcan and lost his breakfast.

"Celeste watched it?" he asked quietly as he sat back down.

"She did. She watched the videos. Testified before the Council. Helped pick new leadership. Even assisted in the executions. And then had all the records sealed. The only thing that you will find in the official open records are the charges, victims listed as either male or female, adult or child and a number. And she kept the worst of the truth away from you and her family."

"He was executed…." Malachi was thinking about how old Celeste would have been.

"She was 19. Still a child herself. But she is the true Alpha of your pack. She had a duty to her sister and her pack. Even when we deployed, she and Sirius found a way to talk at least once a week about pack business. Not once has she ever turned her back on the Silver Lake Pack. Even though you turned your back on her."

"I never knew she did all of that."

"Of course not. You said a weak female. She may be female, but she's not weak. She's survived IED explosions, being shot, nearly being kidnapped, the death of two K9 partners, several fellow marines and other service members, four deployments, fought against the mate pull and was abandoned by her father. That's not even mentioning the shrapnel that is permanently embedded in her leg."

"You've known her a long time," Malachi surmised.

"About six years. My mate has known her longer. Jill is her best friend."

"Are you also mated to a wolf?"

"My mate is a werecat. You kicked your daughter out for being herself. Jill was kicked out of the pride for the same reason." Jack pointed to a couple at a nearby table with a warrior discreetly watching from a slight distance. "Isn't that your youngest?"

"Yes, Portia."

"The hunters were given some rules before coming out this morning. They cannot be the first to initiate any type of physical contact. It's up to her. If he touches her first, even if she is okay with it, he will be brought before Alpha Wyatt. He was a medic in the navy. He treated lots of women who were beaten, abused or raped. Add in the fact that at 17 he saved his sister from being raped. And he has four sisters. He's very protective of women and girls."

They watched the couple for a few minutes as they talked. Portia laughed at something that he said and then accepted the phone from him. She laughed even harder at whatever was on the screen and then handed him his phone back. As they started walking again, the young man tucked his phone back into his pocket and Portia tentatively took his hand.

"Wyatt's right." Jack said quietly. "It's harder to win a mate than just take them. Tell me, Malachi, how did you meet Aislinn?"

"The Hunt," he said, remembering the year of her Hunt. "It was my fourth and her first. I remember how excited I was. They led the maidens through the fields first. As we started through the first field, I smelled her scent almost immediately. I had to find her. Once I did, I took her back to the room I was staying in and made love to her."

"Have you ever heard her side of the story?"

From the look on his face, Jack could tell that Malachi had never considered that his mate would have a different version of events. After several minutes of contemplation, Malachi reached out to his mate.

Aislinn, I need to ask you something.

Ok. Even through the mate's link, he could tell that she had been drinking. Her Irish accent came out when she drank. What do ya want ta know?

Tell me how you remember our Hunt.

Oh, Malachi, I've had just enough Margarita to do that. Me mum told me to give in ta me mate. And that was you. Ya caught me, and I was scared. You were so much bigger. And I had seen plenty of naked men. If they were big in body, ya were big in other places.

Ya took me back to ya room and bedded me. I'd never touched a mon before. Nor been touched by one. I knew it would hurt. Ya were gentle. In yer own way. It hurt. Ya marked me as ya came. Then ya went to sleep. It wasn't until the next day that I even knew ya name.

Malachi sat there for a moment. Surely, I told you my name.

Ya never did. Yer da, when he called ya up, he said me son Malachi has met his mate. And ya drug me up, an me da, he blessed us. Me mum, she asked if I was okay, I said I was. An then, I left wit ya, that were that. When we got back to yer pack, yer mum took me oop an made me stay in me own room until the ceremony. Ya barely spoke to me in those two weeks.

No, I couldn't get enough of you. Malachi said.

Aye. Ya snuck into me room at night. I was barely 17. Had been told to never deny me mate. What could I do? I didn't know what ya wanted. Other than between me legs. I didn't know what I should do.

Were you scared, my mate?

Aye. I was terrified.

Why did you never say anything?

What would I say? I was a virgin and knew nothing. I was the daughter of a Gamma, mated to an Alpha.

I'm sorry, Aislinn.

Tis in the past. Oh! We have a bottle of Jameson.

Go enjoy, my love.

54 - LESSONS FROM A LITTLE GIRL

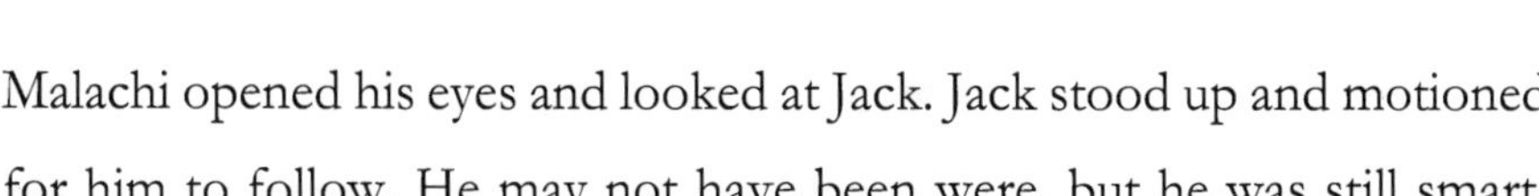

Malachi opened his eyes and looked at Jack. Jack stood up and motioned for him to follow. He may not have been were, but he was still smart. He could read people. And he knew when someone was hurting. They stepped out of the pavilion and Jack shielded his eyes.

"Sun is so bright, it could damn near make you cry," Jack said and Malachi agreed. "Something I'd like you to see." Jack led the way down to a little park area where several pups ran around playing. As they approached, a little girl lit up and ran towards them. Jack scooped her up and she wrapped her arms around his neck.

"Who's that?" she asked, indicating Malachi.

"This is Alpha Malachi. He's Aunt Sles' dad."

"Are you going to present her?"

"I don't think she wants me to."

"Of course, she does," the little girl said. "When I get older and I take a mate, my dad's going to present me." She beamed at Jack, "Aren't you?"

"If that is what you want." He sat her back down on the ground. "Go tell Miss Eliza that you're going with me." She ran off towards a middle-aged woman. The woman looked over and waved at Jack. The girl ran back and grabbed both men by the hand.

"Daddy, can we go see the house?"

"Yes, we can. How much longer until we get to be a family?"

"Twelve days!" she squealed.

"Did you introduce yourself to Alpha Malachi?"

"I'm Amberlee."

"Little lady," Jack said gently.

She let go of their hands and stepped in front of Malachi and offered her hand while also tipping her head slightly to the side as a sign of submission. "My name is Amberlee Nicole Johnson-Williams. It's nice to meet you, Alpha Malachi."

Malachi took her hand gently. "It's nice to meet you Miss Amberlee Nicole Johnson-Williams."

She smiled and then went back between them, grabbing their hands again. "Is Daddy Jill with Aunt Sles?"

"He is. Do you know what that means?"

"We get to see the house before he does!"

"Exactly," her dad confirmed as they turned down a residential street.

"Daddy Jill?" Malachi asked, a little confused.

"Most little girls only get one dad. I'm going to get two!" Amberlee said excitedly.

"His real name is Matthew, but he's gone by Jill pretty much since we got married." At the confused look on Malachi' face, Jack gave a small laugh.

"It's like Jack and Jill," Amberlee said. "My first parents were Amber and Nicholas Johnson. They were killed last year in a rogue attack. I'm an Omega. Nobody wanted me. But last time Daddy and Daddy Jill were here, they came with Aunt Sles. Daddy Jill said that he fell in love with me before he ever saw me."

"He did. And I'm glad." Jack said as he motioned towards a quaint little ranch-style house.

"And you can't tell Daddy Jill no," she said as Jack smiled as he opened the front door. "Can I go see my room?"

"Yes, little lady, you may. Right down that hall." Jack pointed and she took off running. "I should tell her no running in the house, but I'm excited for her to see her room." He said as they followed down the hall.

She popped back out of her bedroom; her face was all lit up with excitement and adoration. "Daddy!"

"Do you like it?" he asked as they joined her.

"I love it, Daddy!"

Her room was the only one in the whole house that had any furniture in it. When Wyatt had seen how quickly the pair had bonded to Amberlee, and she to them, he offered them a place to stay. And for them to be able to adopt her. It was that excitement of becoming a family that had them, Gunny and Doc up until three that morning making her room perfect.

Malachi looked into the room and found a wrought iron four poster canopy bed with several layers of sheer curtains on the canopy rails. The silver iridescent and pink curtain sets were tied to the posts, while the purple ones hung free all the way around. It had a light purple dust ruffle and a pale pink comforter. And the head of the bed was stacked high with pillows and stuffed animals.

A doll house stood in one corner and a play kitchen in the other. A dresser stood between the two doors on the wall opposite the bed, he assumed one was the closet and the other a bathroom. On the wall with the door that they now stood in, was a princess toy box and small dress up area complete with plastic jewelry and heels, dresses, uniforms and a full-length mirror.

The hardwood floors were sparkling, and the room still held the smell of fresh paint. Now that he looked a little closer, the walls were the lightest pink, just barely away from being white. Malachi looked at Jack who was smiling at his daughter. The little girl came and grabbed his hand and pulled him to the dress up area.

"Alpha Malachi, will you put my necklace on me?" she asked, handing him a plastic necklace.

"You didn't wait for me," a deep male voice said softly from the doorway.

"I should have. But I thought maybe Malachi needed a little distraction after the day he's had," Jack replied.

Malachi finished putting on the necklace and watched as the little girl twirled in front of the mirror. She stopped and looked at the door. "Daddy Jill!"

The Alpha turned and found a large black man with his head resting on Jack's shoulder and arms wrapped around his waist.

"Hey, Pumpkin. Do you like it?" Jill asked, smiling with as much pride as Jack had.

"I love it, Daddies!" She ran and hugged their legs. Jill rubbed her back while Jack gently stroked her hair.

Jill handed her a small jewelry box. "Why don't you ask Alpha Malachi if he'll help you with this?"

She took the little black velvet box and walked over to where Malachi sat on a stool. Handing over the still unopened box, she quietly asked, "Alpha Malachi, will you please help me with this?"

"Yes, ma'am, I will." He accepted the box and opened it. Inside was a platinum necklace with a small sapphire heart pendant on it. He removed the plastic necklace and then replaced it with the new one. "It looks really pretty on you."

"It matches what Aunt Sles will be wearing." He reached behind him and produced a small hanging dress bag. "It also matches this."

She stood uncertain for a moment before slowly stepping forward to take the bag. Malachi helped her hang it on the dress up rack and unzip it. Inside was a white satin dress with sapphire satin peeking from underneath the skirt. There were also small bows on the sleeves and a sash with a large bow on the back made of the same blue.

"You spoil her," Jack said as he turned his head and kissed his mate.

Jill kissed him back and then smiled at his husband. "Not me. Wyatt." He rubbed his nose against Jack's cheek, leaving his scent on his mate. "All the nieces got the same necklace and a matching dress. All the nephews got tie tacks and cufflinks."

"You've been drinking," Jack said, enjoying the nuzzling.

"A little bit," Jill admitted.

"You only scent me when you've been drinking."

"Complaining?" Jill asked, nipping his ear.

Jack turned in his husband's arm and put his own arms around the other man's neck. "A little."

"For me scenting you?" Jill asked between kisses. "Or not scenting you?"

"Not," Jack admitted as his mate inhaled his scent. Jill purred deep in his chest. His eyes met Malachi who motioned that he was good with their daughter. Smiling his thanks, he led Jack to the master bedroom on the opposite side of the house.

55- THE BACKYARD

"I like it when Daddy Jill purrs." Amberlee told Malachi. "It means that he's happy and he loves us."

"It does." Malachi agreed. "Does anyone make fun of you for having two dads?"

"Not at the orphanage. Wyatt said that I was to tell him if anyone ever gave me any shit about my daddies. No matter if it's for having two, or them not being wolf."

"Should you be saying shit?"

"That's the only time I can. How come you're mad at Sles?"

"She did something that I didn't agree with."

"But you still love her. Right?"

"Of course, I do. I love all my kids. I have thirteen altogether. And I say that I love them the same. But secretly, I do have a favorite."

"Is it your oldest boy? Timothy at the orphanage said that the oldest boy is always the favorite of the Alpha."

"Actually, Celeste was always my favorite. I always thought that of all my girls, all my kids, Celeste would be the one to go out and take on the world. And win." He booped her nose to emphasize win.

"Is that why you got so mad at her? Because she was your favorite and it hurt so much?"

Malachi sat stunned for a moment. Was that why he got so mad? How could a six-year-old be so much smarter than himself?

"Don't you think that you hurt her too?" Amberlee asked him.

"I probably did," He admitted as tears came to his eyes again.

"Aunt Sles won't let any of orphans call her Luna. She said that she is the mother of the pack, and until we have a family again, we belong to her." Malachi saw the tears in her eyes and could hear them in her little voice. "She said she knows how bad it hurts to lose your family. To lose your parents. It's not anything that we as her littles should know about. We can go to her anytime we need. When my daddies had to leave, I was so sad."

"She came and got me, and we made cookies in the big kitchen. A whole lot of cookies. She said that the best way to make yourself feel better, is to make someone else feel better. So, we made cookies and took them to the hospital and the orphanage. And the police and fire stations. Both here, and in the other town. I felt better after that. And when I talked to my daddies, they were so proud of me. Someday, I'm going to be able to make cookies without a recipe too. And I'm going to make people happy with my cookies."

"Oatmeal raisin and chocolate chip?" Malachi asked, his voice thick with emotion.

"Yeah. And she said that some Friday, she'll help me make them, and we'll take them to the warriors when they are done with Saturday morning training. But she says that I can't go during training because they say things that a little girl should not hear. Uncle Wyatt said that she is one of the worst."

"Worst fighters?" Malachi asked, a little confused. Before she had left, there was no one in the pack that could take her down.

"Worst potty mouths," Amberlee clarified. "Uncle Wyatt is the only one that can take her down. Sometimes, he can't even do it. Want to see my backyard? Uncle Wyatt said that he'd have them put in a fort with a swing set and a little area for a garden."

She led the way out of her room and to the sliding door in the living room. As she was moving the security bar to open the door, Malachi saw the two men in the kitchen with drinks from a local coffee shop. They both nodded and smiled in acknowledgement as Amberlee rambled on about her Alpha and Luna as she dragged the older man outside.

"Alpha says that he always gives kids things like this in the backyard. But Aunt Sles says it's usually only the swingset and that Alpha is spoiling me."

"And who do you believe?" he asked as he stepped behind the swing to push her.

"Aunt Sles." She giggled as Malachi pushed her. "I want to go really high!"

After swinging for a few minutes, Amberlee took him over to where the small garden and greenhouse was set up. She was telling him what would go where.

"My parents worked on the farm. That's where they were killed. Some rogues were trying to steal some food, and my parents walked in on them. Since I'm an Omega, I will probably work there too when I get older. Or maybe I'll go to the Marines."

"What do your daddies say?" Malachi asked, suddenly wondering how many kids were in his own pack orphanage. He was pretty sure that his son knew them by name.

"Daddy Jill says that I can do anything that I want. Except for mate with someone who treats me bad."

"And Daddy Jack? What does he say?"

"That she can do anything she wants and marry anyone that she wants." Jack said from the doorway where they had been watching for the last few minutes. "The first time they treat her wrong, I'm beating the hell out of them. And there won't be a third time."

He may not be were, but Malachi knew that he meant what he said. Jack would allow her mate to learn from his first mistake. But if it happened again, he would kill them. With 22 years in the Marines, he had the skills and knowledge to do so. And the protectiveness of a father.

"Do you know where my daughter is?" Malachi asked suddenly. "I need to fix something that I messed up."

The two men smiled.

"I need to get Pumpkin to her hair appointment. Sles should be there."

56 - SPLIT ENDS AND NEW BEGINNINGS

The ladies in the hair salon cheered when Jill walked in with Amberlee on his back. After the Margaritas at the Mexican restaurant, and a toast of Jameson, they had wine at the nail salon. Wyatt had sent champagne to the hair salon. Thankfully, they were all were, and would be sober by the ceremony.

When Jack entered there were some calls that it was girls only.

"I promise, ladies, I am not staying. I'm just the driver." Jack stepped out of the way and Malachi stepped inside. The whole place went still and silent.

"I promise, I'm not staying either. I just came to beg forgiveness from my daughter." Malachi looked at Celeste and fought back tears. "All my daughters. And my wife. I never listened to you. I never considered what you went through. I never even considered that you might want to do something other than get married and have pups. To become a Luna or the wife of a Beta or Gamma."

"I never really considered that you had hopes and dreams of your own. Celeste, you tried to tell me. You weren't ready for a mate. You wanted to see what was out past the pack. There was a whole world out there. I always said that you would be the one of my girls to take on the world and win. It was pointed out to me earlier, and shown to me several times, that not only did you win, but you also made it better."

"I should have listened. I'm listening now and I ask that you forgive me. I know what you did for Aria. You were so damn young, but you went after the truth. Not just for her, but the other victims. You have helped improve the pack, after seeing a few things here, I see what you did through Sirius. I should have given you more credit. You have the markings. You were chosen by the moon goddess to lead our pack. I should not have questioned her."

"Sky," he said started as he turned his attention to his next daughter, "you had every right to fear your Hunt. I should have listened to you. I should have listened to Aria. If I had, she might still be alive. If I had, it might not have taken so many years before you could let your mate even touch you. If I had listened to you, let you come home and get to know him, instead of forcing you to go with him, maybe, just maybe, things would have been much better for you."

"My beautiful, wonderful wife," Malachi turned to Aislinn. "I have realized that I was no better. I just took you to a more private place before forcing myself on you. Don't tell me that I didn't. You didn't even know my name. Just like we did to our girls, you were taught to submit to your mate, no matter what happened. And to submit the instant he found you. Just because it's in a bedroom with candles, doesn't mean it's not rape."

"Portia, I saw you earlier with your mate. I'm assuming that was your mate?" Malachi asked his youngest and she nodded. Just like the rest of the women in the room, she too was crying. "If you want to come home for a while, you may. I am not going to force you to go with him. It's up to you. It should have always been up to you all."

"And for all my girls, you are welcome to come home anytime. Whether you are my daughter, or my son is being an asshole. If he's being an asshole, I'm sending Jack to deal with him. I now understand why you all wanted to go to Council events and meetings. You wanted to find your mate before you had to do a Hunt. And most of you did. Because I was not smart enough to listen to you."

"I just hope that all of you will forgive me."

Celeste was the first to move, she went over to him and hugged him tightly. He returned the hug and finally gave in to the tears that had been threatening for quite a while.

"I'm so sorry," he whispered in her ear. "I missed you so, so much."

"I've missed you too," she sobbed. "There were so many times that I just needed my daddy."

"I'm here now. I'm here now," he said as he cupped the back of her head.

"You should hang out with gay men more often," she laughed as her sisters joined the hug.

"Amberlee is pretty smart herself," Malachi admitted as he kissed the top of heads around him. "Celeste, do you still want me to present you for your Luna ceremony?"

No longer able to find her voice, she simply nodded. She caught both Jack and Jill's eyes and mouthed thank you. They both smiled back at her.

57 - OFFICE CHAIR

Celeste smiled at Paul, the current warrior manning the elevator, as she stepped out onto the top floor. She went straight for Wyatt's office, where voices and laughter flowed out of the open door. She stepped inside and looked over at the group sitting on the couches and chairs. Her Marines, brother and the Marine Corps Alpha were crammed onto the couch and chairs. Including the ones that had been pulled from her office on this floor.

"I've been married long enough to know that when you come back from the hair salon, I should tell you that you look good." Gunny said, tipping his beer at her. "Which you do. But I also recognize red rimmed eyes from crying."

"If there is such a thing, they were good tears." She looked at Sirius. "Dad said that you tore him a new one."

"Let's just say, he knew that I was not happy with him."

"Most of the Council was not," Alpha James said. "Does your dad not know that you spearheaded everything against Mesa Verde?"

"My dad and Sirius just found out today," she said while taking Doc's beer.

"What did you have to do with Mesa Verde?" Sirius asked and the other Alphas in the room looked at him like he had lost his mind.

"Come on Sirius," Gunny said standing up. "I think she wants some time with her mate. And I think it's time that you learn just how badass your sister really is." He looked at Wyatt. "Don't mess up her hair."

"Feel free to do anything I would do," Doc teased as he closed the door behind them.

Celeste turned around and looked at Wyatt. His eyes followed her hands as they moved to the button on her Jean shorts. His eyes darkened as the material slid down her legs and she stepped out of them and her shoes. She leaned in close, and he put his hands on her waist.

Stopping just a breath away from his lips, she softly commanded, "Hands."

He groaned but he obeyed, placing his hands on the arms of the chair. As they kissed, she undid his belt and pants. He lifted his hips to help her as she pushed his slacks and boxers down. He heard the now familiar sound of a condom package and then felt her hands on his throbbing cock.

"I need to touch you," Wyatt growled against her lips.

"No," she said as she straddled his lap. She braced herself with her hands on his shoulders as she lowered herself onto him. They both moaned as she took his full length into her. She began to slowly move on him, slow methodical movements.

"Hands." She reminded him when he reached for her hips. As she moved on him, she held his eyes with hers. She could feel her orgasm growing and she smiled at him. She leaned in, rubbing her breasts and hardened nipples against his chest. Wyatt groaned as he tightened his grip on the chair arms.

"I'm so much more sensitive on my heat. Even with the suppressants. You feel bigger. Thicker."

"You're so fucking tight." He gritted out, the chair arm cracking under the pressure of his grip.

"I'm going to come." She panted, "you don't come until I say you can."

She began to pulse around him, milking him, tempting him to come with her. The other arm cracked as he fought against the need, desire and want that was in him. Her body calmed down and she began moving again.

"I'm going to let you touch."

"Thank the goddess." He started moving his hands and she shook her head.

"One hand. Play with my clit." Celeste locked her hands behind his neck and leaned back. Wyatt let out a shaky breath as he placed his hand on her and began to tease her clit with his thumb. Now he could look down and see her sliding on him, her cunt stretched around him and her cum on his lap and the condom. A deep growl was ripped from his chest. That pushed her over the edge.

"Oh, goddess, Celeste."

"Not yet."

Wyatt shifted his hand on the chair and let the broken piece of the arm fall to the floor. They both looked at the broken arm. There was another growl that rumbled in his chest.

"I'm starting to really like this chair." He grumbled.

"We'll have to see what else we can do in it."

Wyatt groaned and his cock twitched inside her.

"Thinking of other things to do in this chair?" she asked huskily. He nodded and she added, "Tell me."

"Bending you over it and fucking you from behind." The pressure and intensity on her clit increased. "Watching you suck me off." Her speed picked up a little more. "Eating you out. Your heat is so fucking tempting. I just want to throw you on the bed and bury my face in your pussy for hours. That's it baby, come for me."

"Don't you come yet." She quietly commanded.

"Not yet. But just remember, I can tell you not to come either." He pointed out. "Like when I have you in this chair, legs splayed wide while I finger fuck you until I can get you to come for me again." A shiver of anticipation ran through her body. "You like that idea, don't you?"

"Yes." Celeste Admitted.

"Maybe even put my whole fist into that tight pussy." He let go of the chair and moved his hand around to her backside and popped her ass cheek. "Maybe you need a spanking." Another tremor shook her body. With her reactions to his ideas, he knew that he was playing with fire. But they were both enjoying the game.

He moved his hand and found her completely soaking wet. He slid his finger getting it wet before slipping it into her ass. The intensity of the orgasm that caused shocked them both.

"Celeste." Wyatt pleaded.

"Yes." She breathlessly gave permission, and he joined her with an earth-shattering orgasm of his own.

She pulled closer to him and pressed her body to his. He wrapped his arms around her and held her as close as he could. They were still catching their breath when there was a knock on the door.

"Celeste. We need to get you ready, and he needs to go to Stephen's house." Viviane said gently.

"Just… just a moment." Wyatt called back.

She rested her forehead on his. "We need to schedule a week with nothing during my next heat."

Wyatt gave a little chuckle. "Your next heat, we'll go somewhere with room service and no Hunts or ceremonies or obligations except you fucking me senseless and me trying to survive."

"You think that I would kill you?" she teased with a kiss.

"Well, in the maybe three hours that we have been awake and alone, we've spent all but maybe 15 minutes fucking. And most of it was started by you, my sweet mate. And that's with you on a suppressant. Pretty sure that if you were not on one, your heat would have you fucking me to death."

He grabbed her chin and brought her in for an intense kiss. "But what way to die."

There was another knock on the door. "Wyatt, leave the girl alone." His mother called out this time. "You have the rest of your life to do… yeah, all that. So, get it out here now and get your ass over to Stephen's house."

"Tuesday." They both muttered to each other.

Reluctantly, Celeste untangled herself from him and stood up. When he looked up at her, he saw his Luna. The love of his life. The other half of himself. His soul. His heart. His everything.

"I love you," Wyatt said, his voice thick with emotion.

She leaned down and kissed him. "I love you too."

"Your hair looks really good. Even better now." He brushed his finger across her cheek. "Can't wait to see you with your dress. And later, to take it off you."

"There you go, thinking with your dick." she teased.

The door opened and Elizabeth walked in holding it open as Jill walked over and scooped her up. He looked down at Wyatt's lap and his growing hard on, and then the broken chair. "Good thing I only gave her one."

Jill started walking towards the door, "Okay, girlfriend, how did make him break the chair?"

"I wouldn't let him touch or come," she said as she was carried out the office.

"If he's smart, he'll keep you away from Sammi," Jill laughed headed down the hall. "Then again, she has some really good ideas."

"Chair breaking ideas!" Wyatt called after them. "Maybe I should talk to her!"

"You should talk to Doc!" Jill and Celeste called back to him.

58 - THE GATHERING

Wyatt stepped out of Stephen's car and looked around at the transformation his sister and mother had caused. Trellises surrounded the stage, more scattered around the edges and an archway at the front of the aisle. They were all covered with fairy lights and climbing rose bushes rooted in attached planters.

Platforms were set up with rows of chairs upon them. The platforms had fairy lights along the edges, tucked just out of the way. Every other row was draped in either sapphire blue velvet or diamond white satin. The same material was draped in intertwining loops all around the base of the stage.

A steppingstone path led up the center aisle. He found himself hoping that she would be wearing some of her stilettos so he could enjoy the sight and sound of her walking across the stones. He had always liked a woman in heels, probably because of his height. But since the night that she had come to his office in nothing but heels, his shirt, and jewelry, he had loved stilettos.

He was pretty sure that she liked them also. Or at least what they did to him. She still wore her trainers, flip flops, and combat boots. But he had also noticed that her collection of stilettos had expanded to a myriad of colors. His favorite was still the sapphire blue. Followed by the black heels from the bar.

Stephen touched his shoulder, bringing him back to reality, directing his attention to his left. Cody stepped up to him in his navy dress whites. He removed his cap and offered his throat in a submission.

"Alpha."

"Ensign. I heard that you found your mate."

"Yes, Alpha," he said, replacing his hat. Neither paid much attention as the Beta walked away. "Portia. She is your Luna's youngest sister."

"Congratulations. What are your plans?"

"She wants to become a teacher. I was hoping that she could have an apartment while attending the college in the human town."

"No," Wyatt said, which surprised Cody. "She can have Wynne's old quarters. I'll make sure that it is cleared out by the end of the week.

When you're ready to move in, let Celeste know. She will arrange for painters and furniture. When do you report back?"

"The twentieth of July," Cody said with eyes widened. "What do I do about Navy regulations?"

The Alpha chuckled and waved over Admiral Kingston. The Admiral stepped over and nodded at Wyatt while brushing away the salute from the ensign. "Alpha Ian, young Cody here has found his mate and is needing to know what to do next."

"Congratulations. Are you part of the navy pack?" Ian asked.

"No, sir. Up until recently, I was in the Annapolis pack."

"Graduation and a mate. Congratulations again. Why don't we have lunch tomorrow?" he said as a beautiful woman stepped up to him and he placed his arm around her shoulders. "This is my Luna, Michelle. My love, this is Cody, I think that we should probably have lunch tomorrow so that we can discuss how the Navy pack works."

She smiled and offered him her hand. "Annapolis?"

"Yes, ma'am."

"The Alpha is a total douchebag." She grinned and the two Alphas laughed while Cody looked uncomfortable.

"I'm telling your brother you called him a douchebag," Ian said before kissing her lightly.

"He'll probably take it as a compliment since I didn't call him a fucking douchebag asshole." She grinned. "He's my twin. I've been insulting him since before we were born. Including, being hidden the whole pregnancy and then being first born."

"Yes, ma'am," Cody said as Portia walked up.

"Forgive the intrusion and informality, Wyatt." Portia said as Wyatt kissed her offered cheek. "Your Luna is hot!" She gave him a quick hug before stepping back and looking up at him. "I don't know what the details are, and I don't even think that I need to, but thank you." With the last few words, her voice began to crack and tears filled her eyes.

"And just what are you thanking me for?" Wyatt asked as he brushed tears away from the corners of her eyes before they fell.

"Our dad…" she whispered. Her guard, Hadrian, pressed a handkerchief into her hand before stepping back again. "Our dad apologized to all of us. And… and…"

"And he will be presenting our sister," Sirius said, stepping in and gathering his youngest sister into a hug. He kissed the top of her head before nodding to her guard, dismissing him for the night. "And I learned that my sister is truly one hell of a badass."

"She is," Ian agreed. "She was stationed on my ship once. Not long after you left my command. Her and Rory were on their way home. That was right before…"

"I know what happened," Wyatt admitted. "It is sad that a wolf would feel so intimidated by a dog."

"But she has so much more than just a dog now," Ian said watching Jack and Jill walking towards the chairs in Marine dress blues with a happy pup between them. "I'm glad they found some happiness."

"Is that Jill?" Michelle asked.

"If you're talking about the big, black, gay Marine," Wyatt chuckled, "that's Jill."

"I've got to see his tattoo," Michelle said.

"Place dick here." Portia said and the four men looked at her in surprise.

"That's the one," Michelle confirmed. "Let's call it legend. And if it is to be believed, they lost one of their best, I don't know what it was, but she got puddy tat and he got instructions."

"You'd think that since he can deep throat, he'd know where it goes." Portia stated and again the men looked at her in shock and surprise.

Michelle laughed heartily. "You have been around the six pervs for a while."

"I thought it was five," Wyatt said, confused.

"Sammi is just as bad as the rest," Michelle said. "The only difference is that she doesn't get a lap dance." She chuckled at how Wyatt's eyes darkened. "Nice memories?"

"Very much so," Wyatt admitted as he shook his head to clear it. "Something highly recommended."

Michelle looked at Cody. "She spends much more time with them, and she will be a virgin in act only."

"Talking about us?" Doc asked, kissing Michelle on the cheek.

"Only my favorite pervert," she teased.

"Sammi is waddling her way over," Doc said and Michelle chuckled.

"Poor thing," Michelle said, seeing the woman in question as she tried to keep up with her husband who was wrangling their three children while trying to keep his uniform clean.

"Excuse me," Wyatt said and walked over to the heavily pregnant huffing and puffing Sammi. They watched as the Alpha offered her an arm. She placed a hand on his arm and paused to catch her breath. He scooped her up as if she weighed nothing and carried her to their seats.

"Show off," Doc grumbled.

"Behave, Medic," Michelle teased her old friend.

"Yes, nurse," he replied with their regular banter. "Anything you say, Nurse."

"And don't you ever forget it," she said as he kissed her cheek again and nodded to the men, then walked over and kissed Portia on her cheek. Cody growled at the man who then kissed Cody's cheek and walked away. Michelle laughed and grabbed Cody's arm. "Calm down, Romeo. Portia is Celeste's sister and is therefore Doc's sister. He will lay down his life and will protect her from anything. Including you. And although he's sweet, Adorable and playful, he was a navy medic embedded with the Marines. He'll fuck you up, and then patch you up."

"Isn't he gay?" Ian asked.

"Bi," Sirius answered.

"Not helping," Cody growled.

59 - CARRIAGE RIDE

Malachi stood outside the bedroom door, waiting for his daughter. The other women had slowly wandered out. Now there were just the Lunas in the room: Elizabeth, Aislinn, Laura and Celeste. Laura walked out carrying her youngest pup, Muriel, and hugged him.

Moving the blanket out of the way, he looked down at his granddaughter with silver eyes and black hair. "How is our future Alpha?"

"She's doing really good." Laura pressed a light kiss to his cheek. "You have no idea how happy it makes me to hear you say that."

"Took me too long to realize that I was wrong. I keep telling everyone to trust the moon goddess." He sighed and kissed his daughter-in-law's temple. "I should have taken my own advice."

"I love you, dad."

"I love you, too, Laura. Forgive my stupidity?"

"Of course," she said as the door opened and Aislinn and Elizabeth came out.

Laura stepped away as Aislinn stepped up and kissed her mate. "I'm so glad you changed your mind."

"Me too." He twirled one of her red curls around his finger. "I have a lot of mistakes to make up for."

"I always told the kids that there are no mistakes, only learning opportunities." Elizabeth quipped.

"I may have missed some lessons." He mused.

"You can always get extra credit or tutoring." Aislinn offered.

"I love you, mate. And I don't deserve you," he said, cupping her face in his hands.

"It takes a hell of a mon to admit he's wrong. I love ye, tu." Aislinn kissed him again and then walked with the other two women to the elevator. Once the elevator doors closed, he knocked on the bedroom door.

The door opened and he admired his daughter, in an elegant dress and her tattooed arms showing. Somehow, with Celeste, it seemed right. She was a lady, a Luna and elegant. But she was also a warrior, an

Alpha and rough around the edges. She could be soft and accommodating but could also be as strong as steel. After the moment at the beauty shop, he had spent more time with the two men and their daughter. All three sang praises for Celeste.

Although she had always been his favorite, he now realized that he had never gotten to know her. Or any of his kids. It was past time to remedy that.

She smiled nervously at her dad, her heels making her just about even with his six foot three. He looked down and there sat her dog, her hellhound, who was currently wearing a white shirt collar and blue bow tie.

"You look wonderful, Celeste," he told her, fighting back tears.

"Thank you, Daddy."

He offered her his arm and then led her to the elevator. "This pack is lucky to have you. That man of yours is special himself."

"He is," she Admitted. "Daddy, I wasn't ready for a mate. I was still a child."

"I know that now," he said as the elevator went down. "Portia found her mate today. As of right now, she's going home with us. I would have never considered it before." The doors opened and they were greeted by a warrior who handed her a white rose.

"Thank you," Celeste said, accepting the flower. He then led them outside where an Omega handed her a white carnation. "Thank you." When the Omega stepped away, she saw the horse drawn carriage. Tears filled her eyes.

"That man is going to spoil you, my little star," Malachi said as a warrior lifted her up into the carriage. As he stepped up himself, she was picking up a small bouquet of red and yellow flowers tied up with red ribbon, a golden Marine Corps emblem in the center of the bow.

Celeste buried her face in the flowers to hide her tears. Malachi squeezed her hand as the carriage rolled down the street. "Look up, sweetheart." He whispered as they came around the corner. She looked up to see veterans from the pack lining the street saluting as she passed.

"I'm guessing that you didn't know about this?" he asked, brushing a tear away from the corner of his daughter's eye. She gently shook her head no. "But it means a lot?"

"Yes," she whispered. "Since I've been here, I've trained with these warriors. Taught them. And this? This tells me that they accept me. Not only as me, but as their Luna."

The carriage came to a stop as he said, "I should have accepted you as you, a long time ago."

60 - LUNA CEREMONY

The carriage door opened, and Celeste turned to see Sirius and James waiting to help her down. Malachi stepped down and out of the way as the other two Alphas offered their hands. Gently, the two men lifted her up and sat her on the ground. She hugged Alpha James who wore his full-dress blues with his impressive rack of ribbons and medals. She then hugged her brother who wore a black suit with the Silver Lake Pack Crest on the left breast.

Celeste took her father's offered arm, and he escorted her down the aisle. They went through the archway, and she looked towards the altar and her breath was caught in her throat. Standing at the top of the stairs, waiting for her, was Wyatt in his dress whites. Oh, dear goddess, he looked magnificent. He also had an impressive rack of ribbons and medals. Not as impressive as the general, but still quite a bit for only serving for 12 years.

As they walked down the aisle, people on either side rose to stand as she passed. Fairy lights twinkled at their feet, lining the platforms that the chairs were sitting on. An occasional cool breeze would ripple the sapphire blue and bright white chair coverings and bunting around the stage. It also carried the scent of the roses in the planter boxes that encircled the large crowd.

The platforms with chairs stopped several feet before the stage and the path that she was walking down with her father doubled in width. Tears were already filling her eyes as her throat filled with too many emotions to name. Just before she reached the end of the aisle, her mother and Elizabeth stepped into the aisle and gave her the Luna blessing.

"Blessings on you and your new pack, may your marriage and your pack be prosperous and grow in your strength. Blessed be," Aislinn said, her accent thick with emotion. "I love you, Celeste."

"I love you too, Momma," she said, hugging her close. As they broke apart, Celeste bent her knees lowering herself to accept her mother's kiss on her forehead.

"Blessings on you and your new pack, may your marriage and our pack be prosperous and grow in your care. And I want grandchildren." There was a little ripple of laughter from the crowd at her not-so-subtle request. "Blessed be. I love you, daughter."

"I love you too, mom." She hugged Elizabeth and then bent down for a kiss on the forehead. She straightened as the two Lunas stepped out of the way. Between her and her mate stood a saber arch. Gunny and Jack stood opposite each other with their swords high in the air. After they had passed, the two Marines lowered their swords keeping them crossed and preventing her from leaving or anyone else from coming forward.

She spotted Doc and Jill at the far end of the short saber arch. They also lowered and crossed their swords effectively trapping her and her father. The other four members of the bridge were pack members from all the branches.

The priestess stepped forward in robes with the Crystal River pack. "Who presents this woman?"

"I do. I am her father," Malachi declared.

"Do you find her pure of heart and soul and worthy of serving as Luna for the Crystal River Pack?"

He looked at his daughter. "Without a doubt, I do."

"And do you give her to this Alpha and this pack of your own free will?"

"I do. And I do so proudly," Malachi said looking at his daughter with all the pride a father could possess.

She smiled a watery smile as she lowered her head and received his kiss on her forehead.

"Who represents the pack that this woman comes from?" the priestess asked.

"I am the acting Alpha Sirius of the Silver Lake Pack," Sirius said from behind them.

"I am Alpha James of the Marines Corps Pack," James added from next to Sirius.

"Alpha Sirius, do you find her pure of heart and soul and worthy of serving as Luna for the Crystal River Pack?"

"I do."

"Alpha James, do you also find her pure of heart and soul and worthy of serving as Luna for the Crystal River Pack?"

"As long as you don't ask about her language, yes, I do." The warriors laughed and Wyatt's eyes also shined. Grinning, she turned to glare at James who just shrugged his shoulders. Even the priestess was grinning when Celeste turned back around.

"Alpha Sirius, do you and your pack give her to this Alpha and his pack of your own free will?"

Sirius was quiet for a moment and with a voice heavy with emotions, he finally confessed, "No. I lost my sister, my own Alpha, for ten years, I do not want to let her go. But she is no longer just my sister, my Alpha. She is now also a mate and a Luna, and I will let her go." He took a deep breath and Celeste looked up fighting back tears. "I, acting Alpha Sirius, give my blessings to this union."

"Alpha James?"

Alpha James gave a small smile as he looked at his friend and comrade in arms. "Yes, with a heavy heart, I, Alpha James, give my blessings on this union."

The two service members on either side of her stepped back and allowed Sirius and James both to step forward to kiss her forehead and give her their blessing. Then her father gave his blessing and a tight hug before he also stepped away. The other four stepped back into place and Jill and Doc raised their swords, allowing her to pass.

As she stepped up onto the bottom step, Jill swatted her butt with his sword. "Get him, girlfriend."

Celeste smiled and shook her head as she took Wyatt's extended hand. Tiffany, her oldest niece stepped up and took her flowers. Stepping up on the platform, she found herself being pulled up against her mate and her mouth being captured by his.

"You look wonderful," he murmured.

"You don't look to bad yourself." She slid her arms around his neck and gently scratched him with her nails.

He reached up and gently touched the heart pendant that lay in the hollow of her neck.

61 - VOWS

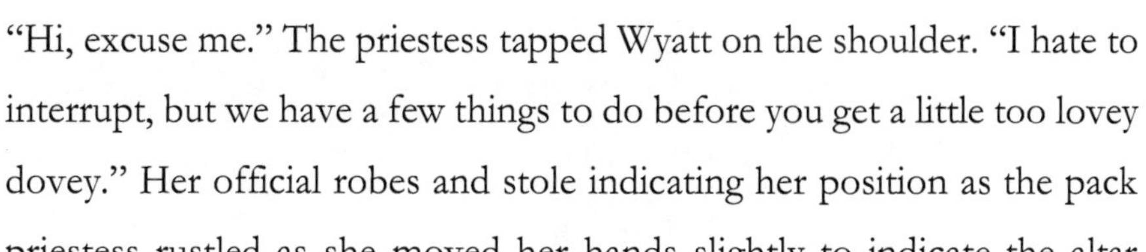

"Hi, excuse me." The priestess tapped Wyatt on the shoulder. "I hate to interrupt, but we have a few things to do before you get a little too lovey dovey." Her official robes and stole indicating her position as the pack priestess rustled as she moved her hands slightly to indicate the altar behind her. "You know," she shrugged, "the actual ceremony that follows the blessings. Ring any bells?"

Celeste tried to step away but found herself anchored to his side. The priestess gave a little chuckle and shook her head.

"For those of you who don't know, this day has been in the making for ten years. And in fact, exactly ten years." The priestess explained. "I fear that my Alpha believes that if he lets go, she will disappear. I have seen the way she looks at you. She will not disappear."

Wyatt pressed a kiss to her hair. "I'm not risking it," he said softly.

"Alpha Celeste, do you come to this pack of your own free will?" the priestess asked.

"I do."

"And do you join into this union of your own free will?"

"I do."

"Alpha Wyatt, do you join into this union of your own free will?"

"I do."

"Alpha Celeste, do you accept the role of Luna for the Crystal River Pack, to be the mother of the pack, to lead and guide the pack, protect the land and the pack members and if needed, lay down your life?"

"I do so promise."

"Alpha Wyatt, I'm pretty sure I know the answer, but are you willing to accept Alpha Celeste as your Luna, your mate, your partner and your equal in your life, your heart and your soul?"

"With every fiber of my being."

"Do you promise to honor and treasure your mate from this day forward until the moon goddess takes you both from this world?"

"In this world and the next."

"Alpha Celeste, are you willing to accept Alpha Wyatt as your Alpha, your mate, your partner and your equal in your life, your heart and your soul?"

Looking up at him, she replied with the same answer, "With every fiber of my being."

"Do you promise to honor and treasure your mate from this day forward until the moon goddess takes you both from this world?"

"In this world and the next." She smiled and reached up to cup his cheek. He turned his face and kissed her palm.

"Okay, you're almost there. Then you can get all lovey dovey." The priestess said drawing their attention back to her. She picked up the ceremonial dagger and handed it to Wyatt.

He stepped forward and sliced his left palm and let the blood drip into the crystal goblet with red wine in it. Wyatt picked up the black and silver satin sash, the colors of the Silver Lake Pack.

He handed the dagger back to the priestess who wiped it off and then handed it to Celeste. She stepped forward and he noticed the Crest on her back. Without thinking, he stepped to her and gently touched the skin that was still slightly irritated.

Celeste sliced her left hand and as she squeezed the blood into glass, she turned and smiled at him. Wyatt smiled back at her and placed a light kiss on her shoulder. The priestess stepped around and took the dagger from her. Celeste picked up the sash with the Crystal River Pack, pale blue with blood red trim.

The couple clasped their left hands together, each holding the other pack's colors. The priestess intertwined the sashes as she bound their hands together. Once completed, she picked up the crystal goblet and offered it first to Celeste and then Wyatt.

"Now you can kiss her and mark her, I know that you already marked him, but you can do it again."

With his free hand, he grasped her chin and tipped her face up to him. "I love you," he whispered right before he gently kissed her. He let go of her chin and moved his hand to the back of her neck. Wyatt started to bury his hand in her black hair before remembering his sister threatened his life if he messed up her hair.

"I love you, too," she panted out softly once her mouth was free. She offered up her neck to him. He kissed her marking spot, the same place that he had placed a hickey almost daily. Celeste moaned lightly as he teased her with his lips and tongue. He lightly scraped his teeth across her neck. Then, he extended his fangs and sunk into her.

My beautiful mate. My Luna. My love. My wife.

All yours my Alpha.

Before lifting his head, Wyatt licked the puncture wounds to seal them. He offered her another kiss before also offering her his neck. She sank her fangs into his neck and reveled in the taste of his blood. Celeste sealed the wounds and then kissed his neck.

To finish the ceremony, the priestess unbound their hands and handed them their rings. Wyatt slid the Luna ring onto her right ring finger.

"I, Alpha Wyatt Nicholas O'Donnell, take you, Alpha Celeste Starr Moore, as my Luna, mother and protector of the pack, under the blessing of the moon goddess."

"I, Alpha Celeste Starr Moore, take you, Alpha Wyatt Nicholas O'Donnell, as my Alpha, father and Protector of the pack, under the blessing of the moon goddess," Celeste said as she placed his Alpha ring on his right ring finger.

"I take you to be my wife, my mate and the mother of my pups. I take you as my partner and my equal. I have waited for ten years for you to find me. It was a very long decade. But one that I would do again to be able to stand here with you. With your colorful personality you won over my family and pack. You have a wild streak that reminds me to just let go sometimes. And yet, you will face down those who would oppose you. And do it with incredible grace and style. You have a heart of gold and a backbone of steel. You, my love, are perfect for me, and now that we share a last name, there is nothing that I would change about you." Wyatt slid her wedding ring on and then kissed her. "I love you, mate."

Celeste tried to blink away her tears and when she failed, Wyatt wiped them away with his thumbs.

"I take you to be my husband, my mate and the father of my pups. I take you as my partner and my equal. You are so patient and thoughtful. You've let me run wild, even after I finally found you. You've never complained about my Addictions to coffee, whiskey or ink. You encouraged me when I needed it. Held me during my nightmares. Accepted my strange ass friends. Oh, shit! I was trying not to cuss."

Wyatt smiled at her while the guests laughed.

"You accepted me. Just as I am. Something that I thought no one would ever do. You helped to heal my family. To heal me. Goddess knows you have the patience of a saint. She also knows that you will probably need it. I love you, mate."

After pushing his ring on, she pulled him down for a kiss. When it ended, he rested his forehead on hers and smiled at her.

"You look gorgeous."

"We already went through this."

"That was before you were my wife."

"Flattery will get you everywhere."

"Everywhere?"

"Typically, I would suggest that you two get a room, but I think that you would take that as a literal suggestion." The priestess joked.

"They will!" Doc yelled out.

The adults and older kids laughed. It was especially funny for the group who had gone to the strip club with them. They just smiled at each other and exchanged a few light kisses.

"I don't need pups conceived before my altar," the priestess said, trying to push a little space between them. "Ladies and gentlemen, I present to you the Alpha and Luna of the Crystal River Pack, Alpha Wyatt and Alpha Celeste."

Teuf finally made a sound from where he lay curled up just a foot away from the couple. He lifted his head, looked at the priestess and gave a small whimper.

"No. I did not," The priestess said to Teuf before rolling her eyes and looking out to the crowd. "And Teuf. Is that better?" she asked the dog who made another small sound and then laid his head back down. "Diva. I just wasn't going to mention you," she grumbled quietly.

Wyatt and Celeste both turned to look at the priestess.

"You understand him?" Celeste asked quietly.

She smiled at the new Luna. "I speak with the moon goddess herself; do you really think that I would not understand him?"

"When you put it that way, I guess not."

62 - CLOSET

The party had gone on well into the early morning hours. There was dancing, plenty of food and lots of drinks. After the formal ceremony, everyone changed into casual clothes. At midnight, there was a run through the woods. Afterwards, everyone began making their way back to their cabins or homes.

Breakfast was served late because most everyone was still asleep at sunrise. Wyatt and Celeste were still in bed as everyone began moving around. She lay on her stomach as he applied lotion to the new pack crest tattooed on her back.

"This is one of my favorites," he said softly.

"Because it means that I belong to you?" She stiffened a little at the thought of being a possession.

"Because it means that I belong to you," he corrected next to her ear. "That we belong to each other."

"I like that too," she purred.

"We belong to each other," he said as he trailed kisses down her back, "and the pack."

The door opened and Teuf made his way to the bed. "You have a house full of guests and this is where you are?" Elizabeth asked her son as she swept into Celeste's closet.

"Tuesday," the couple said to each other from the bed.

"Yes, you can stay with Gunny," Celeste said and Teuf's ears perked up. "Do not chew up their fort in the backyard." He whined and laid his head down. "You ate the tracks off a tank!" She sat up and looked at the dog who turned away from her and refused to look at her. "So, yes. I find it very necessary to tell you not to chew on certain things."

"I don't think that the Marines sent that over as a chew toy," Wyatt said and then his eyes widened as his mate and the hellhound both looked at him. "I just heard him, didn't I?"

"Yup." Celeste grinned as her mother-in-law stepped out of the closet with the outfit that she picked. "Find different shoes."

"But they look good with this outfit." Elizabeth argued as her son said, "Keep the clothes, give me the shoes. In fact, take the clothes, leave my Luna."

"That's one of his favorite pairs. So, if you want me out of this bed, pick a different pair."

"Quit calling me a horndog." Wyatt told Teuf.

"You kind of are one." Elizabeth said from inside the closet.

"And he would know." Celeste gave a pointed look at the dog who turned his attention to the balcony doors and sniffed. Wyatt got up, wrapping the sheet around his waist, and opened the door and he also sniffed. "Did she not feed you?" Celeste asked, pulling the blanket around her.

"I'm sure she has some sausage down at the grounds for Sir Teuf," Wyatt said. "I guess we should get up and go to the games so that he can eat before he wastes away."

"He had an omelet this morning," Elizabeth said as she handed a different outfit and shoes to Celeste. The dog in question turned and lay down facing away from the two women.

"I know, Buddy. Women don't understand how hungry a man gets." Wyatt scratched the dog's head as he passed on his way to his closet. "I still like the idea of you in those heels."

"Tuesday," she told her mate as she too started to get dressed.

"Mom?" Wyatt called from his closet. "Leave."

Elizabeth started to object as Celeste dropped her shirt on the bed and walked into Wyatt's closet. Closing the door behind her, she grinned at her husband. He was sitting on the oversized ottoman. The sheet lay discarded on the floor.

"I have something for you to wear," he said with a smile. His hand slowly stroked his cock.

"Really?" her eyes were following the motion of his hand.

"Top drawer. And lose the shorts," he said motioning towards the drawers on the side.

She undid her shorts and let them fall. Then she stepped over and opened the top drawer. Inside was a large assortment of jewelry boxes in all sizes and colors.

"Which one?" She asked, looking at all the boxes.

"Pick one." He told her grabbing a condom from the box on the shelf. "They're all yours."

Grabbing a box at random, she went to him as he was rolling the condom on. Wyatt took the box and then helped her onto his lap. Once Celeste was settled on him, he guided her with his free hand to start moving on him. With a rhythm set, he opened the jewelry box and removed the platinum and onyx necklace.

The chain was made of tiny stars with even smaller diamonds in them. Fixed on the center of the chain was a two-inch onyx circle. A platinum wolf howling at the moon was fixed over the stone.

"It's beautiful." Celeste murmured as Wyatt fastened it around her neck. It lay at the base of her neck with the stone in the center.

"So are you." He agreed and kissed her. Trailing kisses down, he captured a breast in his mouth. Releasing it he stood and laid her on the ottoman. "Put your feet on my chest."

She did as he said, and he shifted them so that she was practically folded in half with her knees by her ears. Bracing himself with his hands on either side of her head, Wyatt began pounding into her deep and hard. Reaching between them, Celeste began to play with her clit.

"That's it, baby." He encouraged as she cried out in pleasure. Her body quivered as her walls pulsed around his cock. With a shaky thrust, he joined her in the abyss of pleasure.

63 - TUESDAY

By Tuesday morning, Celeste was coming out of her heat. This angered Angel in a way that neither had anticipated. Wyatt woke up to a growling she-wolf in the bed. He found himself face to face with a large silvery white wolf.

"My love, what is wrong?" Wyatt asked as she bared her teeth, growling even louder. Wyatt rolled until he was over her. He shifted as he moved, and Demon held her to the bed with his large paw.

You are my mate, Demon declared.

I'm not going to submit to you.

I don't want you to. He admitted. We want equals. Not slaves.

Weakling.

SILENCE! He warned and snapped his teeth at her. Do not force me to make you submit.

Although she did not submit, she stopped struggling against him. He laid down, keeping her beneath his large black fur covered body.

Shift. He commanded softly. She growled, letting him know that she would not obey. He snapped at her and when she did not stop, he clamped down on her shoulder. The more she fought, the harder he bit her. His teeth broke her skin, and she began to bleed. Shift!

After several moments, she shifted and then he joined her. Wyatt remained above her as they shifted and lay on the floor. Releasing her shoulder, Wyatt kissed the healing wounds.

"I never came to force you to be my mate. I never took your autonomy away. I have not made you submit to me as your mate or your Alpha," Wyatt said quietly. Just as quietly, but with venom, he warned, "Do not force my hand in this matter."

She nodded slightly and closed her eyes briefly. He could tell that she was fighting with her wolf who was vying for control. Angel was driven partially by her base needs and partially by her need to produce the next Alpha of the pack.

"I need you to stay in this form, but we need to speak with both of you." Wyatt shifted his weight slightly but did not let her up. "Celeste, my love, can you hear me?"

"Yes," came the soft reply.

Angel, can you hear us also? Demon asked and Angel snarled at him through the mind link. "If you want to get out of here, you will listen to both of us," Wyatt warned.

Fine. Angel replied and he couldn't help but smile at the attitude.

"When we found you, we knew that you were not ready for us. We were patient and trusted in the moon goddess. She had a plan for us, we just had to wait for her to bring us together. I sent you letters and gifts. We went to see you when we could. Got updates and shirts with your scent on them. We loved you from a distance, waiting for you. We could do nothing less."

You left us in New Orleans, Angel accused.

"We did. We had to," Wyatt agreed.

Demon growled at the memory. I did not want to leave. I wanted us to claim you and mark you.

"You would have been no better than those who mark without consent." Celeste pointed out and Angel added, Might as well have just raped us.

The incident from a dozen or so years ago when Whitney was nearly marked without consent flashed through his mind. He could still feel her fear and his own as she had called out for him. He knew that she herself had to be thinking about her own sisters. One was murdered. The other was terrified of her mate for years.

"Marking without consent is a form of rape. Maybe even the worst kind of rape."

We're not a rapist. Demon argued. Just because the goddess named me Demon doesn't mean that I am one.

"We knew that when the time was right, you would come to us. And then, we hoped that you would choose to stay with us. Choose to give us a chance." He moved off her and leaned up against the headboard. "Come here, mate. Let us hold you."

With a warning growl from Angel, Celeste moved to sit in his lap. Strong arms held her close to his chest.

"Four years ago, I came home, finished my two years with the navy as a reservist and started taking over as the Alpha. Then two years ago, I became the Alpha. Last year, when our pack was selected to host the Hunt, I began to hope that the moon goddess was bringing you to me. I would go to the temple every week and ask the priestess if the moon goddess had said anything to her."

"Every week, it was the same answer. Keep your eyes on the heavens, you'll know when the star comes to you. I was so confused and then one day, Terry told me that Perseus Moore wanted a meeting with me." Wyatt chuckled. "I thought of the book and movie series about Perseus and the Greek gods. Terry automatically thought of the stars. He started telling me about the stars that make up the constellation Perseus. And he loved to tell me about Algol, the demon star."

That's my star, Demon declared.

"He also told me that Virgo was also called the Angel Constellation. And that what my Demon needed was his angel."

That's you, mate, Demon told Angel as he nuzzled her in their minds. I need you, my angel.

"We were born under Virgo, August twenty-ninth. Born under the Angel. Made by the moon goddess, for my angel." Wyatt pressed a kiss to her hair and took a deep breath of her scent. My Angel. Demon reiterated as he also breathed in his mate's scent.

Angel finally turned towards Demon and took in his scent. Why would you not come to me? Even if they could not be together, we as beasts could have been.

How fair would that be? Demon countered. Even if I went to you, and goddess knows that I wanted to, he would have had to be close to her. Almost close enough to touch. Could you have allowed her to be that close and expected her to stay away? Would you have wanted her to?

Angel laid her head between her front pads and sighed. No. Demon lay down next to her and rested his jaw on her neck. No, mate. I could not do that to her.

I know. Her pain is also our pain. As is yours, mate. The past ten years have been hell for us. As we are sure it was for you. But now, we are together, we are whole.

Wyatt lifted Celeste's chin and kissed her lips. "I love you, mate. Never doubt that. We suffered from the distance just as you did. But we could have your scent and occasionally could see you. Not once did we want you to suffer, which is why we sent you letters and shirts with our scent. But we wanted to be your choice."

We wanted you to choose us as your destiny, Demon added. Not just accept it and be miserable.

"I would have eventually accepted it," Celeste whispered. "It's what all she-wolves are told. Give in to the mate pull and submit to your mate."

"How fair is that?" Wyatt asked softly. "Wolves are allowed to do as we please. We are allowed to take lovers and go see the world. She-wolves are to submit and have babies. Your life is laid out at your birth and your worth is based on how many pups you have. You are worth so much more than that."

"Why are you not an asshole?"

He smiled at her. "I grew up surrounded by she-wolves. I was probably thirteen or so, young, cocky and full of myself. Stephen and I were at Momma's and an Omega girl came in and we were downright cruel to her. And I mean, horribly cruel. Momma tore into our asses. Made us apologize to her. You can imagine how that was for two young teenage Alpha blooded boys, being forced by a human to apologize to an Omega."

Celeste couldn't help but give a little laugh.

"Yeah. And then she did something even worse. She asked us what we would do if someone treated one of our sisters like that." He took a deep breath to calm himself. "Still makes me mad to think of one of my sisters to be treated like that. Momma then told us that if we wouldn't treat our sisters like that, don't treat someone else's sister like that. Made one hell of an impression."

"What happened to the girl?"

"My Beta married her two days after her seventeenth birthday."

"Ellie?" Celeste asked and Wyatt nodded.

64 - NOT TWINS

Wyatt walked into Anna's office to find her kicked back at her desk reading a novel. She looked a little embarrassed as she sat the book on her desk. Her job was not to read, but to assist the Luna in any way that was needed. Being caught by the Alpha reading a spicy romance novel made it worse.

"The Luna is not feeling well," the Omega whispered. "My typing was too loud for her. So, I was told to go to the library and find something quiet to read."

He chuckled and shook his head as he motioned to the sitting room door. "I assume she's in there?"

"Yes, Alpha," she answered, starting to get up.

"Why don't you take the rest of the day off? I'm going to take her upstairs."

"Thank you, Alpha." Anna replied as she gathered her bag and prepared to leave.

"And Anna?" pausing at the door, he looked back at the woman gathering her belongings. "Destini Martin is not only my mom's favorite author, but a close friend. Take the book. I'm sure we have at least one more copy."

Smiling at him, she whispered her thanks before placing the book in her bag.

He opened the door and saw his mate asleep on the couch on the far side of the room. His eyes automatically fell to the wood and glass cabinet under the TV. It was her retirement footlocker and had only grown over the years. Big Jake came in one day and modified the cabinet with glass and other customizations.

A shadow box with her patches and insignia sat on one end, the same for Teuf sat at the other. Between the two was a long case with her officer's sword. Inside the cabinet, were commemorative mugs and a custom challenge coin display built into one of the two long drawers. There were other gifts and mementos in the case. Including a special case holding the long receipt signed by the dancers and staff of the Safari Club; one of their favorite clubs next to Camp Pendleton in California.

Lucifer, the runt of Teuf's litter, lay on the couch, curled up at Celeste's feet. Teuf and his mate, Lucia, were curled together on the dog bed. Six years ago, Teuf disappeared for several days, and Celeste was devastated. Then he showed up one day with a mate as if he had not been missing for nearly a week.

Their own pups had been excited that Teuf was back. Celeste broke down in tears, afraid she had lost her old friend. The first litter of hell hounds were quickly adopted by warriors. As were the following litters. The latest litter had already been claimed, except for Lucifer who Celeste refused to part with.

Sometimes Wyatt thought about that first Saturday when John had threatened Teuf. At the time, the pack was leery about having dogs around. Now, the Crystal River pack was also home to a growing pack of hellhounds. The adult pups from the first litter were now taking mates of their own.

Looking on the opposite couch, he watched the other five pups from the latest litter. He looked at Teuf and again thought that although everyone else had aged, he still looked the same. No one was certain how long hellhounds would live, but he was assuming it would be a while. Even the priestess could only say that he would live if his bonded werewolf lived.

Lucia lifted her head and thumped her tail when she saw her master. He scratched her under the chin and Teuf behind his ear before he shooed them out of his way. Once they had moved off the dog bed, he pushed it out of the way with his foot as he moved the blanket off his mate.

Lucifer got down, nipping his father's tail. Teuf was patient with were-pups and even more with his own. Wyatt occasionally felt sorry for Lucia since it seemed that she was pregnant shortly after weaning a litter. His mother pointed out that he did not have much room to talk since his own mate was pregnant with their fourth child in ten years.

"Wyatt…" Celeste murmured as he scooped her up. She was nearly forty and this pregnancy had been hard on her.

"Yes, my love?" he answered as he left the office through Anna's still open door. As he went down the hall Teuf, Lucia and their five pups followed him into the elevator.

"I went to the doctor today," she said, snuggling into his embrace.

"Everything okay?"

"Sammi said that I was having twins, so I had to prove her wrong."

He chuckled as the elevator opened to their floor. It was an argument that they had with every one of Celeste's pregnancies. Alpha pups were always bigger, and she always looked like she was having twins. This pregnancy, she was even bigger than usual. "Was she finally, right?"

"No," she said as he carried her into their room.

"That's good." He told her as he sat on the edge of the bed and toed off his shoes before laying down with her. "Do you know if I'm finally going to get a little girl?"

"No," she said with a smile. "You're getting three."

Wyatt laid on the bed holding his mate with his hand on her belly. He was processing this when his hand was kicked.

"Three?" he whispered in shock.

"Three. All girls," Celeste confirmed. "Sammi deserves an award of some kind. Four sets of twins. I don't know how she hasn't killed Gunny."

"I will get her several awards.

"Why were you asked to take Jill with you?"

"I was asked about taking in an orphan werecat."

"At the Council meeting?"

"Mmmm-hmmm. Six weeks old. Mother abandoned him. And since we have a werecat living with the pack, the Council asked if we could take him."

"What did you say?"

"Nothing."

"Nothing?"

"There was nothing to say. Jill already had the cub and was purring so loud I thought that the answer was clear." He smiled and kissed the top of her head. "Even Jack told me I better not even think about saying no." he chuckled as he pressed a kiss to her temple. "Looks like we now have two werecats in the pack."

Celeste chuckled. "That's my bestie."

"When I met them, I would have never thought that those two would take over the orphanage." Wyatt admitted. "Then again, I was not expecting a gay couple."

She tried to hide a yawn by turning her face into his chest.

"I'm going to lay here and hold my girls while you take a nap."

65 - CHILDREN

After twenty-three years of marriage and six children, Celeste and Wyatt still enjoyed spending time with each other. And sneaking away from their duties and children. As they lay curled together on one of the couches in the private movie room on the top floor, a movie played on the screen illuminating the dark room. Their clothes lay strewn across the dark tile floor.

Holding back her laughter, she wondered which of her five children that were home would find them. Their second son, Martin, was home from his studies at the college in the neighboring pack, Little Ridge. Jacob was helping with the summer athletic camps that the pack hosted every year.

Their daughters, Diana, Electra and Selena, would, no doubt, be in one of two places. The triplets were very different from one another. And very much exactly the same. They all had the endless energy of young Alphas and an unquenchable thirst for knowledge. Which meant that they would either be at the sports camp. Or the library on the first floor.

The only child that she did not know where he would be was the oldest, Aiden. He had followed his father's footsteps into the Navy as a medic. Since he was nowhere on pack lands, he was the only one that she did not expect to interrupt their midafternoon tryst.

Celeste looked at her phone and smiled before answering it. "Hello, Aiden."

"Mom, what if I don't want to be Alpha?" her oldest asked from wherever the Navy had him.

She smiled as their suspicions were confirmed. "Have you talked to your dad?"

"I don't want to disappoint him," He admitted with a sigh. "Mom, I passed the test. This is what I want."

It was the same test that his dad never took. He too was the only son and the next Alpha. Wyatt had joined the Navy with the hopes of becoming a SEAL. Instead, he became an embedded medic.

"Aiden, there is only one thing that you can do that would make your father disappointed in you." She said as she snuggled into her mate.

They were hidden away in the movie room on the bottom floor of the pack house with the lights off and no movie playing. Their clothes were scattered around the room where they were discarded hours earlier. Now she sat across his lap with a blanket covering them.

"Not becoming Alpha," came the resigned answer from the phone.

"Not being true to yourself," she corrected gently. "Talk to your dad."

"Okay. I love you, Mom."

"I love you too." She ended the call and looked up at her husband. "We were found by a kid. Just not the one that we expected."

He leaned down and kissed her as his phone rang. Moving away from his wife of twenty-two years, he clicked the icon to answer the call. "Hello, Son."

"Dad, I took the test. And I passed. I can go to SEAL training."

"I'm proud of you."

"I want to do this. I want to make a career of it."

"Okay. You have until your twenty-fifth birthday to abdicate and pick a successor."

"That's it?" Aiden said in surprise.

"You'll have to get the approval of the Council and blessing of the priestess."

"You're not mad?"

He gave a soft chuckle. "Like your mom said, we'll only be disappointed if you're not true to yourself."

"Of course, you're with mom," Aiden said exasperated. Wyatt pictured him rubbing his forehead. "You're not having sex, are you?"

"Not right now," he said with a little chuckle. "Now, who are you thinking as your successor?"

"Martin has already accepted the position of Beta for the Silver Lake Pack and Jacob has absolutely no interest in the position," Aiden said thoughtfully. "I couldn't force them to do what I don't want to do either."

"So, no to either of your brothers. You also have three sisters." He pointed out playing with Celeste's black hair. There was now a sprinkling of silver in both of theirs hinting at their ages.

More than just their hair color has changed over the last two decades. There were a dozen or more female Alphas leading packs now. Celeste snuggled in against his chest and was proud of the changes that they had helped to come to fruition in their lifetimes.

"They're too young," Aiden argued.

"I would agree with you about Diana and Electra. But Selena was born for the role. When the girls were born, she wanted to name them after goddesses. She looked at Selena and said that she would be the next Alpha for the pack. I never doubted your mom."

"How would she know?" Aiden asked, confused.

"Son, let me tell you a secret to life. Never question your mate," Wyatt advised as he placed a kiss on her head. "Okay, two secrets. Moms know everything."

"Yeah…. Ummm…." Wyatt could feel his mate smiling just as he could hear the guilt and uncertainty in his son's voice as he stammered for a response. "Layla is an Omega. I'm Alpha."

"And the moon goddess knew what she was doing when she made you two. You two were friends as soon as we took in the rogue child. You already felt the pull. Don't let her tiger of a mom-dad scare you off."

"It's not the werecat that scares me."

"Terrified of the gay human?" Wyatt asked, looking at his mate as she fought back laughter.

"You have no idea how much Uncle Jack scares me," Aiden finally admitted.

"Come home when you get a chance. We'll see what happens and we'll talk to your sister."

"Okay. I love you, Dad."

"Love you too. Be safe."

There was a grunt at the other end of the line before the call ended.

"Our babies are growing up," Celeste lamented.

"They are. And we did good with them all. Including the overgrown human who won't move out."

"You'd miss Doc if he left," she pointed out and he kissed her before agreeing that he would miss their old friend. "You ever wonder what life would be like without my friends from the Corps?"

"Boring. It would be boring with no ridiculous bets, nights at the strip club, outrageous bonfires or the random person or couple doing the walk of shame out of Doc's quarters." He stroked her cheek with his knuckles, and she smiled at the familiar gesture. "I wouldn't have our life any other way, Mate."

ABOUT THE AUTHOR

Amy Worcester spent the first half of her childhood in a small west Texas farming community and later moved to the city where she learned to retreat and hide from the world in books. Books were an escape from the trials and tribulations of teenage life, but also a place where she learned the power of imagination. She continued to read and started to play around with short stories in college and young adulthood. She put that on hold when she met the love of her life, and they raised their son. She put all her energy into giving him the best childhood and now that he is grown, she has begun to write again hoping that her stories offer solace and escape from your everyday life.

Currently, Amy lives in Greenville, Texas, with her husband, their son, small pack of dogs, a colony of honeybees and a growing collection of tiaras.

YOUR REVIEW MATTERS

Remember to leave a review. It's the best way to get others around the world to find this book and join us on the journey. It only takes 96 seconds to leave a review (yes, we timed it!). Thank you for your support!

Made in the USA
Columbia, SC
25 July 2024

38689079R00285